The

Richard T. Kelly is the author of the novels *Crusaders* (2008) and *The Possessions of Doctor Forrest* (2011). *Eclipse*, his first script for television, aired on Channel 4 in 2010. He has written several studies of film-makers: *Alan Clarke* (1998), *The Name of This Book is Dogme95* (2000), and the authorised biography *Sean Penn: His Life and Times* (2004). In 2013 he collaborated with Judith Tebbutt on her memoir of hostage in Somalia, *A Long Walk Home*, a *Sunday Times* bestseller and National Book Awards nominee.

www.richardkelly.co.uk
@richtkelly

Further praise for *The Knives*:

'A gripping read from start to finish. A rich, multi-layered account of the complexities of modern government where personal, political and cultural realities mean simple choices are hard to come by.' Alastair Campbell

'[A] fantastic new political thriller.' Amber Rudd MP, Home Secretary

'A story that is dramatic and, at the same time, faithful to the facts about British politics. This is a remarkably rare feat in English letters.' *The Times*

'An exciting novel . . . A finely honed slice of modern political drama . . . it grips from the off. This book could not also be more timely, with the threat to MPs personal safety and radicalisation on British soil as alive on these pages as they are in tomorrow's headlines.' *Esquire*

'A tale of political jeopardy . . . [Kelly] is admirably unjudgemental in his portrait of Blaylock and his politics, and admirably nuanced . . . A sympathetic portrait of a man adrift in the swirling sea of politics.' *Sunday Times*

'Truth is stranger than fiction, and no one knows that more than Richard Kelly . . . while Kelly followed Theresa May's career closely for his research, even he couldn't have predicted quite how timely his tale would be . . . Kelly is now an accidental expert on the new Prime Minister.' 'Londoner's Diary', *Evening Standard*

'This is a sharp and engaging tale . . . Kelly makes lives the reader can believe in. Novels are thrilling in the truest sense when they feel as if they are built of flesh and blood; it's Kelly's success in doing so that makes his final twist of the knife even more shocking.' Erica Wagner, *Financial Times*

'[Kelly's] fluently written and often highly absorbing novel is an emotive reminder that, against the implacable, unpredictable momentum of modern politics, simply trying to do good is rarely anywhere near enough.' *Metro*

'A timely political psychological drama, neatly capturing national fears around immigration, terrorism and privacy . . . Well-paced and filled with enough red herrings to keep you guessing almost to the end.' Graeme Smith, *Herald*

RICHARD T. KELLY

THE
KNIVES

FABER & FABER

First published in 2016
by Faber & Faber Limited
Bloomsbury House
74–77 Great Russell Street
London WC1B 3DA

This paperback edition published in 2017

Typeset by Faber & Faber Limited
Printed and bound by CPI Group (UK) Ltd, Croydon, CRO 4YY

A CIP record for this book
is available from the British Library

ISBN 978–0–571–29667–5

2 4 6 8 10 9 7 5 3 1

For C.M.

'I must do my work in my own way,' declared the Chief Inspector. *'When it comes to that I would deal with the devil himself, and take the consequences. There are things not fit for everybody to know.'*

JOSEPH CONRAD, *The Secret Agent*

There's a story I used to tell years ago where I'd say, if I were a revolutionary leader, and they came up to me and they said, 'We've got a dilemma, we don't know whether to execute these five men or cut down these five trees', I'd say, 'Well, let me look at them.'

NORMAN MAILER

'Over Westminster Bridge and past the House of Commons,' he said exultantly. *'Into Whitehall and up the steps of the Home Office. Right into the fortress of reaction.'*

NORMAN COLLINS, *London Belongs to Me*

CONTENTS

NOTE TO THE READER

This is a work of fiction, though it reflects some matters of public interest in the time when it was written. The UK government that it depicts is imaginary, and both the legislative framework and the political calendar within which that government conducts its business are not those of the UK, past or present – or, at least, not in every respect. Moreover, the geography of Westminster, and of many other places, has been re-imagined (the real Home Office is not found on 'Shovell Street', there is no such parliamentary constituency as 'Teesside South', nor towns near the Tees named Maryburn and Thornfield, et cetera). In other words, while I have borrowed things recognisable from life in the aid of plausibility, this story remains, of course, make-believe.

DRAMATIS PERSONAE

David Blaylock MP – The Home Secretary

And in alphabetical order
Caleb Aldrich – US Government's Director of Counter-Terror
Sir James Bannerman – Commissioner of the Metropolitan Police
Geraldine Bell – David Blaylock's private secretary at the Home
    Office
Alex Blaylock – seventeen-year-old son of David Blaylock
Cora Blaylock – thirteen-year-old daughter of David Blaylock
Molly Blaylock – nine-year-old daughter of David Blaylock
Diane Cleeve – founder of charity Remember the Victims
Richard Colls – Chief Constable of Kent Police
Ben Cotesworth – special advisor ('spad') to David Blaylock
Dame Phyllida Cox – Permanent Secretary (chief civil servant)
    at the Home Office
Bob Cropper – 'chief of staff' for David Blaylock in his Teesside
    constituency
Norman Dalton MP – Junior Minister for Policing at the Home
    Office
Chas Finlayson MP – Government Minister for Employment
Nick Gilchrist – documentary filmmaker
Andy Grieve – close protection bodyguard to David Blaylock
Snee Gupta MP – Government Minister for Education
Sheikh Hanifa – Government consultant on 'inter-faith
    dialogue'
Abigail Hassall – newspaper journalist/political correspondent
Seema Hassanli – Communities officer at the Home Office

Susan Rivers MP – Government Minister for Defence

Sir Alan Ruthven – Cabinet Secretary: chief civil servant and advisor to the Prime Minister

Belinda Ryder MP – Government Minister for the Arts

Duncan Scarth – businessman, co-founder of the Free Briton Brigade

Amanda Scott-Stokes – chartered clinical psychologist

Griff Sedgley QC – barrister frequently engaged by the Home Office

Brian Shoulder – Head of Scotland Yard Counter-Terror division

Mark Tallis – special advisor to the Home Secretary

Caroline Tennant MP – Chancellor of the Exchequer

Patrick Vaughan MP – Conservative Party Leader and Prime Minister, known to his Cabinet as 'the Captain'

Francis Vernon MP – Leader of the House of Commons

Adam Villiers – Director of MI5

Guy Walters MP – Junior Minister for Immigration at the Home Office

Lord Waugh – Lord Chief Justice, head of the judiciary in England

Simon Webster MP – Government Minister for Justice

PROLOGUE

1993

'Gentlemen, these are your rules of engagement. You'll carry them printed on a card in your pocket – I'd prefer you keep them etched behind your eyeballs. They are not hard to remember, they could even be of use to you in other places. One, you will at all times show purpose. Two, you have the means to protect yourselves, so use them. Three, do not tolerate aggression – if you are fired upon, return fire. Be that said – four – never give an order that can't be obeyed. Five, in the unlikely event you find yourselves notably outgunned, and a safe route exists to remove yourselves – remove!'

Whitewashed and clean-stamped with call-signs on turrets, the trio of Warriors rumbled in convoy down raw muddy tracks lately carved for their passage through the Lašva Valley. Holding to a steady speed, keeping twenty yards apart, their heavy treads powered over the rough road – thirty-ton weight driving down dirt and loose stones, engines emitting full-throated roars.

From his jostled vantage, chest-high to the turret of Bravo Zero, Captain David Blaylock surveyed the Bosnian countryside. The sullen skies that had met the Yorkshire Regiment in late April were, today, a cool cloudless blue. In the air was the good resin smell of the conifers lining the roads and clustered on the hillsides. The modest villages, the thickets of wan, reviving birches, the hawthorn and the elm – in all, Blaylock felt, it wasn't so wildly unlike North Yorkshire. Except that hardly a single bird was ever seen or heard. Except for his sharpened sense that round any bend, over any crest, one could come upon something dreadful –

foretold by the whistle and boom of mortar fire, or black smoke climbing in a billowing column over trees.

Blaylock had lived with this foreboding since the regiment's arrival – their first ride into the valley, past ruined houses and hamlets with their mournful air of despoil. He was ready, now, for the sight of ruined bodies – men and women and children. He bore it, uneasily, as a platoon captain's duty. Twenty-six years old, he commanded twenty-seven men.

A stubby pencil in hand, braced against the Warrior's motion, Blaylock drew lines on tracing paper nestled into the fold of his logbook, hand-amending the company map of local routes and villages. His convoy was headed for Fazlići, then west to Suhi Dol, his mission to explore and log hitherto uncharted terrain that lay off the rebuilt roads, places that had yet to see a UN presence. Today, then – so Blaylock briefed the boys – was 'Operation Show-A-Friendly-Face'.

Trev, his gunner, sat beside him in the turret, staunchly in charge of the Rarden cannon and the mounted machine gun. Down below was Cookie, the driver, a study in lip-bitten focus. In the back of the wagon, behind its metal cage, sat Gordy, Jinks and Chappo – keeping watch out of the Warrior's raised back hatches, trying out their wit above the engine's din for the benefit of Tamara, their dark-eyed and seemingly biddable Bosnian interpreter.

Up top Blaylock was just glad to be moving, breathing the air, away from the garrison at Stari Vitez – not stuck on guard or escort duty. The garrison, a disused school, was a crowded mud-hole – a Muslim enclave, moreover, within a Croat-held area, such that the sense of siege was palpable. Blaylock had yet to get comfortable with peering out through the mess window to see Bosnian forces in sniper positions, barrels trained on Croat lines half a mile away.

His men, he knew, were even more perplexed by a set-up far removed from what they had seen lately in Belfast. That had been a simple sketch on a chalkboard, Her Majesty's armed forces against skulking paramilitaries. Bosnia, though, was civil war – a two-way conflict that had recently and strangely split into three. And since they wore blue UN helmets on their heads, the Yorkshire Regiment declared for no particular dog in the fight.

Blaylock's main piece of leadership before today had been a chore he found hateful: overseeing the safe passage of Muslim refugees – standing idly by, in other words, as miserable parents and dazed children were trooped off trucks and onto coaches for further 'dispersal', all their worldly goods in plastic bags, their wary eyes betraying that they had seen bad things and were braced for worse, that their sense of peril was in no way relieved.

And so in this morning's task Blaylock felt a kind of liberty – there was no radio link to base, the umbilical cord had been thrown a bit wider, the challenge distinctly different.

Bravo Zero chuntered on through a small village of a dozen or so houses. Suddenly a flurry of children, all matted hair and holey pullovers, darted out of an alley between dwellings, waving their arms excitedly. To his left Blaylock saw Trev was digging into his pockets.

'No sweeties, Trev, remember? Wrong message.'

Trev did as he was told. What Blaylock gave the expectant children instead was a smart salute, before the convoy left them in its roaring wake.

At the foot of the Bila Valley the Warriors rolled up to a Bosnian Croat checkpoint, a lean-to hut manned by three HVO soldiers and marked on the road by a blunt cordon of black anti-tank mines spaced out across the muddy track. Blaylock slid unhurriedly down from his perch and strode toward the men, smacking his logbook into his palm, Tamara hastening behind him.

'*Doba dan, kako ste? Ja se zovem Captain Blaylock*. United Nations? You have to let us through. We are not involved in combat. Humanitarian purpose only, yes?'

The guardsmen waved surly hands, made surly noises. Blaylock inclined to Tamara and she murmured translations in his ear. It was the usual issue of local compliance – demands to see papers bearing the scrawled hand of local commanders, a tiresome delay. Blaylock had his standard-issue riposte good and ready.

'No, no. We're not at your disposal, okay? We don't run back and forth fetching paper. Our way through has been agreed with your command, you've no right to stop the UN.'

The men coughed and spat on the earth in the manner Blaylock had come to consider singularly Slavic. Though he spoke the truth he couldn't quite blame them for their suspicious minds. These Warrior tours were, after all, a kind of spying. So he watched them impassively while they conferred. They had the look of a peasant army – ill-sorted villagers, schoolteachers and bus drivers who had been handed rifles and pressed hastily into ragged green fatigues like schoolboy football bibs doled out of a bag. Less naïve to his eye, though, were the red-and-white chequered badges pinned to their camouflage vests, insignia that struck him as undyingly fascistic.

He had seen more menacing Croat forces on his travels – tough twenty-somethings, gun-toting spirit drinkers, bristling with skull-and-crossbones logos and commando accoutrements. Blaylock found it easy to imagine the worst of them. His view had been coloured by tales from the departing Cheshire Regiment about the miserable task of 'clear-up' after a massacre in a small Muslim village – extracting blackened bodies from burned-out houses in white bags while Croat neighbours looked on, hard-faced, their own hearths unscathed.

By contrast his encounters with Bosnian Muslims had been affable. These were the people from whom the army was renting its roof, who did the chores around camp. The Bosnian forces he met at checkpoints struck him as reasonable people, rightly aggrieved, and badly under-resourced for war. If Blaylock had not exactly picked a side in this three-cornered fight, he had certainly formed an opinion.

The Croat guards began grumpily to poke their mines toward the roadsides with the toes of their boots. Blaylock was glad to see them roll over without a fuss. Insofar as he understood leadership in this strange moral quagmire, it meant sticking by the rules of engagement the Major handed down: *You will at all times show purpose, et cetera.*

With the way past the HVO checkpoint cleared, Blaylock clambered back atop his Warrior and pressed the intercom.

'Cookie? Howay, let's roll.'

'Any chance of a piss-break, boss?'

At a suitable remove the convoy halted and Blaylock's boys lined up like racehorses to urinate in spattering style up against the Warrior's tracks. Out of sight Blaylock shared a smoke with Tamara, half a red Marlboro he didn't much want. But the mood of the garrison seemed to have sucked everyone into the habit – this, and the sheer usefulness of smokes as checkpoint currency, the proffered gratis pack often pre-empting exchanges about 'papers'.

Small talk with Tamara was fitful. Blaylock asked after her doleful little daughter, a recent visitor to the garrison. Tamara replied shyly. Blaylock could sense that she considered herself on duty at all times: this job was a big deal for her, maybe a ticket out of Vitez. She was a grafter and had, clearly, earned the respect of the troops, since Blaylock had overheard no unprintable nicknames for her, no excessive banter about her breasts or backside.

He kicked a stray rock as he waited for his men to zip up. From backgrounds only marginally tougher than his own, they seemed at all times ready to be led by him – so long, he felt, as he made plain his concern for their welfare.

Belfast had been useful in that line – for all its bone-chilling shifts of surveillance on top of Divis Tower, the tedium and perpetual brew-ups, the observation post becoming a kind of confessional box. When Cookie had haltingly sought 'a personal word', Blaylock had heard him out soberly, without judgement, and had been much relieved a week later when it transpired that the lad had not, in fact, impregnated his girlfriend's sixteen-year-old sister. Such cares were repaid the day Blaylock led his men into a terraced house purportedly rammed with IRA weapons and instead ran into a command-wire bomb-blast – mercifully mistimed. He had suffered no worse than to see his world turn white and then black for some moments; and when he swam back to his senses he found Cookie already bandaging up his bleeding foot.

This was leadership as Blaylock had come to understand it: not just to be the biggest dog with the loudest voice, but strong enough to show kindness and make mistakes – albeit never so weak as to let anyone give out shit. He would never forget his first weeks at Sandhurst, moments when the discipline was so inflexibly unforgiving he felt a gulf in his chest and the ground of his resolve giving way beneath him. Failure was inconceivable – the jack wagon back to County Durham would have stamped him indelibly as second-rate goods. And so he had rallied, 'found his bollocks', learned to take a bollocking from the Colour Sergeant, to swear he would do better then focus on nothing but that – to swallow the mindless neatness and oppressive order, to zone out the stinging rain and the leeching mud. He had dug just enough of what was needed from himself, and felt himself change in the process. A sense of kinship with his comrades – stoic, striving fellow sufferers! – had settled on his shoulders like the rain.

Now, in the mess at lights-out, when he studied his men stretched out in their vests and combats, Metallica bleeding from their Walkman headphones, he felt some kind of conservative instinct he thought he could call parental.

He trod his cigarette into the mud and banged his fist on the glacis plate. 'Right then, you's. Tie a knot in it.'

It was midday and five miles further on when Blaylock saw another checkpoint coming into view, markedly different from the last. Here was a barrier and sentry post, a guard-hut of nailed logs and planks with a clear plastic roof. Earth was banked at one side of the road, the bank of a stream ran opposite, the effect being to narrow the passage ahead.

Blaylock frowned to see significantly more bodies milling around the hut, too, more than a dozen men – surely surplus to requirements? They were dark-skinned, dark-browed, many bearded and with chequered *keffiyah* wrapped around heads, shrouding faces. Some wore fatigues, camouflage trousers and jackets, others were in loose khaki pants, embroidered waistcoats, banded turbans. Several appeared to be nursing assault rifles, others yet more hefty weaponry.

This was not regular Bosnian army. In wash-ups the liaison officers had spoken of 'irregular forces', mercenaries – *mujahedin*. Blaylock knew in his gut that he was looking at them now.

'Bloody hell, boss, Ali Baba and the forty thieves . . .' Cookie's vision of the road ahead from his driving seat, magnified ten times by the Warrior's powerful raven sight, far outran Blaylock's.

As the Warriors slowed up to stop thirty feet before the checkpoint, one of the guards hefted his weapon to his shoulder.

'Geezer's got an armed RPG there, boss.'

Blaylock swallowed, hoisted himself out and clambered down the slope of the Warrior's glacis plate, trying to execute the move with assurance. Tamara hastened along beside him, her eyes notably wide. They passed a large muscular African man, staring at them from his perch on the grassy bank beside a heavy machine gun on a tripod. He wore a bullet belt draped across his chest, and a machete stood propped against one of his fatigue-clad legs. That knife troubled Blaylock – it was a spade-like blade of dull silver, maybe fifteen inches long, surely intended for the slaughter of beasts.

As he drew near, a handful of guardsmen jostled forward in the manner of confrontation. One, with prominent teeth, close-cut dark curls and the gaunt mien of East Africa, came furthermost, shouting irately. '*Kuffar*' was the word burning through the air.

Tamara looked anxious. 'I can't . . . what he's saying?'

Blaylock, keeping eyes front, touched her arm lightly. Another man shouldered forward – bearded, eyes very blue, cheeks pock-marked under an Afghan hat of reddish felt. Blaylock extended a hand. But it only hung there, met by a stare, until he withdrew it.

'My name is Captain Blaylock. United Nations protection force.'

Tamara began to translate. The Afghan put out a flat peremptory palm in her direction and shook his head at Blaylock.

'Her, no, she not speak, she go.'

Blaylock looked steadily into his translator's eyes as he addressed her. 'Go back to the Warrior, Tamara, it's okay.'

As Tamara trooped away Blaylock turned again to the Afghan. 'We have to pass through here, my friend. Get on our way, yes?'

His antagonist again shook his head and took a hand from his rifle to wave it disdainfully at the retreating Tamara. 'On your way, yes.'

'You have no right to stop the UN. We're not part of this conflict, all we do here is observe and carry aid.'

'All you do. Yes.'

Just as Blaylock began to fear his words would merely be volleyed back at him, the Afghan made a more expansive gesture in the direction of the guard-hut. 'This, you see? This is ours. You no go as you want. You go back. This is ours.'

'Yours? You are Bosnians, are you?'

'We are *Muslim*.'

Now the Afghan made a beckoning gesture of sorts, clapped his hands, and his fellows began to draw closer. Two who had sat on a mound of earth rose and sauntered over as well. As the Afghan continued to clap Blaylock realised with a start that he was being treated to sarcastic mock applause. And now he was confronted by a cordon of men, bristling with bullet belts and knives worn at the waist.

'Crusaders, uh? Crusaders! They come!'

Blaylock's pistol was holstered inside his flak jacket. He fought the urge to reach and feel it. 'Our mission', he said, 'is peacekeeping.'

'No fight?'

'No, no fight! Peacekeepers!'

'You too late! Too late!' The Afghan prodded a finger at Blaylock's epaulette. 'You look, you look, uh?' He mimed the bewildered shaking of a head. 'Where is peace? Where? You don't fight, what good are you?'

Blaylock ransacked his brain for some bridge-building language. 'Why we are here . . . is to deal justly. You will deal justly with us, no? In Islam all men are brothers, right?'

'You know Islam?' He gestured sharply between them. 'You tell me what is Islam? You not my brother. *These* are my brothers. You, you deal with Croat, with Serb. Killers of Muslim!'

One of the Afghan's comrades stepped forward suddenly, shouting and gesticulating with a pointed finger to the skies. Blaylock could feel his heartbeat, could sense movement behind him, and wanted not to turn, and yet turned. And so he saw the muscular African man coming at him, machete held loosely at his side. As Blaylock went to reach into his flak jacket the *mujahid* hefted up the huge knife and thrust it under Blaylock's chin to within an inch of his Adam's apple.

He felt an injection of dread, dosing down like melting ice from his scalp to the soles of his feet.

In the same moment he heard a heavy *clunk* and a hydraulic siren-sound, and saw past the African's head to where Bravo Zero's gun turret was traversing with stunning speed into position to fire.

Meeting the African's gaze as he had been trained, seeing

nothing there but dispassion, Blaylock was conscious of motion all around, the sounds of rifles being slipped from shoulders and cocked, then the sight of men scampering onto the facing banks on either side of the Warrior.

As the blood hammered in Blaylock's temples his mind raced to compute, to conjure a proper leadership decision, the correct procedure to rescue a man at sea, the man being himself.

Kill them all, God will know his own.

'Alright, cut it out, man, cut it out, cool it, yeah?' A young man was shouting as he came toward Blaylock from the bank, also bearded and turbanned and in camouflage, yet his accent was of the South Pennines, and the hand gesture he was making seemed to signal an end to the skirmish. Glancing to the African, Blaylock could tell the big man had seen something meaningful behind him. His machete was lowered, though his dispassionate gaze stayed in place.

'Sufficient unto the day . . .' Blaylock heard himself mutter. He turned to face the Afghan, who glowered at him. *Never give an order that can't be obeyed,* he thought, and stepping back he saluted smartly. 'Another time. We'll meet again, I trust.'

Then he turned and felt his feet moving under him, his guts tightly clenched. In motion he gestured to the Warriors to start the business of turning round as best they cumbersomely could. At his back he heard dissent, jeers, and a rising chant, '*Allāhu Akbar!*'

'Fuck me,' Trev offered, as they rumbled back down the trail to Vitez. 'That was a moment, eh, boss?'

'Yep. Focuses the mind, doesn't it?'

Blaylock, though, could not quite hear his own voice. He placed a Marlboro absently between his lips, bit into the butt, then removed it and tossed it away. His body's alarm mode had receded, the panic rush from the adrenals had slowly turned course and been transformed, somehow, to a belated and low-burning rage.

He retrieved his notebook and smoothed out his tracing-paper map with an unsteady hand. He extended his pencil lines to Fazlići and there drew a circle; followed, on reflection, by a star; then, encircling it like a safe harbour, a crescent moon.

Then fury surged in him again and he scored it out with hard strokes.

'Another time . . .'? Yeah right. Fuck me. It had been, he knew, a poor riposte. Were there to come 'another time' then, no doubt, he would have to do better.

PART I

1

2010

Howay you slack bastard. Up and at 'em. Fight the losing battle.
So Blaylock's inner voice drove him on.

London at sunrise wore a lacklustre look. The weather was turning, autumn insinuating – the greyness of air and sky he saw as the city's natural state, slowly retaking hold over the careworn streets of Kennington. Wearing shorts, tee-shirt and the disregard for cold that he took as his birthright, Blaylock pounded the pavement and the pavement pounded him back. Alice in Chains raged into his ear from the iPod Nano affixed to his right bicep.

He was thinking, again, of the ludicrous levels of fitness to which Sandhurst had raised him twenty years before – tabbing twenty miles up a hillside, thirty-kilo Bergen on his back. It was a laugh, a short one, at his expense. All that had been a stiff ascent to a peak with nowhere to go: a hard-won accumulation of physical capital that he had spent, steadily, ever since resigning his commission. These morning runs were a rear-guard action, a Maginot defence against the gravity of time. Still, the wish to be again that lean and focused force going forward, parting the air in his wake – Blaylock felt it keenly.

Yesterday had been a bad day at the office, and another unpromising one lay in the offing. The whole week, in truth, looked like trouble. But he clung to his conviction that to put in a good shift on a bad day was a virtue that repaid itself tenfold. Whenever he said this to his colleagues they smiled and nodded, as if they would follow him into the thick of any fight. Somehow, though, whenever he glanced back over his shoulder, he didn't see them there.

He looked behind him now – looking for the other running man he knew to be close at his heels, the dependable presence, his reliable rival. And there was that man, in his black tracksuit, looking plenty lean and focused and air-parting, albeit twenty yards short of Blaylock.

That's right, kidder. You stay in your lane.

Blaylock ran on through gates and into his circuit of Kennington Park, upping a gear to dart by a young blonde swaying languidly down the path, still in summer clothes, wand-like from behind. As he did so he witnessed a conjuror's trick – a stunning *trompe l'œil* – for from the front she was bulgingly pregnant, to the point of capsizing.

September baby. You'll have a clever one. Just like my September boy. Too bloody clever . . .

Exiting the park and heading up Kennington Road he lengthened his stride. It wasn't a race – he was daft to think so. Yet the thought did persist. Some streak was driving him to outrun his fellow jogger yards behind – shake him off, leave him in the dust – if only to change the given, rock the guy's apparent complacency.

And so Blaylock accelerated, hitting the pavement harder, past the yellow-brick Peabody Estate, past Toni's Caff and the shabby corner-shop cluster, past the fine Georgian white-stucco terrace, the squat pub, the unloved low-rise flats, doorsteps where bagged rubbish aggregated.

A throb in his calves was on the cusp of outright painful. He could feel, could hear, his rival behind, pacing himself like a solid middle-distance man, as if poised at the shoulder for the toll of the bell.

Abruptly Blaylock eased down, having reached the short promenade of local shops – Colin's Furniture, Ranjiv's Chemist, Dev's Corner News. He jogged over to Dev's show-bin of the daily newspapers in their grid behind a scuffed clear plastic flap.

My sacrificial altar, my daily pound of flesh.

The tabloids all proclaimed versions of the same thing: 'SYLVIE: TOP COP COVER-UP?' All ran with the same now-familiar photo of the victim, the sunny fair-haired sixth-former in her heartbreaking school pullover and tie. Blaylock, father of two daughters, couldn't stand to see it any more. But the summer's banner news story wasn't going away, and the papers had found grounds to revive its pain. '*Every day brings reminders,*' Sylvie's father said. '*We're haunted.*'

One bright day in April Kevin Clail, twenty-eight, had struck Sylvie Jordan, sixteen, with a half-brick then dragged her unconscious body into parkland where he had raped her and stabbed her to death, and where her body was later found by a group of younger children from her school. A woman who saw Clail hasten from the park had helped police to find him, as had CCTV. Police had further found that a DNA sample from Sylvie's skin 'strongly supported' a match to her killer.

As for what else might constitute justice, the papers all seemed to support a case that someone in the Metropolitan Police – even its Commissioner, Sir James Bannerman – ought to pay with their job. For on that day in April Kevin Clail ought already to have been in prison: five years before, he was accused of raping another sixth-former, arrested, released on bail, then removed from enquiries due to 'lack of evidence'. Bannerman was now making clear that the force would refer itself to its own Directorate of Standards. For the time being, though, the Commissioner stood arraigned in the court of public opinion.

Blaylock flicked on through the tabloid pages until he saw: 'Hate Preacher's Home is His Castle!' This story, too, was illustrated by a familiar photo: the dark-eyed, gently amused visage of Ziad al-Kasser, former nightclub doorman, lately fiery leader of prayers at a north London mosque, believed by the British state to have 'non-provable terror links'. A refugee from Syria who cried persecution by Ba'athists, he had been refused asylum but granted 'exceptional leave to remain', and remain he had, however fierily he preached against the British state; for British judges had upheld his human right to make his home in England, for fear of persecution should he return to Syria.

Today's report concerned some who disagreed with al-Kasser sufficiently to gather and chant at the foot of his driveway. These people were also pictured, their incensed pink faces frozen in mid-shout, unmistakably the 'Free Briton Brigade' – a white working-class group seemingly composed of football hooligans at a loose end plus others who spent most of their lives in pubs, now making a decent fist of fomenting disorder on the streets of various English towns and cities.

The FBB's protest had prompted Mr al-Kasser to petition police about the distress caused to the second Mrs al-Kasser and their five children. At the High Court the FBB had argued for their rights to free speech and assembly; but the judge had ruled that they conduct any future protests at least five hundred yards away. 'The law is an arse', was the comment of the FBB's main spokesman, one Gary Wardell.

Blaylock had to smile. The law was complex, it weighed in the balance vying reasoned wishes and ideas of the public good. Today it favoured the Hate Preacher. On another day, maybe not.

Belatedly he saw a reference in the story to 'the error-prone and volatile Home Secretary' and he decided he'd seen enough.

He made a cursory paddle through the broadsheets, Left and Right, where he found similar material reported but in polysyllabic words: ' . . . rends in the fabric of society', ' . . . the precarious balance between security and liberty', ' . . . rhetoric bordering on racism'. Chancing on a column that hotly defended Ziad al-Kasser as a benighted man of faith, Blaylock looked to the heavens for strength – and observed his fellow jogger, at ease over the road, gazing into the middle distance, idly stretching his calves like some aged thoroughbred. There was something smug about this black-clad man – of his own age but taller, leaner, with a better head of hair and so much less sullied by sweat.

A stream of cars was drawing near down the road between the two men. Mischief seized Blaylock: he tossed aside the *Guardian*, turned and took to his heels, off the main drag and down a side street leading into a social housing estate. At his back he heard scraping tyres, angry honks, crunching footfalls. The chase was on.

He hurtled across the car parking spaces and ducked down a cramped concrete-bollard alleyway into Falstaff Court. Bombing along, he exulted in his prank. Childish, for sure – but weren't grown men, too, still keen on games? And now, at last, he could feel sweat on his brow, his heart properly thumping in its cage. His calves were straining but he didn't care. Exiting Falstaff Court he could hear gaining strides at his back but still he ploughed on, darting across a road ahead and directly down a narrow, secluded residential street, taking the first available left, increasingly sure he had lost his pursuer.

As he rounded another corner he heard a jarring shatter of glass.

Within twenty paces he had clear sight of the evidence on the road ahead – a shower of diamonds glinting on the deteriorated asphalt, and the hooded, bent young man rummaging in the back-seat of the Volkswagen Polo through its smashed window.

'Oi!' Blaylock shouted as he ran nearer.

The youth emerged in full, a wrecking bar protruding from his hoodie sleeve, held firm in his right hand.

'What've you done that for?' Blaylock shouted louder as he pulled up, sounding preposterous even to himself.

The youth was affronted. 'Fuck off out of it, man,' he spat, then the swathed arm drew back and swiped. Blaylock recoiled to evade the blow, bounced on his heels and threw an instinctive left jab that caught the youth's chin such that he reeled and toppled onto his backside. Blaylock darted in to plant a foot on the youth's forearm, feeling some old instincts to be dependably present and correct.

Then from nowhere he felt a rugby tackle piling into his side, stealing his breath, and he hit the asphalt heavily with weight atop him.

Mayday. Contact.

Even as he tussled on the deck he could hear reinforcements coming. Abruptly the writhing weight was yanked off him, and as he clambered back to his feet he saw that black-clad Andy Grieve had the second youth very forcibly restrained.

Now the black Mercedes was pulling up and the Met Police tag-team coming forward at speed, radios to their mouths. Glancing to the young man held fast in Andy's bulging arms, and at the grimacing bar-wielder being helped up into custody, Blaylock noted their widely amazed eyes – flabbergasted, understandably, by this rapid reaction, and by their incredible ill fortune in having selected this particular target on this particular morning.

Blaylock saw curtains twitching behind glass. Certain residents of Milner Street, SE11, had ventured out onto doorsteps to watch the two young men being patted down by police officers. Andy Grieve, relieved of his share of custodial duties, looked quietly perturbed. Blaylock stretched and massaged his grazed elbow and sore knuckles, letting the adrenalin beat its retreat back through his creaking body.

A regular police car turned into the street and burned to a standstill. As the two suspects were being passed over, Blaylock approached his Scotland Yard watch team.

'Can I give you my statement or do I need to talk to them?'

'We'll probably want them to take this, sir.'

'Okay, just let me get it done, eh?'

And so Blaylock lingered and described his intervention to a sober-sided young Asian constable.

'So, to be clear, *you* hit *him*, sir?'

'Well, yeah. I saw he'd a tool in his hand and was fully intending to hit me with it. So, yes, I gave him a tap first . . .'

Blaylock would have preferred some short verbal commendation for citizenry beyond the call and whatnot. But he wasn't surprised. He had always struggled a little with how to talk to police: some vestige, maybe, of having had his collar felt aged sixteen, all mouth and full of beer, back in Newton Aycliffe, County Durham.

He was glad to see his chauffeured Jaguar cruise into Milner Street at last. As he moved, so Andy moved smartly to his side, and the Jag's darkened passenger window slid down to reveal his Met-issued driver, Martin Keeble, sandy-haired, his pug face tanned as an Algarve golfer's and wearing a ghost of a smirk.

'Blimey, sir, what've you gone and done?'

In the cool, cushioned backseat of the Jag Blaylock retrieved his BlackBerry from the strongbox, called his private secretary Geraldine Bell and explained that his arrival to work would be delayed on account of an unforeseeable incident. A vicar's daughter, Geraldine's manner was impeccable, always concerned, never ruffled. Since she was required to know more or less his every waking move, also where and how he slept, Blaylock was ever reassured to have Geraldine as the safeguard of his secrets and foibles, and vaguely proud of the fact that in his conduct to date he had done nothing to cause her disappointment.

Andy, sat stolidly at his side, was a trickier case. They had not exchanged a word since the arrest, and Blaylock wondered if his silly scarpering stunt was felt to have been grievously out of order. It nagged at Blaylock, though – this permanent watch on his movements, the advance team plotting and reviewing wherever he might roam. For eighteen months Andy had been Blaylock's close protection officer – sharing his private life, such as it was, a patient presence in Blaylock's home, car and hotel rooms.

And as much as they had in common – same age, both divorced dads, a Forces man and a Special Branch man – Blaylock was never fully at ease in their relations. There seemed something basically unmanning in the requirement that he be flanked by toughs at all times – thus his queer longing to slip the leash.

He had suffered the regimen ever since Patrick Vaughan summoned him to Number Ten on the morning after the election, to confirm what they both expected. Blaylock had left his count in Stockton-on-Tees to catch the first train from Darlington. (A simple life it had seemed, back then.) After the most perfunctory of chats amid the removal-van turmoil of Downing Street, and directly upon his firm handshake with the new Prime Minister, Blaylock found himself flanked by detectives. He stepped outside to the armour-plated Jaguar, coppers and police dogs all over him, and knew it would be this way morning, noon and night for as long as the Fates decreed he be Home Secretary in Her Majesty's Government.

The rotating pairs of police guards were familiar faces now, and no real bother. They all struck him more or less as no-nonsense law-and-order Tories. He even wondered, on occasions, if he was sufficiently Tory for their tastes. Andy Grieve, though, was not so easily read.

'Must say, boss,' Andy spoke up, finally, 'you stuck a pretty good one on that lad.'

Blaylock exhaled in relief. 'Well, I don't reckon it puts any hairs on my chest taking a pop at a teenager. But he'd have wrapped that wrecking bar round my head if I hadn't. Or his mate would, if you and the cavalry hadn't shown up.'

Andy clucked his tongue, ever calm and solicitous about misfortune, as Blaylock imagined he was with his teenage son. 'Funny, though. I could see, soon as I rocked up into the street – you were up on your toes and weaving. Did you box in the regiment?'

'Christ, no. In the *regiment* they really boxed. I'd have had seven bells knocked out of me.' Blaylock chuckled, relaxing as a normally suppressed version of himself returned to the down-stage of his person. 'I did box in college at Durham, mind you. For a lark. I got roped in.'

'How'd that happen?'

'Oh, I was drinking in the bar one night and this lad I half-know staggers up, starts saying the boxing team's one heavyweight short for a match the next day. I must have been half-cut 'cos I said, "Aw aye, I'll step in, no bother, kidder." I was thinking, "He's more pissed than me, we'll forget this by the morning." But, oh no. No one forgot. So that was me in the ring the next night.'

'How did you get on?'

'I . . . got by. I remember that climbing through the ropes felt like a big, big act of willpower. But the lads just said, "Get out in the middle and throw punches for as long as you can breathe." And right from the bell I just knew, the other lad was as green as me, he'd clearly been told the exact same thing. We were like two bloody windmills. Clinging to each other by the third round.'

'Did you win?'

Blaylock affected a visor-eyed look of affront. 'Of course, Andy. Points decision, like. I'd say there was *marginally* more blood streaming out of his nose than mine. I got back in the dressing room and the other lads – bastards – they just shook their heads and said, "Bloody fluke".'

'And after all the guidance they'd given you.'

'Exactly. I did learn a fair bit, though, just from that one bout.'

'Such as?'

'Such as how to get yourself braced and ready for someone running up to give you a massive clout.'

'That *is* a good lesson, boss.'

'Aye. And remains so.'

It was good to josh, in Blaylock's view, though he knew he had to keep watch on the rougher things that amused him. He had been told so by the Prime Minister. *'David, not everything in life is a fight. And not every fight is necessary.'* He accepted the critique – and yet resisted it, too, feeling an urge to push back. At times his basic view was that the way he carried himself, all things considered, was a net-positive to the people he served, and that his critics on the touchline – *the bystanders who grab megaphones and make some noise, all the Twitterers and the gobshites* – they could take it and shove it.

He knew, nonetheless, what Paddy Vaughan meant. Others closer to him had made similar observations, with far less forbearance.

As the conversation ebbed in the car Blaylock's ears tuned in to the *Today* programme on the radio, where news anchor Laura Hampshire was quizzing someone on the topic of Ziad al-Kasser.

'. . . Is it not the case that Mr al-Kasser argues for independent Muslim emirates within the UK where sharia is law?'

'That is so, and if you are a Muslim in Bradford or Dewsbury or Tower Hamlets then sharia is what you should want . . .'

Blaylock recognised the debating tones of the self-styled Abou Jabirman, *né* Desmond Ricketts, a former plasterer known to old friends as 'Snowy' – a Jamaican-British Muslim convert with a criminal record, now oft heard expounding in the media on matters of church and state.

'. . . and in fact sharia is what a big, big part of our community does want and is comfortable with. So that wish should be considered legitimate and not to be, ah, interfered with or, ah, demonised.'

'Yes, but do all Muslims in Bradford – even anywhere in the UK – do many Muslims consider, as Mr al-Kasser appears to, that women must accept Allah made them inferior, and that thieves should have their hands cut off?'

'Well, you put things in your own words and out of their contexts but if you read the actual sermons of Ziad al-Kasser . . .'

Blaylock had already fished in the strongbox for a pen and a torn envelope, and now began to scribble notes for a letter to the BBC's Head of News. Still, he overheard the next item – a report from the annual Chief Police Officers Conference, where Lancashire's top cop was complaining of government cuts to their budgets.

'They're coming too thick and too fast. Just on my patch, month to month, thefts are up, burglary's up, car crime and shoplifting up. So the government need to realise—'

Laura Hampshire cut in coolly. *'I'm afraid, Chief Constable, I must stop you there, because Daniel Manningham is in south London for us, and we have reports coming in that the Home Secretary David Blaylock has been involved in a police incident near to his home in Kennington, an incident, I believe – is this right, Daniel? – in which Mr Blaylock helped to apprehend a criminal suspect?'*

'Yes, as we understand it, Laura, just before 6.30 a.m. police were called to this street by David Blaylock's Scotland Yard protection team and bystanders have confirmed . . .'

Blaylock's phone trilled and he checked the caller ID – Becky Maynard from his press office.

'Good morning, Becky.'

'Home Secretary, good morning, my god, are you okay?'

'Of course.'

'Are you okay to talk about it?'

'Really. I've not got a scratch on me.'

'Great, I mean, about how we handle it? The story? It's going crazy here but my sense is the balance will come in positive for you, so it's a definite opportunity to do something . . .'

Blaylock interrupted, seeing in his head the tumult of press officers now fielding five hundred calls. Briskly he dissuaded Becky from anything other than a brief statement. Slipping his phone back into his jacket he saw that Andy was regarding him with a half-smile.

'Sir, just to say, in any sort of emergency – there's really no point in your getting involved. I've got your back, y'know.'

Blaylock weighed his response for a moment or so. 'Howay, Andy. We both know if I saw a real threat coming down I'd have that Glock off of you in two ticks. And I'd secure my own defence. But, cheers, yeah?'

Andy reclined sizeably into the Jaguar's leather, as though to signal his ease at a ribbing from the boss; just as likely – Blaylock was sure – so as to let his tracksuit jacket slip fully open, the better to display the butt of the semi-automatic holstered snugly under his arm.

Back at home Blaylock showered, shaved and donned his navy Austin Reed suit, dodging the long mirror's reflection, since it rarely lifted his spirits, and he needed to keep lively. The morning's adrenalin rush was worn off, and familiar gloomier thoughts had moved back in.

He packed his ministerial red box with the day's major pieces of paper. His speech to the police chiefs needed final sign-off. The latest – last? – round of objections to his legislation for identity cards had to be rehearsed. Cabinet would meet at 9.45 a.m. In two weeks' time the House would rise for party conferences, and umpteen policy positions needed to be settled in advance. He had never felt more challengingly employed. And yet nor had he ever known such deep, overpowering moments of futility – not even at the lowest ebb of his tour in Bosnia.

As he was knotting his tie he heard Andy's courteous rap on the bedroom door. He looked around the silent bedroom, to which he would retire, alone, come the evening – the unmade bed, the identical pressed navy suits hanging from the armoire doors, the desk stacked with colour-coded files, the panic button by the bedside lamp, the greying view through bulletproofed glass onto the Kennington square outside. This was the life he had made for himself

– its duties and burdens, its powers and restraints, its solitude and confinement. He threw the duvet across the mattress – *Box your blankets, sir! None of that civilian sloth!* – and opened the door to Andy.

Downstairs as he exited the front door he recognised a hand-addressed envelope atop his private mail on the console table, and he doubled back and slipped it into his pocket.

2

The Jaguar rolled up to the great glass-box estate of the Home Office on Shovell Street, SW1, and Blaylock shifted from the backseat. Evidently, word of the morning's ruckus had spread. By the entrance the press had mustered a scrum – men in anoraks, some with heavy microphones, which they wielded as if to disconcert more easily jostled females. In his peripheral vision Blaylock clocked a second minor threat – a handful of placard-waving demonstrators, chanting in the standard spirited manner, but seeming now to shuffle down the pavement toward the entrance from the far-flung pitch where they had surely been told to stay put. Taken together, the two groups made a fair din.

'STOP DETAINING WOMEN! RESPECT THEIR RIGHT TO BE FREE!'

'Minister! Any comment on your punch-up this morning?'

'STOP DETAINING WOMEN! RESPECT THEIR RIGHT—'

'Mr Blaylock! Is this the first time you've hit someone?'

Andy muscled a path through and Blaylock, blinking under the barrage of camera flashes, pressed on. Yet before he could get to the door a diminutive young woman in a smart woollen coat, striding forward from among the chanting demonstrators, succeeded somehow in ducking through the press pack to point a bullhorn at his ear.

'Home Secretary, do you think it's right to deport an innocent woman to certain death?'

The wincing reporters seemed to care no more than Blaylock for the query or its volume. And with that Blaylock was safely inside the relative hush of the reflective sanctum.

He negotiated the full-body security gate through to the vaulting atrium that looked up to four floors of hive-like activity. Never did he cross this space without thinking of his arrival at the Home Office eighteen months previously: the formal 'Welcome' from staff, many of whom had thronged the atrium, more of whom stayed close to their posts, such that he had peered up and around the walkways and balconies while tight-lipped faces gazed down at him, and he had been struck by a mental image of himself brought before them in a torn shirt, bound by the wrists on the back of a tumbril.

His route to the lifts was intercepted by Becky Maynard, tripping lightly down the stairs from Level One, a gleam of resolve in her eye such that Blaylock had rarely seen. It occurred to him he ought to hit somebody more often.

'Bravo, Minister,' said Becky, politely but firmly. 'Just to say, I hear your position loud and clear, and if any big requests come in I'll only run them by Geraldine just so you're aware.'

Then she was off again, before he could instruct her not to bother Geraldine either. Not for the first time Blaylock had the strange sense of being surrounded by women – formidable, all, with cool heads and level gazes. From their assessing looks he somehow always took the meaning that he ought to take a moment to turn aside and tuck himself in.

He made it into a lift unhindered, ascended to Level Three, stepped out and strode past the cluster of offices occupied by his junior ministers and, more substantively, the department's Permanent Secretary, before reaching the comfort zone of his own private office team: the engine room of the building, his eyes and ears and buffers, clever young people sifting high stacks of paper while speaking clearly and intently into phone receivers cocked between shoulder and ear.

Geraldine – bespectacled, her unmanageable hair primped into a frizzy nimbus – came forward and greeted him with a nod toward his office door. There, arms folded, clearly wanting a private word, stood his special advisor Mark Tallis. Tall, dimple-jawed, privately educated, Tallis was his spad with special responsibility for 'press liaison' and the one among them most aggrieved by having to sit out in open plan desk space, fully separated from his master by a stairwell. Civil Service fiat, however, had forced the spads away from any closer proximity, as if to degrade the imagined powers of their dark arts.

'David, bloody good effort this morning, *patrón*.'

'Cheers, Mark.'

'You saw the *Post*, though, that toe-rag having a go—?'

'Easy, just give me five minutes with Geraldine, okay?'

She had moved silently to their side and Blaylock bade her into the office then shut the door behind them. His desk sat before the furthest window so as to make a dauntingly long walk for any bearer of bad news. But he and Geraldine took seats around the oval group meeting table parked midway, and she passed him the usual sheet of A4 confirming his day's schedule. He frowned at an unexpected Item 1.

'Sorry, but can you squeeze in Sheikh Hanifa and his friend from Russell College before Cabinet? Fifteen minutes?'

'You mean they're on their way?'

'It did seem urgent . . .'

Blaylock nodded. Geraldine then presented him with a pair of letters and he scanned them. The first, from Sir James Bannerman, politely notified him of what he had already read in the papers: that the 'Sylvie Affair' would be scrutinised internally. The second was on the letterhead of the Mayor of Tower Hamlets but ran to several sheets, with the unmistakable look of a petition:

We, the undersigned call on you to ban a proposed march by the Free Briton Brigade in east London on September 30. Clearly this march has been planned to disturb community

*preparations for Eid-al-Fitr, and in such a place as to revive
an ignominious tradition of fascists seeking to parade through
multi-cultural east London. The FBB bring a message of hate
to our borough. We call on you to secure our streets, protect
our citizens, and ban this march!*

The list of signatories was long and staunch. Blaylock passed the
pages back to Geraldine with a nod. 'Okay, I'll need to speak to
Bannerman, if His Holiness will grant me five minutes.'

'Got it. The Inspector of Constabularies would like to ride with
you in the car to the police conference tomorrow, is that fine?'

'Tell him I'd be glad of his company.'

'And can we tell Number Ten you'll be at the black-tie do at the
Carlton on Thursday night? They're chasing all Cabinet members.'

'Aye, if I really can't get a better offer.'

Geraldine nodded and left. Blaylock moved to his desk, where
a laptop sat dormant – his immovable note to self that all important exchanges in the building take place face to face, all important information pass from hand to hand. '*I don't want people in
this building lobbing grenades over email*' had been his day-one
decree.

Setting Geraldine's one-sheet down he glanced to the silver-
framed photo of his children: a posed studio portrait, their gift to
him last Christmas, decently done. He liked to imagine the kids
had come up with the idea, but suspected it was their mother's
initiative. Alex's irked eyes betrayed displeasure in having to pose;
Cora's querulous look rather challenged the lens; but at the foot of
the pyramid Molly's smile was so wide she was probably saying
'Cheese'.

Hearing footsteps Blaylock looked up to see the Permanent
Secretary bearing down on him, having entered without a knock.

'Good morning, Home Secretary. Heavens, if you wanted to
come in late you needn't have gone to such lengths.'

Thus Dame Phyllida Cox's version of Managing a Situation with Humour, accompanied by a smile that didn't reach her eyes. Possibly she had learned it from a manual. From Cambridge via the fast stream, Phyllida had always commanded big jobs in big departments. Not that 'command' was a term she acknowledged. 'By golly' – she had assured him at their first meeting – 'we are here to serve our Home Secretaries, not to make problems for them.' That plural, though – *Secretaries* – had stayed with Blaylock, in its sense of successive ministers as mere fly-by-nights passing through a far more entrenched world.

Dame Phyllida stood six feet tall, her robust frame routinely softened – as today – by furled and pinned scarves, gemstone brooches and heathery-tweedy coats. Her nose was prominently curved and her cheeks coloured easily, whether from pique or discomfort or a generalised sense that things were not being done as the manual decreed. Blaylock saw her as a Head Girl type: her voice must have carried at assembly, and she would have been a useful bully on the hockey pitch. But he could imagine, too, the unrulier girls ganging up after lights-out to truss her vengefully into her bedsheets.

'I've drafted this,' said Blaylock, thrusting at Phyllida the envelope on which he had composed in the car. 'A letter to the editor of *Today*, copied to the Head of News and the chairman of the Trust.'

She held it between finger and thumb as she perused. 'Yes. I heard this. You're really concerned? Laura Hampshire didn't let the Jabirman chap get away on anything.'

'Phyllida, I know newsrooms. Desmond speaks for nobody, but someone at the BBC either finds him very impressive or else they reckon he livens up their show. So they let him talk a load of garbage that's totally detrimental to what we call "social cohesion", right?'

'Do you not think he's rather beneath your paying attention to him? Or dignified, let's say, by your picking a quarrel with him. You are a scalp to him in that sense, no?'

[32]

Not caring for Dame Phyllida's tack, Blaylock was glad to see Mark Tallis sauntering up behind her, furled papers in one fist. But Dame Phyllida held her ground. 'I expect you heard the complaints about police funding from the Lancashire Chief?'

Tallis eased into the single armchair set before Blaylock's desk. 'David's already got his rebuttal in. Actions speak louder and all that. I just told Rob Gritten at the *Mail*, "Our message is that every citizen has a part to play in reducing crime on the streets, and the Minister has shown us this very day that he doesn't exempt himself from duty . . . ".'

Dame Phyllida, ignoring Tallis, gave Blaylock some moments' worth of a meaningful look, then turned and left. Mark unfurled and passed the papers he carried to Blaylock.

'My polish on Phyllida's draft of your speech to the cops.'

'The last draft wasn't Phyllida's, was it?'

'Not formally, but didn't you spot how what had been crystal-clear was suddenly turned into mud?'

'Right. So, what's your beef with the *Post*?'

'Didn't you see? "The error-prone and volatile David Blaylock"? And Martin Pallister got two whole inches just to whack away at you.'

Pallister, Blaylock's shadow on the Labour frontbench, was a seasoned media performer with aged-heartthrob looks and the dim aura of a lost leader. But Blaylock was unbothered by him, and vexed to see Tallis fret – hopeful of one day conveying to his spad that what the papers called a 'crisis' was usually manageable, and that he would pay no heed to such panicky language until the morning they had gathered sufficient dirt on him as to run a big thick-eared close-up of his bleary 6 a.m. face with DISGRACE etched above in big capitals. And on that day, maybe, they would be right – maybe he was a disgrace, maybe more than he or they knew. Today, though, was not that day.

'Mark, listen – I don't want you forever on the blower to the hacks and hounding my critics on Twitter. Okay? You could use a bit of Deborah's sangfroid. You're not an attack dog. I see you as a deep thinker.' He smiled. 'Will you sit in with me and the Sheikh?'

Mark – having stiffened at the comparison to Deborah Kerner, Blaylock's policy-specialist spad – seemed mollified by the boss's jocular compliment and clasp of his shoulder, as Blaylock rose and moved to the door where Geraldine stood wearing her brightest 'Now?' face.

'I was sorry to hear al-Kasser's praises being sung on my Roberts radio this morning,' said Sheikh Hanifa, making pained and rueful shapes with his hands. 'Poison in the air. He speaks for no one. And it so *wearies* most Muslims. To be tarred with his brush.'

Blaylock had once assured Sheikh Hanifa that his door was always open, and the Sheikh had taken this literally. But his sexagenarian presence – round-faced, mild-eyed, silver-haired under a green-banded turban – was no burden, and his credentials were unimpeachable. Chaplain of Russell College, a twenty-year veteran of 'inter-faith dialogue', Hanifa was a man on whom successive governments had relied to provide reliable definitions of what in British Islam lay within the pale and what lay beyond.

As the tea trolley was trundled into the office Blaylock took the chance to discreetly look over the stranger Sheikh had brought with him, introduced as Ashok Mankad, Russell Professor of History and Head of Pastoral Care – a slight, doleful man in big blackframed spectacles.

'Home Secretary?' the Sheikh ventured. 'We have, of course, just had our freshers' weeks, and in chatting with Ashok I saw that both he and I noticed similar things, disturbing things, that have caused us concern. We have often spoken of the Islamic societies? Their calibre varies from college to college, some of high standard and great value to Muslim students. Others . . .' The Sheikh shrugged and slowly set a glossy printed leaflet down on the table before Blaylock. 'Our society at Russell, we have had some disputes. Who keeps the key to the prayer room, what content is put on social media ... But, it has been okay. Now, the society has connected itself to an organisation that is new to me, and already they have booked a series of talks that, well ...'

Blaylock looked at the leaflet. It advertised a list of Islamic Society debates scheduled up to Christmas. The billings – 'Does the Media Understand Sharia?', 'Can a Good Muslim Be Gay?', 'What Is Preventing a Palestinian State?', 'What is the Real Meaning of Jihad?' – had a uniformity to Blaylock's eye, as did the repeated listing of one Dr Ghassan Doumani as guest speaker. At the foot of the leaflet was the legend 'In Association with the Institute of Islamic Praxis'.

'Is this Institute by any chance headed up by Dr Doumani?'

Professor Mankad nodded. 'A remarkably busy man.'

'You can sense, I think,' said Hanifa, 'the tenor of what is proposed, the attitude to non-Muslims, to Israel, to same-sex relations ... For the first-year students newly arrived to Russell, keen to join in activities ... it sends a confrontational message, I think.'

Silently, glumly, Blaylock agreed. It was Russell he hoped his son Alex might attend to read Law in a year's time.

'Now, Home Secretary, I have of course tried to speak to the society president, but he has been persistently avoiding me.'

'I see.' Blaylock shifted in his seat. 'The issue, it seems to me, is the one you raise about the duty of care owed to your students. We don't want to be painted as Orwellian bullies. But it may be that universities and student unions are a bit out of date on free speech issues – certainly if we've got parties who want to use free speech as a platform to argue that other people shouldn't speak freely.'

Mark Tallis was clicking his pen. 'Are female students welcome to attend these sorts of events?'

Hanifa winced. 'They are, though lately there has been this business of separate seating, if the invited speaker wishes it so.'

Blaylock threw a pointed look to Tallis. 'Well, then, it may be past time to look more closely at the validity of the invitations. It's been on our minds, in fact – the idea of some second-level order to bar certain kinds of gatherings on campuses.'

'On what grounds?' Professor Mankad looked very alert.

'On the grounds of their being un-collegiate. We won't abide segregation. No union within a union, no state within a state.' Blaylock turned to Geraldine, who sat taking notes. 'I need a report done on the college societies, nationwide. And I want to see the Director of Counter-Extremism Strategy tomorrow for a catch-up.'

'Shall I invite the Minister for Security?'

Blaylock knew why Geraldine asked. His Security Minister Paul Payne was zealous in his junior brief yet apparently unsatisfied, possibly seeing himself as a Laertes miscast as Osric. Blaylock preferred to keep Payne out of the way by tasking him with issues such as cyber-security, which Blaylock never really understood.

'No, just me and Rory Inglis. Sheikh, Professor, forgive me but—'

The two visitors rose to go. Mankad, though, looked at Blaylock very directly. 'Where I live in Stepney, I understand this "Free Briton Brigade" intend to march?'

'Yes. I am just in receipt of a petition to ban it.'

'You have a view?'

'It's the view of Scotland Yard that counts. You have a view yourself?'

'I do. These rallies, they are an incitement to violence.'

'Well, there is a right to demonstrate. But if, as you say, the intent is to provoke disorder then we won't be having it. We treat thugs as thugs. No exceptions, no excuses.'

Sheikh Hanifa sighed loudly. 'I am guilty, perhaps, of rosy spectacles? But when I first came to England, the seventies? It seemed to me that people could just get on with things in their own way, following their custom. Then came all this anger, the attacks, the "Go home!"'

Mankad nodded, intensely. 'The white fascists, they made a climate of intimidation. There had to be a defence of our rights. But, we were different communities. So how could we speak with one voice?'

'Islam,' Blaylock murmured.

'That's right. All the things we did anyway, believed anyway, we had to start shouting about. In the name of Islam.'

Mark Tallis, silent and seemingly restive until now, leapt in. 'That's interesting. God, yes, white people say the same, that's the time it started going wrong, when integration went backward.'

Blaylock winced, not liking Tallis's analysis or his choice of words.

'So who is to blame?' asked Mankad, eyes unblinking behind his thick lenses, seemingly very desirous of something other than a politician's answer.

'Evil in the hearts of men,' said Blaylock. 'What else?' He extended his hand to Hanifa. 'We fight on and fight to win, my friend.'

His courtesies having made Blaylock a few minutes late for Cabinet, he moved at pace to the private lift, but Mark Tallis stayed at his heels. Coming toward them from the Level Three kitchen were Mark's fellow spads, Deborah Kerner and Ben Cotesworth – Deborah cupping her double-shot espresso, Ben bearing his chipped pint mug of tea.

'Ride down with me,' Blaylock said, gesturing to the opening lift. The three young people did as they were told. They were bright and ambitious, and Blaylock found them endlessly willing to surrender their time and privacy in return for his trust and preferment.

'You're all ready for some dust-ups this afternoon?' he said.

'Maybes not as ready as you, gaffer,' offered Ben, the dogsbody of the team – a sharp, serious, recessive Geordie with an endearingly daffy laugh. Blaylock had handpicked Ben as an exemplary figure of the mission to rediscover Tory votes in northern cities. He was a large lad with a straight back and a sensible haircut and Blaylock saw in him a sort of loyalty that suggested a platoon commander in waiting.

'Okay, Ben, so we do immigration figures after lunch, I'd be glad of your input there. Deb, I need you in with me for the team meet on the Identity Documents Bill.'

'You want me to drop a bomb on that bunch of deadbeats?' This in her Georgetown drawl, from over the rim of the espresso. 'I saw some of the figures they've got, I told 'em it's bullshit.'

'Let's see the lay of the land. I have to keep the troops motivated.'

Deborah rolled her eyes. There was a cosmetic appliqué aura around her – her mask of pale foundation and red lipstick, her long black hair worn in a visor-like fringe with long side bangs, her striped and belted dress. She was so overtly feminine Blaylock had to stop himself stealing second glances at her; and yet he had come to believe she neither cared nor noticed. Deborah was impervious to charm, intently focused and seemingly – like himself? – unencumbered by a private life. Her appearance seemed merely a sort of armour she donned to do battle. Blaylock wondered if her sexuality wasn't wholly sublimated in politics.

They exited to the underground car park where Martin waited at the wheel of the Jag. Blaylock turned.

'Listen, you all need to remember to respect the system. Geraldine is my voice, right? She's the weapon of choice. Whatever noise I kick up, nothing much seems to work round here. But when Geraldine asks someone to do something for me, they do it. A lesson for us, eh?'

His praetorian guards nodded, in unison, however unhappily.

3

The implacable black door swung wide, admitting Blaylock to what he never failed to think of as Wonderland – a rabbit's warren, a hall of mirrors, its chequered marble floor made for games. A glance to his wrist told him it was 9.39 a.m. and he was nearly back on schedule.

As he hastened down the plum carpet of the long corridor to the Cabinet anteroom, Downing Street Head of Comms Al Ramsay was sauntering across from the press room, fingers pressed to his slow-shaking head as if the world were really just too much this morning.

'David, for your info, Scotland Yard have issued a statement about this morning's . . . incident? That two young persons were arrested on suspicion of robbery and affray?'

'That sounds as I remember it.'

'I hear you've seen some trouble?' Caroline Tennant, Chancellor of the Exchequer, had materialised at Blaylock's side as if by magic, in a tailored black suit and extravagant heels that gave her ash-blonde head an inch over his. She addressed him as she addressed everyone, like an admired head teacher who wore her authority lightly.

'No more than usual, Caroline.'

Since neither of them did small talk they were condemned to stride together silently down the hall – Blaylock, per his custom, nodding slightly toward Churchill's old leather armchair – until they reached the anteroom, where Caroline swayed off ahead.

Her Majesty's ministers were helping themselves to teas and coffees, some ducking in and out of the empty Cabinet Room.

Blaylock craned his neck to see who had already set out their stall and strewn their papers around a place setting. A few ministers already sat pensively, like candidates for examination. The cooler customers loitered and chattered. Loudest and most expansive, as usual – 'So I said to him, "Come *off* it!"' – was Business Secretary Jason Malahide, broad of shoulder and trim of beard, hands in the pockets of his double-breasted suit as he rocked and guffawed.

Needing a substitute for adrenalin, Blaylock poured a black coffee and knocked it back, then took care to exchange nods with those few ministers he counted as friends. There was Chas Finlayson, Employment Minister, lean and bloodhound-eyed. An ex-officer in the Territorials, Finlayson was big on schemes to put shiftless young men to work and had won Blaylock's support for some new version of national service. Then there was Simon Webster, Justice Secretary, who seemed honestly to approve of Blaylock's reform of British policing, at least to the degree that it saved money for the courts.

Now Peter Kitson, balding button-eyed Secretary for Health, stepped aside from a *sotto voce* exchange and hastened over to Blaylock.

'David, did you *deck* someone this morning?'

'Yep. A very, very minor ruck.'

Sir Alan Ruthven, Cabinet Secretary, with whom Kitson had been conferring, now stepped over too – crisply turned out as ever, in his pale spectacles, a look of freeze-dried patience under his parted grey fringe.

'Yes, so we hear. It really is an admirable thing about you, David, this way you just – leap into the fray.'

Blaylock smiled, thinking how Ruthven might whisper a subtly transformed version into Patrick Vaughan's ear. *'I have to say, Prime Minister, it does concern me somewhat, this keenness of the Home Secretary to just . . . leap into the fray?'* Blaylock thought Ruthven simultaneously aloof and over-engaged, the

Prime Minister's watchman–gatekeeper, forever on manoeuvres so as to preserve his own share of power.

'Rocky!' Jason Malahide, passing by, slapped Blaylock's arm with a big phoney bonhomie. 'That eye of the tiger of yours, I don't know. Look alive, here comes the Captain.'

Malahide's ears had been the first alerted to the sound of the Prime Minister and his entourage from down the hall. 'The Captain' now appeared, patiently at the centre of that buzzing retinue, and the ministers made their show of snapping to order. Patrick Vaughan dismissed his retainers and cocked his head as if to lead the officers into Cabinet. They filed in, took their places round the long table with much shuffling of the Gladstone chairs – the Captain in centre place under the gaze of the portrait of Walpole, Ruthven assuming his inviolable perch on the Captain's right, Blaylock to the left.

Glancing right Blaylock appraised Vaughan's familiar profile – the prominent nose, the well-tended fleshiness of his features, the hair stiff-brushed off the temples – like a top-order England batsman retired early to well-paid TV work and a newspaper column on wine.

Caroline Tennant sat composedly opposite Vaughan, as if to mirror him. It always seemed to Blaylock that they were symbiotic, complicit, sharing in the true loneliness of executive leadership, their fates entwined. *The rest of us are expendable*, thought Blaylock, glancing around the table. *We happy few, gathered in this seventeenth-century townhouse to turn our minds to the nation's ills.*

There was an apparent ease to the table, it being largely a gathering of university contemporaries and schoolmates, Vaughan the *primus inter pares*. Though no class warrior, Blaylock had by far the humblest background of them all – his father a colliery mechanic, later a repairman running a hardware shop, but always a Conservative voter. '*Don't rely on the state to put food on your table, son. Elseways you'll starve.'* Back when he had gifted Blaylock his first promotion, to shadow Defence Minister, Vaughan had praised him as 'a tough character, plain-speaking, with a common touch'. *What you mean,* Blaylock had mulled on leaving the room, *is 'You're from the north, you're working class, you were in the army, and we could never, ever have too many of your sort.'*

But now the Captain was calling the table to order with a sidelong look in Blaylock's direction. 'Okay, so first, we're relieved to have the Home Secretary with us today, and not in Accident and Emergency. As I always say, it goes to show they shouldn't get you angry . . .'

A rumble of perfunctory chuckles from heads bowed over paperwork. Vaughan sat back, never cheerier as leader – so it seemed to Blaylock – than when chairing a meeting. Yet it was Ruthven, relishing his role as lieutenant on deck, who now took over the running.

'The Chancellor, Prime Minister.'

Caroline Tennant murmured her way through just-published and not-especially-terrible GDP figures, her expression one of mild satisfaction, though she cautioned fellow ministers with the continued need for all departments to practise 'self-restraint'. For most of them, Blaylock included, this had meant cuts of a quarter or more to their annual departmental spending in the last twelve months.

The Captain chuckled, running a hand over one gleaming temple. 'Well, the nation can be assured at least that the grown-ups are in charge . . .'

Minor guffaws. Vaughan sought Caroline's cool smile in return. Blaylock glanced round. *Is that us? The grown-ups?* On the issue of spending he more often felt that he and his colleagues were like errant children, inasmuch as whenever they were insufficiently abstemious then Caroline Tennant did the job for them, wielding an axe of veto to policies that bore too high a price tag. She did so very gracefully: not gratuitously, nearly apologetically. But axe them she surely did. Blaylock was never sure of her true motives. To save the taxpayers money, or massage some headline figures toward the higher calling of re-electing the Captain? Something in her style was unreadable.

'The Foreign Secretary, Prime Minister?'

Ruthven now invited Dominic Moorhouse – an ageless boffin in black-rimmed specs, his thick hair in meringue-like waves – to brief the table on the state of the game of nations. France had been pressed into a military operation in a former colony: the Palais de l'Elysée had politely asked after the possibility of British boots on the ground and, instead, had been politely offered advice from the counterinsurgency manual. US Special Forces, meanwhile, were conducting targeted drone strikes against alleged Islamist *groupuscules* in the Horn of Africa and northern Nigeria, in which direction the UK had gestured its support.

Any minister was welcome to dip a finger in the blood of the Foreign Secretary's position, or else to demur. But the Defence Secretary Susan Rivers, who had entered politics from management consultancy, had no military expertise to offer. Blaylock had long ceased to imagine his own ex-services opinion carried any special weight: nobody in Westminster valued any sort of life anyone had before politics. In any case, his view here was as everyone's. Penetrating the arid centre of Somalia was a risky errand. Drone strikes, remote-controlled death from above, were perturbing, but met the need to injure and disrupt the enemy. The likelihood that they worsened the purported grievances of said enemy was not a matter one could afford to countenance, any more than one could really afford to address those purported grievances.

Cabinet was clicking along with customary briskness, a handful of agenda headings despatched per the Captain's wish to be done in forty-five minutes. Vaughan retook charge of proceedings.

'So, the headline figures on net migration will be known today and, Home Secretary, we hope the good work will continue and the target for reductions kept on course, just in time for party conference?'

'I am hopeful also,' Blaylock nodded.

'The Business Secretary, Prime Minister?'

Jason Malahide, by dint of his black beard, always seemed somehow piratical when he bared his teeth. 'I feel, again, I must point out that any reduction in immigration to this country shouldn't be cheered from the rafters if the figures show we continue to deter the best business people from overseas, and foreign students, damn, sorry—'

Malahide had been interrupted by the ringtone of a phone – his own, the bleeping notes of 'Why Was He Born So Beautiful?' The table made noises off and Vaughan his patented 'Give me strength' face, until Malahide had fumbled into his jacket and silenced the offender.

'Sorry – yes, overseas students are the wealth creators of the future but our policy is driving them elsewhere and, frankly, hurting our economy. We are *seriously* inconveniencing the Chinese by forever taking their fingerprints, and wasting the time of our top banks on endless visa applications for overseas hires. I mean, old colleagues of mine in Zurich and Frankfurt are *laughing* at us.'

Malahide, Blaylock knew, was not so much of a European, having made his money with a company that mined iron ore in Brazil and copper in Chile, was headquartered in Zurich and registered in Jersey. What did seem noteworthy to him was Caroline Tennant's firm approving nod to the bit about 'hurting our economy'.

'Home Secretary?' Ruthven tossed Blaylock the ball.

'Obviously I share the Business Secretary's desire that this country be a mecca for entrepreneurial talent—'

Obviously we prefer wealthier foreigners, we've plenty home-grown poor.

'However, he knows as well as I do what are the parameters

within which we are obliged to make our decisions—'

We swore we'd keep immigration low, so since we can't do a hand's turn about movement within Europe we have to hit the rest of the globe instead.

Ruthven, to Blaylock's annoyance, was busy as a racetrack bookie taking note of ministers now wishing to speak. Whenever Caroline Tennant or Dom Moorhouse addressed the table it was to give mere briefings on decisions already made – courtesy calls, letting colleagues know roughly what they were up to. Blaylock's share of government business, though, seemed forever an invitation for all-comers to jump in with boots on.

Valerie Laing, petite and flame-haired Communities Minister, tapped her folder vexedly with a biro. 'Whatever happened to that idea of reserving job vacancies for our people? That we only let in an EU candidate where a UK national had first dibs?'

Ruthven made a show of turning pages before him. 'Those discussions were had, but never without the caveat that any such policy would require us to prepare for legal challenge, at some cost.'

Malahide scoffed. 'Our voters will say, "We've got a Tory government, so what's it for?" Why don't we just do what we think is right and let Europe sue us?'

'Whatever any of us may think,' Vaughan sighed theatrically, 'we are bound by law.'

Blaylock checked his watch – thirty-three minutes gone – and fell to gazing through the window at the rose garden. They had had this argument, fruitlessly, so many times. What he knew, what they all knew as grown-ups, was that it was folly to lump together all who migrated to Britain – from within Europe or without, for whatever reason – and, worse, to then subtract the numbers who left and consider the difference a target to be assailed and reduced. *Never give an order that can't be obeyed.*

He was called back to proceedings by the irascible Malahide.

'David, come on, how hard is it to ensure proper immigration checks get done on people before they can rent a flat, or use the health service, or get a driver's licence?'

'The legal advice my department received', said Blaylock, bridging his fingers in a style he thought judicial, 'was that if identity checks were made compulsory in that way then they would have to be applied to everybody. Including "our people".'

'So they'd have to lug their passports around while EU citizens get to pony up any of a hundred IDs they use on the Continent?'

'Quite. That's why we're scrapping all that rubbish and just having one.' Blaylock was cheered that the obvious rejoinder had fallen so easily into his lap. But not one nervous laugh was raised. He pushed on into the silence. 'It's why we want one biometric identity card, to get in and out of the country, to access state services, et cetera.'

Ruthven's pen was poised, the clock on the mantle ticked.

Finally, Malahide chuckled. 'Well, yes, over to you on that one, David.'

Blaylock rubbed his jaw-line, looking from face to solemn face of his colleagues, feeling a cramped wrathfulness in his chest. ID cards had been a manifesto pledge, and yet the very mention of them, he knew, remained venomous to a whole swathe of people – some of whom were supposedly working with him to legislate the idea into existence, others of whom were sitting quietly with him around this Cabinet table.

'The Leader of the Commons, Prime Minister.'

Francis Vernon, Vaughan's dependable right hand for all unpleasant business, fixed Blaylock with his usual restive frown. 'On that point – the prospects for the Identity Documents Bill are a concern for all of us. MPs are unsure what's going on. There's a raft of legislation before the House, Home Secretary, and you were given your slot some time ago. So what's the big hold-up?'

Blaylock felt tension through his still-linked fingers as he gave a gritted response. 'I have said, more than once, that regrettably there has been political briefing against this bill from within our own ranks. So I'm not surprised backbenchers are confused. However, it is quite true that the bill carries special complexities with regard to human rights, data, cost, security, privacy—'

'Yes, and yet, amazingly, we press on.'

Blaylock looked sharply at the interjector – Arts Secretary Belinda Ryder, in her former life a popular historian oft seen on television hiking up Greek hillsides, now the most conspicuous Cabinet rebel on civil liberties issues. Ruthven and Vaughan, however, were also glaring reproof at Ryder.

'Belinda, with respect,' said Blaylock, intending none, 'these risks have never been taken lightly. We work to ensure the right solutions.'

'David,' Ryder rejoined, with the condescension she might show a layabout student, 'those risks will never be resolved. To get the bill through is one thing, to live with it as law is a risk far greater.'

'The Business Secretary, Prime Minister.'

Jason Malahide grinned. 'David, it's your baby, I'm sure you know all too well how much work needs doing to sort the mess out. And if your department's mutinous I'm sure you can rough them up.'

Blaylock gave Malahide a long look, irritated by this show of support clearly meant to undermine, and by how much Malahide seemed to know about his department.

'We will resolve the difficulties, and this bill will move forward.'

'You say that, Home Secretary,' Francis Vernon persisted, 'but the perception is that it's being put off and off while we struggle to work out how to do it. Meaning there's a case we should just pull it.'

Now Blaylock was lost for words. The silence extended. The room then looked to the Prime Minister, the only man who could 'pull' a bill, and thus banish it to the boneyard forever – the only man from whom *'Sort the mess out!'* was truly an imperative.

Finally, the Captain pronounced. 'Let's be clear. We know the Home Secretary is doing what he believes in. I believe in it, too. If it were just the two of us who believed, that would be enough.' With that he shut his folder, seeking no further comment. 'So, I expect to see you all at the Carlton on Thursday night, a big gathering of our clan, show of strength, all that.'

Blaylock checked his watch – forty-four minutes. It was remarkable. To be precise, it was leadership.

4

Andy Grieve stood waiting by the Downing Street gates, where Blaylock advised they would walk back to Shovell Street. Andy conferred with police, the route was briskly agreed and Blaylock strode out, stiff from the morning's exertion and his cramped seat at the Cabinet table. He was irked, too, by some of what he had heard.

Malahide was right: it was 'a Tory government', but by a gnat's whisker and no more, propped up by deals cut with Ulstermen, and it was silly to pretend such a thin mandate permitted high ideological posturing from commanding heights. The party was comforted and emboldened overmuch by Labour having elected a new leader from its most pharisaical wind-bagging tradition. Still, the odds of Vaughan losing the next election to such a figure could not be discounted. The Captain, for all his wiles, had earned no laurels on which to rest. The pollsters said he was not seen as 'popular in the country', nor as 'tough and no-nonsense', nor even as 'basically decent' – much less 'the choice of a new generation'. But the job, if thankless, had been keenly sought, and to Blaylock's mind there was no use moaning about it.

Reaching into his jacket for his phone, Blaylock felt instead the envelope he had snatched from his hall table, and he seized the moment to part the seal and read. The letter was from Tamara Sahbaz, his old interpreter in Bosnia: she sent news that her son had begun college.

Tamara had informed him shyly of her pregnancy on the day Blaylock's company departed Bosnia. Nine months later, in the week he resigned his commission, she had written to say she and her husband had named the boy Davilo. *'And that is from gratitude to you, David.'* A photo was enclosed. Davilo was dark-haired and dark-eyed like his mother, though he towered over her. Blaylock felt something in his chest, some offshoot of the pride in one's own, and a gladness that the boy was growing up with such promise.

It disturbed him, still, to think of how easily this might never have happened – by a hair's breadth, a hair-trigger. Stari Vitez had been a vulnerable outpost. If the Croats felt they were losing ground elsewhere in the war, it was simple redress for their snipers to take it out on the villagers of Stari Vitez, who tended to stay indoors lest they offer a target. Tamara, though, had to be always on the move, and gradually Blaylock realised – from the bullet-holes pocking every bricked surface – that the snipers considered her a prime scalp. Each time he had watched her go warily on her toes across the duckboards over the mud he had felt a special dread, fearing the sudden crack and thump of sniper fire.

Even now, under a milky sun in Westminster, Blaylock had to shake his head sharply to dispel things he wished never to think of again, things that squatted there daily and nightly and reproached him.

He folded and re-pocketed Tamara's letter as he turned into Shovell Street. Outside, the morning's protesters had grown a shade more populous and louder still, and some of the reporters who hadn't got him earlier had remained, doggedly. But Andy cleared his path.

As the lift doors were closing upon Blaylock Becky Maynard stuck a hand through the gap and pressed in beside him. 'Oops!' she sang, as if she hadn't meant to intrude. 'George Morley from the *Sun* called to ask if he could send one of his reporters on a jog with you tomorrow?'

'Aw, not in a million years, Becky. I mean, howay.'

'O-kay. So you know, there's been some malicious editing of your Wikipedia entry this morning but we're onto it.'

'Sorry, my what?'

She passed him an online print-out, a potted biography of himself with a passage ringed in red ink.

> Blaylock, a British Army captain in his twenties, is known for his commitment to ex-services charities, also for his ugly temper and acts of thuggish aggression toward people smaller than himself. Colleagues refer to him, without affection, as 'Rocky'.

'We're on it, as I say,' Becky said to Blaylock's frown. 'Also, the *Correspondent* have a new politics person, her name's Abigail Hassall and she's been on about wanting the big interview with you? It would be one sit-down, maybe a day's shadowing?'

'Why would I do that?'

'She said you're "a fascinating character".'

'Bet you spat out your coffee at that, Becky.'

Becky, however, merely blinked. She did not waver.

'No. If it's a woman and I'm "fascinating" it means she wants to talk about my ex-wife and all that. No chance.'

In his sights was the larger meeting room adjacent to his office and it was filling up, key personnel of the immigration team slipping past him and Becky, giving half-smiles and rather wide berths. Blaylock turned away, knowing nonetheless that Becky would not roll over.

'I expect she'll do a profile on you in any case.'

'Then she can get all she needs off the internet.'

'Would you go for a run round the park with her?'

Turning once more he saw Becky's tongue was in her cheek.

'As of tomorrow – and, so you know, for the foreseeable? – I'll be doing my morning run in the gym.'

Eric Manning, Director-General of Immigration, was a neat and tidy fellow with gentle manners and a tendency to dress up bad news. Blaylock watched him polishing his designer spectacles as they sat, and he knew what was coming.

'Well,' Eric said and blew out his cheeks. 'The figures are in and we do have a notable year-on rise in new migrants over the first six months of this year. Twenty-one thousand or so, to be precise.'

'The net total of newcomers being?'

'One hundred and seventy thousand, two hundred and nineteen.'

Blaylock pressed his forehead into the palms of his hands, involuntarily. *What if that was a city? How big would it be? York? Luton? My constituency?*

He was surprised upon looking up once more to see faces round the table bearing expressions of concern, in particular his Junior Minister Guy Walters, the young, loyal, not terribly bright MP for Kingsworthy.

'Home Secretary?' said Walters. 'Are you—?'

'Sorry. Go on, Eric.'

Manning continued. 'The rises are equal in EU and non-EU, but the latter remains ahead overall. But, there are some encouraging trends. Numbers of foreign students are down again.'

Bloody Malahide will be all over that, thought Blaylock.

'That said, some concerns in the other direction are a nine per cent rise in asylum applications, and a notable fall in the numbers of illegal migrants forcibly removed or leaving of their own accord. Also fewer Britons have gone off to live abroad, but we have rising numbers coming in from Spain, Italy, France – the wine belt, oddly.'

'I'm all for southerners heading north,' Blaylock murmured. Someone chuckled – Ben? But he was disconsolate. He yearned to see this issue afresh, not so wearied by the years, but it appeared intractable. And he had come to understand how it told on longer servers than himself – why staff who could hardly be considered departmental veterans nonetheless looked suddenly aged and helpless.

The immigration system creaked. No available resources could be thought adequate, no figures truly accurate. And no truly talented staffers wanted anything to do with it, while those who were politely forced into it just served their time counting beans down in Croydon. Blaylock could all too easily imagine some of them, overwhelmed by the workload, afflicted by paralysis, pushing obstinate figures into a drawer and turning a key. He could picture secret lock-ups – warehouses, even – jammed with cabinets full of abandoned immigration case files. It was one of his second-order stay-awakes at night.

Indisputably of the first order, though, was the fact of party conference in a fortnight when he would be required to say that immigration was falling, which would, on present evidence, be to say that black was white. It was a party political problem, thus not one shared by the permanent civil service round the table, yet he was compelled to make everyone feel the urgency.

'This is not good,' said Blaylock, finally.

Eric cleared his throat. 'It's not *ideal*. But there is, if you like, an upbeat story to tell here, about people wanting to come to this country – hard-working people, contributing to our economy.'

'Eric, I'd love to have that view, it's obviously a sweet deal for coffee-shops to get their baristas from Bucharest. But the public think immigration's too high and that it makes problems, and we said we'd lower it, so that is our mission and anything shy of that is a failure.'

'That people believe it doesn't make it so, not statistically. And it overlooks the wider benefits.'

'In my constituency, in all the old industrial areas, people seem to feel it can reduce their opportunities in life. They're not bothered by how cheap it is for Londoners to get a nanny or a cleaner or a loft conversion.'

'Minister, we should be wary of broad-brush caricatures—'

Blaylock felt the reproof – dimly aware, as of a backache or toothache, that the picture he bore in mind of the hypocrisy of Londoners was near enough a picture of his ex-wife. Still, he rallied.

'We also have to be wary of discounting what people say is their experience. They're not to be damned as bigots or belittled as fools just for objecting to the rate of change in a place they thought they knew.'

He pulled up, judging from the looks round the table that he had begun to beat on a drum in a manner his audience found strident.

'Look, if we all want to be relaxed about immigration we just have to show we have control of the numbers. Over a decade we've had several million more guests in this country than the public were bargaining for, and the levels keep ticking up. So, we need to ensure our guests are good guests. Right? And that we manage those levels, in a way that speaks well of diversity – not adversely. We have a sensible target of what the levels ought to be. Right now, we're missing it. By a mile.'

Guy Walters, frowning, elbows on desk, raised a hand. 'Eric says forcible removals are in decline. Then isn't it time to get the troops out?'

'What do you have in mind, Guy?'

Walters's whole frame roiled with keenness. 'As I understood it, we've got a database full of tip-offs from the public about illegals. Let's get our Enforcement teams out on the road, make a big day of hunting these people down – house calls, spot checks at dodgy workplaces. Send a message, yes? If people think all we ever do is talk about clamping down then, hey, let's get clamping!'

Blaylock pondered. The plan had a brute simplicity, rather in the manner of its author.

Ben Cotesworth, though, looked rattled. 'David, there's a big, big problem with that kind of tactic. People will say we've gone fishing – just based on gossip, on nosey neighbours. In that database you'll have a whole load of hoax calls, malicious calls, rival curry-houses having a pop at each other. You'll be taking the word of narks. And, yeah, bigots.'

'Ben, I don't doubt there'll be a few wrong steers but, howay, we're not Gestapo. If people have their papers on them then they can go about their business.'

'It's a *stunt*, but. It's showbiz. A big hassle knocked off in a day just for headlines. If we want to do this we should at least do it right – review the data properly, plan it, use some stealth.'

Blaylock felt sharply what Ben was accusing him of – of trying to look big and tough and, rather, appearing cowed and small. He would not have suffered the charge from anyone but his protégé.

It was true: he believed he was responding to steady silent pressures exerted from beyond the door. He loathed the idea of decisions made solely to get out of a short-term hole, for naked political interest. He loathed it especially because he had done it before, once or twice or three times. And now – he could feel it coming over him – he was going to do it again. Because, in the end, he didn't hate expedience half as much as he loathed inertia.

'Guy, you're sure we have the data to hand, in good order?'

'Oh yeah. Fifty thousand tip-offs reported by the public. If we don't get a thousand expulsions I'll walk naked down Whitehall.'

'We'll see about that. But, yes, let's get it done. How soon?'

'God, I mean . . . why not this week? Friday?'

Blaylock nodded assent, and looked to Ben, who had folded his arms, sunk his chin in his chest and tilted back in his chair – a posture Blaylock used to observe in his son during the final grim months before divorce and exile from the family home.

As the team filed out Geraldine was there, looking custodial, and she steered Blaylock lightly by the elbow toward his office.

'Some interception warrants have turned up in quite a batch, maybe you could sign them off now?'

Blaylock sat at his desk so as to treat with seriousness two dozen or so requests from MI5 to approve intrusive surveillance on select individuals – wire-tapping, room-bugging, plain-clothes observation.

The subjects were suspected Islamists in the main, plus a couple of Irish republicans, and a suspiciously shiftless Russian 'tourist'. Blaylock read as carefully as he could. He refused to be cowed or made star-struck by the spooks – wanting, rather, to form his own judgements based on the evidence. He could not, however, scrutinise every warrant line by line. More often he was resigned to trusting these secret, untested hunches, these informed suspicions of conspiracy and wickedness. He felt some sort of force steering his hand as he scribbled his signature – the duty to protect, his duty as minister for the interior, hardened by the fear of what failure might constitute. The spooks were nameless and faceless to the public, but he was the poster-boy for national security; and if wickedness came to pass then the public would require a public figure, like a target, on whom it could pin the tail of blame.

The various Islamist suspects depressed Blaylock especially. Some looked like little more than young men with talents for delinquent nastiness, and driving ambitions, apparently supported by holy writ, to become nastier still. These were petty-criminal converts, for whom Islam seemed to be a handy means of rebranding the society against which they offended – the authorities that had, quite reasonably, punished them – as a den of corrupt *kuffars*. Others in the pile of warrants, though, appeared to be model pupils, 'clean skins', and yet observed to have been keeping company with existing 'subjects of interest'.

Blaylock found himself staring at one such application, made against a youth whose sins amounted to 'accessing extremist material on the internet'. Considering it a worthwhile exercise to query the spooks once in a while, Blaylock picked up his secure telephone to MI5. In the next moment his BlackBerry beeped and he checked the screen. It was a text from his ex-wife Jennie: *Just heard the news about your run-in this morning!? You okay? Jx*

He thought for a moment, picked up the device, and started to tap out a reply. The effort to sound both laconic and glad of her concern took him some moments more than he had planned for, such that when Geraldine knocked and re-entered he had forgotten his qualms over the stray warrant. He signed it and passed the pile *in toto* over to Geraldine.

At lunch-hour Norman Dalton, Minister for Policing, rapped on Blaylock's door, back from the first morning of the Chief Police Officers Conference and instructed to debrief Blaylock on the mood. Dalton bore two bacon butties from the greasy spoon in the next street, and he and Blaylock stepped out to seek one of the seated areas dotted round Level Three where staff members could eat lunch. Passing the line of black pod-like soundproofed cubicles provided for quiet solo work, Blaylock found himself, as ever, imagining staff accidentally trapped inside and shrieking for help unheard; or else stealing crafty naps with their heads cradled in their arms.

They found chairs and Dalton unwrapped his treats. Blaylock found Dalton canny and competent, a seasoned fifty-something albeit with the look of an outsized schoolboy, perpetually pushing his spectacles up the bridge of his nose.

'So, Bannerman's speaking tomorrow?'

'Yes, that'll be your pleasure if you get there early. I hear he'll go big on reasserting the Met's operational independence. Anyone would think he was feeling threatened. I had to listen to Martin Pallister being his irrepressible self, giving it the full class war. "Them bloody Tories, looking down their noses at the honest British bobby, they just want a better class of officer what talks proper, don't you know?"'

'He didn't actually *say* that?'

'He certainly said that Tories have a problem with the, I quote, "ordinary working-class make-up of our rank-and-file police".'

'Well I never . . .'

If pushed Blaylock would have said he had greater problems with the Rotarian *petit bourgeois* make-up of police chief constables. He had suffered enough dinners with them as they dawdled over desserts and *digestifs*, their waistlines and self-estimations swelled by six-figure salaries and gold-plated pensions.

'Anyhow, Pallister got cheered to the rafters. I dunno, it feels like a bit of a *goading* atmosphere in the place, chief. Take your tin hat.'

'I've a few bones to throw. It's not all make-do and mend. We're saying there's money for hi-tech innovation; there must be some in the crowd who think it's better the cops have gear that's at least as good as the phones they've got in their pockets?'

'Maybe. But, you know – stick a camera on every copper and there'll be some reckon it's there to watch them, not the baddies. You might need one or two more bones . . .' Dalton wiped ketchup off his fingers. 'You know, after you they've given the big evening speech to Madolyn Redpath? She'll give us a pasting, you know what she's like.'

'I don't. Never heard of her.'

'You sure? She was outside the building just now waving a bullhorn in people's faces . . .'

Dalton struggled to his feet and jerked a thumb toward a long window with a vantage on the Shovell Street entrance. Blaylock got up and followed.

'And, sorry, who is she?'

'She leads on policy for Custodes, the civil liberties lot? Quite the crusader. And hardly out of school uniform.'

They peered through the window with their heads close together and could still make out a gaggle of demonstrators massed at the correct remove from the entrance. But the young woman with the bullhorn appeared to have abandoned her post. On returning to his desk, however, Blaylock saw that a newly lodged petition sat atop his in-tray, calling for change in the conditions of women inmates awaiting deportation at detention centres. The covering letter bore the insignia of Custodes and the signature of Ms Madolyn Redpath.

Blaylock spent an hour on pointed business calls – 'recorded meetings' – with Cabinet colleagues, while Geraldine listened in on headphones, taking minutes amid pin-drop silence. Needing bones to throw to the cops, he secured from Simon Webster Justice's continued funding for 'neighbourhood courts' to relieve police of processing blatantly guilty young offenders. Webster was blithe: 'David, it's a million saved in admin and court orders, so we'll get top marks from Caroline.'

He was done in time for his regular briefing from Griff Sedgley, leading silk at the chambers that took a lion's share of Home Office briefs. Hawkish of feature, fastidious of collar and cuff, Sedgley exuded a leather-bound quietude by which Blaylock was always assured.

Their chief item of business was the protracted extradition to the United States of Vinayak Khan, a Londoner wanted for trial by Homeland Security on charges of aiding and abetting known terrorists. Khan had committed his alleged offences nearly a decade ago in front of a computer screen in Willesden Green – a 'web-spinner', as Blaylock saw him, joining up cyber-threads such that bomb-making instructions could be cleanly relayed across continents, or a weapons training camp disguised as outward-bound adventure in the wilds of Oregon. The European Court of Human Rights maintained that extradition should not happen before the outcome of a final appeal to the Grand Chamber in Strasbourg, to which Khan's lawyers had made strenuous presentation that he be tried in the UK.

'I'm not withdrawing the extradition order,' said Blaylock.

'If you don't,' murmured Sedgley, 'you could be found in contempt of court.'

'That would be a not madly inaccurate assessment of my view. Let's see how the judge responds to Strasbourg tomorrow.'

They moved on to domestic business: eleventh-hour applications to overturn deportation decisions, most of them drawing on human rights law. A reformed Jamaican drug dealer, already booked on a flight back to Montego Bay, was poorly and pleading that he couldn't hope to subsist anywhere but England. A Somali man with form for assault now awaited a plane to Mogadishu, but his lawyer argued that he would thence be in mortal danger from Islamist militants. To Blaylock the process always seemed a ladder, very often one step up and two back, there to tread on a snake and slip back to the start of things, where the press and MPs lay in wait to curse the Home Office for incompetence.

'Geraldine, when do I get my sit-down with the new Lord Chief Justice?'

'Lord Waugh's office say he's been chock-a-block but I'll chase,' said Geraldine, scribbling.

'Now this one', said Sedgley, 'is at Special Appeals and you should know it's looking . . . problematical.' He passed Blaylock a set of papers marked *Bazelli v Secretary of State for the Home Department*. 'Mr Bazelli is a Bosnian who came to the UK with his father twenty years ago.'

'Fleeing the war?'

'Indeed. He got indefinite leave to remain, since when his adult life has been a stream of convictions – theft, assault, handling stolen goods. After four years in Scrubs he was meant to go back to Sarajevo; however . . . in the patented manner, before going down he impregnated his then-girlfriend and the child was born while he was inside.'

'So he's claiming "right to family life"?' This expression never failed to cause a clenching sensation in Blaylock's core.

'Yup. The child's British so, clearly, has a right to carry on being schooled here. And to have a father, even one so very derelict as Mr Bazelli. The first tribunal took our side, the second took theirs, tomorrow it's back at the Special Court.'

'Well, that's a drag but hardly a novelty, right?'

'Not on paper. However, on this go-round he's being represented by a proper heavyweight human rights silk. Namely, your ex-wife.'

The news struck Blaylock in the manner of an uppercut from close range, but he did his best to act like he could still see straight.

'I thought she'd not done this line of work in a while?' Sedgley continued. 'Busier fighting foreign tyrants in Strasbourg than defending exclusions? Do you have any idea why this now?'

Blaylock felt the silk's courtroom gaze now turned upon him. 'No. It makes for an odd situation but . . . what can we do but put our paws up? It'll be a little story for the papers, win or lose.'

'Quite. I just wanted you to be aware.'

Blaylock saw Deborah Kerner and Mark Tallis were at his door. He made his apologies to Sedgley and headed with the spads toward the urgent meeting of the team preparing the Identity Documents Bill – for which, he knew, he needed to have his head screwed on and facing forward – and yet pulsing through his head all the way was one obdurate note: *Why has Jennie picked this fight?*

'Sorry, say again, Deb?'

'I said you should look to give 'em the silent treatment for this one. Be cool, let them do all the talking 'til they trip themselves up.'

'Okay. I'm cool.'

Deborah looked sceptical. 'Sure you are. Just so you know, I can hear you cursing under your breath.'

As it transpired, Blaylock found that a brooding silence came naturally to him as he sat inking pyramids on a page while colleagues whose names he persistently forgot – the lead legal advisor, the bill drafter, the communications bod, the note-taker – took their seats. His attention was reserved for the bill's 'delivery manager', Graham Petrie – a big-bodied, perfectly bald, softly spoken fellow whose manners belied a steeliness of will – and on Phyllida Cox, whose support in this matter he did not count upon. As the last chair was scraped under the desk Blaylock looked up.

'Right. Graham. Where the hell have we got to?'

So began the reporting back: the counsel of despair. '*The costings remain, frankly, on the side of hair-raising . . . The guarantees we need for the security of people's personal data remain elusive . . . Communities still haven't signed off on our using their computer system . . . It's hard to see past these anomalies we have over our travel treaties with the Irish Republic . . .*'

Blaylock looked to Deborah and saw that she was struggling to heed her own advice, full of fret and straining at the bit to query the evidence. When Petrie was done Blaylock frowned at him.

'Graham – why don't you tell me something new? Counsel needs to get drafting this bill. The timeline is clear: a year from today anyone who wants a driver's licence or a passport gets an ID card. I know the issues, I understand other departments want tweaks. We need to write it up and crack on. The trouble is I listen to you all and I almost detect the sound of your – trying to talk me out of this? Like it's too much bother?'

Blaylock saw that he had now obtained all of the silence he could have wished for, and he leaned in.

'Understand, the die is cast – we will do this. Yes, we will make contingencies. No set of costings can be called cast-iron – they will change. But that cost is to be weighed against what we gain, fighting fraud, crime, illegal immigration. We may be sure Parliament in its wisdom will find the right amendments to keep us within EU law and satisfy the guardians of our ancient liberties, all of that. But we're not here to debate principles. Just to resolve technical issues. Now, does anyone in this room not get this? If not then speak now, speak freely.'

Graham Petrie looked from face to face around the table, then at Blaylock. 'Minister, this is a bill where . . . I feel we have to be wary of haste to implement the policy unless it is absolutely adequately worked out. I don't say this one *can't* work—'

'Of course not. If you said that then I'd have to throw you out of the room.' Belatedly Blaylock ventured a smile – *Joke!* – but too late, for Graham had not taken it lightly.

'I happen to believe, Minister, that we are obliged to be honest about gaps or logical wrinkles in a policy. Also, to weigh the time and effort it will take to craft this bill, as against the risk of public suspicion of it, the potential for major budget overruns *and* for judicial rejection.'

'Graham, all I see is a weird unwillingness round this table to put forward a set of clauses in order to be tested. I repeat, it will cost what it will cost. Data security will be the best we can make it.'

'Minister, are you so confident our "best" will satisfy the concerns of the public about what the state will do with their data—'

'Graham . . .' – Blaylock shook his head – 'you talk about the state like it's a villain in a movie. The state is *us*. We, the people's servants. Legitimate by contract, with the right to command. And we're not such an awful bunch, are we?'

The room stayed silent, no one visibly impressed by Blaylock's oratory. He wondered if he had confused Hobbes and Locke – or Rawls? – to the distaste of all these First and Upper Second PPE graduates.

Finally Mark Tallis raised a hand. 'David, just thinking aloud here but – might it be a help if we just, well, called the cards something else?'

Turning to his spad with an expression of intrigue, as if to encourage him to continue, Blaylock was suppressing a laugh.

'"Identity cards,"' said Tallis, as if turning the words in the air for the first time. 'Okay, I can see why people might think it's got a Stasi feel to it. But what's the card really for? Just a simple way to say you've the right to be here, and you're entitled to work here and claim services here. Why not call them "rights cards"?'

'That's a thought, Mark. Or "freedom cards". Or "citizen cards".'

Deborah winced. '"Entitlement cards" isn't totally terrible.'

But Blaylock could read from the room that it was time to end the sideshow of he and his spads versus the rest. Graham Petrie looked affronted. 'I don't see how cosmetic alterations will pre-empt the parts of this bill that are going to be politically unacceptable.'

Blaylock heard Deborah in his head. *Be cool.* 'What's your solution, then, Graham?'

'In my view? It's not too late to park this bus and look afresh at how to make simpler provisions that will serve us perfectly well – say, if we just made it compulsory for all adults to hold a passport? Most people have got them already. They feel comfortable with them. The application and issuing processes we already have are rigorous. I took the liberty of preparing a paper . . .'

Graham thumped a bound document of near-cuboid proportions onto the table. Half of the room seemed to lean toward it as if suppressing admiring coos.

Phyllida Cox wore her driest smile. 'Well, you did invite the table to speak freely, Home Secretary.'

Blaylock could feel his temples thrumming with blood. 'You're right. I asked for it. I underestimated the mood in this room. I get it now, obviously – it's a sort of boring, low-level, let's-just-kick-this-one-into-the-long-grass obstruction—'

'Minister, that's—'

'I'm talking now, Graham. Get this straight, you all need, collectively, to get out of that mindset and get yourselves on a war footing. Get focused on delivering this policy, on doing what's expected of you. The mission is not refurbishing passports – that's not what this government promised or what we have committed to do. That is a national biometric identity card, whatever the bloody hell we call it.'

His pen clenched in his fist, he thumped the desk, conscious of speaking through gritted teeth.

'Next time we meet, and that had better be sharpish, I don't want to be having some bloody college debate, I want to be reviewing a draft bill ready for parliamentary counsel. Now, do you lot think you can manage that?'

Phyllida's eyes were full of an alarm that Blaylock had wholly wished for. 'Home Secretary, you know everyone in this department performs in a professional—'

'Yeah, "perform" is the word, it's all "Let's pretend" and no action, *that's* what I'm weary of, *that's* what I'm saying—'

Blaylock felt – the room heard – his pen crack. He looked at the broken bits in his palm and felt all eyes, which had looked away during his tirade, now upon him. He tossed the debris at the wastepaper basket in the corner of the room, and missed. Then he stood.

'David,' said Phyllida urgently, 'let's reconsider—'

'Naw, let's pack it in. Eh? Let's all get out of here and see if we can't make ourselves useful.'

People were still sitting, still staring at him somewhat. Finally they stood and shuffled out in silence. They would be talking soon enough, Blaylock knew that much.

Blaylock paced to and fro across the tiles of the Level Three men's room, end to end, until he was sure his teeth were no longer on edge, his hands no longer curling reflexively into fists. All the while he was mentally replaying his conduct in the meeting. He believed he had expressed himself correctly, that his concerns had been appropriate. And yet the anger in him still flared like an affliction. For a second time he stooped to the sink and spattered his face with cold water.

Still he could feel it in his chest – that old familiar, heedless urge, pressing him to the brink of an act he knew to be ill-fated, even as he pushed ahead and did that thing which, on sober contemplation, he surely ought not to have done. This urge he called the urge of What Should Be, and he was borne along by it regardless of a quieter voice that struggled to plead caution. He shuddered at how he managed, over and over, to carry on as if 'rightness' itself could suffice in the teeth of a storm of wrong outcomes. And yet, simultaneously, some part of him shrank from the true reckoning of what this mindset might have cost him, again and again throughout his life. In his head now, unbidden, was a veritable photo album of times he had reduced his children to tears and taken some black satisfaction in it.

He straightened from the sink, breathed deeply, met his reflection in the glass and was repulsed by the grim furrow of his brow, the small red veins in the whites of his eyes.

For the remainder of the day Blaylock sequestered himself behind a closed office door, annotating a draft of his party conference speech with red ink. Soon it was past 6 p.m., for Geraldine knocked, entered and began diligently to pack up his ministerial red box with layers of colour-coded folders, correspondence for review and signature, briefs for diary meetings, a big night's homework.

Blaylock stood, stretched, went to the threshold and gazed around Level Three. Still uniformly lit, it now had a deserted aspect, cleaners' black bin bags dumped outside many a door.

'Mr Blaylock, sir! So sorry for your team!'

Fusi, a rotund and jocund Nigerian security guard, was ambling down the corridor. Blaylock joined him in cheery chat about the weekend's defeat suffered by Middlesbrough FC, whom Blaylock affected to support for constituency purposes – though Fusi, having fastened onto this fact, believed him a diehard fan. Thus they mulled further over the prospects of Joey Folari, a Nigerian lad on loan to Boro from Chelsea, the team Fusi had adopted keenly since arriving in the UK from Lagos, having learned his trade passing inspection mirrors under cars at the gated entrances to hotel compounds. Blaylock observed that Joey had yet to get a first-team game; Fusi believed the lad would be homesick, struggling to get a decent bowl of *ogusi* soup on Teesside; Blaylock did not doubt the scale of the problem.

As they talked, Blaylock's spads slipped past them into his office and Geraldine, coat on, went the opposite way with a mouthed 'Goodnight'. At last Blaylock stepped back inside, to see Ben at the meeting table reading a hefty document, and Deborah hunched over Blaylock's laptop, the glow of the inbox across her fretting features as she performed her routine recompense for Blaylock's inattention to email by logging in to his account and clearing his backlog. Mark had switched on the usually dormant TV screen fixed to the wall and BBC News 24 played to no one as he paced about while talking to his phone. 'Obviously, don't write that, just know I've said it, okay? Yup.'

Blaylock surveyed his charges with affection. 'While most head home for supper, here we burn the lights late like *Il Duce* on the Piazza Venezia . . .' The spads eyed him curiously. He shrugged. 'Okay, at ease.'

As they sat together at the oval table Mark pushed the evening paper toward Blaylock. 'You made the front of the *Standard*.'

He inspected. 'THE HAVE-A-GO HOME SEC' was the headline illustrated with a shot from the morning's scrum outside the building.

Deborah was eyeing the pages of his red-inked conference speech on the table. 'You ready for a fresh pair of eyes on that?'

'Not yet. I'm still working on the bits meant to be from the heart.'

'Hey, I can do heart.'

But Blaylock wished to crack on. 'Listen, about the ID cards team meeting, did I come over like a mental case?'

'No, David.' Mark winced. 'You were great. It's not the worst idea to come on like a loose cannon once in a while. For one thing people might start to live in fear they'll get shot.'

'Some of them you really do need to get shot of,' remarked Deborah, moodily. 'What did Cox say to you afterwards?'

'I think Phyllida and I are non-speakers for the moment.'

'Well, it's her system you're attacking. All these schlumps need to understand that if you can't deliver then you don't just get a hug and a nice change of job.'

Deborah was forever calling people out on failures to 'deliver': 'delivery' was perhaps her only concern. While liking her stridency Blaylock felt it lacked the needful finesse – the talent for backstage palm-greasing – by which politics routinely got done. And yet her dream of a stiff-broom sweep through the building didn't displease him. He allowed himself the occasional fantasy of what he might accomplish with a permanent secretary he could call an ally, a proper tactical commander. *Let's get this done, chop-chop, no buggering about.*

Ben Cotesworth was looking pensive. 'I don't reckon it's the worst thing for our processes if we just take a moment to consider whether the nay-sayers have a point.'

Blaylock had to respect Ben's pluck, even as his other two lieutenants threw him hard looks. 'You mean Graham Petrie's idea? Passports for everyone instead of ID cards?'

Ben gestured to the fat document in front of him. 'He did ask me very politely to have a read of this.'

Blaylock scoffed. 'Polite of him to have typed up that bloody telephone directory instead of working on my bloody bill.'

'No, no.' Deborah sounded galled, now twisting her silk scarf between her hands as if fashioning a garrotte. 'He just pulled that out of the drawer it's been sitting in since the last time they stopped a Home Secretary doing ID cards. He put a new fucking *date* on the cover . . .'

Blaylock shifted in his chair, wanting to unseat the block of frustration inside him. 'Ben, I got us pregnant with this bill, it was done for love, and we're just going to have to carry it to term whatever the bairn looks like. The point is that the schedule's slipping, the Captain's hearing voices that say jack it in.'

'But if the Prime Minister isn't right behind it—'

Tallis jumped in. 'Number Ten gets the principle of the bill, they just get jumpy at the complaints. But if we make it work, they'll love the results. Our trouble is this idea that we're going to mess it up. That's what the media says, and that's who Vaughan listens to. We need to work on the press. If I get someone tame to interview you, you'd do it?'

'What am I meant to say, though?' Blaylock shook his head and silence reigned for some moments, in which Blaylock realised that Ben was very diligently tapping the bridge of his nose with his forefinger.

'I think I know what this bill needs,' he offered at last.

'Oh yeah?'

'We need to invite the Home Affairs Committee to do a full interrogation of the draft, get all its enemies in to give evidence, the civil liberties groups and tech firms and what have you – the works.'

Blaylock had the sudden surreal sense of entertaining at his table some strange angel who had assumed Ben's approximate shape. 'Are you having a laugh, Ben? You want Gervaise Hawley's committee to chew the bill up clause by clause? Do you *want* us to lose?'

Tallis, though, was looking as pensive as Ben. 'No, hold on. He's a clever boy. People think we're not listening. Let's show how much we listen, let's have the debate, make it clear how serious we are. So our critics have to show how serious they are, too. Then we'll find out what's a real concern and what's just sanctimony. I mean, come on, David, if it's a proper debate don't you think we'll win it? Whatever Hawley says, that committee will get pregnant with the bill, too. Sure, they'll have recommendations, we'll make a big show of appearing to take those on-board, yadda yadda. Meanwhile I bet a few things happen in the real world that make our case for us . . .'

Blaylock wondered what sort of horror Mark had in mind. Inwardly, the troubling incompleteness of the thing had begun to haunt him. He had a firm-to-middling conviction on identity cards. Yet in his heart he knew there were other shades to the story, consequences unforeseen or unforeseeable. The world changed while he slept, then he woke and lumbered onward into a new dawn with 'the policy' designed to address yesterday's problems. There was a bottle of red wine on the office sideboard and he was suddenly thirsty to crack it.

'Okay,' he said finally. 'If nothing else then Ben's idea will get the draft bill written faster, by god. I'll get on to Francis Vernon, get the committee scheduled.'

Deborah appeared disapproving. 'Gervaise Hawley's just going to complain his committee's being forced into an unreasonable timeframe.'

'Oh, but', Tallis tutted, 'in his arrogance Gervaise won't be able to pass up his big chance to kill the bill. Then we put David on the witness stand and, boom, David fucking kills Hawley.'

Surtout, pas trop de zèle, thought Blaylock as he raised his palms as if in benediction. 'Enough. Mark, will you draft something for Francis?'

Mark darted to Blaylock's desk and set to typing out an email. Blaylock wanted to dismiss the others for the night, and yet they sat there seemingly expectant of further overtime.

'Deb, will you have a last look at the cops speech? And Ben, would you have a read of my conference draft? It's got the hymn-sheet stuff. Needs a bit of the salt of the earth, but.'

Blaylock stood, uncapped the bottle of wine that had sat there like a challenge, and offered it around. Mark and Ben shrugged why-nots and he splashed out glasses for them. Deborah, eyes fixed on the page, gave her customary curt head-shake.

'I hope your day finished up better than how it got started, boss . . .'

Blaylock was distracted at last by Andy Grieve, dependably upright and so rarely deterred. But from his slumped place in the back of the Jag, he continued to brood on the view from Vauxhall Bridge under sodium light.

Martin dropped him by his doorstep, whereupon he and Andy shook hands for the night. Within, Terry the night-shift guard was already in situ downstairs, seated with a crime novel in an armchair by the kettle in the kitchen.

In his first floor study Blaylock cracked the red box to find a great sheaf of EU papers requiring his tick of approval. He didn't bother to scrutinise them, faithfully checking the boxes then settling down over Ben's emendations to his conference speech.

'As Home Secretary it is my duty to always carry in mind the safety of the British public. It's the first thing I think of each morning I wake, and the last whenever I turn in.'

This felt laid on too thick, if it had the benefit of being half-true. Blaylock did bear such worries daily – images of the shadow-world, the terror plot, the lone wolf in the crowd clad in the suicide vest, the car edging through traffic with a lethal payload. His first waking thought, though, was always to remember who he was. Come night-time he was more concerned by his growing agglomeration of aches and pains.

His eye was drawn to a rash of red ink: *'Number Ten will query!!!'*

The offending line was *'Play for the team, and if you think you can lead the team then give that a go and see what you're made of.'*

He was pondering whether the sentiment could be salvaged when his phone vibrated. On the line was the former Jennie Blaylock. He stabbed the answer button.

'Hi, David. Listen, the kids saw all about your fracas this morning on the news – your citizen's arrest? They're hoping you're okay?'

'Oh aye, you should see the other fella, et cetera.'

'I'm sure you did what you had to. It'd be a shame if you got your block knocked off by some little car thief, after all the trouble you've seen . . .' Jennie's lilting Durham tones implied, as ever, that she had seen it all herself.

'Well, I'm relieved you approve.'

'Molly's here, she wants a word before bed.'

'Great, put her on.'

'Hi Daddy!'

After a cheering exchange of endearments he heard Jennie retake the handset and felt there was no point messing around.

'So you're chasing me through the courts again tomorrow.'

'The Bazelli case? You know how it is, I'd told chambers I was available for a bit and that was just the bus that came along.'

'What, with your seniority you couldn't have ducked it?'

'Well, let's also say, I don't see that I should have to? Am I supposed to renounce my living, David, just because you've got yours? We've been through all this, haven't we?'

'Yeah, we have. I just keep thinking one day you'll see reason.'

She laughed down the line in the throaty manner he had always adored and which felt, in the circumstances, almost worth the grief.

'Okay, look, I don't want a row.'

'That's good. Because I wanted to ask a favour, actually.'

'You fucking what?' he said, feeling his mood improve further.

'Can you come pick up the kids an hour earlier this Sunday? There's just an errand I have to run.'

'You can't get Radka to call in for an hour?'

'Oh David, you know full well . . .'

He had known his folly even as he uttered it – a needless show of unwillingness on his part, when he only had the children every other Sunday and half of the school holidays; compounded by his perennial forgetting that Jennie's young Croatian nanny would never do anything but the very least she had signed up for.

'Okay, we can get a milkshake or something before the cinema. Have they picked a film to see?'

'I think there's some sort of documentary about nocturnal animals Molly's keen on? Cora's amenable, being a nocturnal creature herself.'

'But what about Alex?'

'He'll suffer it. Okay, yes, bedtime. Listen, thanks David, goodnight.'

Putting down his phone Blaylock felt, as usual with Jennie, that he had been bested somehow. He chastened himself for having responded with such little grace to what was, really, the offer of an extra hour with his children. The visitation terms he had accepted were not generous, and yet the truth – though he wished it otherwise – was that he didn't always claim his entitlement in full.

A crystal decanter and glasses – an old wedding present – sat atop a low shelf next to Blaylock's desk. He went and lifted the decanter, then caught himself, set it down and walked away. Then he walked back, poured out three fingers of single malt and swallowed his medicine – lavender, heather, Virginia tobacco and a hint of engine oil. His eyes watering agreeably, he poured again.

He had first met his future bride at the University of Durham. Even years later he could never quite confess that he carried always in his mind the first time he saw her – early one morning in the college canteen, the radio playing 'Sweet Jane', she in candy-stripe pyjama bottoms and some lucky beggar's cabled sweater, smoking, laughing throatily, running hands through her hair. His heart was near enough set on her then, before he had any inkling of her finer qualities.

Jennie came from Barnard Castle, ten miles whence he hailed himself, and yet something between them made for a gulf. Both reading history, they met weekly in a tutorial room, where they tended to disagree about the causes and effects of near enough everything from the Peasants' Revolt to the Sykes–Picot Agreement. They were both ever ready to speak out, she always with composure, he sometimes hotly incoherent. She was as assured as he was recessive, to the Left as he was Right.

The first in his family to reach a university, Blaylock had hated the idea that higher education was any kind of refuge from the 'real' world. But that was, more or less, how he felt about the left-wingers he ran across in student politics. Their crusading sureties vexed him: most issues seemed to him murkier than that. Though the Conservative Association seemed to him a crowd of braying snobs, such was his faith in the individual over the collective that he signed up – something that Jennie observed with mirth in their weekly jousts.

Come their final year he had gleaned what Jennie had in mind for her immediate future: to travel, write, observe elections. She had met a guy who seemed as bothered as her by global imbalances of power, and their closeness looked to Blaylock like a stronger connection than any he had enjoyed with the handful of girls whom he had dated listlessly and failed to treat very well.

Feeling increasingly unmanned by his unrequited love, Blaylock found a seed growing in his mind. There was another man lurking inside him whom he needed to meet – to invite, even, to the forefront of his person. He convinced himself he could achieve the great change by self-mortification, by shifting himself into harm's way, a challenge that didn't scare him as it might, for he saw himself as having only so much to lose as matters stood. At a careers fair he sat down with the man from the British Army. On paper he had promise. A bursary was available. He travelled to a Wiltshire army base, donned a numbered bib, scaled walls and scribbled his way through mental aptitude tests. A letter came to inform him he had Category One consent to start at the Royal Military Academy after his degree was done.

The last time he saw Jennie before their graduation she materialised before him from out of the throng on Saddlergate, for once without her boyfriend at her side but going the opposite way on a thoroughly drizzly late June day.

'Seriously, David? The army? Oh my lord. Why?'

He had been so resolved and yet suddenly he was back in the seminar room, struggling to sound coherent. She spared him.

'Look, I really hope you'll do all what you say. Really, David. Take care of yourself, okay?'

His fellow cadets at Sandhurst came to consider him a monkish figure – 'a stiff-necked sort of a prick' in one hostile view. He quickly understood that to be in the army and yet seemingly indifferent to the quest of screwing anything in knickers was to put oneself in the line of a particular kind of fire. But one by one the others' long-distance relationships had failed the further they travelled from the civilian world. Blaylock, though, stayed true to the girl he had left behind – or who had, rather, left him standing in the rain. However mad his scheme of self-overcoming had seemed, it had been made on a wager he would meet Jennie again and things would be different. And the plan had worked, on the surface. Yet there had been, in its origins, a fatal flaw.

*

In his bedroom Blaylock flicked on the television to catch *Newsnight* and found a panel in keen debate over a filmed package they had evidently all just watched on the subject of 'Britain's Secret World'. The filmmaker, Nick Gilchrist by name, was in full flow, describing a 'surveillance state' into which Britain had sleepwalked, and calling on the UK's secret service – if Blaylock heard this right – to appoint human rights campaigners in key roles overseeing its operations. A big, lantern-jawed, expressive man with a luxuriant mane of greying hair, Mr Gilchrist struck Blaylock as the sort who oughtn't to be so paranoid.

Blaylock stripped off his clothes and repaired to the bathroom. There he felt the gaze of his reflection – his double – in the long mirrored cabinet, and he turned and gazed back.

Nowadays he didn't much care for the look of himself. The muscled gauntness he'd acquired in the army was long gone. His brow and jaw arguably retained some 'character', but with jowly traces of gloom that seemed to him the manifestation of some creeping, unreliable element in his personality. Likewise, the tremble of flab round his waist seemed to spell a succumbing to the earth and its earthiness that felt to Blaylock unmanly – as, weirdly, did the sag of his undercarriage, formerly a good virile weight, increasingly in his eyes a disused, rather mournful oddment. Idly he rapped his penis with his knuckles – a gee-up gesture of sorts – and it swayed, a glum pendulum.

He shut off the light, settled under the covers, and had not lain long before he felt the usual hard sheet of discomfort behind his shoulder blades. He turned and turned again, massaging himself, but the ache resisted manipulation or any effort to 'lie flat'. Gradually, though, he felt his weight sinking across the mattress, breaths steadily coming shorter, his fatigue rolling over him like the tide over shingle.

He was rudely awakened by his phone and knew straight away that it was the early hours, darkness still heavy behind the blinds as he scrabbled about to locate the slim pulsing oblong on his bed-side table.

'Hello?'

His ear was stung by a blast of incoherent babble. He looked at the screen ID – UNKNOWN – then pressed phone to ear again. The babble was breaking into parts: he could make out wailing sirens, stray shouts, street noise, a war-zone ambience of mayhem and panic.

'Hello? Who is this?'

Out of silence he was answered by a voice that was female, albeit a robot's monotone. *'Do you hear that, Mr Secretary? It is – terror. It is – your future. It is – going to happen. Mr Secretary.'*

Blaylock sat up, kicking the cover off his bed. The voice in his ear became high, sinister in its purity, a choirboy reading from the Bible.

'And when it happens, you will have to ask yourself – what did I do to prevent it?'

'Listen, whoever you are, you're making a big mistake.'

The voice changed again – so thickly sepulchral it could have issued from a crypt. *'Proud of yourself? Big man? You should be ashamed. You should die of shame. This country is run by vermin and you're the biggest rat of them all. The trap is set. Look out!'*

Blaylock moved for the door, hearing an approach outside.

'Your time is up.'

The last thing Blaylock heard coming down the line was the mad clamour of an alarm clock, then Terry was rapping at his door.

The kitchen clock read 03.17 as Blaylock brewed a pot of tea for Terry and his police team plus the new arrival, a trim and shaven-headed detective from Scotland Yard Counter-Terrorism who introduced himself, in politely estuarine tones, as Detective Neil Hill.

'May I have a look at your phone, sir?'

Blaylock passed over his battered BlackBerry, feeling a similar sheepishness as when his son cast a jaundiced eye over the ageing device.

'Am I going to have to lose that?'

'No, sir, what I'm thinking is we'll install a bit of software on it that tracks and records calls? Obviously we'll get what we can from the original call. But the payday will be if they call back.'

Blaylock nodded, having long been vaguely of the assumption that his phone was already tapped. 'Okay. Fine.'

'You feel alright, sir? Not too spooked?'

'Oh yeah, sure. It'd take more than that.'

'We'll get the handset back to you before the morning's out, sir. We just have to sort out the surveillance authorisation.'

'You mean I'll have to sign a warrant on myself?'

The officer nodded, clearly seeing neither harm nor humour in this simple procedure. Blaylock tipped his tea into the sink, thanked Detective Hill for his efficiency, bid goodnight to his minders and trudged back upstairs in search of sleep.

Original script, check against delivery

*I know that change is painful. This government does not seek
change for its own sake. When economies are forced on us I
accept these will be unpopular. I don't want a confrontation
with police, only a conversation. And be assured, I hear you.*

*But I cannot simply heed your wishes. My budget is not
quite nine billion pounds. Policing receives nearly half that. In
recent years police numbers reached record levels, but those
levels were just not affordable to the public purse. They have
had to come down, and they will have to come down further.*

*Despite that, I am – yes – asking the police to achieve
more. But let's try to meet that challenge, together. Even in
straitened times, with intelligence and purpose and fresh
thinking, we can cut crime.*

*It can done by better teamwork, co-thinking and
partnership across forces and regions.*

*It can be done by better technology. You need the right tools
for the job, and on this I back you to the hilt.*

*It can be done by initiative. My commitment to 'restorative
justice' has given officers the power to use their own
judgement over minor offences – to give swifter satisfaction
to victims of those crimes. Any good police officer wants to
take the lead that way.*

*And leadership, above all, is how the thing can be done.
I'm asking you, the leaders, to lead change. Part of that is
appreciating how money gets spent; maybe you see this more
clearly than the rank and file. But you will make the big*

decisions, based on the consent of the people, whom you serve, just as this government serves. We know what needs doing, and our duty is to do it – not to complain or dissent. So let's none of us try to hide behind whatever office we hold. It <u>can</u> be done.

PART II

1

'Easy now, you'll not hit an unarmed man?'

Philip Nixon, the lean and silvery Scot who was Her Majesty's Inspector of Constabularies, grinned from behind palms raised in mock surrender as he climbed into the backseat of the Jaguar.

'Howay.' Blaylock waved the leg-pull aside. 'I've not got it in me this morning.'

Nixon gave Blaylock a sharper look from under his critical Caledonian brow. 'You look beat, right enough. Did you not sleep?'

Blaylock shook his head, wishing to leave it at that. From the front seat Andy glanced back to ensure Nixon was buckling in, then gave Martin the signal to pull off and begin the journey up the M1.

In truth Blaylock felt his etiolated mood to be less a result of the abusive caller and the broken night's sleep than the content of a 6 a.m. phone chat with Patrick Vaughan about the procedure of taking his Identity Documents Bill through 'pre-legislative scrutiny'. The Captain, sounding horribly unimpressed, had instructed him to get things under way in tones that left Blaylock sure he would be paddling this canoe alone.

'So,' said Nixon, 'you've got your story straight for the day?'

Blaylock nodded. 'Plain words. It's not like we mean anything so drastic, is it? As we well know, if I was such a hatchet-man I'd be cutting the number of constabularies in half.'

'Aye, and you'd have twenty unemployed Chief Constables after your blood.'

'Quite. For now I've got enough enemies. Speaking of which,

I've got a quick meeting with Bannerman once we get there.'

In his past life Nixon had been a blue-chip accountant specialising in privatisations, foreclosures and associated redundancies. As such Blaylock found him an easygoing ear on the subject of difficult choices. However, as he now studied the broad blue backs of his police-issued driver and bodyguard, Blaylock was reminded to curb his language.

'Thing is, all the best Chiefs know we need reform. You look at a guy like Richie Colls in Kent. There's a copper who's come through the ranks, earned his spurs. He's just had to cut a quarter of his staff, it's not pretty. But he sees the opportunities, too, he gets the best from what he's got. He's got crime down by twenty per cent. That's why I asked him to lead the trial of lapel cameras on every officer.'

'Man after your own heart . . .'

'Oh aye, he's a good guy, Richie. Few more like him and we'd be merry. Plenty problems round his patch but he's all over them – he takes responsibility, he motivates his team. See, that's the real problem with the cops – it's leadership. It's not identified in them, it's not fostered. So they'd rather bang on about money than just get on and . . .'

Blaylock, having warmed up anew to his theme, looked again at Andy's broad shoulders, and tailed away.

Nixon clucked his tongue. 'Aye, well. What money you've got and how you spend it, it's a test of character, no mistake.'

Silently, conspiratorially, Nixon placed his newspaper open on Blaylock's lap at a story concerning the Chief Constable of Lancashire and a disputed claim for personal expenses incurred while attending a 'special convention' in Las Vegas.

Blaylock felt his phone vibrate near to his heart – felt his pulse move, too. Friend or foe? He withdrew the device with care, saw with relief that it was Geraldine, but was vexed to note this new sense of apprehension he was storing around his person.

Geraldine conveyed problematical news for him from Number Ten. The Captain had been alerted by Al Ramsay to the counter-immigration operation planned for Friday, and now wanted him and Blaylock to attend proceedings together, media in tow. Not for the first time Blaylock felt chastened by having to put his face to a course of action he had waved through while rating it highly dubious.

Even in the foyer of the Excelsior Hotel Blaylock could hear applause emanating from the convention suite, but he parted from Philip Nixon and was ushered by men in black to an upstairs seminar suite, as if this were a papal audience or an appointment with the *capo di capi*. There the Commissioner of Police of the Metropolis awaited him, fresh from the stage in his navy regalia but already seated and sipping tea. Bannerman's *consigliere* smartly withdrew some papers he had been waving under the boss's nose. Blaylock surveyed the smartness of the room and the numbers in attendance. *Are we comparing entourages here?* he thought. *Respective hefts?*

'Nice venue you picked for this. Will have cost a pretty penny.'

Bannerman didn't flinch. 'I shudder to think what it'll cost West Midlands to police your party conference in a couple of weeks. But if a thing's to be done then it costs what it costs, haven't I heard you say . . . ?'

Bannerman bore the chilliness of one who had never bothered with any charm school diploma on his path to power, but he undoubtedly knew how to deliver a line. Blaylock had heard that he dabbled in drama while reading Engineering at Oxford, and some of his college friends now held top jobs in the arts. If Bannerman likely cut a greyish figure in their company, he had won big points with the liberal press for his crisp delivery in media rounds, where Blaylock struggled to lay a finger on him. Since their audience today would be brief, Blaylock got to the point.

'I need your view on this proposed march through the East End by the Free Briton Brigade.'

'I've seen the petition. Knowing that patch, I don't think it can be allowed to happen. But – I will speak with the gold commander and get back to you. They don't worry you so much, do they? This "FBB"?'

'I see them as a not insignificant effort to take white racism upmarket.'

'Maybe so. I'm sure we've all seen tougher problems on our streets. It's not like they've got a political wing. Or a quartermaster.'

Blaylock had noted Bannerman's wont to allude to past experience of run-ins with the Provisional IRA and other hairy moments in the job – as if one day they might sit to trade war stories and compare scars.

'Yeah. No danger of them invading Poland. The issue, of course, is how we reassure communities.'

'On that, Home Secretary, we wholeheartedly agree.'

'Another thing. The Sylvie Jordan case concerns me. It's not going away. Are you sure the public concern has been correctly addressed?'

Blaylock saw winter descend in Bannerman's look. 'What's on the front page of the papers this week will not dictate our response. We have a human tragedy, yes. These tragedies are blown up by the media in ways I consider exploitative. "What if it was your kid?" and all that. Murder of this sort is a middle-class fascination. It ignores the larger profile of violent crime that we deal with every day.'

'I hear you. The point is whether this murder might have been averted if procedures had been better.'

'The point is that the previous allegation against Kevin Clail was investigated. The complainant did not wish to press charges.' Bannerman got to his feet. 'This is a tragic business. But I'd ask you not to make any overhasty contribution to it.'

'We agree, too, that public figures must be held to high stand-ards, ourselves included?'

'Of course. Though, what is a policeman but a human being doing a job? I know you understand this, whatever your criticisms.'

'Home Secretary, it's time . . .'

Blaylock heard his summons from the rear then looked back to see Bannerman had drawn nearer.

'Yes, time for you to preach parsimony. Please bear it in mind, how much you ask us to do for less. Our officers take on heavy burdens, big sacrifices – risks, every day. Please be careful how you repay them.'

'I believe those burdens and sacrifices are shared around.'

'Well, there comes a point – a price point – when things just can't be done properly. And at that time it becomes beholden upon me and my colleagues to fight our corner.'

'I'm always wary, James, of capable people telling me that things just can't be done.'

'Ah yes, they never say that in the army, right?'

'Not as a rule. Well, no, I take it back, I used to hear it a fair bit at Sandhurst, usually from the cadets who dropped out, got on the jack wagon – decided they needed a slightly easier life? What they did most often was join the police.'

Bannerman emitted a scoffing sound but offered no other riposte, to Blaylock's grim satisfaction.

Blaylock assumed his front row seat in time to hear the President of the Association of Chief Police Officers lamenting 'hard times' for policing, replete with figures that Blaylock broadly recognised, though some came as news to him.

'Every ten per cent drop in police numbers leads to a three per cent increase in property crime, in anti-social behaviour . . .'

Blaylock scribbled this figure down in mild wonderment, then glanced absently round the plush convention suite.

'We, like the public we serve, are members of hard-working families. We work overtime, we give up our leave when we have to. I urge the government to preserve our good relations. Don't seek confrontation with us. Don't take our goodwill for granted. Hear our message. When funding is next determined, fight for us, not against us.'

Blaylock followed the President onto the stage, and soon found his speech a long trudge uphill to its peroration. The gifts he had wrapped up – the rewards for initiative, the hi-tech investment – barely warmed up the room. He had the sense of being a bad father, his paternal efforts spurned and read as insincere, while for his own part he knew he could not force the child to be inquisitive or self-sufficient.

And as he lavished praise on Richard Colls apropos the successful trialling of new technology he knew the move had backfired. Blaylock had hung a coat of many colours on Colls's back, and by the black looks on the faces of the Kent Chief Constable's brethren they seemed to fancy casting their brother into a pit. Blaylock's mood worsened and he was not inclined to dress up his parting message.

'The Met start their trial of lapel cameras across ten London boroughs this November. I look forward to a camera on the lapel of every officer. We've learned from the Kent experiment that it improves conviction rates. The camera brings scrutiny to bear, and scrutiny is good for all of us, myself included. Every day we should be asking ourselves, do we meet the standards the public are entitled to expect, so ensuring we have their trust? In light of some issues lately arisen, I will ask Philip Nixon to make a new and thorough review of standards and conduct in policing. We will know truthfully where we stand, and none of us have anything to fear – only a lot that we can learn – from the truth.'

He accepted a derisory ovation as he left the stage.

*

In the adjoining reception area where restive delegates milled and took coffee Blaylock snatched a glass of fizzy water, and sipped on the move as Andy came to his side.

'A sharp exit, right? I don't want to get collared.'

Andy nodded. 'When we hit the foyer we'll go out by the back way, Martin's waiting.'

He was pleased, though, to see Richard Colls approach through the crowd, hand outstretched. Colls leaned to his ear as they shook.

'You put me in the spotlight a bit up there.'

'I'm not wrong, though? The cameras are working, yeah?'

'Yeah. We're seeing more people charged, more people admitting the offence. My lads are getting like filmmakers, they leave a scene worrying if they got the shot they needed. To be honest? One or two would prefer if the bloody things had an off-switch. But yeah, if you could stick some sat-nav features in there, bit of face-recognition? Every officer would be a walking CCTV.'

'We'll do what we can for six hundred quid a pop.'

'You should maybe think about a sponsor. Get the big insurers on-board. If they saw what my guys have been seeing there'd be an awful lot of claims going up in smoke . . .'

Colls winked, they shook again warmly and Blaylock, spirits lifted, made for the exit, Andy flanking him down the carpeted foyer, past the central staircase to a seemingly deserted rear reception with glass doors through which the Jaguar was visible.

There, though, a diminutive young woman emerged from out of a deep sofa and came unerringly toward Blaylock, blinking expectantly. The enquiring eyes and pale elfin features were familiar to him as she thrust out a hand.

'Mr Blaylock, I'm Madolyn Redpath. From Custodes?'

He shook with her. 'Yes, you're speaking later on?'

'I dropped by to hear you first.'

'How did I do?'

'I've learned not to expect much liberalism from Home Secretaries. But I must say you seem to be plumbing new depths.'

The veteran tone and tough words – delivered in the high clear tones of an Oxbridge chorister – left Blaylock bemused.

'I'm sorry I couldn't please you.'

'Not at all. Clearly you're more concerned with chasing headlines than trying to do what's right.' She was smiling slightly, hands thrust into the deep pockets of her woollen coat. Blaylock found the effect doubly pert and self-pleased.

'The two things can coincide, you know. Forgive me, I must—'

'Will you forgive me? I do need to talk to you about Eve Mewengera. She's currently languishing in Blackwood Removal Centre, and you're deporting her back to Harar.'

'I don't have perfect recall of every case.'

'You saw the petition we handed in yesterday?'

'Glanced, yes, but my response times are—'

'If you don't act now she will die.'

'Sorry, she—?'

'She's a political activist, she came here fleeing persecution and all she's been given is more of the same. If she's deported she'll be locked up for sedition and in prison they will *kill* her.'

'Look, I can't comment . . . Detention and removal are part of our system; obviously the case you're citing has been through a process, so I'm afraid you'll have to let me review it in my own time.'

'Time? Okay. Thank you for yours.'

Again she thrust out a hand, this time her left, and Blaylock thought that odd even as he took it, then found it odder still that her light grip became a clutch – but this was as nothing to his surprise when, dreamlike, he saw her right hand fly from her coat pocket to press and clasp something cold and hard round his wrist. Recoiling, he met resistance, and saw the steel handcuff conjoining him by a snaking chain to its twin around hers.

'Aw, for crying out loud, what do you think you're doing?'

'Sorry, do I have all of your attention now?'

Andy had muscled in rapidly to seize Madolyn's arm. 'Give me the key, miss.'

'Not until – don't touch me! – this is a peaceful protest, okay?'

Blaylock gestured ruefully as far as his shackled hand would permit. 'So what's your next move?'

'I would like five proper minutes of your time, please.'

It struck Blaylock that no one was watching – that Andy might yet hoist up this slip of a girl and haul her to the car where they could conceivably hack off the links. And yet, he thought better.

'Okay, five minutes, if that's the end of this caper.'

Andy's brow furrowed. 'Sir, this is not—'

'It's alright, Andy, Ms Redpath and I will go and speak in the back of the car, so long as she's got the key.'

Ms Redpath nodded curtly. And so they stepped out together, absurdly linked, and trotted down the short steps to the Jaguar, Martin at the wheel looking thoroughly tickled by the spectacle.

'Where did you get these?' Blaylock asked her, to break the stiff silence.

'From a sex shop in Soho. Surprisingly sturdy, aren't they?'

As they sat, Blaylock massaged his wrist and could see Andy's stern eyes in the rear-view mirror as Madolyn unbuttoned her coat so far as to reveal a plain grey pinafore dress.

'You're a lawyer, right?' he tried scolding. 'Why couldn't you just arrange to come talk to me like everyone else? I'm not such an unreasonable man. But Andy here is a tougher proposition.'

Madolyn only raised her eyes as if summoning the strength to have congress with fools.

'Okay, five minutes then, tell me about . . .'

'Eve Mewengera. She's from a poor village but she went to Nas-ret, studied, became a journalist. Her village has farmed for generations – mango, banana, papaya. She went back there and found the army had moved in, was pushing her family and everybody else off their land for some big-money foreign interest. Anyone who tried to protest was harassed and beaten. Eve tried to report it and she got arrested for sedition, did three months. In prison she was raped by a guard. Friends of hers died. Once she got out they arrested her mother. So she scraped some money together, flew to London, applied for asylum – and she was arrested. After the usual back and forth with your offices her application was rejected and they hauled her off to Blackwood, where she's now awaiting a flight back to hell. And she is being treated appallingly.'

'The facilities are as functional as we can make them. That's not taken lightly.'

'We can argue that another time. I'm taking about Eve being sent to her death.'

Blaylock felt pressed to think quickly. There was something in the narrowing of the gaze she trained upon him, the forensic bullets she fired, that he found impressively focused, even daunting.

'If we and the courts felt she didn't qualify for protection then she can't stay. She has an appeal, surely? Things can happen right up to the wire.'

'Based on what she's been through, she has no grounds for hope.'

'Ms Redpath, you talk like her fate is sealed. This is not a dictatorship we're talking about, it's a government with whom we have bilateral agreements, we can get assurances she won't be harmed.'

'Oh please, they won't be worth the toilet paper they're written on.'

'Well, then what can I possibly do for you?'

She produced a thick black ring-binder from her bag. 'It's not for me. Just look at Eve's case. Obviously you can stop her removal.'

'No, no, it's not for me to interfere with a case that's gone through the proper process. If I open up one—'

'I know, act justly once and you'd end up acting justly all the time. Anarchy, right? Then you would have to stop being oblivious to human pain and start seeing people as people, not just statistics that get in the way of your send-'em-home regime—'

She had riled him. He raised a reproving finger. 'Now you're out of order, I am not "oblivious to human pain". Where do you get the nerve?'

She considered. 'I'm sorry. I withdraw that.'

The ring-binder lay between them. Blaylock stared at it, sceptical, feeling her eyes still on him.

'Okay. I will read your material. If I find grounds for concern, that something ought to be done that could be done – I will get back to you.'

'Thank you.'

'But, to be clear, this is between you and me. If I read in the papers that your organisation has "got me on the spot" or "backtracking" or whatever, then all bets are off.'

'Fine. My organisation doesn't need publicity. This is Eve's life, but there are many more like her, I won't count it as some triumph to get you to pay attention. But if you can't see the injustice here then you don't need me to make your life any worse.'

Blaylock, tired of the joust, accepted the black ring-binder.

Andy, visibly unhappy, turned in his seat. 'Sir, can I just confirm, you're really content to leave the matter this way?'

'Yeah, I'm fine. Restorative justice, right? I've no big issue with Ms Redpath's behaviour. Consider me a satisfied victim.'

Madolyn nodded coolly and slipped from the car. Blaylock watched her re-pocketing her sex-shop handcuffs as she trotted back up the steps to the Excelsior.

2

Geraldine and Becky Maynard both stood by Blaylock's door wearing matching looks of mournfulness as he strode toward them from the lift, still clutching Madolyn Redpath's dossier.

'Griff Sedgley just called,' said Geraldine. 'To say the Supreme Court granted the Bojan Bazelli appeal. Unanimously.'

'Right. Great. Does Griff think we're beaten, then?'

'He said no further action would be in our interest.'

Becky pressed in. 'I'm afraid a few papers have been on at me about your ex-wife. Too late for the *Post* but we can expect the broadsheets to say something. What would be our statement . . . ?'

Blaylock exhaled his displeasure. '"We are disappointed with the court's decision."'

'Is that it?'

'Obviously if they want to say my ex-missus has given me a kicking round the courts then they're welcome, whatever.'

Geraldine tried a soothing tone. 'David, the Judicial Office says could you possibly see Lord Waugh at his *squash club* tomorrow morning? Eight thirty? It's in Highgate.'

'Jesus. Okay. Whatever. Am I meant to bring kit?'

'I'll check. Don't forget you need to be at the Commons for seven?'

Blaylock grunted, having managed to forget the three-line whip that required him to attend the evening vote in support of government amendments on a Schools Bill. Worse – he now recalled – he had agreed to meet a delegation of backbenchers afterward, at the behest of his Parliamentary Private Secretary Trevor Parry, a notably sharp-elbowed Member who had coupled his fortunes closely to Blaylock's own.

'Rory and Seema are waiting for you inside.'

'Eh?' Now Blaylock was vexed. He had not requested a delegation.

Rory Inglis, Director of Counter-Extremism Strategy, rocked gently backward in a chair at Blaylock's meeting table, his fingers laced contemplatively across his white shirt. A Foreign Office veteran, still youthfully bright-eyed and pink-cheeked under a thinning flaxen fringe, when he was not notably deep in thought Inglis specialised in tossing pitying smiles in the direction of those who failed to think so deeply. It was with such a smile that he now greeted the Minister.

Blaylock, though, was looking at Seema Hassanli, one of Inglis's most diligent 'community officers', sober in her black suit and Calvin Klein spectacles, her grave face framed by a black *hijab*.

'Hi David,' Inglis chirped. 'I asked Seema along because she has a good eye on what I guess might be bugging you.'

'There's a few things you and I need to discuss first. If you don't mind.'

'Okey-doke. Seema, sorry, give us ten mins?'

Lips pursed, Seema gathered her files and departed. Absently Blaylock walked to his desk and set the Redpath file atop his in-tray. Hearing his door click shut he turned back to Inglis.

'I had Sheikh Hanifa in yesterday, all het up again about Islamic societies on campus again. With good reason. And, of course, with al-Kasser back in the media – I feel I need to get my head straight on our counter-extremism agenda. What we're doing and why.'

'Gosh. As drastic as that?'

'I don't understand what we spend and what we get back. For instance – the Council of Student Societies, we work with them, right? We fund institutes who go and put inflammatory speakers in front of students. Some of those students, we've got them on surveillance, I sign warrants on them. There are so many groups, and bloody acronyms, alphabet soup. Then I find one that we thought was fine is peddling anti-Western sentiments, and one I never trusted anyway has guys talking out of both sides of their mouths . . . And we get shot of one lot then they resurface under another bloody acronym . . .'

Blaylock felt he had gone on too long yet was waiting for Inglis to nod, indicate some sympathy or at least un-bridge his gnomic fingers. He waited in vain.

'My point, Rory, is that we pitch a big tent and some strange birds come in to shelter. Do you disagree? Or are you fine with it?'

'Some of these groups . . . Remember, they're not monolithic, not exclusive, some of them find it as hard to run their ship as we do ours, right? They can't always get everyone on-message. But, on the whole, it's better we know what they're up to. And show them we're listening.'

'I don't want tolerated snakes in our midst.'

'I hear you, David, but ask yourself, who *do* we want? Some kindly dragoman to reassure us? A nice old-school guy like Hanifa? Sure, but there's a limit to what he can do. Or we could just talk to all the bright young Muslim guys and girls who are into liberal democracy and separating church and state. But that's just what we want to hear.'

'The justification for this spend is to counter extremist views, Rory. What's that for, if not precisely to say that liberal democracy is better?'

'It's a lovely aspiration. But a long, long game. You have to try not to get agitated, see this as an ongoing operation. I understand you got in a strop with the Beeb over, what's-his-face, Abu Blah-Blah?'

'Abou Jabirman – Desmond.'

'Right. I just wouldn't go there if I were you.'

'That's exactly what Phyllida said.'

'Well, there you go. My point is, don't imagine young Muslims are filled with radical fire whenever he opens his big mouth. Radicalisation is a far more complex process, it takes peer group approval—'

'Listen, you don't need to tell me these guys' knowledge of Islamic theology is shallow. I don't imagine they're impressively devout. I get that their thing is violence.'

'Well, again, I wouldn't assume Desmond is the messenger. He's just working at his own career. He's not stupid, Desmond. You need to be at least as astute as him.'

'Are you saying I'm stupid, Rory?'

Inglis laughed, a little too long and loud. 'My simple view, David, my sincere advice, is that an ounce of prevention is worth a pound of cure.'

'I've never understood what that means. And you need to be aware, Rory, I'm still looking for cuts in our budget. What we're spending in your area looks vulnerable to me.'

At last Blaylock felt he had succeeded in yanking the rug out from under Inglis's hauteur. 'Before you do anything hasty I trust you'll take on-board my view?'

'I will hear you but my decision will be final. Do you want to get Seema back in?'

Seema returned, seeming no cheerier. *Join the club*, thought Blaylock, drumming fingers on the table.

'Seema,' said Inglis, resuming his thinker's posture, 'the Minister's been looking at some of the groups we work with and basically he doesn't like all that he hears – fears we're throwing good money after bad. Is that fair, David?'

Seema jumped in with assurance. 'With respect, Minister, it could be the cheapest money you'll spend. In my view you maybe need to hear more of what's being said for yourself, not have it mediated.'

'A degree of mediation is necessary,' Blaylock offered, 'if what's being said is in Arabic, or Punjabi, or Urdu.'

A silence followed. Blaylock sensed he had set the room on edge. Even Inglis now sat up straight. Seema was looking closely at him.

'Minister, how many Muslim friends would you say you have?'

Blaylock stammered slightly. 'Obviously I know any number of leaders, representatives . . . I have contacts from community visits.'

'Which community do you think you're visiting when you go? Pakistani, Bangladeshi? Somali? Arab, Kurdish? Sunni, Shia, Ahmadiyya? Or just, y'know, a load of Muslims?'

'I concede, I'm no expert in the regional or theological variations of Islam. The point is, I go wherever I'm invited. I'll always gladly spend time with good people who sincerely want to make a difference.'

'With respect – you don't go there as a man. You're behind a shield. You think your audience doesn't know that? They see you doing your duty on the big "Muslim problem" . . . and they're made to feel like just functionaries, too. Try treating them as people for a change.'

'Well, I . . .' Blaylock swatted his knee in mild exasperation, for his day seemed to be acquiring a theme. 'It's not easy.'

'Not for any of us. So much of what I have to do has this narrow focus on young men and their discontents. I mean, what about women? They are passionate about issues, they can be agents for change. I spoke to a Muslim women's group today—'

Blaylock pointed to her head. 'Hence the *hijab*? You felt the need for a flag of convenience?'

'I'm sorry?'

'You don't wear it to the office routinely, do you?'

'It was appropriate for my audience today, yeah.'

'So, is that not a shield of sorts for you?'

'It's not a hard thing for me to have honest exchanges with Muslims. For you, Minister, that's maybe something to work on . . .'

'I repeat, I'm always, always ready to have the argument.'

'That's been established, Minister. I put it to you that you might want to look like you want to understand, not just to have a punch-up.'

Blaylock could feel the black umbrage steam up in him at Seema's words; if Inglis had not been sitting nearby, seeming to study him very intently, he might have let it boil over. Yet Seema herself seemed undeterred – un-possessed – by any fear of how he might react.

'If you wanted to meet some people who are honestly trying to do good, there's two great guys I know running a project out in Stapletree in Essex. Sadaqat and Javed? Sadaqat's a qualified youth worker, mentor; at his local mosque he set up a seminar and a bookshop, and now he's set this place up with his mate Javed, and it's really impressive. If you met them and heard them out about what they've done and why, I bet you—'

'Stapletree? Fine. Seema, you set it up and I'll be there.'

'What are you doing tomorrow night?'

Blaylock looked to the ceiling. 'Aw, come off it. Guess what, I have a prior engagement, as you can imagine . . .'

'And is it really so important?'

'Ha.' Blaylock recalled the Captain's insistence that his ministers all be present and correct in black tie at the Carlton Club.

And then he thought again.

'Actually, when you put it like that . . .'

'So, come to Essex with me. It can be simple. Low-key.'

Blaylock had to laugh even as he rubbed exasperation from his eyes. '"Low-key", aye. I hope these lads will be happy with my security crawling all over their gaff tomorrow morning. But, yeah, consider me happy to take your advice, Seema. Don't make me regret it.'

Geraldine was at the door and gesturing. Blaylock rose.

'Geraldine, sorry, there may just be a tweak to my schedule tomorrow night . . .'

With matronly precision, minutes in advance of Blaylock's last engagement of the day, Geraldine packed up his ministerial box and Blaylock, belatedly remembering his pledge to Madolyn Redpath, shoved the black folder down into the red box's maw. Finally Geraldine presented him with details of the squash club where he was due to meet with the Lord Chief Justice early the next morning.

'He says he'll happily hit with you if you're up for it,' Geraldine added as Blaylock peered perplexedly at the scribbled address.

Blaylock had never been much of a 'House of Commons man'. On his arrival as a new Member seven or so years previously, pacing around outside committee rooms while he waited to be allotted a cupboard from which to represent Teesside South, he had found nothing instantly endearing. He was no Westminster anorak, and found the procedures of the place to be fustian, hidebound, irksome, utterly unimproved by the fulsome provision of subsidised dining and drinking. The quaint etiquette of Parliament being hardly more efficient than the manuals of the Civil Service, Blaylock felt himself further restrained from telling Phyllida Cox how much better he thought the machine could run.

Still, at certain rare moments, he had felt Westminster exerting some large and poignant charm over him. On one evening during his drear weeks of orientation he had wandered the low-glowing corridors of the Palace alone, finishing up in the vastness of Westminster Hall where he looked up to the great hammer-beam roof and felt a kind of piety toward all that had been raised there in the name of representative democracy.

Now, just in time, Blaylock strode from the Members' Lobby into the Chamber, took the nod from the sergeant-at-arms and paced past the long and garrulous lines on the benches – Members anxious for their dinner, easily made miserable. Taking his frontbench berth he acknowledged his PPS Trevor Parry, keenly in the row behind him, and Government Chief Whip Tim Charlesworth perched hawk-like by the gangway, a black Moleskine notebook held ominously to his breast.

'The Question is as on the order paper,' bellowed the Speaker. 'We will move to division. Clear the Lobby!'

Back on his feet he moved with the throng out to the Aye lobby. Having given his name to the clerk Blaylock was shortly back out in the Members' Lobby, whereupon Gervaise Hawley dallied over, smoothing his salmon-coloured tie between his finical fingers, a slight and acerbic smile pre-arranged on his face.

'So, David, you'll soon be prostrating your Identity Documents Bill before us?'

'That's right, Gervaise. Our day in court.'

'I knew the day would come. Empires fall, great men come and go, tides rise and recede and yet, once again, as the deluge subsides, we see a lonely Home Secretary clutching an identity card and crying that everybody must have them . . .'

The allusion, too, had clearly been prepared in advance and Blaylock shrugged his acceptance of Hawley's mockery just as Trevor Parry appeared at his side. Together the two repaired to Blaylock's office behind the Speaker's chair, a poky, perennially musty room with green leather Pugin furniture and a sideboard at which Parry busily dusted wine glasses and uncorked a Saint-Émilion Grand Cru.

Then they trooped in, the Honourable Members for Twining, Newhampton and Thanet, all bright new boys in the last parliamentary intake, keen to have their interests noticed, susceptible to blandishments. They paid their respects and took their glasses, and then Thanet stepped a few paces forward to make the demonstration to the Minister.

'We want to reassure our constituents that the government hears the message from parts of the country that don't shove themselves forward . . .'

Thanet struck Blaylock as a good solid constituency man. He listened with care.

'We must be seen to have the interests of the public first, the rights of innocent victims, not those of dangerous criminals. Our rights were won at Runnymede. They're not a gift from Strasbourg judges with an overweening self-opinion.'

'I share your concerns. It so happens I am meeting the Lord Chief Justice tomorrow.'

'You cannot direct judges, you need to change the law.' This was the contribution of Newhampton, a pale, porky, bespectacled chap, to Blaylock's eyes the obstinate sort who might fancy himself as a rebel.

'A British Bill of Rights is what we'd favour,' purred Twining, a posh-sounding Scot. 'The best of all possible worlds.'

Blaylock nodded as to indicate he had heard, then switched, in the style of the questing journalist, to one last thing he might have said at the start. 'As you're aware, we expect in the next sitting to bring forward the Identity Documents Bill. I trust I have your support.'

'You'll hear some say, Minister, that it might do the government a greater service to vote against the bill?' Thus spake bold Thanet.

'Never, ever believe that,' said Blaylock, tilting his brow in a show of veteran displeasure. 'Loyalty, for me, is the only virtue.'

'"To the country, always. To the government when merited."' Thus Twining, who, Blaylock decided, might have to be watched.

But Thanet thrust his chin forward cheerfully. 'We are dependable *freikorps*, *Kapitän*. And we are ready to be led. Strongly.'

Blaylock wanted to wince but thought it wiser to smile, aware that he sometimes used equally dubious allusions after half past six and half a glass of wine. They drained their glasses and exited the office in decent spirits, there to see the Chief Whip loitering watchfully in the corridor.

'Tim. Sufficient unto the day the evil thereof?'

'Well, quite, David. Quite.'

Rapidly Blaylock strode out to New Palace Yard where his Jag awaited, fully expecting the Chief Whip to tell Patrick Vaughan that his Home Secretary was conducting secret manoeuvres among younger MPs, conspiring for a tilt at the throne – the standard power-paranoia of politics, in which Blaylock had not the slightest interest.

At home he was compelled to spend a good half-hour on wardrobe choices for the following day. What with a morning squash game, a community run-out in Stapletree and a black-tie do at the Carlton, he had the sense that the Jaguar might have to function for the day as a sort of four-wheeled changing room.

With suit-bag and kit-bag packed, he sat and perused Madolyn Redpath's file on Eve Mewengera. Documents from the Foreign Office and Habesha's High Commissioner in the UK were both clear she had to go and rejected her complaints, asserting compliance with international conventions. Yet Blaylock found himself seeing the thing from the other side. What had befallen the woman was evidently grim, iniquitous. How could she expect anything to get better? The thought in his head was clear and chastening. *It shouldn't happen.* And yet, to reverse this state of affairs would be a huge deal. He simply hadn't the willpower to think about it, not tonight.

He had begun to glance anxiously to his silent phone set on the desk by the file. Now it rang, and he jumped. But it was only Mark Tallis, with his customary briefing on the next day's newly set headlines.

'Your honeymoon in the papers didn't last, patrón. The Mail's *gone big on the immigration figures, says you're "presiding over failure". And the* Sun's *made a headline out of your ex-wife's win in court.'*

'What sort of a headline?'

Tallis cleared his throat. '*Uh, "Home Sec Decked By Legal Eagle Ex"*.'

'It scans, right enough,' Blaylock muttered, rolling his eyes, finding that they came to rest on the whisky decanter.

3

Feeling a mite exposed in shorts and polo shirt Blaylock swished his borrowed racquet experimentally as he jogged up decked steps and down the central aisle separating the gleaming cell-like courts. On reaching Court Six he found a lone figure peering wryly back through the glass at him – Lord Waugh, a hairy-kneed sexagenarian with the craggy look of a matinee idol from Blaylock's parents' era, one who might have played Heathcliff and Hamlet before settling into middle-age and saturnine villainy.

'Shall we knock up?' asked the Lord Chief Justice.

Sure, thought Blaylock, nodding. *Let the weirdness begin.*

Blaylock had not struck a squash ball in anger for twenty-odd years, and had to reacquaint himself with the little rubber pellet and the needful speed of the racquet head. Conversely he was surprised, and not pleasantly, by the relative nimbleness of the older man. Having stooped to retrieve a shot he had failed to return, Blaylock straightened upright to see his opponent clearly impatient to get to business.

'What's on your mind this fine morning, Mr Blaylock?'

'Human rights law. How our courts interpret it, following Strasbourg. I wanted to be sure I know your view.'

'You feel there's a problem? Been upset by a reverse or two lately, perhaps? On the distaff side?'

'No, I never mind being beaten fair and square. But quite often the pitch looks to me like it's prepared in the opposition's favour. The public have a similar sense, I think. The effect can be to give human rights a bad name. Or do you never think that?'

'Well, perhaps you'll define for me the unfairness you describe?'

'Oh, take the old lag's plea of right to family life . . . Hardly a cloudless defence, is it?'

'You get the odd generous decision, true. Still . . . in the specifics of each case there is often quite a tangle of thorns, as the great man said.'

Blithely Lord Waugh smacked another serve, and hostilities resumed. The older man's deftness of touch was quite a thing, and quickly Blaylock was once more scuttling from wall to wall of the cramped court. After savouring a couple of cleaner hits, he swung and missed, and heard a vexing *Tsch* at his back as he reached for the ball.

'It gets thorny, as you say,' Blaylock recovered his breath, 'when foreigners who lied their way into this country and committed serious crimes get to hang around even after they've done time.'

'Oh, be assured, I no sooner forgive wickedness than you. But I can't ignore an Act of Parliament. We are signatories to a Convention.'

'Meaning we're bound to follow a foreign court.'

'No, simply to consider any judgment or opinion of the court. We arrive, however, at our own decisions. And I would say the public still like the fact that judges are independent – not in anyone's debt.'

'You don't think judges find it useful to keep their noses clean with the powers they know litigants will end up appealing to?'

'You have no legal training yourself, do you, Mr Blaylock?'

'I took the basic course given to all ministers.'

'Basic indeed . . .' Lord Waugh served again, and soon enough Blaylock was playing fetch again, Waugh standing over him.

'It seems to me', said Waugh, after a noisy clearing of his throat, 'that the fraction of cases that go against the government is probably a salutary thing. It means our law gets good scrutiny.'

'What's the need? When we have a so-called Supreme Court?

How many referees do we want in-between the state and the people?'

'Tell me this, Mr Blaylock, if Mephistopheles called on you and said, "For the price of your soul, I guarantee you the government will never lose more than one in every two hundred cases" . . . wouldn't you call that a deal worth shaking on?'

'I'd need to look at that one case we lost.'

Waugh let loose a rheumy chuckle. 'Well, you may need to lower your sights.'

As they resumed, Blaylock felt his calf muscles twanging with the strain of the sudden moves from standstill. He played and missed again.

'Try not to thrash, eye on the ball, sir. You know, this Europe we have now, this common ground we've found . . . I think of it especially when I'm in Tuscany. My father fought with the partisans, you know. His father was of that generation who said, "Never again." Now we have a Europe of five hundred million citizens sharing rights and freedoms guaranteed by an independent court. It seems to me we should be proud of that. Otherwise, what are we? Little Englanders?'

'Where I want to be standing', said Blaylock, trying to take charge of his erratic breathing, 'is with law-abiding people in this country, who expect to be protected from the non-abiders. They're the people I tend toward when I'm thinking about who I serve.'

Waugh grounded his racquet. 'Tell me, what is it that you want to see happen? The UK leave the Convention?'

'No. But our own Bill of Rights? A different matter.'

'Oh, best of British luck with that. It wouldn't tame the judges, you can be sure. If you ruin their sport they'll just make up a new game.'

'This is not a game, Lord Waugh.'

But Waugh met Blaylock's hard look with a grimace, then struck another serve. Blaylock stepped in and lashed a backhand low to the corner. For once it was Waugh who lurched in vain to reach the ball and Blaylock, in His Lordship's way, did not wholly step aside in time, such that the older man bumped off him and staggered slightly, occasioning a coughing fit that bent him double. Blaylock stood over him silently. When Waugh's eyes flicked upward his gaze had lost its geniality.

'Well now. I do believe you're developing a game of your own.'

'Strange, isn't it? To be arguing over who's got right of way? Speaking for the democratic assembly, if I thought our democracy really relied on the scrutiny of judges I'd have got into another line of work.'

'You'd have stayed in the army, perhaps?'

'No, but—'

'Look, Mr Blaylock' – Waugh, straightened, abruptly revived – 'the only people I've ever met who think politicians should have fewer limits on how they carry on are politicians. I quite understand that were I in your shoes I mightn't care much for seeing my exercise of power made inconvenient. But that is the law.'

Lord Waugh hit a whiplash serve, to which Blaylock's return was ill struck, and Waugh's fierce forehand drove him back to the far corner of the court where he found he had no shot yet made a furious slash backward – only to instantly feel and hear a jarring crack against the court wall. With the ball rolling at his feet, he dumbly inspected his racquet's broken head. Lord Waugh trotted up to his side.

'Dear me. If you'd like to play on I'm sure you can borrow another.'

'Another day, maybe. I'm due at my usual meeting with MI5.'

'Oh, Mr Blaylock. You must hear some stories . . .'

Showered and suited and back in the Jaguar to Westminster Blaylock took a call from Griff Sedgley, thoroughly expecting to hear of new obstructions and affronts. In the event the news, in relation to the attempted extradition of Vinayak Khan, was better.

'*The court has considered Strasbourg's view and basically it wants top-level assurances from the Americans that Khan's condition is accepted and that nothing will be done to jeopardise his health in violation of the Convention.*'

'Meaning?'

'*Meaning he won't be treated like a soldier, won't be put in super-high-security or end up on Death Row. We need to guarantee that on arrival in the US he'll go to a psychiatric referral centre and stay there until trial.*'

'I see no problem.'

'*The catch is we have thirty days. Until four p.m. on the twenty-fourth of October.*'

'Oh, conceivably it could be done overnight.'

'*The Americans aren't always so prompt.*'

'No, but they're in town right now, as it happens. I'm seeing Secretary Aldrich later today, so I'll have a word . . .'

They were a mere three round the table of Blaylock's office, since no one else in the building had sufficient security clearance, and so the usual air of surreal decorum closed over their weekly session as dictated by the finical demeanour of the Director of MI5.

Adam Villiers bore the air of a thinker, his head befitting a Roman bust, hemmed by a monastic tonsure. He was robustly constructed yet with something of a dancer's off-duty elegance in how he carried himself; and however grave – at times pallbearer-like – were his manners, a dark humour was often discernible in his eyes and at the edges of his remarkably ruby-red mouth.

In the chair beside Villiers was Brian Shoulder, Scotland Yard Head of Counter-Terror Command, who put Blaylock less in mind of the Emperor Diocletian and more of an Islington market trader, with his tidy crop, boxer's nose and narrow eyes as grey as nail-heads.

'So, Home Secretary,' murmured Villiers, 'you have joined the ranks of the surveilled? Vis-à-vis your threatening phone-caller?'

'Yes, I'd forgotten about him,' Blaylock lied. 'If "him"' it is.'

'Let me not alarm you any further, but in the overnight chatter we did pick this up . . .' Villiers slid his trusty matt-black tablet device across the table-top and tapped PLAY on a paused video. Blaylock peered down at footage of a sun-bleached African scene: two men in flowing garments and headgear, rifles in hand, clamouring and gesticulating at the lens.

'What am I looking at?'

'Zanzibar. The gentlemen are clerics, members of a recently formed Islamist sect. Their rhetoric calls for attacks on all foreign tourists, occupying forces, local apostates—'

Blaylock grunted, assuming this shopping list might run on.

'They wind round, however, to making quite a specific threat against you, Home Secretary? The gist of what the chap in the blue turban says is that, should Ziad al-Kasser be thrown out of Britain, then not only will all Westerners be "erased" from East Africa but you personally will be made to pay.'

'They can join the queue.'

'Very good,' said Villiers, appearing to think that agenda item had been settled. They turned to consideration of the broader watch list of individuals and groups being monitored, individuals lately arrested on suspicion of preparing offences, the perpetual focus on London and the Midlands. Villiers expressed a mild frustration over a months-old, still fruitless watch over members of a suspected cell in Birmingham. 'We approach the moment where we wonder if we should carry on . . .'

Blaylock appreciated that the picture didn't easily cohere, the joins often inexact. A dozen or more officers assigned to each subject made him chary of the price tag, the manpower, in every case. They moved on to the roll-call of suspicious individuals whose movements were electronically tagged and monitored for set terms, the statutory process they called 'risk certification'.

'Mr Nadir Hamayoon breached his conditions yesterday. Decided for whatever reason to take a stroll near Brimsdown Substation? He may have done it to annoy us, as some of them are wont to. I am rather more concerned about Abul Rahman. His term is just about up for renewal, he's kept his nose remarkably clean.'

'So finish the risk certificate but put him back on surveillance?'

Villiers nodded. 'Yes. To have these chaps just pacing the length and breadth of a cage can be counter-productive. Whereas if the cage is unlocked, and they resume former associations, old habits . . .'

'And if we don't take our eyes off them . . .' Blaylock added, since this part seemed to him sometimes neglected. But Villiers was moving on to a summary of concerns about suspected British-born extremists overseas, an issue over which Blaylock generally felt lesser levels of unease on the grounds that individuals who quit the UK to fight and die for a caliphate could, to some extent, be left to their fate.

The trio were then driven to Downing Street for a Cabinet Room meeting of the body Patrick Vaughan called his 'National Security Council', adorned by the heads of GCHQ and MI6, Dom Moorhouse, army chiefs and senior mandarins. The whole high-level shooting match had long smacked to Blaylock of homage to the White House; and tonight that sense was exacerbated by the guest-of-honour presence of Caleb Aldrich, US Director of Counter-Terror.

Having met Aldrich before, Blaylock approached him directly before the meeting was called to order, and explained his situation over the extradition of Vinayak Khan. Aldrich made a pronounced show of listening as statesman-ally, exuding *gravitas* and *empathia*, though with his good suit, ivory cufflinks and widow's peak he reminded Blaylock rather more of a glad-handing real estate broker.

'I don't anticipate a problem, David. Our interests are the same. We won't bend over for Strasbourg but, yeah, I expect we could ensure Mr Khan goes some place where he'll get a mint on his pillow.'

Once all were in place Vaughan dispensed with an agenda and offered the floor to Aldrich, who stood and, hand in pocket, held forth on the American vision of the globe. His delivery had urgency, yet something about his eyes, dark-ringed and strangely inert, was suggestive of some vital missing part. He then offered to take questions.

'Can you clarify the White House position on drones?' asked Dom Moorhouse. 'As a tool of policy in counter-terror?'

'Sure, no problem. Always, we'd prefer to take the subject alive, debrief 'em, prosecute 'em. But let's be clear, there are locations where the risk of committing US troops is unacceptable and local law enforcement can't be trusted. There are just some jobs where only Hellfire missiles will do.' He paused to let some nervy laughter pass. 'Be that said, the bar we got to clear is high, we got to know we're taking out a priority target, or significantly degrading enemy capability, or disrupting a planned attack. That doesn't have to be, y'know, forty-five minutes away . . .'

Blaylock cocked a hand as to speak. 'What do you say to calls for greater transparency on your targeting policy?'

'If we had to go get a warrant on every strike . . . ? Listen, if we've seen behaviour on the ground by military-age males that gives us sufficient concern, our view is we don't need to know the guys' names.'

'What about collateral damage?'

Aldrich shrugged. 'Sometimes in the nature of a strike-zone. We hate that. We go to great lengths to avoid it – we have the means to be extremely precise. But the risk will not deter us. For reasons I just said.'

The talk turned to developments in Yemeni bomb-making technology and surveillance systems in US airports. Then Blaylock felt a familiar twinge of irritation. His junior-level Security Minister Paul Payne, evidently emboldened by his researches into state-sponsored cyber-terror, made an enquiry about some recent theft of fingerprint records from US Customs, allegedly the work of Chinese hackers.

Aldrich, for once, appeared rattled. 'We don't envisage that stolen data as having any kind of real use-value to an enemy.'

Payne persisted. 'But if one were proposing a national identity card based on biometric data, such as fingerprints – the risk of such a compromise would be far greater, wouldn't you agree?'

Aldrich looked to Vaughan, grinned and spread his arms in supplication. 'Ah, forgive me, I'm pleading the Fifth on that one.'

Blaylock bristled at Payne's arrant disloyalty. As the meeting broke up Vaughan zeroed in on him, but only in the high-flying mood that National Security seemed always to foster in him.

'So we're on for tomorrow morning in Slough, David? Shoulder to shoulder with Border Force? Shall we have a word about the drill at the Carlton, before dinner?'

'I'm sorry, Patrick, I'm afraid I'll be coming late.'

The PM sniffed. 'Why? What've you got on?'

'Just a, uh, counter-extremism exercise.'

Vaughan nodded soberly, as though he had a clue.

4

It was near 7 p.m. as they drove into Stapletree, and peering through the window Blaylock felt that the dusk cloaked much but arguably not enough of the vistas of characterless houses, garage forecourts, fast food huts and out-of-business pubs. He looked to a pensive Andy Grieve, and recalled that Andy had grown up nearby in Ilford. Seema Hassanli also sat in silence, *hijab* faithfully in place.

They passed the Goresford Islamic Centre's awning and parked around the corner. As they walked the fifty yards, Blaylock took a notion and yanked his tie loose, rolling it up and stuffing it in his jacket pocket.

'Do I seem relaxed, Seema?' he ventured.

'As far as it goes,' she murmured, glancing backward to Andy.

They were buzzed into a cramped reception space, its lino wearied by footfall, walls plastered with ill-sorted posters and advertisements for meetings and services. At the threshold of an office a young man in a baseball hat appeared, wary-eyed and bucktoothed. Blaylock saw past him to peeling walls and listing shelves of box-files.

'Hi Sid,' Seema greeted him. 'We're a little early, you seen Sadaqat and Javed?'

'They're takin' *shotokan* class in the extension? I show you.'

He led them down a corridor, and Blaylock began to hear the muffled sound of high-pitched, strangulated cries and grunts. He exchanged bemused glances with Andy as Sid opened a door for them into a long fluorescent-lit studio space of whitewashed walls and laminated wooden floor space.

A gaggle of Asian boys in white karate pyjamas and belts of various colours were striking poses, stepping forward and feigning kicks and punches, emitting falsetto martial cries in response to barked instruction from their coaches – two young Pakistani men standing shoulder to shoulder, whom Blaylock took to be the proprietors, Sadaqat Osman and Javed Mukhtar.

Both wore intent expressions as they took turns to issue prompts. One was tall and muscular as a basketball player, his eyebrows a black line, mouth set straight as a blade. His dark head swivelled to meet Blaylock's gaze for a fleeting instant, then faced front again.

The other – shorter, wirier, more luxuriously bearded – suddenly crouched and raised his hands, and the boys began to step forward in turn to land slapping punches into his palms. His taller colleague's face broke into a delighted grin, baring uncommonly white teeth.

'Okay, green belts! Bow to me, bow to each other!'

As the children dispersed the two young men approached Blaylock, and Seema conducted introductions. Sadaqat, it transpired, was the taller, Javed the shorter and more self-contained.

'*As-salam-o-alaikum,*' Blaylock recited as he thrust out his hand.

Sadaqat's eyes filled with mirth. '*Wa alaikumu s-salam wa rahmatullahi wa barakatuh,*' he replied as they shook. 'We are, uh, pleased and honoured to welcome you to our centre.'

'Thank you. I like the look of this class.'

'*Shotokan*? Yeah, it's one of the most popular things we do. Everybody likes to throw a punch now and then, yeah?'

Blaylock smiled. 'I've never had the discipline for martial arts.'

'Me neither. My boy Javed here, he's the proper eighth *dan* man.' Blaylock took the cue to shake with Javed, too.

'This is a fine-looking extension you've got, Sadaqat.'

'Thank you. We raised the money in the community, and the

community helped us build it. So, yeah, we're proud. May I take you upstairs, show you what else we got?'

As they threaded back down the corridor Blaylock ear-wigged Sadaqat's cheery exchanges with Seema.

'Did you sort out that bother you had with the little *hisbah* patrol?'

'Oh yeah . . . Nipped that one in the bud.'

'What was that?' Blaylock enquired.

'Ah, one or two of the boys we get in regular got it in their heads to go around locally like a bit of a gang – giving out to people they knew that their behaviour was, uh, not sufficiently Islamic? Telling their sisters' friends to dress more modest, knocking cans of beer out of guys' hands and that.'

'How did you manage?'

'Peer group pressure, innit? It's amazing how people can be shamed.' Sadaqat flashed his pearly smile. 'Nah, we just had a word, told them to grow up and act like men. Not sad little boys trying to get back at girls who don't fancy them, yeah?'

Blaylock was amused by the tale and the telling. Back out in the reception they now mingled with a stream of men coming in from the street, clad in down-filled coats, who joined them in climbing the stairs.

'Prayers,' said Sadaqat. On the upper floor he indicated a good-sized carpeted room into which the human traffic was headed, then took his guests aside to show by turn a 'quiet room' ('for one-to-one counselling?'), a 'seminar room' ('for short courses?'), and what he called 'the den' ('to shoot pool or watch the football').

There was, as it turned out, no football showing in the den, its walls painted black but enlivened by spray-paint murals. Rather, the flat screen fixed on high showed a young imam in waistcoat and hat, holding forth in Urdu from behind a desk piled with heavy tomes: the recognisable format of a TV phone-in. A big, pallid, stocky young white man, luxuriously red-bearded under his *taqiyah* cap, was alone and peering up at the television with notable intensity from a capsized black leather sofa.

Sadaqat steered Blaylock over to a pool table where two young men stood swinging cues in anticipation. The first – 'Mohammad Abidi, call me Mo' – wore a lightning flash razored into his hair, a pair of perilously loose fit jeans, and the general air of one who liked his reflection. The second, one Nasser Jakhrani, was bespectacled, duffel-coated, shy-smiling.

The TV imam, though, was sounding ever more irate, since the young ginger-haired man on the sofa had suddenly jacked the volume right up. Sadaqat winced and strode over to him; the youth leapt to his feet in a manner Blaylock thought combative, and a sharp if muted exchange ensued before Sadaqat rested a solicitous hand on his shoulder. Then with an imploring mien he beckoned for Blaylock to come over. Blaylock exchanged looks with Andy before obliging.

'You should shake this man's hand, Finn,' said Sadaqat, his own calming hand still in place. 'He is the Home Secretary of the government, yeah?'

Blaylock saw a near-comically averse look cross Finn's face, as one who had been told to pull on the leg of a live tarantula. Yet he took Blaylock's hand.

'Hi Finn. So, you like this centre here? Find the facilities good?'

Finn appeared to treat the simple enquiry with high seriousness, looking about him as one whose opinions were insufficiently heeded locally. 'Gah. Ought to be more *rigour* in this *dawa*. Too many brothers know more about . . . *rappers*, and *footballers*, than know the companions of the Almighty Prophet, *alayhi as-salam*. But, uh, yeah, in my view, on the whole – my brother Sadaqat's place is a proper reverent place. For a brother seeking the purer life and that. Sanctuary, from the cursed *Shaitan*, you get what I'm sayin'?'

But Blaylock did not, and so was relieved when Sadaqat engineered their exit, bidding his visitors adjourn to the quiet room and closing the door behind them. There was a table with six chairs and a whiteboard that reminded Blaylock of his own set-up in Shovell Street. As the party chose seats Andy stationed himself by the door. Blaylock realised Sadaqat was looking at him ruefully.

'I apologise for Finn, he's, uh – he has problems.'

'Of what sort?'

'Bipolar disorder. Which they thought was just drug psychosis. No one figured 'til he pulled a knife on his foster mum. Said she was possessed by devils. Finn's big on devils . . . He did three months in prison for it and when he got out – nobody cared about him, man.'

'He seems to listen to you.'

'I've picked up a few techniques, how to talk him down a bit, stop him listening to the other voices he's got banging round his head.'

Glancing to a shelving unit rammed full of thick manuals Blaylock noticed a framed photograph: Sadaqat posed with a smiling redheaded woman and a beige-complexioned boy.

'Your family?'

'Yeah. My wife Rosie, we met at college? Our boy is Sacha.'

'Huh,' Blaylock smiled, liking what he saw.

Sadaqat smiled back. 'You thinking to ask me how it is with my wife being English and that?'

'Not at all, I—'

'It's not a thing. My dad moved us to England in the seventies – he knew it wasn't rural Pakistan no more. Like, he's an observant man but he doesn't live in the dark ages. He said to me, where you grow up, that's home. England is home, London is home.'

'You've no . . . issue, thinking of yourself as British?'

'British Asian Muslim, is how I'd put it. I tell you this, I'm not interested in race, it's not meaningful to me, as a divider of men? All I care about is ideals we can share in common.'

Struck by this answer, Blaylock nonetheless found Sadaqat's gaze so peculiarly intense that he wished to change the subject. 'So this centre, it was all set up by the pair of you?'

Sadaqat glanced at Seema. 'Yeah, originally I'd got something going at the mosque near me, a place for young people – they offered me their basement room, was meant to be for hang-out and discussion group but . . . a lot of the boys wanted to get fit, so we got in some gym stuff, then the imam got fed up with all that clanking metal, yeah? Boys shouting out, trying to bench their own body weight? Thing was, we wanted an open-door policy, but not everyone who came had their manners down perfect? And for work like this, in a community, you need somewhere people can come without feeling they're just upsetting everyone by breathing.'

'The mosque was a bit too rigorous?'

Sadaqat winced. 'I'd call it – fussy? Hidebound. At least here we, me and Javed, we are responsible, we say what goes.'

Blaylock sought to engage Sadaqat's taciturn partner. 'Javed, Seema told me before this you were running your own business, but things got tough?'

'Yeah. I had a corner shop. It was trouble, all the time. Drunks and druggies coming in. I don't like to talk about it now. Even to think about it. But it made me want to do something, to address that problem. I'm happy now, doing this project, not dealing with all that . . .'

'Poison,' Blaylock filled in.

'Poison, yeah. Ignorance. *Jahiliyya*.'

Sadaqat appeared eager to ride over Javed's simmering silence. 'What we do here is about instilling some discipline, some self-respect, some self-improvement. Of the mind and the body. This neighbourhood, you can see, we got problems. My Islam is about showing a way up and out of those problems. Helping young Muslims make better choices, stronger choices. To believe there's something better, even if you start from nothing. The guys you just met? Mo, he might have nicked a car or two in his time . . . But now he runs his own clothes shop. Nasser, he's in a call centre now, but he's applying to study medicine.' Sadaqat sat back, shaking his head. 'The curse of this generation is nihilism – not seeing the deep meaning in things. What we say to guys who come is, you can live your lives with honour. And that's not about fussing over whether or not your *beard* is the right length, you know what I'm saying?'

A horn sounded. Blaylock's hosts both got to their feet.

'Will you excuse us?' said Sadaqat. '*Maghrib*, we gotta go next door. But I'd be pleased to talk some more.'

Blaylock stood and paced the room, aware Seema watched him.

'Are you glad you came, Minister?'

Blaylock nodded. 'Yeah, sure. Great guy. He gets it. Uses his initiative. Good for him.' He studied a handmade poster on the wall that called for volunteers to sign up to an outward-bound excursion, caving on the North York Moors. When Sadaqat re-entered the room with Javed minutes later Blaylock enquired after it.

'Yeah, our guys, they don't see a lot of fields or cows . . . It's good to get them out and about. To stretch themselves, yeah? Their horizons. It can be a spiritual experience down there in them caves, man. But, whether we get enough bodies to go, or the cash, even . . .'

'Look, it's a terrific idea. If you can't get the money let me know, I'll see what I can do for you.'

'Hey, if you help us out, you gotta come along too, yeah?'

'Deal.' Amused, Blaylock checked his watch somewhat regretfully and went to Sadaqat with his hand out. 'Listen, I've been pleased to meet you both. Really impressed by your work.'

Sadaqat shrugged, with the look of someone who knew his own worth. 'Eh, the day will come when we die, Mr Blaylock. Nothing belongs to us then but our deeds.'

Blaylock had reflected anew. 'I hold a big regular meeting at the Home Office, a forum on extremism in the community, how we deal with it? I'd like it very much if you would come along to one if you could.'

Sadaqat, for once, looked abashed. 'Uh, I'm not so big on speaking for people that way. You know? Making speeches like I'm telling everyone else how to do it?'

'I'd be interested in your view. Let my office send you the details, please at least consider.'

While they filed from the room a hubbub was emanating from downstairs and as they descended – Andy moving firmly to the front of the party, Javed at his shoulder – the source of the disturbance became clear. A small throng, two dozen or so bodies, had gathered just outside the centre's doors; a TV camera was jostling around, backed by lights; and young Sid seemed to be struggling to hold a line and keep calm against protest, assisted by Blaylock's Met police team. With a sinking heart Blaylock recognised the burly *taqiyah*-sporting man at the front of the crush – 'Abou Jabirman', the former Desmond Ricketts. Clocking Blaylock in turn, Jabirman began to stab his finger over Javed's shoulder.

'You! Why are you here? What do you think you are doing?'

'I was invited here, Desmond.'

'My name is Abou Jabirman, call me by my name!'

'You'll always be Desmond to me.'

'Shame on you, to show hospitality to this man!' Ricketts's associates aped him in wagging their fingers in unison at Sadaqat, who had resumed the stern mien Blaylock had seen in *shotokan* class – the brow a black line, the mouth straight as a blade.

'This is not the way to do anything, brother,' Sadaqat responded.

'Traitors and collaborators! Allah has no time for them, their shame will be *immense*.' Jabirman resumed his harangue of Blaylock. 'Why do you come to a Muslim area, how do you *dare*, when you persecute Muslims? Muslins you call "extreme"? What is extreme? When you spy on Muslims, arrest them, deny their rights, when your government goes abroad and murders Muslims in Muslim lands?'

Andy Grieve pressed forward. 'Sir, you need to get back—'

'Be quiet with your mouth, fool, get your hands off me. Where is democracy and freedom you talk about, you would deny it me?'

It was Blaylock's turn to speak over a shoulder, Andy's. 'I'm not denying you anything, Desmond, it would be nice if you'd let me pass.'

A shoe flew over Andy's head and skimmed Blaylock's shoulder. But now sufficient bodies were pressing the throng back. As Blaylock moved to the Jaguar he could hear Seema receiving her own dedicated broadside behind him – 'Go suck the Home Office, *qahba*!'

Once Martin had them safely onto the A13 signposted for central London they sat in gloom and relative calm.

'That went well, I think,' Blaylock offered.

He insisted Martin drop Seema at her door in Bethnal Green, and since they were parked up he changed into his tuxedo in the backseat, Andy assisting him with his bow tie. Martin, meanwhile, took a call warning him of some disturbance on Pall Mall, where a student demonstration of sorts had been dispersed. But by the time the Jaguar pulled up before the Carlton Club there was nothing to see but for a trampled banner on the pavement, and a girl with a painted face remonstrating with a police officer. By now, just a shade before 9 p.m., Blaylock was light-headed with fatigue.

As applause from the gathering attended the end of a suitably Churchillian passage in Patrick Vaughan's speech Blaylock endeavoured to slither unseen through the Churchill Room and seek his seat with minimum fuss. A brisket of beef with savoy cabbage materialised before him, via a deft young waiter. Casting an eye across the two dozen tables, however, he knew he was the last Cabinet member to have presented himself, and that he had not evaded the Captain's eye.

Vaughan, nonetheless, rolled on, relaxed and fluent in the absence of journalists, at ease before the fundraisers and donors who were his meat and drink, and who appeared to want much the same things as he wanted for Britain – less red tape in Whitehall, fewer wind turbines in the countryside, and a proper respect for the blessed energy of private enterprise throughout the land.

If the public could see us up close and unbuttoned like this, Blaylock wondered, *would they think better of us? Or worse?* Given the rich fare on offer, dog-tired as he was, Blaylock filled his wine glass and drank. It was an elite experience, for sure, and the disparity with the place whence he had come could not have been more glaring to him; yet in the face of such glares he had learned to be phlegmatic.

Upon the serving of coffee and cognac Blaylock got to his feet and exchanged glad hands and polite remarks with bankers and hedge funders, grocers and MDs of car firms, a witty milliner and a restaurateur with a svelte Bosnian Muslim wife. He had only just been introduced to 'Duncan Scarth, from your part of the world, Home Secretary' and felt his hand grasped by a tougher-looking customer than the crowd usually contained, when Al Ramsay stalked over and beckoned him aside, clutching a printed schedule for the next day's showpiece immigration raid.

'It'll be good for you and Paddy to spend more time, David. I know he'd be pleased if you'd show up once in a while for the 4 p.m. daily meeting. The whole team would like to see you there more.'

'Come on – that's a polls and media meeting, Al, I've got sod all to contribute.'

'With respect, David, why is that?'

Left alone again, Blaylock accepted a brandy, glanced around the room and gradually grew conscious that his eye was falling on young women: a leggy but stationary waitress idly tossing her ponytail, a blonde in a fitted blue dress unabashedly retouching her lipstick, a pale-skinned belle engaging in conversation with her copper-haired head tilted lazily aside as if awaiting a portrait painter.

He shook his head in self-wonderment. How long, after all, had this been going on? How many months had he spent in abstinent *get-behind-me* mode, self-drilled to resist the slightest carnal urge, doggedly faithful to something he couldn't quite stand to admit?

'Decent show on the pulchritude front, eh?'

Chas Finlayson was at his side, more bloodhound-like even than usual and seeming to have put away a couple of Courvoisiers himself. He thrust a letter upon Blaylock. It was from the office of Martin Pallister, subject: 'NATIONAL SERVICE'.

'*I applaud your sensible and progressive proposition,*' Blaylock read. '*I see the good it may do for disadvantaged young people, and you have my support. I hope the seeming opposition of the Prime Minister, Chancellor and Education Secretary will not be allowed to prevail.*'

'That's the thing fucked, isn't it?' said Finlayson sadly.

'If the only way it can be won is with Labour support then – yeah, the Captain won't be having that. Politics, eh?'

'You and I know what it was for, David – for the young people with nothing going for them, no hope of a half-decent job – get them out of their deadbeat homes, give them a chance to use the body and mind they were given. '

'I know, Chas, I'd have happily seen my own boy do it.'

'Right. The point being that it be led by the armed forces. But, somehow, once my department got their fucking mitts on it, it became all about . . . *charity* work. Like some gap year. They said, "It has to lose the army angle, it puts young people off." And the thing of it is, David, the whole fucking *reason* I wanted to do it was the fucking "army angle" . . .'

Finlayson's tipsy, choleric gloom was hilarious to Blaylock. 'I know, bonny lad,' he offered consolingly. 'I know.'

'Just that bloody thing of making the best of yourself. That's why you and I joined the forces, right?'

With a few good belts of brandy on-board Blaylock felt his tongue loosen. 'Aw, for me, Chas? Truth is – it was all because of a woman. I could as well have joined the Foreign Legion.'

For a moment Finlayson looked as if he might cough up his dinner. Then he chortled and slapped Blaylock's shoulder.

Back home, gloomy in the grasp of his armchair, Blaylock threw back three fingers of malt then repaired to his desk, where awaited a set of briefings for the next day that he had been resisting. Following whatever the morning brought in Slough a group of campaigning women were coming to see him at Shovell Street to discuss the issue of domestic violence. Blaylock had ensured that Phyllida Cox and Deborah Kerner were booked to be at his side for moral support.

The offence, he was in no doubt, was a wholly ugly and lamentable thing. He fully recognised that one might not know the half of a person with whom one had decided to partner and co-habit. He wished to give a fair hearing to the women's concerns. On some level, though, he was troubled.

It troubled him as to what more he could usefully offer beyond the existing laws, checks of police records, injunctions, et cetera.

He was troubled, too, by a sense of the domestic sphere as a murk of inevitable disputations and conflicted emotions, a hard place for the state to invigilate relationships between two people in their full gamut of complexities, privacies, intimacies. It seemed to him that two people might so easily drift into a malaise and not realise it fully until far too late – whereupon one might then be too ashamed or frightened to do anything about it, perhaps feeling all the while that she would be sealing her partner's fate, handing him over to the law, while still feeling love for him. These elements, in his view, made intervention so hard to judge.

Undoubtedly, too, he was troubled by the undeniable historical fact of an occasion when police officers had been summoned by concerned neighbours to his and Jennie's marital home, to attend the scene of a domestic disagreement that had escalated rapidly in both volume and passion and had seen Blaylock put his fist through a panel of their bedroom door that Jennie had locked from the other side.

There were mistakes, he knew, that outlived and stayed impervious to apology or remorse, and lived on behind the blackness of your eyes. You re-watched and re-watched yourself making them, just as you had watched yourself in the original sinful act, and yet failed to lay a staying hand on that second self.

Realising that he had done nothing but hold his head in his hands for some long moments Blaylock closed the folder and shut off the lights.

5

In the back of the parked Prime Ministerial Jag Patrick Vaughan was crisply turned out and rehearsing his lines, albeit frowning somewhat at the pages of the script on his lap.

'"Be very clear, there is no hiding place if you're here illegally." I should swap the clauses, shouldn't I? I will . . . "You will be found and you will be sent back where you came from." Could I get away with "from whence you came"? Or does that sound fusty? Grammatically it's just "whence", isn't it? David?'

'Just sounds old-fashioned, Patrick. Stick with what you've got.'

'Okay. Yes. "Much the better for you that you leave by your own accord." Right . . .'

Blaylock peered out at the drear aspect of residential working-class Slough an hour since a grimy sunrise. The houses were good-sized, all stone-cladded or pebble-dashed, fronted by scruffy lawns. The Jaguar was parked next to a shuttered kebab shop, round a corner from the street where the action was scheduled to unfold. Theirs was a small cortege, dominated by two big chequered and crested vans around which the Immigration Enforcement team now milled – six officers, bulky in their navy flak blousons and boots, seeming to find the morning unexpectedly warm and visibly anxious for kick-off.

Al Ramsay, in a huddle with a handful of press, strode over and tapped the glass. Blaylock swung the door open.

'Okay, I think we'll roll in ten minutes.'

'Why the delay? If we're not careful the targets will have had their porridge and got off.'

'The ITN van is still five minutes away. If you're after something to read, David . . .' Ramsay handed him the *Guardian*, folded and plumped at the op-ed page, which asked in eighteen-point type: 'What did Blaylock think he was doing in Stapletree?'

'Getting out of listening to another bloody speech by me, I believe,' offered Vaughan, suavely.

Blaylock tossed the paper aside. 'It was a scheduled visit, with proper advance security, which got hijacked because somebody grassed.' He drummed on his thighs, riled. 'Sorry, Paddy, I just fancy a quick look out.'

As Blaylock moved from the car Andy Grieve broke from chatting with the Enforcement officers and moved to his side. One of the officers followed, frowning. 'Sir, I think the guys are thinking we ought to move in before the whole postcode's got wind of us?'

'I think they're right. Howay, let's get cracking.'

After the briefest of conferences the Enforcement team headed round the street corner en route to the first address on the jobsheet, ignoring the vexed gesticulations of Al Ramsay. Blaylock looked to Andy, shrugged, and followed the officers.

Soon they had fanned out across the front of a property and were rapping lightly on doors and windows. Watching from the pavement with Andy, Blaylock saw a female officer emerge from inspection of a narrow side alley running the length of a breezeblock wall. He glanced up to a second-storey window, the glass blocked out by what he recognised as the Moroccan flag, a green pentagram amid a wash of red.

Suddenly the front door creaked open in its metal frame. One officer stepped inside, and his colleagues followed him. Blaylock heard Andy emit a long sceptical exhalation.

'Six lads, why are they all going in the front . . . ?'

Instantaneously two close-cropped men – wearing hardly more than sports vests – came hurtling down the alleyway. The first, seeing Blaylock and Andy, feinted to his right and raced out into the street, Andy taking to his heels in pursuit. The second hesitated before Blaylock in the manner of a cornered mouse, then ducked his head and rammed at Blaylock like a bull. Blaylock tried and failed to get a hold of the man before crashing down to the cracked concrete.

He heard crunching boots and grunts all around and was quickly helped to his feet, whereupon he saw that Andy had the first runner already in custody, the second was being hotly pursued by blue-jackets, and a photographer was maniacally snapping away and reframing while Al Ramsay sought to dissuade him.

After ten fraught minutes – during which the big vans pulled round, the two runners were cuffed into the back of a police car, and Al Ramsay seemed not to want to acknowledge his existence – Blaylock accompanied the Prime Minister on a guided tour of the property.

The instant they were through the door into the narrow darkened hallway Blaylock could hear a child's panic-stricken crying coming from the kitchen. The atmosphere felt wrong: Blaylock felt himself to be the invasive presence.

One interrogation was being conducted in the living room – Blaylock made out decent soft furnishings and a big telly, and heard 'Who's renting this place?' repeated insistently. They were led on upstairs, met by a wall of sour unaired odour, where all the curtains were drawn and blankets and pillows were piled up across every floor, a ringtone diddled away unanswered and in the master bedroom four swarthy men in pyjamas sat, glumly constricted, on a bed, an officer standing over them, seeking to determine their names and ages.

'Come on now, gents, you're gonna get me cross.'

Their officer guide spoke quietly. 'So, we have an Indian gentleman whose passport is a fake. A lady with a visa that expired several months ago. And it doesn't appear these young Albanian men have any paperwork at all.'

'So they're all here illegally,' said Vaughan, as if helpfully. 'What next?'

'Straight to detention, pending removal, no passing go.'

'Well, I call that a fair morning's work. You'd wonder why can't it be like this all the time?'

Because this is showbusiness, thought Blaylock, but then the Captain touched his arm and jerked a thumb in the direction of the stairs.

Back outside Al Ramsay took Vaughan into his care and stared critically at Blaylock. 'I'm not sure you can face the cameras, David.'

'Look, I okayed this operation, so I'm prepared to defend it.'

'What I mean is, there's a rip in your bloody jacket.'

Blaylock touched his shoulder and realised that Ramsay didn't lie. 'Whatever. I'll do it in shirt-sleeves.'

Ramsay laid a hand on his arm and Blaylock was irritably minded to bat it aside. In fact he was being steered aside, for two officers were emerging from the house, flanking a crushed-looking woman with a sobbing four-year-old boy clutched awkwardly around her.

A fair morning's work, oh yes, Blaylock thought.

Once the stage was clear Ramsay approved the shot and Blaylock stood begrudgingly, arms folded, at the Captain's side.

'We came to Slough today to send a message. Be very clear, if you're in this country illegally, there is no hiding place . . .'

On the M4 the corteges separated and Blaylock saw the Captain's Jaguar power ahead, flanked by motorcycle outriders. He took a call from Mark Tallis, guessing correctly its import.

'You've gone viral again, patrón. *Your security guy, though, he should know people are starting to ask who he is.'*

Blaylock chuckled as he hung up. Andy looked questioningly.

'You're getting famous, Andy . . .'

The phone pulsed again. Blaylock put it to his ear without thinking, only to recoil from a blast of discordant noise, out of which resolved a terribly familiar quasi-female automated monotone.

'Mr Blaylock, when will you die? When will you die, Mr Blaylock? Every second you're alive, other people pay. Time for you to die, Mr Blaylock.'

Andy clocked Blaylock's grim expression and leaned in. Blaylock shared the handset with him, seeing that the screen read ID – UNKNOWN. The voice had mutated into a sinister childish treble. *'We see you, going around, stomping on the weak and the sick, calling it courage. Still so proud of yourself? Have a care, Mister Rat!'*

Grimacing, Andy made a cutting gesture with the flat of his hand.

'The trap is set. Your time—'

Blaylock pressed END CALL and pondered the muted device for some moments.

'Well, that's that, for what it's worth,' Andy muttered. 'He's toast, whoever he is.'

Blaylock slumped back into the leather.

Badly wanting a place where he could close a door, change out of his torn jacket and hang a sign for an hour, Blaylock went to his ministerial office in the Commons. In a few hours he would head up to his constituency for the weekend, and a review of the itinerary in store for him offered such drabness as to dull the ragged edges of the morning's run-arounds.

Last night's *Tees Gazette* had been sent down for his attention and with a black coffee in hand he flicked through the paper to see which local stories had traction. A 'Hands Off Our Hospital' campaign, protesting the mooted sale of an A&E department's land to a commercial developer, was ticking along predictably well. Blaylock's Labour opponent, meanwhile, had pride of place on the letters page, accusing him of 'gambling with police numbers and public safety'. Labour, he had to admit, ran a good machine, its sights perennially trained on his exposed flanks. They believed Teesside South belonged rightly to them – that Blaylock merely had the seat on loan, and that the electorate would finally succumb to buyer's remorse.

And yet he had won with a solid swing after an effort of which he remained proud – eighteen months of touring every ward with a clipboard, trudging up and down the stairwells of every social housing estate, listening to whatever concerns were proffered, promising to investigate them all. Where previously doors had always been hastily closed on Tory faces, people seemed to give a hearing to a local man, ex-army, who had worked for a living once. 'Blaylock: A Different Kind of Tory' was the helpful headline on an early *Gazette* profile.

Once installed, though, Blaylock had been made to look a pinch-penny after years of public subsidy that had improved Teesside South both materially and cosmetically. It remained a seat where the council and the NHS were the biggest employers, with equal numbers of people out of work long term. Now the place clearly could benefit from fresh funds, a few coats of paint, more troops to pluck the weeds and spear the litter. But Caroline Tennant had decreed there was no money this year, nor the next; whereas some floating voters clearly believed Labour might cough up. 'Blaylock: Same Old Tory' had been a recent and rather hurtful *Gazette* letters banner.

He put his constituency papers into one neat set and asked his PA to get the chief executive of NHS Teesside on the line.

Striding from the lift at Shovell Street Blaylock saw the short, compact figure of Paul Payne lurking by his door, unsmiling as ever, his backcombed blonde hair a significant addition to his height. Blaylock found Payne a baffling mix of insecurity and cockiness – subdued for long spells before popping up to create some trouble he had carefully crafted at his desk. Though Blaylock thought Payne pretty lucky to hold a junior ministerial brief, the man himself clearly thirsted for further recognition, despite his seeming lack of friends and the void where a personality ought to be. Yet Payne was nothing if not determined; and here he was, popping up again.

'David, about that jaunt of yours to Stapletree last night?'

'Yes?'

'I wish you would have told me about it.'

Blaylock shrugged. 'It got fixed up at short notice, Paul. And you'll have seen, it was nearly a debacle – I'd say you were lucky to miss out.'

'But didn't you think going there was worth discussing first here?'

'You mean discussing with you? What would you have said?'

'From a Security view I'd have said it was maybe a rash choice – not going to somewhere more considered, better vetted.'

'Good job we didn't speak, then. I might have missed meeting someone who was worth meeting. Since we're doing gripes, Paul, if you've some issue you want to share related to the Identity Documents Bill, start by sharing it with me, not with the PM in front of visiting dignitaries. You got that?'

Payne nodded diffidently, clearly unapologetic. Blaylock, immeasurably irked by a self-styled rival he didn't remotely rate, pressed on by.

'Home Secretary, we face a crisis in this country – a crisis of violence against women in the home. It accounts for one in five violent crimes committed nationwide, and every week two women are murdered by a partner, ex-partner or lover.'

'That two women a week stat is out of date,' Deborah Kerner intervened. 'The recent trend is down a little?'

There was then a chill meeting of gazes between Deborah and Gail Hurd, the Kiwi-accented chief executive of Women United Against Domestic Abuse. Blaylock winced inwardly, feeling the instant rebuttal had struck a wrong note too soon.

'Let's say', he offered, 'that if it were one and three-quarters we agree that's still too many. Please, Ms Hurd, go on.'

Lean, thin-lipped and black-suited, Gail Hurd held her acidulous look another beat before resuming. 'As you know, there is a long, tragic history of cases where women died because warning signs were missed or ignored. Susan Hart, Emma Watts, obviously Marjorie's daughter Vickie . . .'

Blaylock didn't recall every case, but Mrs Marjorie Michaels was a subdued presence at Gail Hurd's left – further supported at her other side by a solicitor, introduced as Anna Mann, a woman so large Blaylock had wished he could offer her a bigger chair.

'We campaigners have heard assurances and apologies for years, and yet still women suffer because the same mistakes are made over and over. Government needs to show it understands, takes responsibility and offers leadership. At the moment, only you can do that.'

It didn't seem a ringing endorsement. Blaylock cleared his throat. 'Be assured, this is a priority. We do need to ensure women know how wide-ranging the police powers already are to pursue a suspect and make an arrest. But there are key areas where we seek improvements. You'll know I will bring an Identity Documents Bill before the House—'

'Yes,' asserted Anna Mann. 'We'll be giving evidence on your draft to the Select Committee. Do we understand right that your database will hold all an individual's old addresses? Because a security hack in that case could be catastrophic for women trying to escape an abuser.'

'The security of the database is of paramount importance. You may know, too, within a year we expect to have cameras on the lapels of every police officer. That'll make for a powerful record of victim statements at the time of arrest – even if they're retracted later.'

'You trust the police to manage that system?' said Gail Hurd.

'Why wouldn't I?'

'Because', she sighed heavily, 'police still don't respect domestic violence. A camera isn't going to teach a policeman how to spot that kind of behaviour, how to read the signs, take them seriously—'

'Forgive me, but we have to be realistic about how deeply the state can be interposed in the home. Police officers can't interpret every "sign"' when two people, on the surface, seem to have chosen to be together—'

'I trust you're not saying it takes two to tango?' said Anna Mann.

Blaylock was bothered. 'No, what I mean is that we understand these offences are committed within a climate of fear, often masked from the authorities. I would put it to you, though, that things have changed, that police are better trained.'

'In my view there's just a culture of misogyny embedded in the police,' Anna Mann shot back. 'No amount of self-regulation will shift that. It's not even just them; I personally can't see an end to domestic violence until we end sexism in society.'

Blaylock suddenly found himself aspiring to the patriarch's tones of Lord Waugh. 'Well, be that as it may, tell me, what is it that you want to have happen?'

Gail Hurd leaned in. 'We think what's needed is an independent judge-led public inquiry.'

Blaylock groaned inside. 'I see. With what kind of a remit?'

'To hold the police and the CPS to account, look at what social services and health services have to deal with, take evidence from families, victims, stakeholders like ourselves . . .'

'What do you hope that'll accomplish?'

'Well, the issue will get the national prominence it deserves.'

'There's something else, from my point of view, can I just say . . . ?'

Mrs Marjorie Michaels, silent until now, had spoken. Blaylock shifted to face her. She was small and hunched in her black jacket and skirt, her facial features oddly reminiscent of a pubescent male, her complexion worryingly red as if from a persistent medical condition or the drugs needed to treat it.

'I know money is such a thing,' she continued haltingly. 'It's money often as not that keeps women from leaving a situation. But having somewhere to go and call home, just for a bit . . . Someone there who understands, who'll listen, who knows how to talk to kiddies who are scared? I think it makes such a difference.'

'You're talking about refuges?' said Blaylock.

'Yeah, oh yeah . . . They're golden, I think. Golden. If you could do any one thing that's what I wish you'd do. More of those? Or just save the ones they got. I know what Anna means, the trouble with men . . . But I don't know how you train 'em out of it, if you can. I don't know how you change someone who's that bad. And I do take your point, what the police do, they're not far off what you'd want. But sometimes . . . a woman just needs to leave, straight away, or she and her kids, I mean . . . they could die, Mr Blaylock. They could die.'

Blaylock, having made sure to meet Mrs Michaels's eye, now felt himself swallow uncomfortably hard. 'Yes, refuges, qualified staff, they do require significant resources . . . But I do note your comments, Mrs Michaels, I do, and I ask you to leave this with me.'

Phyllida Cox had made no contribution to the meeting but once the delegation had reached the lifts she made for the door, turned back to Blaylock, and said, 'Can we speak before you head north? There are a number of things.'

'Of course.'

'You okay with that?' asked Deborah when Phyllida was gone. 'You're really going to try and do something for refuges?'

'Oh, I can't afford it. Caroline would kill me. It's just . . .' He gestured helplessly to the air, as if to some cosmic dimension of the problem.

Geraldine was at the door. 'James Bannerman on the line for you.'

'*Good afternoon, David. To advise you, the march that the Free Briton Brigade planned for east London – we can't let it go ahead, usual rules, section thirteen of the Public Order Act. I'll be saying the right to protest is countervailed by the threat of public disorder, also by our wish to protect local communities and premises.*'

'Great,' said Blaylock, absently. 'Shall I get a legal opinion here, to be safe?'

'*Why bother? I would say in all candour, the intelligence on this outfit now seems a little more concerning than I first thought. Over and above the usual concern for damage. Frankly I don't want them gathering anywhere.*'

Blaylock was puzzled by Bannerman's unusually ominous tone but, before he could press, the Chief rang off.

Kept waiting outside Phyllida's closed door he loitered like a minion in the seated area, gazing at the portrait gallery nailed up in an orderly succession round the walls – the Home Office boneyard, the honour roll of his predecessors, a poisoned chalice passed from Liverpool to Peel, Wellington to Walpole, Palmerston to Churchill.

'Do you have a favourite?'

He turned to see that Phyllida had materialised in her doorway. 'I realise I never asked you before.'

'Aw, they're all so different. Except that they all left, in the end. I just hope there'll be a nail up there for me when my time comes.'

They stepped into her office, distinguished by the building's best collection of aspidistras and by Sir Robert Peel's antique clock atop her bookcase, its gilded aspect seeming to belong to a different building. She took her place behind her desk with what seemed to Blaylock a distracted air.

'Thank you for the draft of your conference speech.'

'How did you find it?'

'What you say about immigration figures, you're quite sure you want all this business of "The buck stops with me"?'

'I'd feel anything else would be dishonest.'

'It's just a hostage to fortune. One never knows . . .'

'When I started here, Phyllida, you warned me never to set any store by my plans. Because things would just happen, the last item on the agenda would suddenly be at the top?'

'Yes. That is the job. We will always be fire-fighting.'

'Yeah. And yet, I find I can't live like that.'

Surprised that he offered nothing more, she looked down to her notes. 'You remain so confident about identity cards?'

'"It can be done, and it will be done. Beyond any possibility of doubt." What matters is the atmosphere in which we work. In which we fight. I need you to see that it permeates the building.'

'Clearly the policy continues to face huge practical difficulties. Were Number Ten fully aware how big it would be?'

'Maybe not, and you and I may see it differently, but still we are mandated to enact the policy, and you need to be helping me deliver it. I feel I'm still hearing unnecessary notes.'

'David, I am not just some cheerleader. In policy matters I believe I can be a useful counterweight. So I would like you to at least hear me out. Ms Kerner seems to have your ear perpetually, and I must say I question the wisdom of some of what she's pouring in there.'

'I hired Deborah for her strong voice, and I find it bracing.'

'David, I've seen a fair few special advisors in my time. The ones with the loudest voices, strangely, are always the ones least adept at crafting workable policy. She stomps about firing memos when it's not her damn job to manage people or direct operations.'

'Nor is that what I hired her for. And yet at times I've been left wondering how else I'm meant to get things done.'

'People in this building work long, stressful days—'

Blaylock snapped. 'Sure, yeah, I see plenty of worry on faces – worrying about their own backsides, and how they get out of being blamed for some shambles they watched happening. What I want to see is people firing all their guns to do what I bloody well asked them to do. My private office are here late every night, long after the bloody directors have gone for their tea—'

'Please, *please*, David . . .'

He stopped. Phyllida's face had creased so badly he thought she was in pain. When she spoke again she was quiet.

'Please, not another of your – eruptions.'

'My what, sorry?'

'When the black clouds cross your face, when you start to bash things . . . We've worked together long enough for me to see it coming. I'm sorry, this is a delicate matter but I have felt the need to raise it, for . . . quite some time. It's not a position I want to be in, as a woman . . . But I urge you to please be calmer. People hear you round this building. They hear you and they . . . they think the worst.'

Blaylock had struggled to come to terms with her harrowed tone, but now something admonishing in her face made something inside him push back. 'Phyllida, with respect, if I'm not satisfied with work, with attitude – I want people to know about it. And if I give someone a very minor shellacking I don't expect them to curl up and cry about it. Jesus, you'd think—'

She stood up, not even looking at him. 'Forgive me. I was mistaken to try to raise this.'

'Hey, look, I am more than happy to discuss it.'

'David – I see no point.'

6

Gazing at the darkening window of the First Class carriage Blaylock felt a familiar sensation of racing in transit between rival kingdoms – up from Wessex through Mercia to the welcoming borders of Northumbria. Andy sat opposite him, his police team as a foursome behind. Before him was as much paperwork as he'd felt he could face on the journey. His red box was travelling separately, solo, in the back of Martin's Jag and would await him under police protection at Darlington.

He stared down, eyes swimming somewhat, at the now substantially red-inked pages of his draft conference speech.

'For the most part the electorate are hard-working people who want to live in a society that is tough-minded but fair, where you get out what you put in, and people can be what they want to be if they play by the rules . . .'

He had written that, true enough; and yet the thought of saying it aloud was beyond risible. He put a clean red line across the page and asked Andy if he fancied fetching them each a can of McEwan's Export.

From Darlington Martin drove to Blaylock's constituency office, sited amid a drab concrete-and-wire-mesh business park part-funded by the European Union. Finding himself famished, and it being Friday, he phoned ahead to the office and enquired if anyone would care for a fish supper fetched in. Though he found no takers, Blaylock nonetheless hopped from the Jag outside Val's Caff just before the turn into the park.

He was next in line as Val spooned virulent-looking chicken

tikka onto a jaundiced potato before dressing the sides of the polystyrene box with limp lettuce leaves. Her customer, though, was crestfallen.

'Aw, ya put salad in? Aw, didn't want that. Tek it out, yeh?'

Blaylock felt a crushing fondness for the customs of his tribe.

He strode into the lamp-lit park, noting a new VACANT lot, a call centre that had evidently ceased fielding calls. But shutters that had been long drawn down in one sullen corner of the forecourt were now raised to reveal an ad for a small engineering firm, which cheered Blaylock immensely. If all jobs were equal, he felt, some were more equal than others.

In the office the team was assembled, blinds drawn down over the cheerless view, fluorescent lights blinking over the cramped space. Blaylock shared his bag of chips with the table.

In the chair, preparing a digest of the weekly postbag, was Bob Cropper, Blaylock's veteran election agent, past master of minding the office expenses, fielding intemperate callers to the office and gauging local opinion by putting a wetted finger in the air. At Bob's side was Margaret Whitton, special case worker, delegated to any constituent who presented with a couple of quid or less in their pocket on which to subsist for a week. Holly Robson, office manager, sat with the ring-bound notebook. Jim Fisher, constituency party treasurer, looked as if he'd rather be in the pub. Placed beside Blaylock was Chloe Herron, a quiet, pretty sixth-former in a smart coat, on work experience and visibly still getting the hang of office routines.

'People have written in quite dispiriting numbers', Bob Cropper tutted, 'to ask if there'll be a Free Briton Brigade candidate at the next election. They leafleted here this week, actually spent some money.'

Bob passed Blaylock a full-colour flyer in bold shades of red, white and blue, replete with portraits of apparently ordinary people looking with wounded eyes into the lens. On the back was an unflattering snapshot of Blaylock himself, caught as if just told his flies were undone.

100s of Asylum Seekers SWAMP our towns, waiting for our courts to throw them out. HIS government pays our council to put them up for FREE!

Thinking this crude stuff, Blaylock nonetheless felt fleeting panic as he tried to imagine how he would spell out what was so vitally different about his own political view.

The FBB are the TRUE voice of YOUR streets that David Blaylock PRETENDS to come from! We want YOU to stand up and speak for YOUR community too!

'Yeah, well,' Blaylock offered, 'if they ever hold a pen for long enough to write some proper policy we might have to pay attention.'

'What's the bet they stand a candidate here next time?'

'You worried, Bob? Is it time for me to go hunting a nice safe seat in North Yorkshire?'

Familiar chuckles rippled round the table, yet Blaylock thought he saw worry in certain tired eyes. Margaret, seeming even wearier than usual, rallied nonetheless. 'There are thirty-six thousand households in this constituency, we know them all and we've directly helped out twenty-two thousand of them. So if the ungrateful buggers want to . . .' She could not bring herself to the dispiriting conclusion. Bob reasserted his role in the chair.

'Well, turning to the green ink brigade . . .'

Every week there were loners who wrote in strangled prose with blasts of hyperbole. But Blaylock never took them lightly. In his days of 'How to Be an MP' inductions he and fellow newbies had been urged by a junior whip to attend to every scrap of constituency correspondence. '*Always, always read to the end, even if the whole first side is about what a cunt you are. Because if you don't turn the page there's always a chance the second side will begin, "And just because of you I'm going to kill my wife and kids."*'

'Someone put a bit of graft into this. I don't know how you want to take it, David.' The vintage look of the thing nearly made Blaylock smile, the message spelt out by a cut-out collage of newspaper capitals.

BLAYLOCK – 30 DAYS TO MEND YOUR WAYS OR ELSE!!!

'Andy.' Blaylock beckoned Grieve from his guardsman's post by the door. 'Does this constitute a threat?'

Andy came across and peered down. 'In the current market I'd call it a low bidder, boss.'

Driven a few darkened miles back to his constituency home in Maryburn Blaylock observed the nightlife as he glided through town, amused still by the cut of the youngsters just starting their northeast Friday night out – packs of likely lads strutting along in smart shirts, gaggles of girls tottering toward minicabs, amusedly about the business of trying to stop their stretchy skirts from riding up.

At home he took a shower and made the mistake of looking at himself in the mirror. To be here was a blessed removal from his Westminster routine. But the Maryburn house seemed to embody, and not happily, the life for which he had traded his marriage. With five bedrooms, garden and garage, it had been a snip when bought seven years before. The state-installed videophone and panic room had doubtless added to its value. It had been bought, however, not as a mere constituency perch but as a proper weekend residence for a family that, as things turned out, had hardly set foot in the place.

Jennie had been pregnant with Molly when Blaylock was first sounded out about contesting Teesside South. Possibly, when she agreed to let him have a go, she envisaged him failing. But the closer he edged to the breakthrough, the more the schism between them widened. It seemed to Blaylock they had overcome so much to be together that it was crazy to come apart for so little. But political differences, for so long the source of spirited, principled disagreements, now assumed gigantic proportions. Jennie made a number of negotiated appearances at his side on the stump, with Alex and Cora. But he knew with sickened surety that she would not accept the part. Six weeks after he won the seat, Jennie served notice that she and the children would not be shifting from Islington. The manner in which he reacted to the news only made clearer to her that things would be better if he left.

There was another dimension to the tale, he knew – Jennie's narrative of his thuggish temper, on top of his brute self-absorption. It was undoubtedly the case that during the campaign – when he was supposed to be minding Cora and instead had his mobile pressed to his ear discussing with Bob Cropper the way Ottersdale Ward might be tending – Cora had stepped precipitously off a curb, been glanced by a passing car and suffered a broken leg. That was a headstone-like marker in their decline. He had never left the doghouse after that.

'You're the MP, yeh?'

'That's right.'

'Okay. Hadn't a clue who you were before th' day.'

His first Saturday surgery appointment was with Mr William ('It's Billy, yeh?') Darrow, a taxi driver from Port Clarence – and really, actually, a forklift driver, but then there wasn't the building work there used to be. Sat before Blaylock with his beefy forearms formidably on the table between them, Billy was so pronounced in his unhappiness that Andy – always uneasy in the hurly-burly of Arndale Shopping Centre – was visibly attentive.

Billy, though, was subdued. He was already in dispute with his ex-partner, and now he was losing his socially rented flat, with a spare room he had kept for visits from their daughter, because it was judged too big for his needs.

'I don't think of myself as a victim, right? But, fact is, I *am* a victim. It's all been tek off us. What's left for me, eh? I'm just – it's like I'm going down and I dunno what to grab onto.'

Blaylock valued this constituency business and yet it could feel like a dismal turning of a wheel, a sack of distress one might suffocate in. If people were getting the benefits they were entitled to, there was little else he could tell them. But he promised Billy Darrow his office would assist with an appeal against the ending of his tenancy.

He had to move on – to the woman who was keen on 'Hands Off Our Hospital' and didn't fancy travelling to get seen to – to the man who sat down and said, 'How do you live with yourself? Putting people out on the streets?'

In a break he surveyed the lackadaisical Saturday shoppers, the already tired-looking cleaning woman with her mop and cart, the hand-lettered SALE! signs in windows, the urchins with faces buried in candyfloss. It was the community, right enough, and to be encountering it here in this manner was an improvement on the office, which could seem, at times, like a police station. But sat behind a desk in the thoroughfare he could never quite escape the feeling that his business was hardly superior to that of the grafters selling raffle tickets or fake Gucci watches or cable TV subscriptions with an unbeatable offer on the weekend's big title fight live from Vegas.

Just as he could see lunchtime ahead, he realised Margaret Whitton was fending off a pained-looking woman of Sub-Saharan complexion under her *jilbāb*, clutching a crying baby. He stood and hastened over.

'She's not on the list, David, I'm trying to explain—'

'I'm sorry,' he winced at the woman. 'You're not my constituent, I can't give you the time I owe to them.'

Bob came through the swishing doors, looking gaunt, and stalked up to the table. 'Oh, David, sorry, I've just had the police round, someone's only gone and done the office overnight.'

'They broke in?' Blaylock looked to Andy, thinking about computers, hard drives, classified files.

'No, they just put all graffiti on the outside walls.' He passed Blaylock his phone, on which he had snapped a photo of said graffiti, daubed in high, lean red letters: WHO DOES BLAYLOCK SPEAK FOR?

'Now, not to worry, I've got 'em slapping the whitewash on.'

'There must be CCTV of it?'

'The bloody thing of it is, the police reckon they've knocked the one in the car park off its pole. It's full-on criminal damage, right enough. They must have brung a twenty-foot ladder.'

'Any theories on who "they" are?'

'Well, I said, didn't I, I thought they've been getting organised . . . ?'

When lunchtime came he was driven a mile or so to attend a 'culinary festival' of 'fresh local produce' – there to drink half a glass of bitter beer and eat a baked savoury slice glutinous with gravy. Then he dropped by a newish 'extra care' apartment complex for the over-sixty-fives, bought a couple of bracelets and a wooden doorstop fashioned by some handy retired residents, joked with the old-timers about the merits of 'armchair exercise' and listened quietly to an ashen woman whose grandson was forever calling in to tap her up for drug money. He just made it to Bishopton Road for 4 p.m., where Bob was waiting outside the ground bearing scarves for each of them, and together they watched Thornfield Town take on Ryhope in the day's big Wearside League clash. At half-time, with Town two goals down, he had to get going if he was to catch the 17.55 from Darlington back to London.

'Fucking Town's had it,' he heard from a sedentary position as he mounted the steps to the exit. Then a crumpled betting slip whizzed through the air before him. He stopped to note the offender, a bloke in a bobble hat who returned his look with interest.

'Aye, you an' all, Blaylock.'

7

So what did we learn about David Blaylock this week? The ex-soldier remains handy with his fists and not afraid to have a go. Commendable as that might be, does it have the slightest bearing on his fitness for the job of managing the UK's borders, protecting its citizens from crime and terror threats, and upholding our cherished rights and freedoms in the bargain? Has he got the bottle – not to mention the subtler political skills – needed for those larger, more complex and crucial encounters with reality?

Yadda yadda, thought Blaylock. Mark Tallis had not let up texting him to the effect that the *Correspondent*'s profile was something he ought to see, so at last he had asked Martin to pull over at the next Esso garage. But the fifteen hundred words of Abigail Hassall's piece read to him like discount psychoanalysis.

'David's big problem', one estranged ex-ally told me, 'is that he sees everything as personal, and everything becomes a fight, from which he never backs down or sees where he might be wrong. He just stands there and flails away. I don't know who or what inflicted the psychic defeat on him that made him that way, but it must have been a sizeable one.'

Who, he wondered, had sung? What 'ex-ally'? How recently 'estranged'? On a handful of prior occasions, friends he counted honourable had warned him of their intention to pass comment.

He was unaccustomed to the anonymous knife in the back. It had the inflection of something Jennie might say, yet he knew her as the soul of scruple whose silence with the press was staunch as his own.

He tossed the *Correspondent* aside, knowing he needed to have his head right for an afternoon with his children. They read him too easily now, saw all too clearly if clouds hung over him, and he had to have them see that they had all of his attention. Otherwise, the risk of further decline in their relations was too grave.

Even from what Blaylock had felt to be the invincibly strange early days of post-divorce, the kids had shown themselves remarkably adept in the new dispensation. For sure, they had favoured their mother, though Alex had for a time seemed to waver – his dad's loyal little lad, back then. But they had all missed him a fair bit at first, he knew as much. He had strained every sinew to indulge them without fuss, playing one off against another if affections seemed to slip. It was with stunning rapidity, though, that the kids grew older and wiser, saw through his guiles, computed his now essentially adjunct status to the family. Nowadays Sunday was a familiar duty, ever much the same, regular as clockwork, handing Blaylock the same old lesson on a plate.

It was then, very sharply, that Blaylock remembered Jennie's request that he come collect the children earlier this week – a request he had disputed, resigned himself to, then forgotten. He fumbled into his jacket for his phone, where a curt text message already awaited him.

For all the difference it made, he ran up the mosaic pathway and hurdled the stone steps to Jennie's door. She had fastened up her hair with a blue brocade scarf. Batting aside Blaylock's apology she blew out her cheeks. 'Listen, Cora's not well, she can't come out.'

'Not well how?' With Cora that could mean a range of issues. Jennie gestured for him to step indoors. 'Female trouble.'

'Oh . . . poor lamb. Can I go see her?'

'She was dozing just now. Maybe leave it and look in at drop-off?'

Across the threshold Blaylock felt the familiar estranging sense of being, for a change, in a real home – a shared habitat crafted with proper care for all persons within it. Jennie directed him toward the living room. Stairs led down to a big basement kitchen and den, the heart of the house, somewhere Blaylock was somehow never invited.

'Daddy.'

Molly was tripping down from the upper floor, shyly smiling, sidling up for an embrace. She remained, with reservations, his fan.

'Get your boots on, Molly.' Jennie moved things along.

'Where's the boy?'

'Up in his room, looking at college websites. Seeing what size of mortgage he fancies taking out on his future.'

'Is he still thinking about filmmaking?'

'Yep, that's the passion.'

'Does he think he really needs to give three years and ten grand to it? When he's already making little films on his computer?'

'Ask him. I know if your lot had your way he and his pals would be square-bashing.'

He watched her reach up and unfasten the headscarf, shaking out her long locks, until she met his eye coolly with a look of *Yes, what?*

She had caught him, for he had quite suddenly and unwisely fallen to thinking of how much he had always loved to watch her divest herself of clothing, in a major or minor way, whether she minded him or not. Then again, he had liked it just as well to see her putting her clothes on – the ritual draping of those curved lines of hers, all the way up to the dark crowning glory of hair, the canny gleam in her eye, that broad red mouth in that pale and fine-boned face.

She was – she remained – the loveliest woman he had ever known. He congratulated himself on the neutral maturity with which he could make this inward acknowledgement.

'So, you bested me in court. With your Bosnian.'

'Not personal, as you know. It was the right ruling.'

'You're totally sure of that?'

'There was a child involved, that child deserved consideration.'

'Right. And as for her delightful father, we're lumbered with him too for the foreseeable.'

He sat back into the deep crimson sofa and glanced around. The *Observer* was on the coffee table, DVDs lined up by the big telly, thick hardbacks spine-out on their shelves, glossy magazines under the coffee table. He knew she was watching him, and what she was looking for, suspecting him – quite rightly – of keeping watch for telling signs about the house, most especially for vestiges of some new male presence.

For a good, long and gratifying while, though, Jennie had been just as single as he. It appeared no man could meet the standard. Previous suitors, certainly, had failed to win over the children – Cora loudest in deploring both 'the geek' who wrote political satire for radio, and the divorced lawyer with two sons, all three of whom Cora rated 'slimey'. As long as Blaylock remained notably alone himself, he knew, he was winning points with the children, if not with Jennie, who seemed not to be keeping score.

'So how was your week? Apart from all the punch-ups?'

'I had a game of squash with the Lord Chief Justice. We talked human rights. He told me off about Europe.'

'Never been much of a European, have you, David?'

'Never had the house in Tuscany, right enough, pet. No, it's a regrettable cast of mind I share with the majority of British people. Backward of me, I know.'

'How did you get on with the cops on Wednesday?'

'They listened politely enough, until I told them I was having an inquiry into how they carry on.'

'Well, no wonder. All I hear about is decline in trust of the police, and from middle-class juries, too. So you're on to something.'

'Yeah. But it's funny, I get talking to you and suddenly I feel like I want to defend them.'

She chuckled, which he appreciated – and yet he longed to get a proper gut-laugh out of her. The same malaise showed in how she would pop her eyes or skew her jaw to show 'surprise' or 'interest'. But it was studied. It had been years since her eyes really sparked at his 'news'. And so much of what he had done with his life had been designed to seek the favour of those eyes.

'I got a letter from Tamara Sahbaz? Young Davilo's off to college.'

But by her *Fancy that* look he knew she had read the gambit, and he pressed no further, for in any case their son was now hustling into the room, his knees poking out of his torn denims, fists thrust into his hoodie pocket.

Cut your hair, son, grow up and shave.

Alex's barnet was short at the sides but with a crest swept over the top – a sculpted and, to Blaylock's eye, overly self-conscious look. From the hoodie Alex withdrew a video camera barely bigger than his fist and began to twiddle with its extendable viewfinder.

'Is that new, son?'

'Give him his due,' Jennie remarked. 'He delivered an awful lot of pizzas to pay for it himself, didn't you?'

'Mum, did you ask him?'

'What is it, son?' Blaylock was ever vexed by indirect address.

'It's just, there's an old movie on that I really want to see, down at the South Bank, it's just on today? And we could still make it.'

'Alex, you know, son – anywhere that we go together has all got to get security-cleared way in advance.'

'It's just you never get to see this projected on a screen.'

'Sorry, what is it?'

'*Battleship Potemkin*?'

Blaylock winced. 'Howay, Alex, think of your sister, eh? No, it's owls for us today, bonny lad.'

In the end the film about one woman's doughty quest to locate a rare species of owl in the Omani mountains caused no pain. 'Good' was Molly's firmly head-nodding verdict. Alex even ventured some approval of the 'quality' use of long lenses. Afterward they sat in a crowded American-style diner, over plates of spicy chicken burgers and curly fries. While Molly embellished the paper menu with doodles Alex appeared pensive under his fringe. Blaylock fought the urge to check his phone, worried, too, that his face was frozen in some absent frown.

'He can sit with us if he likes.' Alex was gesturing to Andy Grieve, sitting upright at a table for one ten feet away, his eyes flicking mildly around the room.

'Never worry. Andy and I see enough of each other.'

'He's a surveillance camera on legs, isn't he? Do you actually worry? About someone, y'know, doing you in?'

'I'm well protected. Over-protected, really. The police do an excellent job.'

'So why are you rucking with them all the time?' Alex offered this as if innocently over the lid of his oozing burger.

'I don't "ruck"' with the police, Alex, there are just some sensible changes I need to discuss with them.'

'Daddy has a *lot* to do, Alex,' Molly offered without lifting an eye from her artwork. Blaylock looked at his youngest child and felt the familiar gnaw behind his ribs – love, desperate and unalloyed. Because she was the youngest, the one still susceptible to his sway?

'But they're not happy, are they, the police?' Alex persisted. 'Do you think they'll go out on strike?'

'Coppers? No, never. They're more responsible than that.'

'Don't you think they're just a *bit* corrupt? Some of them?'

'Oh well, you should ask your mum about that, she'll give you chapter and verse. Have you and her had that conversation?'

But now Alex merely stuffed curly fries into his mouth and turned back to gazing round the restaurant.

'You're allowed to talk about your mother, Alex.'

'Yeah, but we don't need to, do we?'

The silence persisted. Blaylock really wished to improve on it.

'What's your opinion of the police then? I'm not sure I get where you're coming from . . .'

'I expect some are alright,' Alex said at last, having chewed for some moments. 'But, as an institution? I think they're part of a whole system . . . an oppressive system. Like, whenever there's a big demo or protest, about something totally righteous? There's the police, just clubbing people down. They take their pay and they defend whatever the establishment tells them to.'

'By "establishment" you mean people like me?'

Alex shrugged as if to say his father could take it as he liked. 'What I mean is, we're all of us the people, right. So, what I think is, the people ought to be the police.'

Blaylock smiled, feeling himself on terra firma. 'Well, one of my illustrious predecessors said that, yeah? But public order is necessary, you see that, don't you? So ordinary people can go about their business? Of course, people have a right to protest what they think is "righteous"; but a protest has to be policed. Otherwise what have you got?'

'Anarchy. Anarchy in the UK.' It was Alex's turn to grin.

'Right. Fancy a bit of that, do you?'

'I just think there's a place for it. Society benefits by a bit of fruitful chaos. Resistance to the so-called done thing.'

'Well, I agree with you.'

'Oh yeah?' The boy indicated a flash of authentic-looking interest.

'Sure, I've always thought there should be a proper revolutionary party in Britain. There's enough people who feel that way – who think politicians are all shysters and the rich are bloodsuckers or whatever. All that . . . energy? It should go somewhere. It should be tested.'

Blaylock had begun to enjoy the sound of his pontificating voice. His apprentice, though, had resorted to peering beneath the table at his own denim crotch.

'What's up?'

'You mind if I film you?'

Now Alex lifted his video camera onto the table-top, its red REC light already glowing red.

'Alex, no, turn it off, eh?'

'Shame. I could have just done it covertly.'

'Then I might have had to have Andy cart you off.' He sighed. 'Listen, what I was saying, a revolution's not a dinner party, right?'

'I'd bloody hope not.' Alex downed the dregs of his Diet Coke, noisily. Blaylock sat back, now dissatisfied to be sitting where he was, taking the side he was taking, having this barnacle-crusted debate with his adolescent offspring, in language that sounded yet more calcified.

Molly looked up from her drawing. 'I'm just asking . . . but could we maybe do something all together one time? Like a family?'

Blaylock ruffled her hair, but Alex gave his sister a stagey scowl and fell to polishing his lens with the hem of his hoodie. Blaylock gestured for the bill.

He ushered them back across Jennie's threshold. Molly hugged him hurriedly before dashing to the downstairs loo. Alex bounded directly up the stairs, two at a time, as if released from chores. Unhappily Blaylock watched him disappear into his bedroom.

'Go easy on him,' offered Jennie, now at his side.

'Eh? No, he's fine. We had a good chat.'

'Did he say he's had a bit of stick at school?'

Blaylock frowned. This was an old story with Alex, and no fatherly exhortations to 'whack 'em back' had ever been considered helpful.

'God. He's old enough now, I'd have thought. Big enough.'

'It's not a physical thing,' Jennie sighed. 'They do politics in class, he's in the debating club . . . they know you're his dad.'

Blaylock bridled. 'There's not a lot I can do about that, is there?'

'No, okay, and – calm down – Alex can handle it.'

'Yeah well, but you bring it up, I mean – I come here to be with the kids, not just turn over a whole load of . . . dead ground.' Blaylock was properly vexed, could feel his temples pulse.

Jennie's eyes on him, though, seemed like a warning from history. 'Why don't you go into the living room and see Cora?'

Taking the hint Blaylock found his elder daughter lying on the red velvet sofa in a towelling dressing gown. She looked aside from her paperback with the upward twitch of her mouth that passed for greeting, and he stooped and kissed her warm forehead.

'How are you, my love?' he said, hunkering down on his haunches. But there was little he could extract from her. The book was called *Crocodile Soup* and it was 'good'. She was taking Feminax and it 'was helping'. Long and lean as her mother, already exhibiting a comparable brainpower, Cora was nonetheless a troubled girl. Over the past year she had appeared glum, her weight fluctuating like her mood.

Blaylock stroked her cheek, and in the silence she looked aside as if to say the thing was surely done? Blaylock pulled himself up awkwardly and returned to the hall, there to find Jennie waiting with her arms folded and a similar air of closure.

'Alex!' she shouted up the stairs. 'Come and say goodbye to your dad.' No answer. She looked at Blaylock and shrugged, to his chagrin.

'That's how it gets if you just let him squirrel away in his pit.'

Jennie rolled her eyes. The slackness of the situation Blaylock found profoundly riling. He now bounded up the stairs, and turned Alex's door handle, only to find it locked. He knocked.

'Alex? Can we say cheerio?'

'Hang on!' The voice from within was testy, over music.

Jennie had trooped up the stairway to be at Blaylock's side – quite unnecessarily, he felt.

'He's locked the bloody door, what's that about?'

It remained obdurately shut, and had gone quiet from behind. Blaylock bashed on it, hard, with the hub of his fist. *'Howay*, Alex.'

'Don't, David,' Jennie said sharply.

Blaylock was clutching at the doorknob anew when the door was flung open by a glaring Alex.

'"Cheerio",' said the boy. *'Okay?* Jesus!' And he spun round and stalked back to a desk cluttered and piled with electronics.

'Yeah, great, your manners are a bloody *delight*, son. Have a good week.' Blaylock lunged and yanked the door shut.

Jennie was shaking her head, as though in age-old despond.

'Don't give me that look, Jennie, there's no call for him to behave that way, no reason for you to indulge it.'

Blaylock could feel himself talking between his teeth, could feel the tautness across his face. And even now, after all the years, he was hoping she would give in, change her weather, see the force of his feeling as an insuperable argument and surrender to it. She did not.

'You don't understand what you sound like . . . the effect you have. You never do.'

'Well, that's an old one, so . . .' He took the deepest breath he could draw into his tightened chest. 'So, I don't know what you want me to say.'

'You don't need to say anything. Not to me, okay? But one day, you might want to just *try* to change your ways. For their sake,

and for yours. I mean – it would be better for you, to find a solution.'

'Solution to what?'

'To your problem, David.'

'And what is my fucking . . .' – he caught himself. 'What is my
problem, Jennie?'

She was looking meaningfully, authoritatively, head tilted as if
to say the answer was self-evident. Then the phone was ringing
and she turned, she was done with him, she was trooping back
down the stairs.

'Hello, Jennifer Kirkbride . . . ?'

Blaylock took a moment, swallowed, knowing he was alone
and out of place. Once he was back in the Jaguar he would have
returned to his serious life, his packed schedule and hand-tailored
arrangements and weighty responsibilities, and he would leave
behind these hopeless complexities and tangles of ill feeling that,
strictly, belonged to the past and ought really, for the good of all
parties, to be abandoned there. He marched down the stairs and
out through the door directly.

'You okay, boss?'

In the gloom of the backseat Blaylock realised that he ought not
for so long to have been holding his hand over his brow as if to
shut out a painful sunlight. Looking up now he saw Andy looking
back at him with far too much concern.

'Yeah, yeah. Fine, thanks, Andy. No bother.'

'I'm sorry, boss. It can be tough sometimes, I know. Family and
stuff . . . I mean, I don't want to be out of line.'

'No, no.' Blaylock pulled himself upright and together. 'Listen.
There are faults on both sides. It's a long story.'

8

He had always believed he would see her again. When he agreed to troop along to Durham alumni drinks – albeit in what he rated a bloody dreadful basement bar in Soho – it was only with Jennifer Kirkbride in mind. For nearly an hour the rackety music and forced chit-chat were just as bad as he'd feared; but the lift in his chest when he saw her descend into the cramped space redeemed it all.

And it was she who sought him out, took him aside, bought him a pint. There was something new in her eyes. She had heard all kinds of things. He had left the army? Become an aid worker? Worked for a bit as a stonemason? All true, yes, but first he insisted they talk about her.

She spoke forcefully of far-ranging travels and encounters, volunteering with Médecins Sans Frontières, election monitoring in Thailand, time spent in Burma that was so appalling as to focus her mind on the law. While he was in Bosnia, she had been called to the Bar.

Inwardly he admitted: he had thought her narrow in certain ways, 'armchair' in her convictions. Now she had been undeniably seasoned, broadened, by meaningful exchanges with all sorts of people in varying predicaments. Remarkably, she had got a little bit more beautiful, too. But when she directed the conversation back onto him he came to feel somewhat cross-examined.

'I wanted to find out if I could lead men. They call it moral courage. I didn't have enough, sadly. It was more about just getting by.'

'Listen,' she said, rather sternly, rattling her straw around her glass, 'I've met a few good soldiers, and what they had in common is they all said they weren't good soldiers.'

He was questioned very closely about Northern Ireland. Wagering on what he took to be her sympathies, he spoke of how he had intervened to curtail some heavy-handed police treatment of two youths suspected of chucking petrol bombs. He had earned some kudos for that on the streets of West Belfast, also now, it seemed, from Jennie.

'You were in Bosnia how long?'

'Uh, five months. Felt like longer.'

'But you went back after the war?'

'Yeah. To be honest the aid stuff had been what seemed most helpful to the people while we were supposed to be soldiering. Hosting tea parties for children and stuff . . .'

'As a soldier you were stopping ethnic cleansing.'

'No, no, no. We *assisted* ethnic cleansing . . .' He didn't wish to mire her in the bitter recall of it all. Yet he did feel a need to confess, a deep-seated wish that she understand; and so he recounted the hopeless mission of United Nations forces in Vitez.

'The job was just fucking impossible. I mean, I knew within a week why we needed to be there, if we were honest.'

'Why was that?'

'To stop the fucking extermination of a load of Muslims, right in the heart of Europe, by a fucking pact of convenience between two lots of fascists who were more or less open about their intentions.'

He was near to spitting with long-suppressed anger, it felt like an unburdening of truth. Yet, still, he didn't trust himself. The remorse, he knew, was still a kind of mask, or restraint. There remained things he couldn't bear to tell her. His hands on the table had curled into a fist, and Jennie laid her own hand on top of it and looked at him levelly.

'I'm sorry,' he said. 'It's so bleak.'

'Don't be. You'll have seen dreadful things, I know.'

The conjuring power of care in her voice put another image into his head, the face of a slight, toothy little girl looking up at him helplessly, in an instant before the sky fell in.

He felt his restraints snap and got a hand to his face in time, shuddering for a few moments, grateful for the dark oblivious din of the bar but desperate to pull himself together. Her hand went to his shoulder and stayed there.

'I'm really sorry,' she murmured. 'Have you ever talked to any-one about it? Properly? Did the army offer you help?'

The 'it' she had intuited was not what had upset him, but she had given him an excuse, at least, to speak of something else.

'There was a psychiatrist I could have seen, but I never did. I didn't see it would do any good.' That much, he knew, was true.

Not long after, they were standing outside in foot-stamping cold looking very intently at one another as their peers stumbled by, noisy with booze and plans for going on.

'Listen,' she told him. 'I want you to know, it means a lot to me, that you shared what you did. That you've got the strength to do that.'

'To be so weak, you mean.' He laughed softly, but she shook her head.

'Where are you going now?'

'I'm not sure. Do you want to go on?'

She slipped her hand into his and squeezed lightly. They began to walk, in silence, and he had no clue where they would go and kept his eyes doggedly on the stunningly starry night sky. But on a quiet street they paused, and inclined their heads to one another, and the kiss was of a sweetness Blaylock could have believed fatal.

They caught a night bus to her flat, she led him to her room, charmingly cheerful now, unfussily carnal as they undressed, then grinning up at him, breathless yet notably in control, her black hair across the white pillow, her smile full of moonlight. Nonetheless, as he moved inside her she seemed very serious, and he was relieved, since for him the whole business was near enough a sacred rite. What troubled him as they clung together warmly afterward was that there had been some kind of thievery in his capture of her.

Six months later they were married, she six weeks pregnant. At their wedding dinner she, naturally, took a turn in the round of speeches.

'I want you all to know why I love this husband of mine. He is a good and kind man, an honourable man.'

He loved her for saying it, sure, but he could feel fear in his gut, too – fear for her high opinion of him, of what it was founded on, that it couldn't possibly last. He wondered now if their wedding day was indeed the last time she held such a view wholeheartedly. When, exactly, had she ceased to believe in his integrity?

In retrospect he could see that by the time they took their vows – their child in her belly, her hand decisively won – he had resolved that it were a better thing he kept a veil over the extreme starkness of his tender love for her, that low fire he had tended for years. He felt he had shown her quite enough of his vulnerability – believed that she needed to see him as more stoical and load-bearing, per the tough individual experiences of the world that had, finally, brought them together. Thus, in order to be her husband, one final self-overcoming on his part appeared needful. Yet as a consequence of that strange contrivance he seemed, fatefully, to turn himself into a lesser man.

Their marriage – in his view, at least – had been a wordless pact that they would face the world together with a shared sense of what was right and good in it. Yet he had wondered from the start if he could really live up to his side of the bargain. In time he wondered, too, if she didn't question her own part in it. In any case, that first strong bond had been steadily worn, by compromises made out in the world and toward each other, ardour slowly turning to an affectionate familiarity and a taking for granted of their respective services to the family firm; then to withdrawal from one another; then decline into mutual hostility.

However had it got so bad, so debased? That their happily chattering children began to make noise just to drown out their forever quarrelling parents? That he ceased all efforts to comfort Jennie, communicate with her, dry the tears and make things better? That the children came to see him as the man who was absent, who no longer kept promises, who slammed doors and shouted through them? In his head he could hear his own hateful voice, from right near the death: *'You can't believe I would hurt them, you can't say that, Jennie!'*

She had looked haunted on the day she asked him to leave. She wept while he stayed dry-eyed. But when the front door closed on him he could not have imagined something so terminal.

It had hit him the harder, no question – the voiding of all sureties, the sense of irreparable breakage. She had decided their love was done and had acted on it so bravely; he had been trying ever since to catch up. But it was hard work when – with no intention, by the slightest gesture – she could still remind him of a sky full of stars.

9

His phone rang, the hour so late that he flinched.

'*Sir, it's Neil Hill of SO15? I've good news about your hoax caller, sir. We've got him.*'

'You're kidding?'

'*No, sir, the call you received on Friday was from a payphone and the CCTV coverage of the vicinity was first-rate, so we identified our suspect and traced him pretty quickly. We lifted him from a flat in Wood Green tonight, and we have now arrested him on suspicion of malicious communications and of making threats to kill.*'

'My god. Who is he?'

'*An Algerian gentleman, sir, by the name of Yucef Medhkour. In the room he's renting we found some paperwork indicating that he's been going through the process with your department of seeking leave to remain? Basically, he's not had any joy, I dare say he wasn't very happy about it. His thing is sound engineering, all sorts of toys in his room, so we suspect that's how he made those effects you reported.*'

The simple logic of it all flooded into Blaylock's mind and he received it gratefully, thanking the detective for his cares. He was ready to hang up and be done when one stray thought occurred.

'The tap on my phone, that'll come off as of now?'

'*That would be a reasonable assumption, sir.*'

'So will someone come and – take the phone off me, do the business?'

'*No, no, sir, we'll just turn off the surveillance remotely . . .*'

The call complete, Blaylock stood up, paced the room, lifted by the efficiency with which that bit of nastiness had been cleared up, relieved that, for all that he had refused to let it get to him, he could at least forget about crank calls for a while. It was, he accepted, the nature of the job that one had enemies. He preferred them, though, to be visible.

He went to his desk, took the pages of his conference speech and attacked the text anew with red pen. After forty-five minutes of sustained improvement, he rose, stretched, changed into tee-shirt and shorts and bounded down to the kitchen where Andy sat with the *Sunday Times*.

'Get your runners on, bonny lad, I just need to blow off some cobwebs.'

Out on the wet and inky Kennington streets he felt his calf muscles twanging routinely, his back bowing and aching at first, but within ten minutes he was striding cleanly, planting his feet, breathing evenly and feeling a good cold air against his chest. Andy was running more or less apace this time, and that seemed the right place for such an ally.

As vigorous as he was feeling, he found his thoughts snagging on the people and predicaments he knew to be persistently in his way, obstructive, unhelpful, hectoring, even outright pernicious – the ridiculous Desmond Ricketts, the pushy Paul Payne, the conniving Jason Malahide, the wily James Bannerman. He indulged himself for the moment, saw himself running right through them, scattering their plots and plans like ninepins.

Right then, right. I'll not be deterred, not me. Not by the stirrers or the frauds or the nutcases. I'm going to stay my course, do my job. And yeah, I might be wrong, I might be right, but let's find out which. I'm ready to be judged. Let people make their minds up about me on the facts, not on rumours and lies and things that happened aeons ago. I've got my case and I'll stand up and try it – let the jury decide. I'll know by the eyes if I've done it or not. But it can be done. It can all be done, and it will be done . . .

Paddington Green, December 27
Subject: Said al-Allam
Interviewer: DS Neil Hill
#2 of 5

NH: *Can we get you some water?*

SA: *Uh . . . No, I'm alright.*

NH: *Nothing we can get you?*

SA: *No. Thank you.*

NH: *Okay, before we broke off, we were discussing the various things you became aware of through your communications with Mustafa bin Ara.*

SA: *Yeah, but I never knew that was his name, right?*

NH: *Okay, your communications with the person you recognised online as 'Tair'? But we're discussing how it was you became aware of a plot, directed against the Home Secretary, against David Blaylock?*

SA: *No, no, no, that's not what I said. I was—*

NH: *Sorry, what you said—?*

SA: *No, no, listen, I was not aware of nothing at the time. At the time? It was only after. After. When I, you know, put two and two together. That that was what I had . . .*

NH: *It was, it was what you'd heard, without knowing—?*

SA: *Yeah, what I saw, what I saw. Just 'cos of being in the chatroom and seeing messages between . . . them gentlemen who we was just talking about. 'Cos they used a code and stuff, words meant different things – I mean, they talked about a marriage and all that, and it was code. What I mean is, none of that made any sense to me at all, not at the time. Not until, y'know . . . what happened yesterday.*

PART III

Gazing up at a sorry sky he could nearly believe that to be stood as he was – in a school playground, shivering a little, clad in a numbered tee-shirt and tracksuit bottoms – was to have travelled horribly back in time.

The school was a low-rise brick block flanked by HORSA huts, the playground a cracked concrete yard that might have been designed for the grazing of juvenile knees; and set down into its midst was a high metal cage like some medieval touring borstal, around which two dozen thirteen-year-old schoolboys wearing PE kits milled expectantly. In silent contemplation Blaylock felt another shiver go through him.

'Would you like me to fetch you a coat, Home Secretary?' At his side was the smooth-cheeked Tory councillor who had invited him to this community project.

'Never worry, son,' said Blaylock. 'I'm from the north.' He glanced to Ben Cotesworth for approval, but his spad wore a look of suppressed mirth, as if in his mind he were already describing the day's big debacle to some pals across a table of pints – or else posting it, snap by indecorous snap, to Instagram.

This patch, Blaylock knew, was one more place in England where to be a Tory was a tough gig: a deprived ward, largely given over to social housing, worth at most a handful of votes from private landlords renting ex-council properties. Nonetheless, the order had come down from the Captain that for the duration of conference his commanding officers should be seen to be busily engaged all round Birmingham. This, then, was Blaylock's contribution. He only hoped his Cabinet colleagues were playing the game properly, too.

A community police officer, tubby round the middle, was doling out coloured bibs bearing the logo of a local estate agent, and already one urchin was performing quite an expert array of juggling tricks with a fuzzy fluorescent football. Blaylock watched, respectful of the boy's cocksure skills, slightly hoping he would slip and cock up – until the police officer lumbered over to him, so full of seeming contentment at being relatively popular for a morning that Blaylock found it heartbreaking.

'I'll say this, usually when I'm around you'd not see these kids for dust.'

Blaylock had got distracted by one towheaded boy sat forlornly apart on a wall, dangling his feet. 'Somebody's not so cheery.'

'Yeah, well. There's always one doesn't get picked.'

'It's five after nine, David,' said Ben, now fretful. He was media bag-carrier for the morning, Mark Tallis having bigger fish to feed back in town at Conference Centre. The young woman from the local paper was present and correct, camera round her neck, tapping at her phone, but they were waiting still for a crew from the regional evening news.

'Okay,' Blaylock resolved. 'Let's just do this. Just a kick-about to get warmed up, maybe? You, and you, versus you, and *you.*' He beckoned to the disconsolate boy on the wall, who peered at him, first with suspicion then with dawning joy.

'Freddie?' said the community cop. 'But he's not got his gear.'

'They just need bibs, right? Howay, get them bibs on.'

Ball under arm, Blaylock ushered the boys into the cage as a crowd formed all around and faces pressed into gaps between bars. Wishing he had a whistle, he dropped the ball, put a foot on it and rubbed his hands.

'Right! I want to see a good clean game – no bad tackles, no barging, no grabbing. Five minutes starts *now.*'

He rolled the ball into play, darted from the cage and clanged the door shut. The resultant pell-mell was exhilarating to see, and Blaylock's hoarse directives soon passed from officiating ('*Hands off him!*') to coaching ('*Pass it, your pal's right there!*'). Freddie was not much of a player, but keen as mustard, even managing to scuff one toe-cutting shot into his opponents' hutch-like goal before his team ran out 3–7 losers.

As the boys trooped from the cage, grinning and panting, the councillor patted their shoulders and Blaylock shook their hands for the camera.

'Vote Conservative,' quipped Ben *sotto voce* from the sidelines.

'Go piss up a rope,' uttered Freddie under his breath, pleased with himself.

Climbing into the back of the Jaguar Blaylock felt first the enveloping warmth, then a tickle in his nose, and he ducked his head and sneezed convulsively four times in succession.

Martin drove at speed back to the city, ten miles in under ten minutes. Blaylock stared out the window at housing estates flitting by, their weathered facades and blank windows, their separate worlds.

Quarantine, he thought. *We quarantine the poor here, and call that a service. 'You lot stick to the outskirts of town, a good stone's throw from the orderly bit where the rest of us do the business. And try not to call us, yeah? We'll try to keep pushing the basic food and lodgings your way.'*

The view changed to rows of redbrick and whitewashed semis, then to the concrete innards of the Second City. To Blaylock what he saw of the built-up area still spoke to him of decline – over-planning, under-usage, the long-term diminution of productive forces. As they slowed toward the 'ring of steel' around Conference Centre he could see off-duty members of Warwickshire and West Midlands Police Federations thronging on the civilian side of the barriers, bearing placards and banners that decried both government cuts to police pay and the exorbitant cost of policing the conference.

Bannerman will be pleased, Blaylock thought. *Thanks, Chief.*

On the other side of the cordons and berms their police colleagues, numbers boosted by burly private security staff, faced the protesters impassively.

Blaylock took his dutiful place in the hall for Caroline Tennant's big morning speech, but he listened only fitfully. For some time he was transfixed by the huge logo projected behind her – an electrified Union Jack, bursting with light, above it the legend ONWARD TOGETHER. Then he fell to stealing sidelong glances at delegates in the block of seating to his left, who listened far more attentively to the Chancellor.

For years, it felt like, Blaylock had heard well-intentioned people asserting that the day was nigh when the Conservative Party would be remade by the transforming force of generational demographics. He did wish that the revolution would come – if only so he could tell Jennie this was another weighty matter on which she had judged him too quickly. But, plainly, they still awaited that rosy dawn. Here in the stalls, at least, Tories remained an older crowd – well-tended beef, dressy women, fleshy men, sideburns and bald pates aplenty, Rotarians in blazers, a scattering of toffs in Barbours, a proportion of otherworldly jug-eared types and pain-faced gurners, and a cohort of sixth-formers, mature for their age, no doubt, and yet looking awfully juvenile in what could only be their first ill-fitting grey suits.

Even now – staring up at an unmarried, childless, female Tory Chancellor – it seemed to Blaylock that the crowd remained much the same old Tories, only smaller in number and a tad more confused, inclined to nod their heads when told of the regrettably sometime ill effects of the movement of women into the workplace, otherwise to shake those same heads gravely over 'the failure of multiculturalism', just as they applauded attacks on 'red tape' and crooked pension providers, and cheered any defence of the local post office or 'our returning heroes'.

In advance of his own turn at the podium Blaylock first discharged a duty in sitting for lunch in the conference hotel's goldfish-bowl atrium restaurant, with the editors of the *Times*, *Telegraph*, *Express*, *Mail*, *Post* and *Correspondent*. A ritual discussion of issues was enacted. He was given his five minutes' grace to deliver the basic message of a sensible Conservative programme of government staying its course, after which he accepted prods and teases about more complicated messages, coded or otherwise, that the editors had discerned within the speeches of his Cabinet colleagues, and he tried to disentangle himself from these as deftly as he could. He then affected a listening mien as, over coffees, they whacked away on the issue of immigration, especially the 'fishing expedition' of dawn raids before the House rose. To Blaylock's surprise the *Telegraph* seemed to side with various protests that the clampdown had inspired among the settled London communities of China-town and Brick Lane. But the day had yielded results: two hundred arrests, seven hundred repatriations. Guy Walters had not, in the end, streaked down Whitehall.

As he rose for goodbyes and handshakes the *Correspondent* editor was newly solicitous. 'Your fringe event this evening, it'll be chaired by our new political commentator, Abby Hassall? She's a talent, you'd better be on your game.'

Blaylock smiled, thinking only of the profile in which Ms Hassall had queried his 'bottle' and obtained some treacherous quotations.

The editor of the *Post* had kept close to Blaylock's elbow as though a final and private word with the Minister was his paper's special entitlement.

'Domestic violence, Home Secretary?'

'Yes?'

'We've got very much on-board with this, you should know. Our readers are very engaged with the whole issue. They believe in it. I believe in it.'

'Sorry, in what precisely?'

'The calls I believe you've been getting for a large-scale inquiry? We would back those. We'll be keeping a bit of heat on you about this. Obviously I won't stick you on the front page every day, ha-ha. Unless that's what it takes for you to make a decision . . .'

Blaylock made a vexed note to self to take this seriously. As much as Marjorie Michaels had troubled his conscience he had been fudging the matter of lobbying Caroline Tennant for funds to act. Now he could envisage the *Post* trying to force his hand with a campaign that cost them little but spare-change indignation.

With the editors gone, Blaylock drained his coffee in peace and looked about, past the potted palm fronds, observing the jungle and its wildlife. On a flat screen relaying live coverage from the hall, Jason Malahide was delivering a rousing attack-dog speech, decrying a variety of things that struck him as *'waffly'* and *'wishy-washy'*, among them statistics, EU directives, *'all this bossy rule-making, a wholly unnecessary burden on honest hard-working people who want to get on with their business'*.

Then, amid the cheery crowd-pleasing, Malahide's eyes narrowed and his mouth tightened to an indigestive moue – what Blaylock knew to be the Business Secretary's version of gravitas.

'Our opponents don't understand how money is made, because they've never run a profit-and-loss account in the real world! But my experience in the energy sector taught me what business needs! And the business of this government is business!'

The applause was tumultuous. Blaylock wasn't surprised.

Five minutes later he was striding over the elevated walkway from hotel to conference hall, Ben, Mark and Deborah flanking him. They passed Malahide and his entourage going the other way as if pointedly.

'Knock 'em dead, Rocky,' Malahide grinned.

Passing the conference souvenir stall Blaylock clocked for the first time the piles of engraved collectable tat that had been rush-produced in his approximate image: mini-boxing gloves and Lonsdale-style shorts, even a china figurine of himself kitted out for the ring, grinning incongruously and looking about twenty pounds heavier than how he truly tipped the scales.

Restive in the wings, ready to go, Blaylock suffered through a short introduction by a knighted septuagenarian actor, a salt-of-the-earth type lately seen on screens in gritty crime drama *The Guv'nor*. In the flesh this knight was smaller and better spoken, yet the crowd seemed to wish to see him as a tough customer, and he didn't disappoint. '*Tell you what*,' he said, looking up with a studied, punchy pause. '*I wouldn't want to be a villain with this guy around.*'

Blaylock took his place, checked the wafer-thin glass autocue on his podium and the big LCD scroll spanning the back of the hall, and plunged in.

'You know, we talk a lot about pledges to fight for this and fight that. It's a well-worn metaphor and the public can be forgiven for getting weary of it. The fact is, politicians can't fight alone. Nobody can. We fight together for a shared cause or we don't fight at all. It's just as General Patton told his troops before D-Day, "All of the real heroes are not storybook combat fighters . . . Every man has a job to do and he must do it. Every man is a vital link in the great chain."'

The applause came easy for that one, as Blaylock expected, though he knew his audience might have preferred something by Churchill. But he was off and running. He thanked his 'superb' team of ministers, his 'sterling' Cabinet colleagues, his 'inspirational' Prime Minister – even the West Midlands Police; whereupon he came to the 'Policy' section.

'One thing we have pledged to fight is illegal immigration.

That's not to say that the numbers of people seeking entry to Britain illegally are the gravest enemy we face. Some say those numbers are relatively small, so why bother?

'You bother because of the principle of the thing – the fairness of systems, and the trust of our citizens in how they function. Each of us as a citizen has a tacit and conditional contract with the state, for which the state requires our consent. Unless the state deals fairly with us, the systems can't function.

'It comes down to this. Are we a nation or aren't we? Do our citizens have a say in who lives alongside them or don't they? As long as we agree our borders shouldn't be wide open, then the views of existing citizens ought to come first. That fairness is worth a great deal.

'When a system is persistently exploited, people get demoralised – even a bit is too much. So we have to put a stop. And once you've made clear what you won't tolerate – clamped down on the so-called minor offences – it's remarkable how the clamps stick on the major ones, too.

'That a nation's population grows, and diversifies – these are perfectly fine things, but they oughtn't to be the goal of policy, because they create social problems – segregations, tensions – that need careful management. So we need to control immigration, sensibly. And, on that score, the buck stops with me.'

Taking the applause, content that things were going well, Blaylock hastened to the 'Personal' passage.

'I chose this party. I wasn't born to it – I wasn't born to anything much. But I was raised well – I got that much of a start in life. My dad told me to do the best I could, for my own good but for the people around me, too. Try to set an example, pass it on, observe the golden rule. Play for the team, but call your own mistakes your own, be responsible for all your actions, whether they lead to triumph or its close cousin, disaster. In time I wore the Queen's uniform and wore it proudly, and in the army I learned everything about teamwork that I'd ever need to know.

'I went to a "good enough" comprehensive school. I got through. There wasn't much expectation for me or my classmates. But as a young person I wanted the chance to be the person I felt I could be. I wanted respect, though I knew I'd have to earn it. I figured out that I would have to think for myself, that it was beholden upon me – even if that meant arriving at difficult choices.

'So when the time came to exercise my right to vote I studied the facts, made my choice – and it wasn't massively popular round my way.

'We're not widely liked in the north. Mind you, it's not so much our policies that are unpopular. Who doesn't want better transport, livelier town centres, safer streets, proper sentences for serious crimes? No, it's what we seem to embody. Northern people think we're not like them. Why?

'Where I'm from, as I grew up, under a Tory government – jobs were lost, and they haven't come back. Our economy was changing, the things we did for our living, how we paid our way in the world – we had to move with the times. But, my view is, we didn't handle that process of change as well as we should have, we didn't take the needful cares to carry everybody with us. A lot of people looked and decided that we thought unemployment was a price worth paying for an economic uplift. And you can't play politics with people's livelihoods. If we got it wrong before, we have to show we understand now.

'My political obsession is unemployment. It spirals through families, it breeds hopelessness, it drags us all down. Whereas a job, being part of the world of work and all that comes with it? It gives you respect for yourself and for other people. Yes, let's be honest, work can be dull and dreary, too. But the greater part of it enables our sense of worth in society like nothing else – it's a hugely vital thing to a person. And this government is committed to this principle.

'This party is the home of people who want to get on in life by their own initiative, their own labour – people who want to shape their lives by their own choices as far as they're able. Because the exercise of those muscles by everyone makes society stronger. And we really don't need the state to tell us how to do that. We know, as a consequence of decisions we've been making all our lives. We know what's right for ourselves, for our families, our neighbourhoods.

'This party is the home for everyone who feels that way. We need to get that message through. There's no bar on income level. Not the pigment of your skin, or your God if God you have, or your sex, or who you're in love with. This party doesn't work if it operates a caste system. This party doesn't work if we all look alike. Because that's not Britain today. If people don't come to us, or if they do and if we don't make them welcome, we have failed.

'As Conservatives we know what is in our country's best interests: a fair Britain that generates real opportunities to get on for everyone who's ready and willing to seize them. Everyone has it in them to be their best. They need to believe it. But they can be sure we believe in them. This is the party that works.'

He was done – and the air seemed to thrum with an approving clamour. There was a rote element to it, Blaylock knew all too well. Still, the standing ovation thundered usefully on.

At his side for the stride back across the walkway Mark Tallis thrust his iPhone under Blaylock's nose. 'Twitter's on fire. Look.'

David Blaylock CLEARLY the most formidable Tory Minister #OneNation
Punchy stuff from the Home Sec! #Blaylock4Leader

But Blaylock's eye had been caught by something he wanted to scroll to, and he seized the phone to do so. It was something much less laudatory, from a broadsheet commentator.

> We knew David Blaylock wants to be Tory leader. He's just shown he's prepared to win ugly, by blaming all our nation's woes on immigrants.

He repaired to his hotel room, slumped into the sofa, accepted a mug of Lemsip and let his spads talk at him – about fringe events, lobbyists seeking audiences for their clients, 'security industry engagement'. Did he want to see for himself the new cutting edge of radiation screening and millimetre-wave cameras? Did he want to meet 'the new breed of detector dog'? Not this afternoon.

Tallis looked disappointed. 'Well, for what it's worth, Claymore Security have a suite at the Arsenal–Chelsea game next Tuesday, they slipped me a pair of tickets. I wondered about you and your boy . . . ?'

'It's a thought. Cheers, Mark.' Blaylock tucked the tickets into his top pocket. His phone pulsed – Geraldine. She had James Bannerman on the line.

'David, I'm in receipt of a letter from Messrs Gary Wardell and Duncan Scarth, who claim to be the chief operating officers of the Free Briton Brigade? In light of the ban on their marching through the East End they have requested a small "static" demonstration, which I am inclined to grant as a gesture to their freedom of expression. We will offer them a suitably cramped location and a narrow window of time, so as to minimise disorder.'

Blaylock rubbed his forehead, trying to recall where he had heard the name of Duncan Scarth. 'It's your call, Chief. Good luck.'

Deborah Kerner had entered, with a stranger in tow: a shortish but *sportif* fellow in a blue suit and broad-striped tie, with a strong jaw and a rather knowing dimpled smile.

'David, this is Gavin Blount? Gavin did security stuff for the Cabinet Office in the last government, now he's Political Director in Belfast. Ex-Grenadier Guard, don't you know.'

Blount's grip was firm, his gaze level, his accent faintly West Yorkshire. 'I admired your speech.'

'Gavin wrote this great paper on system inefficiencies, and . . . I just thought, hey, you guys ought to meet properly. Coffee, Gavin?'

'Thank you, black, one sugar.'

'Same for me,' said Blaylock, taken aback by Deborah's uncommon readiness to play maid, peering at the cover of the paper she had passed him: *Driving Change: Leadership & Command Structure in the Civil Service.*

Blaylock grunted. '"Command". That's a dirty word in Whitehall.'

'I know.' Blount showed his dimples. 'Those military connotations. I don't say the team should be running round in fatigues. But, too many clever types pushing paper around has . . . limitations. Too many people in Whitehall obsess over "structure" but run a mile from "command", because it's not how the wiring looks in the diagram . . .'

They talked politics a while, and the cold Blaylock had felt coming on all morning began to rasp in his throat, yet he found Blount's company so agreeable he nearly called for a tumbler of whisky. In no time he was being chivvied by Ben about the fringe meeting he was due to attend.

'No, I need a lie down. Cancel for me, yeah? Just give them the full contrite bollocks.' He shook hands with Blount. 'I trust we'll meet again.' The younger man turned smartly, as if with a click of his heels, and Deborah showed him to the door.

Tallis lingered. 'Can we talk about the parties this evening?'

'Nope. Let's see what's the best offer come 6 p.m.'

'You like Gavin?' asked Deborah, returning.

'Sound man.'

'Yeah, imagine him in your team meetings in place of old Cox.'

Blaylock threw her a look as if to say he understood very well that she had been match-making. Tired and achy, he went to his darkened room, lay back on the cool quilted throw-over and checked his phone messages. Jason Malahide had invited him to dinner *à deux*, an impertinence at which he was nearly too jaded to scoff.

He gave in to the temptation to check the BBC News reports on his speech and quickly wished he had not. Someone from the Institute of Directors was quoted as saying that 'after Jason Malahide's big energetic vision of a Britain open for business, it was depressing to hear David Blaylock's little Englandism'. Martin Pallister had gone for the high hand. 'The Home Secretary's empty posturing over an issue where he's already failed barely merits comment. I will just sit here and wait for his words to come back and bite him.'

Tugging absently at the match tickets in his top pocket he thought for a moment, then called Jennie, and knew instantly from her voice that nothing he might say would please her.

'Does Alex fancy coming with me to Arsenal next Tuesday?'

'*He has plans, I believe. Have you done anything about the week of the tenth?*' He realised he was caught in negligence once again. '*Remember, the school's doing "Take Your Kids to Work"? I'm bringing Cora to chambers, have you thought about something doable with Alex?*'

'Fine. Yes. I have. I will.'

'*Okay. You don't sound so cheery.*'

'I'm a bit done in, I had my speech this morning.'

'*Yeah, I heard.*'

'What did you think?'

A heavy exhalation down the line. '*I realise it's the Tory way to say "This is how it worked for me so all you lot need to do likewise." But, y'know, David . . . what are your lot actually planning to do to bring a load of jobs back to the north? And, sorry, General bloody Patton? I know how you felt about the army, how painful it was for you, so it does pain me a bit to hear you trying to package it up and sell it.*'

'Okay, forget I asked, goodbye Jennie.' Riled, deflated, he fumbled for the Actifed bottle, took a swig and hauled a pillow over his head.

Presently the phone vibrated anew. He didn't expect a contrite Jennie, and was not disappointed. It was his friend Jim Orchard, Lord Orchard of Sherwood.

'I'll go to the foot of our stairs. I was expecting the machine.'

'Always at your service, Jim.'

A guffaw came down the line, a jolly collegiate *hur-hur*. *'Well done on your speech. Very purposeful. "Always do your best, lads and lasses, just like my old dad told me to." Hur-hur. Yes, I liked all that.'*

'I hoped you would.'

'Might I possibly have your company this evening? Appreciating you'll have more attractive offers on your dance card.'

'It's a lovely thought but I'm under the weather.'

'Poor you. Can you not be tempted by a rogan josh and a pint or two of fizzy piss at the Raj Doot?'

Now it was Blaylock's turn to guffaw.

'Yes, I sense you are easily swayed . . .'

'You're looking well, Jim.'

'I don't believe you. Bloody politician.'

Closing in on seventy, Jim Orchard still took his pleasures as he found them. Tall enough, he carried a gut not quite cloaked by his generously cut lightweight suit. A railway worker's son and grammar school boy who went into the construction game after a Cambridge scholarship, he had directed millions toward party coffers and enjoyed the ear of every Tory leader since Blaylock was in short trousers.

'Well, believe this, I'm glad to see you. I had offers. Jason Malahide also proposed dinner tonight.'

'Whereabouts? In the library with the lead piping?'

'Yeah. I know an ambush when I see it.'

'It's a shame, how the two of you dance round each other. Much better if you could just demand satisfaction from him, like Castlereagh did with George Canning. Invite him civilly to pistols at dawn on Putney Heath, hur-hur . . .'

Blaylock smiled, and waited for the waiter to take away their plates. 'If I was counting my enemies I'd neither stop nor start with Malahide. There's Belinda Ryder, the civil liberties champ—'

'Oh, that's how it is when you're a possible leader. It breeds resentment. Your successes bring more grief than your cock-ups. They're counted more heavily against you, right?'

Blaylock didn't rise to what Orchard implied.

'But, yes, that civil liberties crowd. It's strange to me, David, once upon a time we had a very, very clear view on the defence of the realm. We were bloody well for it, and the state had to ensure it. Now we have all these strange fish, complaining how tough we make it for people we suspect of evil intent. Defending freedoms their granddads may or may not have died for . . . It's relatively new. Let's face it, *Winston* was a fairly avid phone-tapper long before anyone thought to make it a statutory process.' Orchard had begun to tap impatiently at the table-top.

'I know. Don't get yourself too vexed.'

'Oh, it's just I fancy a smoke. My point is, don't you fuss yourself unduly about Belinda bloody Ryder. Or that lightweight Malahide.'

'Darlings of conference can go a long way. All the way.'

'Well, quite, that is partly why I still seek your company.'

'I'd never expect you to make a lousy bet like that.'

'It is perfectly sound. Of course, the man has to want the top job.'

'I'm not in the running. I have my job to do.'

'Ah, Trollope! "No motive more selfish than to be counted in the roll of the public servants of England" . . . C'mon, David, who do you think you're talking to? Let me run the book on your actual "rivals", if I may be so crass. Caroline Tennant? Needs to get some kids, I'd say. Before that, a husband. Also, a sense of humour.'

'I don't think the public reckon a divorcee is the greatest role model.'

'Wasn't a problem for Eden. Though it might depend on who's the second Mrs Blaylock . . . Where did we get to? Malahide, yes. Pleases conference and speaks to Essex and all that, but we have those votes priced in already. North of Watford he's pretty obnoxious. Which is where you come in, riding astride today's stirring peroration.'

'Home Secretaries don't get to be leader any more. It's the job, there's always something turns up to cut their reputation to shreds.'

'Oh, stop bloody whining. The knives are out for you, always. But that is the mission you accepted, David. So you have to face the knives, with fortitude. Just as we ask of the great British public.'

The waiter was offering complimentary Courvoisiers. Blaylock demurred, and saw that Orchard looked at him disapprovingly, then clear past him altogether.

'Well I never, who's the Jane?'

Blaylock saw Andy half-rise from his neighbouring perch, a hand on his jacket, and he turned to see a woman arrive purposefully by their table – a woman with height and figure, a swishy blonde bob and a boxy black jacket over a cinched red dress, a woman of a sort to make Blaylock sit up straight and hope his brow wasn't gleaming with sweat.

'Home Secretary? I'm Abigail Hassall. You were meant to be on my panel earlier today? Please, no need to get up—'

But Blaylock stood anyway, discarding his lividly turmeric-stained napkin, for he was feeling towered over by this woman in her high-heeled leather boots. Standing, he found himself distracted by the course of her long pendant necklace and made himself meet her eye.

'I'm so sorry you were ill. But glad you've made such a recovery.'

'Oh, you know, the capsaicin in chilli, it's medicinal . . . I trust you managed without me.'

'It was all a bit *Hamlet* without the prince. But, anyhow, I've got the message you're averse to talking to me. Your prerogative, of course.'

'No aversion. I just don't do interviews of the sort you have in mind.'

'How do you know what I have in mind? There are some things I'm keen to ask you but I wouldn't say they're for publication.'

'Oh, if you're just after an off-the-record chat I'll talk to you any time anywhere.'

She laughed, one short 'Ha', and gestured around the busy restaurant.

'Look, I'll buy you a drink, somewhere quiet, if you can wait for me and Lord Orchard to settle up.'

Orchard, though, was studying him closely from seated, his rheumy eyes alight with amusement. 'The bill? Never you mind, a mere bagatelle, dear boy. A mere bagatelle . . .'

They walked abreast down the hotel corridor, Andy five paces behind. One glance through the smoky glass front of the upper floor lounge was enough to tell him they'd get no privacy. And so they repaired to Blaylock's suite; she arranged herself on one of two facing sofas while he, sitting opposite, upended two little bottles of Chilean Shiraz into two long-stemmed glasses.

'OK, are you wearing a wire or any sort of recording device?'

'No.'

'If you're lying I'd have to kill you. Have you killed, rather.'

She rolled her eyes and made an empty-handed gesture.

'To be clear, this is not an interview, not a profile, not any kind of "piece". You wanted a conversation?'

'Well, we can try . . .' Looking mirthful, sceptical, and very attractive, she crossed her legs and brushed an imagined speck from her dress as it rode up.

'I did see what you wrote on me in the *Corresondent*. I guess you dug around a bit, persuaded a few people to sing?'

'Not so much. I haven't been on the Westminster beat that long.'

'No? So who are you? How did you get to this esteemed perch?'

'I've, ah, bounced around a bit, I suppose. Started out with Reuters. Was in Tokyo for a bit, then Bhutan, Turkmenistan. I was a financial journalist, really, until quite recently.'

'You wanted to write about people instead of money?'

She sipped her wine and considered. 'Personae are interesting. But not vastly more than money. Money dictates behaviour to such a degree. Yes, though – the actors in the game have come to interest me more. Plus, it's good to keep changing, I think. Too much of the world is people sticking to their own square yard of experience.'

'What did you study at college?'

'Anthropology.'

'Right, makes sense.'

'Do you mind if I ask the questions for a bit?'

'Shoot.'

'Your having this military background – have you found it useful to you in politics?'

'No. There aren't any transferable skills. The whole methodical thing about recognising you're in a hole and figuring how to get out of it – that ought to be a help, but it's not. The army is all about the team, loyalty, shared responsibility. Basically I've learned in politics to never, ever expect the same standards of behaviour. Politics is just about the individual – the black arts, the slippery pole. You are doomed to failure if you imagine otherwise.'

'How long was your army career?'

'Short. Sandhurst, commissioned, joined my regiment in West-phalia, holding back the Russian hordes a while. Six months in Northern Ireland, the long war, a bit livelier.'

'How lively?'

He liked the manner of her invigilation, and had further decided that her right was her best side. *She's studying me. I may as well perform, the beast in the jungle.*

'A few running gun battles. One time I was stuck in a Saracen that got pretty well perforated. An IED went off under my feet. After that was Bosnia, lively in places. Then my regiment got put out to pasture as a training unit in Canada, and I decided three years had been enough.'

'It wasn't because the army was facing cutbacks?'

'The army is always facing cutbacks. No, I just didn't see it as an environment in which I could function, long term. I went back to Bosnia, first for Oxfam, then Feed the Children. Then home, I took an MBA at Durham, joined a company an old mate of mine had started, stone importing, got to be a director.'

'You wanted to earn some money.'

'I didn't succeed. But, yeah, I tried to be responsible for a profit-and-loss account in the real world. The Tory way, you know?'

'You were married with a son by then?'

'I don't discuss my family. The stone business was short-lived, then I slipped into journalism. Just like you.'

'How did that happen?'

'It had occurred to me in Bosnia, actually. Where my regiment were, in Vitez, the press were close by. I'd watch them and think it was a better gig. Just to shake my head over things, act like someone should do something? I mean, they were capable guys, and girls – one or two of them caught a stray bullet. But it was a comfier position for sure.'

She tapped the rim of her glass. 'As a soldier – did you ever kill anyone?'

He coughed. 'Not that I know of. I used reasonable force to incapacitate. There were times I fired a ton of ammo in the enemy's general direction and didn't have the chance to assess the damage afterward.'

'Do you think the army made you an aggressive person?'

He set down the glass he had been nursing. 'The Colour Sergeant tells you, "If the time comes, you've got to bayonet the baby." That's the deal, you have to do things no civilian would. Your training puts an unnatural level of aggression into you for that purpose. But there are also means by which it's suppressed in you, too. I mean, I'm not an aggressive person, not now.'

'I've heard it said you can be.'

'What, I seem that way to you?'

'You're probably different off-duty.'

'I am never off-duty, Abigail.'

She laughed. 'Listen, I wouldn't blame you. But you're saying everyone's got you all wrong?'

'Me and a hundred others. Listen, I know one or two MPs who are pretty awful, talentless, slack bastards. But more often the way politics is reported . . . I don't recognise the story, and I'm a character in it.'

'What's wrong with the story?'

'A narrowness of focus . . . People being tribal, they'd rather report their kneejerk perception of an issue than the actual information that might make the thing intelligible to debate.'

'So what's to be done?'

'That's why we're talking now. You can change it, Abigail. Start with the bathroom mirror.'

She looked at him from under sceptical eyebrows. Was she offended? She hadn't touched her wine for some time.

'I mean, don't you think you come at things with biases?'

'I don't have any particular politics, if that's what you mean. That would seem to me . . . backward. If you see the big picture then the problems are the same, the differences in approach are quite marginal. That's why one looks to find the interest in individuals . . .'

His phone vibrated. He ignored it but to his dismay she stood up.

'Look, thank you for this. I'm sorry if I seemed . . . testy.'

'No problem. Some recompense for my bad manners. I hope it was worth your time.'

'Well, I still need something to write about for tomorrow. Maybe I should have gone out dancing instead . . .' Indeed she shimmied and twirled lightly on her toes as she stooped to retrieve her bag from the sofa. He felt leaden by comparison.

'Why don't you take a closer look at Jason Malahide? And his head for business? You're interested in money. So is he, but it's quite a short CV for all what comes out of his mouth.'

'I see. Where would I start? With what?'

'Ask what business has he really ever run? He's wheeled and dealed, sure, I don't say he would sell his own grandmother but he wouldn't think twice about selling yours.'

She smiled. 'Why would you want to—?'

'I don't like people who talk big.'

'From the man who said, "The buck stops with me"?'

'I take that back – I don't like people who don't really believe what they say they believe in. Because it's a game to them. It's not a game.'

'Okay. Can I call you?'

'I don't give my number to journalists. Mark Tallis does that stuff.'

'How about you take mine?' She fished and handed him a card.

'Good to meet you, Abigail.' He extended a hand and she took it lightly, slung her bag over her shoulder and was off. He was sorry to see her go. It had been an amusing dance – a minuet, of sorts. Had he been shooting his mouth off, packaging his past again?

Those qualms were creeping over him. But her presence had challenged him, incited him, put him in a curious mood. It was almost too much excitement for one day.

Later, before he drifted off to sleep, he was thinking of her still – the quizzical tilted jaw-line, the violet eyes and the golden bob, the necklace draped languidly between her clavicles, the way she had said 'I wouldn't blame you' that seemed to betoken a tough-minded customer – the sort of woman he had always tended to admire. But while he still felt riled by Jennie's hard verdict on his speech, the pert appraising glances of this Abigail Hassall had rubbed him more the right way.

EAST LONDON FBB PROTEST MARRED BY CLASHES

A Met-approved 'static protest' by the Free Briton Brigade (FBB) in one of east London's most diverse areas erupted in violence last night when disputes broke out between FBB members and 'anti-fascist' campaigners who had also obtained police permission to demonstrate in the same street. After arrangements jointly agreed with police broke down in disarray, officers had to move in to separate the rival groups, culminating in scuffles and arrests.

FBB members gathered as agreed for their static protest at 6.30 p.m. The counter-protest – billed as a 'celebration of diversity' by the Fascists Out! campaign group – set up behind a cordon on the other side of Forest Road where demonstrators made speeches. By 6.45 the FBB contingent had begun chants that counter-protesters later described as 'provocative'. Some FBB demonstrators then began to walk up Forest Road, breaching the conditions of the protest. When counter-protesters tried to intervene they were restrained by police and jeered by the FBB, whereupon some pushed past the outnumbered police to confront FBB members face to face. Eventually police reinforcements arrived to stop the disorder and the two groups were dispersed.

The Home Secretary David Blaylock, who approved the original ban on the planned FBB march, gave a statement: 'In retrospect the police ought perhaps to have imposed tougher conditions on the protest, but the protesters have no excuse for their behaviour, and any attempt to repeat it on our streets will not be tolerated.'

'We're anti-fascists,' one local counter-protester, who asked

not to be named, told the Standard. 'These are our streets, and we're not having the fascist FBB coming round.'

The FBB calls itself a 'human rights movement' opposed to 'Islamist extremism', though critics accuse it of racism. The group today issued a joint statement signed by its co-directors Duncan Scarth and Gary Wardell in which they wrote: 'Our determination to make our voices heard is redoubled. We will not be deterred by Islamists who wish for an Islamic state within the British state, or by their fellow travellers, the risible far-left. Our resistance will turn back this tide. It can be done and it will be done.'

PART IV

1

'All around the world Muslims are targeted, their lives are held dirt-cheap. They live in the crosshairs of drones, man. And them crosshairs are a symbol, of how the Muslim man is forced to be in this world. A target. And why? For what crime? For the crime of standing up and fighting for his brothers . . .'

The unit of display was Villiers's slim black tablet. The video showed a young Asian man, London-accented, clad like a ninja in front of a shoddily slung khaki backdrop. It occurred to Blaylock that a surveillance operative would find the MI5 chief's browsing history to be quite a horror show. Villiers himself was impassive, bridging his fingers as he studied Blaylock's response.

'Your brothers are suffering, paying with their lives. We need to get off our knees, get the boot of the West off our necks. "An eye for an eye, a life for a life", like it says in the Holy Koran . . .'

'So, yes, Mehdi Ahmad,' murmured Villiers. 'We've had him on the watch list three or four months. It was just after five this morning when Brian's boys moved in to nab him at his address in Ruislip.'

'My brothers in Britain, I call on you to join me in jihad. This is war and I am taking up arms, for I am a soldier!'

You're a shit-house, was Blaylock's overriding thought as he tossed his pen onto his notepad.

'The patterns of Mr Ahmad's web use became alarmingly transparent – hate preachers, suicide videos, instructions in explosives. A friend gave him the run of a garage and he tried out a few crude compounds – HMTD, hydrogen peroxide, camping shop blocks of hexamine, supermarket lemon juice. He had made a recce or two on public transport. However, when it came to recording his last will and testament he got somewhat ahead of himself.'

'*This Britain, this filthy island, is a sewer . . .*'

'What do we know of his family background?'

'Bangladeshi. The father owns several takeaways. They claim to be "shocked", though possibly less than some we've come across.'

'*All it requires is a purpose, a plan, to take leave of this world, and then you can be redeemed. Your life, your death, belongs to the master.*'

Brian Shoulder of the Yard leaned in. 'Up to maybe a year ago this was a lad who just liked his tunes and his clobber and chasing young ladies. Then he got pumped up on steroids. Told his folks he fancied going to the Yemen to study. Winds up at Russell College.'

'Not exactly the wretched of the earth,' Blaylock murmured.

'By no means,' offered Villiers. 'And yet his sense of grievance is fairly virulent. At Russell he seemed to take charge of the Islamic Society, favoured the prayer room to classes, started telling his friends they were fools and young women that they were whores.'

'That', said Blaylock, 'is a story I'm familiar with.'

'*Politicians? Not one of them is a man of honour, not one of them is even a man, these cowards . . .*'

'Okay, that's enough of the great orator. Well done on picking him up before he did anything awful.'

Blaylock was pensive once Villiers and Shoulder left him. In a few days' time he would convene his monthly gathering of selected Muslim community representatives for the 'Counter-Extremism meeting'. It had been on his mind already that some hard words would have to be spoken there. Now he had the notion they might have to be harder still.

The shame of it was that he had been looking forward to renewing his acquaintance with Sadaqat Osman, the young man from Essex having indicated willingness to attend in return for Blaylock's honouring of the offer to join the Goresford Centre's November excursion to North Yorkshire. Blaylock had personally approved a discretionary grant that made the trip possible, and thought it money well spent. Other monies in the Counter-Extremism budget, though, he increasingly felt to be of lesser merit.

'You're looking sombre, *patrón*,' observed Mark Tallis once Blaylock had shut himself and his spads into his office.

'Churchgoing,' muttered Blaylock. His dark suit and tie were for the purpose of a special service he would be attending, an annual memorial for young victims of violent crime. But he was, more generally, in a riled state, and over more than just the dismal rhetoric of the apprehended Mehdi Ahmad.

His post-conference return to work had proved a familiar disappointment. It seemed to Blaylock that in those rare stretches of time when he felt charged and fighting fit, the disposition of his department declined – in a manner somehow reciprocal – to its most listless, mulish and glum. He was further haunted by the possibility that some of his Shovell Street colleagues shared Jennie's critique of how he had carried himself in Birmingham – namely, that he had been posturing, showboating, writing cheques with his mouth – and, worse, that the critique perhaps carried weight.

Now courtesy of Mark he had to mull over the front page of the *Post*, whose editor had made good his conference threat to launch a sort of crusade. 'TAKE BACK THE HOME: NO MORE WOMEN MUST DIE OF NEGLECT' was the headline, illustrated by a collage of snapshots of women wreathed in heedless, heartbreaking smiles. Blaylock recognised only a few of the faces, but knew with a sinking heart that all of these women must have met their deaths by violence. Pages two and three were largely given over to an editorial letter addressed to him, crying special outrage over abusive partners – murderers – who had been foreign nationals illegally resident in Britain at the time of their offence.

'So, we understand it's a campaign, and it'll run all this week, maybe next,' said Tallis. 'Obviously they put it out cold to get us on the back foot. But we need a response.'

'We make clear we take it seriously, recap what we already do, tell them I am currently reviewing a number of options.'

'What are those options?' enquired Deborah.

Blaylock gestured vaguely. He had no intention of consenting to set up some talking-shop inquiry; yet ever since his disconcerting encounter with Mrs Marjorie Michaels he had borne it in mind to seek some emergency funding for refuges. He still shrank, however, from the discussion he would need to have with Caroline Tennant.

They moved on with other pressing matters. Roger Quarmby, the Inspector of Immigration and Border Services, was due to deliver his draft report on the Home Office's performance on Wednesday morning. Blaylock was hopeful that all systems and procedures under his watch would be judged competent. He could not quite bear to contemplate the alternative. Monday week, meanwhile, would bring quarterly crime figures. Here, Blaylock felt the hopes for a favourable outcome were on firmer ground, and he intended to make a fuss about it.

'Ben, I want you to fix me up a visit to Richard Colls's patch in Gravesend for that Monday. I want to get out and about, take a look at every policing and crime prevention project we've got a stake in, right?'

Ben reminded him he was already booked to visit an innovative community policing project in Cogwich, Essex, in three days' time. Blaylock remembered this was the day he had assured Jennie that he would find some work activity to which he could escort Alex. After a hasty call to Cogwich his party secured a plus-one.

As much as the occasion filled Blaylock with unease, some kind of respectful solemnity suffused him as he had climbed the steps to the Corinthian portico and entered the church. The worshipful symmetry of the nave, the chestnut pews, the ribbed and vaulted ceiling – all served to persuade him he had a place in a larger piety.

The house was full, up to the galleries. Blaylock was escorted to a front seat and so brought face to face with the weight of the occasion – for beyond the altar rail was a careful stepped arrangement of treasured photographs, a mosaic of faces, candles lit beneath each, so humanising a sight Blaylock would otherwise have thought akin to the wall of a police incident room. The shrine marked the aggregate of pain in the room, people who soldiered on with unanswerable losses.

Choristers proceeded down the aisle, the vicar stepped into the pulpit and welcomed the congregation to 'our annual memorial, for which we are proud to collaborate with Mrs Diane Cleeve and Remember the Victims'.

Blaylock glanced across the aisle to see Mrs Cleeve nod slightly from sedentary, as was her way. Her bearing spoke of a dignity that was fiercely prized and wanted few words to support it. Fifty-ish, white-blonde, black-suited, her glasses darkly tinted, Mrs Cleeve seemed herself an emblem of a kind of chastening, upright remembrance.

Seven years ago her twenty-year-old daughter Mandy had been raped and killed by a man she had been seeing for some months, a Slovakian named Jakub Reznik with a previous conviction, who fled back to Slovakia but left his DNA at the scene. Captured three weeks later he had pled not guilty. Mrs Cleeve had told a reporter that Reznik was 'a filthy coward without the guts even to confess'. He was now serving a minimum-term life sentence, and would be deported on release. Mrs Cleeve had meantime become founder and linchpin of Remember the Victims, her particular stress being an opposition to what she regarded as the unacceptable porosity of Europe's borders. She had stood shoulder to shoulder with three previous Home Secretaries, and Blaylock knew he had to occupy the same ground. He could not afford to have Mrs Cleeve think he was going soft.

When the service was done he went to pay his respects, deterred just a little by the hulking shaven-headed man, unfamiliar to him, who stood by Mrs Cleeve's side. She wasted no time on niceties.

'I want to come and see you, Mr Blaylock, if that's alright by you. There's a matter I'd like to discuss.'

'Of course. Next week perhaps? You'll contact Geraldine?'

She was curt, but Blaylock knew better than to take it personally. In an instant she was shepherded away by her imposing chaperone.

The afternoon brought a fillip, anticipated but no less welcome for that. Blaylock learned from Griff Sedgley that Lord Waugh had pronounced himself satisfied by Caleb Aldrich's assurances and thus supported the 'immediate removal' to the United States of the terror suspect Vinayak Khan. Cheered that he had something in the bag with which to please the government benches in the Commons, at the close of the day he called Jennie, armed with the excuse of relaying that he would take Alex with him to Cogwich on Thursday.

Jennie, though, was still cloistered at her chambers, fretting over a speech she was due to deliver in a few hours' time to a room full of fellow human rights barristers. Touched by the nervy distraction in her voice – however polished in performance, Jennie always fretted over every bout of public speaking – Blaylock idly scribbled a note of the venue she mentioned, a fashionable set of chambers in Bloomsbury.

He reached Alex at home, the nanny putting the boy on the line.

'Sure you don't fancy the Arsenal tomorrow night, son?'

'*Nope. I'm going to see* Battleship Potemkin.'

'I thought you'd missed your chance?'

'Naw. I lied about that.'

'Right. Hope it's all you hoped for. Are you taking a date?'

'Nope, going with a mate.'

'Cultured mates you have.'

Alex laughed brashly. 'This guy? Yeah, he's pretty cultured . . .'

Blaylock hung up in haste for he had seen a familiar silhouette pass his door. He darted out, saw Fusi the football-mad security guard heading down the hall, and hailed him.

'Fusi! Fancy seeing your beloved Chelsea at the Emirates tomorrow night? You'll get your dinner, too.'

As the dark came down he called into Downing Street for the 'Line of Duty' Police Awards honouring acts of major bravery by warranted officers. He had resolved to keep his appearance brief, and then see if he might surprise Jennie by turning up to her speech. But noticing Commissioner Bannerman at the threshold of the upstairs reception room, unattended by *consiglieri*, Blaylock sought a quiet word.

'Can we talk about domestic violence?'

'Ah yes, you're having your turn in the tabloid hot seat? So the wheel turns.'

'You can be assured I've had nothing but praise for the police response. But in your view is there any way it could be improved?'

'Oh, I'm quite sure if constabularies had the funding and the numbers they'd want dedicated units. But that's not going to happen soon, is it? The biggest problem still is when the victim doesn't support the prosecution. Your lapel cameras, they might help with that. But not quickly. Cheer up, though.' Bannerman patted Blaylock's shoulder. 'It could be something for your "restorative justice" wheeze. Where, say, you have a man who wants to spend all the benefit on strong lager, and his wife who'd have him spend half at most? Maybe some negotiated settlement is doable . . .'

'It doesn't seem to me a laughing matter.'

'Nor to me, but as you know, Home Secretary, the way you do your sums is something I find hard to take seriously. So, in answer to your question, on our current resources, no, we will not be able to make a great difference in the matter of domestic violence. I understand if the politics of that are . . . problematic for you?'

Seeing that further exchanges would be fruitless Blaylock went inside, just in time to hear Patrick Vaughan address the gathering.

'This evening is always, for me, a powerful reminder of the purpose and valour that police officers bring to their job, protecting the public, often risking their lives in order to save lives. We could not ask for more. The Home Secretary does his bit, but I know he would admit that his best efforts are only a drop in a bucket . . .'

Blaylock knew the room had zero savour for this line of humour. Even as he winced he caught sight, through the navy-uniformed throng, of Abigail Hassall mingling among press at the rear of the room. They exchanged cordial nods.

Vaughan called on Blaylock to distribute trophies to a procession of constables who had braved house fires or deep waters, or persuaded the vulnerable away from high ledges, or confronted armed men despite having no weapon of their own. While posing for photos he had his hand gripped rather crushingly by one officer who held a vodka-tonic in the other hand, his diminutive wife at his side. This man did not let go, and though the noise in the room was not excessive he addressed his remarks close to Blaylock's earlobe, as if he might bite it.

'It's nice to get shown a bit of respect. Frankly I don't feel we get it from you, Mr Blaylock. That affects how we're treated on the street, is my view. Because of your attitude.'

'Sorry, you think when I talk about reforming the police I'm encouraging villains to have a go at you? Is that what you mean?'

The officer shrugged. 'Sorry if the truth hurts.'

'No need to apologise, I'm a big boy.'

'You don't look so big to me.'

Blaylock looked to the wife as if for support, but she wore the avid look of one inclined to urge her husband into a fight rather than out of it. Blaylock took a deep breath, let it go, and walked away.

He made it narrowly in time to Jennie's talk and sneaked in at the back of the busy seminar room, pointedly ignoring the murmurs and prods that his presence occasioned. Once Jennie had squared her papers and crossed from the top table to the lectern he succeeded in catching her eye and she shot him a somewhat pursed look; but he saw amusement there, too, in which he delighted.

He had gathered from a whiteboard display that the topic for the evening would be her long-running work with UNICEF to relieve the maltreatment of children in poverty, efforts that over the years had seen her trekking and fact-finding from Colombia to Ghana to Myanmar. Her text, indeed, turned out to be laden with citations and stats from UN reports – scarcely Jennie at her full-throated best, and the nodding heads of her audience told Blaylock she was preaching to a choir.

Still, as he listened more closely to her asides on journeys made to Adamawa and San José de Apartadó, he could picture her – not in her black uniform and pressed collar but in old jeans and tee-shirt, hacking down rough roads, unwashed and unguarded and putting herself in harm's way for the good of others. Her dauntlessness, the purpose that made her such a formidable lawyer, the patient cares that shone out of her mothering – they were all there. It occurred to him that had Jennie ever soldiered she might well have made a finer soldier than he. Certainly she had fought her way along a career path, never conceited, never deterred, accepting no masculine bullshit – his own included. In shame he recognised that in the early stressful years of her practice he had never praised her sufficiently for her successes. Within a year of their divorce, however, she had made silk.

When the session wound down he wondered how to interrupt or interpose himself in Jennie's company. Yet she pressed her way through the mingling bodies directly to him.

'Hey. Was that okay?'

'You were great, you're always great. I'm your biggest fan, right?'

Her smile was wan. 'I'm just so knackered. In the office at five this morning, then at the High Court giving your mob some stick for breaking air pollution law . . .'

The familiar sorties, however jaunty, gave Blaylock pause. Jennie leaned in nearer his ear. 'You're going to hurt my image with this crowd, you know. I'm supposed to stick around for a glass of cheap wine.'

He pressed his nose to her ear in kind. 'I couldn't take you somewhere for a glass of very expensive wine?'

She leaned back, then, to his great surprise, grinned. 'Go on, then.'

They were driven to a boutique hotel in Clerkenwell, where Andy settled on some plush furnishing in the foyer while Blaylock and Jennie took high stools at the bar and drank a mineral Chablis. Their chat came easy and unforced. When he ventured his view of the problems her speech had identified – 'It's a matter for the states in question, their lawmakers, their police' – she gave him as much without fuss. She was indeed tired, and keener to grouse about a pompous colleague in chambers and the inadequacies of Molly's Year Four teacher. Blaylock sat and focused on being a good listener, though really he was watching her – enjoying the familiar way she pushed her long locks from her face – and thinking about the two of them, savouring this effortless intimacy that was unattended, for once, by their onerous past.

He felt himself giving in a little to old imaginings. Was there anything really so essential in their past differences? Even after all, did anyone know her better than he, and vice versa? Wouldn't strangers in the bar, seeing them so inclined to one another, take them for a couple?

After Jennie had polished off a second large glass of white wine she busied herself to head off, but with the smile by which Blaylock scored the evening a success. They stood up, and she looked at him intently for a moment. A hug or a peck on the cheek was not out of the question on occasions when they had rubbed along well enough. But Blaylock was dumbstruck when Jennie put her mouth to his, lips slightly apart, then squeezed his arm before turning away, heels clicking as she crossed the foyer and out into the night.

He was left standing at the bar in boy-like wonder. For one thing, he could not deny: the crushing fondness for her he had been feeling had turned in an instant to arousal. That in itself would not have thrown him were it not for the deeper sense of reciprocity he thought he had sensed between them. Fanciful or not, his head was so filled with the urge to be with her that it seemed, briefly, to spin. He had to breathe deep, pull himself together, so as to step out, face Andy, get going.

2

Blaylock's morning preparations for Home Office Questions in the House had less of the rigour he usually applied to them, for he knew himself to be mired still in misty reflection over Jennie. They were disturbed decisively, though, when Geraldine brought in an urgent communiqué from Jason Malahide, complaining about a 'hostile' profile just published in the *Correspondent*. '*I detect fingerprints on this,*' Malahide wrote, '*and be advised that I am looking into it.*'

Blaylock whistled up Abigail Hassall's piece and was amused, not least in the imagining of Malahide's face as he read certain quotes Blaylock had anonymously chipped in to Abigail's research. Really he felt nothing there was so damning as some of the crazed paeans to the free market – '*The state oughtn't to be in the business of housing, or schools, or hospitals*' – that Abigail had dug from Malahide's press clippings.

He handed the letter back to Geraldine. 'I'll see Jason in Cabinet shortly, I'm sure we can heal the breach.'

Geraldine winced. 'David, Number Ten says the PM actually wants to see you and Malahide together before Cabinet starts.'

The Captain – whether by inclination or instruction, but under the glinting eye of Alan Ruthven – subjected Blaylock and Malahide to some focused *froideur*. 'I'm aware of a certain needle between the two of you. And I think we know well enough these things need to be settled in private, not carried on through the papers. We can't afford blue-on-blue conflict, understood? It's a gift to our enemies and it detracts from the work of this government.'

Thinking to fight another day, Blaylock found himself joining in a handshake that doubtless both he and Malahide rated meaningless.

The Cabinet meeting that followed might have been designed to annoy him. First, Simon Webster updated Cabinet on moves by the Grand Chamber of the European Court of Human Rights to declare the sentence of life imprisonment as an 'inhuman punishment' unless the prisoner was allowed the right of review at some advanced stage of incarceration. Webster wore a ring of moral assurance over his raised eyebrows as he trashed the Grand Chamber's proposal. 'It is arguably the most objectionable thing we've heard from Strasbourg in some time. We trust our Court of Appeal will see sense, and Lord Waugh and his colleagues will take a stand.'

Patrick Vaughan weighed in with a matching belief in his own rightness. 'Yes, we're talking a small number of cases, brutal murderers in the main, who – we are all clear – our courts should be able to send to jail for the rest of their lives. There are provisions for exceptional release on licence if the Home Secretary saw compassionate grounds but, well, we know the Home Secretary is no bleeding heart.'

Blaylock, feeling he was being watched, chipped in. 'I will be seeing Diane Cleeve of Remember the Victims before I next go to Brussels – obviously our position has no more prominent supporter than Mrs Cleeve.'

The room nodded in unison. Chas Finlayson's 'national service' white paper was then consigned to the bin, with what seemed to Blaylock a needless aside from Education Secretary Snee Gupta about the folly 'of teaching young people to march when they should be out learning trades'. Belinda Ryder then spoke out against a memo Blaylock had circulated about a proposed ban of segregated meetings at student unions, worrying in her best broadcast voice that she feared 'the precedent of government intervening on campuses'. Minded to rejoinder sharply, Blaylock was relieved that the Captain got in first to declare the matter was, basically, none of Belinda's business.

But he had not heard the worst until Communities Minister Valerie Laing brought to the table a briefing for the local government finance settlement, and indicated that her department's contribution to police funding would be reduced further.

Blaylock gestured across the table, incredulous. 'Sorry, but be aware, the police will say that's going to put basic services at risk, and I wouldn't blame them. I've cut their core grant to the bone.'

If Valerie Laing had fancied a fistfight she did not get the opportunity, for Caroline Tennant sailed into the exchange with a look of high disquiet. 'David, where the police are concerned I thought you had nailed up your reforming colours? Because it's strange to see you now begging exceptions. We all have to match deed to word; there is no point talking tough about a balanced budget then coming back with the begging bowl.'

Blaylock had an urge to lift the candlestick holder by his place setting and hurl it at the wall. Instead he took the measure of a room in which no one was on his side and, seething, swallowed the admonition. He was still quietly beside himself as he half-listened to Vaughan's closing remarks, urging his ministers to 'get out and about around the country on regional visits, spreading the government's message'.

'Obviously', Blaylock uttered through his teeth, 'any of you are welcome to join me for a tour of the northeast's heavy industries.'

'Quite,' said Vaughan. 'Business Secretary, you ought to get up there, I should think. David, you'll host? Cabinet Secretary, will you please minute to that effect so we get their offices talking?'

It had amounted, Blaylock had to admit, to an even-handed rebuke. The Captain's version of leadership went straight down the middle, in that regard as in so much else.

*

At 2.30 p.m. Blaylock got to his feet and approached the Commons despatch box. 'Mr Speaker, I am pleased to report the Lord Chief Justice's affirmation of the proper functioning of our extradition arrangements with the United States, and I can confirm that last night Vinayak Khan left for the US on a plane from RAF Mildenhall.'

He drank in the first noisy 'Hear, hear!' But there was no time for complacency as the Member for Hackney and Shoreditch rose to speak in favour of the *Post*'s campaign for action on domestic violence. 'Will he not act to ensure vulnerable victims get the treatment they deserve?'

Blaylock had been warned by Deborah to treat this question with maximum muted gravity. 'I thank the Honourable Member. I believe a taboo is being broken down in the sense that women are coming forward to report offences. We must agree to view the figures differently.'

And then Blaylock's shadow stepped forward – Martin Pallister, blue-eyed and blue-suited, one middle-aged man who evidently devoted serious time to combing his hair. Pallister was an unalloyed northerner, with a northern accent and a northern way of narrowing his eyes to express scorn.

'As identity cards, another of the Home Secretary's hopeless causes, go before the scrutiny of House Committee – will he please tell us if he seriously expects to convince the House and indeed the wider public that we will all be safer if, for whatever we wish to do, we have to first show our papers to anyone who claims the right to ask?'

Blaylock surged to the box, checking himself not to start speaking before he would be properly heard. Then, composed, he fixed his opposite number with a gaze and arranged his face as if to say that his perplexity and incredulity were growing by the second.

'The Right Honourable Member for North Tyneside is going to

feel the benefit of these cards soon enough when he's claiming his benefits and pension entitlements . . .'

Blaylock forgave himself this, since the benches behind him were so loudly delighted by such a gratuitous dig at a former golden boy.

'And, much as it pains me to say . . .' – he closed his folder and leaned on it so as to suggest this bit was from the heart – ' . . . I am disinclined to do knockabout stuff on important issues of national security and crime prevention, issues that I know were, once upon a time, taken just as seriously by the posturing fraud opposite.'

There was uproar, as Blaylock had expected: the loudest shouts, of course, from the benches opposite. Once the Speaker had restored order he was stern. 'I must call on the Home Secretary to withdraw the word "fraud". It is, as he knows very well, un-parliamentary language.'

'Mr Speaker, I do withdraw it. The Right Honourable Gentleman, I know, used to agree with me on this matter until relatively recently. I accept that nowadays, for whatever reason, he finds he cannot.'

Soon the safe Tory questions were on stream, the reassuring drear flow of MPs referencing their constituencies in pursuit of positive local media coverage, asking Blaylock to commend their local police force and falling crime figures, which Blaylock did most happily. With the first flurries done he ceded the floor for a while to his ministers, Dalton, Walters and Payne, who were generally keen for a share of the limelight, if not necessarily for the more thankless queries.

Martin Pallister, though, was not done. 'Will the Secretary of State say what is the number of foreign national offenders currently at large in Britain whom the Home Office ought to have deported but have not?'

Blaylock considered the handling of his folder a major issue of personal style. He liked it slim, such that it was clear he needed no crammer; and in dealing with Pallister he endeavoured never even to look at it.

'We do not have current figures, but we will have them next time once the Independent Inspector has reported. I will be happy to advise him then. It is certainly the case that we inherited a broken deportation system from the party opposite, and the fight to repair it is a daily burden. I would be glad only of his support in that endeavour, and perhaps a little contrition.'

Blaylock retook his seat conscious that he would have been wiser to cut his answer in half. He would need the Independent Inspector to have thrown him a bone before the 'next time'.

3

It was 9.01 a.m. and Roger Quarmby's long-awaited draft report sat squarely before every place setting of the Immigration Team. Some attendees were flapping through pages as if hunting for scraps of consolation. But the numbers seemed to numb understanding. Blaylock's copy lay open at the summarising bullet points, all perfectly grim. Phyllida Cox was watching him, he knew, for one of his eruptions. The report was, near enough, an unmitigated disaster.

Quarmby had served it up cold, not least with a straight answer to Martin Pallister's perennial query about the number of foreign national offenders at large in the UK: roughly 1,500, it appeared, a steep rise over two years, some of them off the radar, including a dozen convicted murderers and a dozen rapists. Blaylock had no clue how he might explain away those figures to Diane Cleeve, much less his Labour shadow. But then the dangerous individuals were only a sliver of the wider group of illegals – refused asylum seekers, visa over-stayers, those on the run to evade removal or eking out appeals – whom Mr Quarmby estimated to number in all 'anywhere between 400,000 and 800,000'.

At last Blaylock spoke, his voice hoarse from the prolonged silence. 'Does anyone here think this is remotely acceptable?'

Eric Manning let out a trapped, pained exhalation. 'Clearly, the report is bad. But it could be worse.'

'Eric, look, what is this "Lost Register" he's talking about, people who've just vanished?'

'It's not that hard for people to go missing.'

'But what happens to those cases? What action is taken?'

'It depends on resources. We can't look forever, sometimes we have to admit our data is flawed, the trail's cold. In some cases it is just not in the best interests of the taxpayer to continue the search.'

Guy Walters raised a hand. 'I see a case for hiring bounty hunters, frankly. Based on last known addresses, credit checks, whatever.'

'The thing is, Guy,' Manning shook his head, 'you can track them down and they'll just file new legal cases to remain.'

'So the Lost Register is a dumping ground, isn't it? To forget about?' Blaylock rubbed his brow. 'Eric, if we just take asylum applicants – the rise in new cases, and cases awaiting a first decision, and cases older than six months, and the thirty thousand cases older than seven *years* – can I ask, is it your view that our people are just incapable of taking a damn decision?'

Eric now wore the bothered look of one who felt himself unjustly in the hot seat. 'Minister, our officers dwell over quite a lot of cases where grounds for rejection are high, just because we know we may lose an appeal. And we know your views on lost appeals. So, yes, a pile does accumulate, otherwise we'd just buckle.'

Guy Walters, indefatigable in a crisis, spoke up. 'Couldn't we incentivise the case officers to turn down more appeals? Some kind of a sales board, with prizes?'

Phyllida Cox made her wintry entrance to the debate. 'This workforce will not respond to any further pressures. They will only become even more demoralised. To make a system move you need skilled, incentivised staff. As you know, Home Secretary, our budget meant that a great many good people left. I doubt we'll hire them back?'

'Can we not do some blue sky thinking here?' Thus Ben Cotesworth, fretful as usual. 'I've read a submission on amnesty—'

'That's a non-paper', Eric retorted, 'not worth the Minister's time.'

'What? If you invited illegals to come forward, pay the back taxes they owe, get in a queue for permanent residency—'

'Ben,' Blaylock shook his head, 'amnesty's a lost cause. It's the wrong message.'

'It hasn't occurred to you that we already have it? Effectively, unofficially, with all these failed cases we can't pursue?'

'What occurs to me is we shouldn't be in the business of retro-actively blessing criminal behaviour just because we're all too bloody worn out to do anything about it now.'

Blaylock's vehemence turned the table contemplative for some moments. Finally he spoke again, somewhat hoarsely. 'Does any-one happen to know – offhand – if my predecessors were aware of the scale of chaos this report describes?'

'Before my time, Minister,' Eric Manning fired back.

'And mine, of course,' said Phyllida, also unusually hastily.

Blaylock nearly laughed. He began to speak slowly, seeking to measure the effect of his words. 'Okay. We need to now collec-tively take responsibility for sorting out the mess. We are in this together and we must get out of it together. We need an internal review of all procedures. Meanwhile, for our sins, we have to pub-lish this catalogue of misery within a fortnight.'

Mark Tallis spoke up from the end of the table. 'Obviously the press will say the report is a colossal shambles. And I think we should take a moment to consider the message it sends. Clearly Mr Quarmby's initial findings need to be studied carefully. We need to examine our processes, yes. But my view is, this is not yet ready for public announcement. Not as-is. We would be doing a disservice.'

'To what, Mark?' Blaylock was truly curious to see what kind of sorcery Mark proposed.

'For one, there are questionable figures that we need to double-check. I mean, "anywhere between 400,000 and 800,000", what is that? The Home Affairs Committee has the right to expect correct statistics – as right as we can make them. There's a security risk here, too. This report is a virtual crib-sheet on playing the system, what route to take into the UK illegally, when to lodge your claim. We need to consider redactions. We need to study it all, carefully, and get back to Mr Quarmby in due course.'

'When?' Phyllida Cox's tone was tart.

'In due course. But I think it's far too important to say, "Oh, within a fortnight." It will take the time it takes.'

Blaylock, who had sat in silent admiration of Mark's ceaseless guile, now looked to Dame Phyllida. 'Does that seem . . . reasonable?'

Phyllida replied with some weariness. 'Mr Quarmby's reaction, we can safely assume. But ultimately, David, like everything that happens here, it's your decision.'

Back in his office for the briefest colloquy, feeling harassed and edgy, due at a meeting downstairs and hardly wanting to touch the disreputable ruse he was now endorsing, Blaylock instructed Mark to email Roger Quarmby a considered response in his name.

'Write what you just said, Mark. "I have read your submission . . . My view is that it needs consultation before any public announcement."'

'Right. Becky Maynard's asking what's the line for the press?'

'The same, but you can tell Becky the truth, that we're trying to avoid an absolute shoeing from the press on our litany of past fucking failures. Okay? I've got to move, the basement is waiting for me.'

Exiting the lift on the ground floor Blaylock saw through glass that Seema Hassanli was helping Sadaqat Osman, nattily clad in a dark sports coat and tie, to negotiate his way through the entrance security. Sadaqat was saying goodbye to another woman at his side, and stooping to kiss the head of a small boy.

Blaylock forged ahead into the basement conference suite and found the thirty-foot table hemmed on all sides. Scholars, imams, charities, media monitors, women's groups – they had assembled from far and wide, some men in white, some suited, a few in leather coats, most sporting *taqiyah*. The handful of women all wore *hijab*. And all faces appeared ponderous, hardly looking forward to the dependably fractious hour ahead.

Blaylock nodded to Sheikh Hanifa, dependably near Blaylock's vacant chair at the head of the table, then saw Seema enter with Sadaqat. They squeezed together into a space at the far end of the table. Blaylock sought Sadaqat's eye and they exchanged nods.

'This meeting comes at a crossroads,' Blaylock began. 'For some time now we've gone down a road together. Where we have needed to get to is a drawing of the teeth of extremism in British Muslim communities. We have listened to you as representatives, we have sought your ideas on how to prevent radicalisation, we have funded you and trusted your judgement. It has been a complex and worthy undertaking. But in my estimation it has not proved successful.'

He looked around and let the comment work its intended affront.

'As much as we spend – forty million a year – the numbers of extremists plotting atrocities against the wider public are not in retreat. And when plots are uncovered we repeatedly hear groups from whom we expected oversight pleading ignorance. I know people in this room have worked hard. And much has been done. There's no need for anyone here to feel wounded. But the point of our work has been to send out a clear message, that faith in Islam can be a proud part of a patriotic British identity and that violence has no part in it. Has that message been carried properly, clearly, into your communities? I need to know I wouldn't get better results just giving the money to law enforcement. And at the present time, I'm not convinced. So from today I will be reviewing all funding programmes. The total funds available will have to be significantly reduced, and all parties currently in receipt will have to reapply in the next year.'

Arif Syed from the Council of Mosques and Imams was the first among the sea of aghast faces to speak. 'Home Secretary, we have worked with your department for seven years, now you propose to tear that up and cut off funds?'

'Not if your results are demonstrably adequate for the investment. Where a scheme has helped keep young people honest – fine.' Blaylock gestured down the table to Sadaqat, who looked sharply down at the table. 'Where it's amounted to nothing more than talk? Talk is free.'

'You realise we will not just accept this decision – we will fight it.'

'I accept that. But I put it to you that we will be able to agree on an evidence-based assessment of what has or has not been effective.'

Having delivered his bombshell, Blaylock now felt nagged by remorse, seeing people with whom he had dealt affably for some time now bridling, not unreasonably, at being held accountable for matters beyond their bailiwick. He recalled West Belfast housewives whom he and his platoon had castigated for giving succour to IRA violence that, clearly, frightened and appalled them.

'You speak of what we have agreed. You seem to me to be selective here, Home Secretary . . .' The gathering turned expectantly to Zaf Qadir, who occupied the far opposite head of the table to Blaylock. Chief of the sizeable and influential British Muslim Congress, Qadir had the starved, hawkish features of one highly self-denying in his diet, and the severe mien of one who might deny others much else besides, though his fine tailored suit suggested a certain interest in fripperies.

'We have agreed', Qadir continued, 'that extremism is not some "Muslim problem"? That our community is beset by white British fascism, the marches and provocation and hatred.'

'I hope I've never given you cause to doubt my view of that?'

Blaylock replied. 'But, with respect, that is that and this is this. If relations between Muslim and non-Muslim in Britain were only ever concerned with wrangles over the problem of how to prevent violence on our streets then that would be a hopeless, hateful picture. They are not. Our relations are far richer than that problem. This meeting, however, is solely to do with that problem. We have other forums, other monies, devoted to enhancing mutual appreciation between faiths and communities. This is not that meeting. This meeting is about stamping out extremism – ensuring Muslims live fully as citizens of this country, upholding the law and opposing violence.'

'Yes, there is the presenting problem,' said Qadir. 'There are also the underlying causes. Is it not a time for cool heads to look closely at our shared failures? Rather than inflame a situation and, perhaps, just confirm suspicions about how this government really sees Islam? Need we speak of significant disagreements over foreign policy?'

'Of course not. That would be a waste of time. British Muslims are fully entitled to criticise British foreign policy, in public and through the ballot box. They have no right to take it as grounds to plot violence against the public. We all share freedom of speech, freedom of worship, the right to be safe from harm. From these alone should follow good relations. And we make no exceptions, we allow no excuses.'

'Again and again', Qadir shook his head, 'we hear this idea that "extremism" is really just insufficient "Britishness", that Britishness is the cure-all medicine, that Muslims must somehow choose between being British and being Muslim—'

'Well, clearly, one may be both, but only the "British" part entitles you to your democratic say, whether you want to use it as protest or whatever. "Britishness" is what unites us. If you think otherwise, then you may be labouring under a misunderstanding. Citizenship means signing up to the whole, and the whole must be swallowed. We know there are some readings of Islam that don't fit with the values of this country – the sorts of readings hawked around by the Ziad al-Kassers of this world. These need to be challenged. It perturbs me, for instance, how mosque committees don't necessarily do so in their choice of imams. That, too, is something we may have to look at.'

'Forgive me, Home Secretary.' Sheikh Hanifa spoke softly, yet still Blaylock was surprised. 'I am a man of faith, we are people of faith. We did not adopt or purchase that faith. We did not decide on it for personal advancement. We believe that what we believe is the truth revealed. An imam must have legitimacy, must have expertise in sacred knowledge, in the teachings of the Prophet Muhammad, *salallahu alaihi wa sallam*. He cannot be some . . . community worker? Appointed by your office?'

Blaylock looked down the table to where Seema Hassanli wore a disbelieving look. At her side Sadaqat Osman had closed his eyes.

'Sadaqat, thank you for coming today, I'm interested in your opinion as a newcomer to these proceedings. Does what I'm outlining seem reasonable to you? Or not?'

The gathering now turned as one, near accusingly, to the least familiar face around the table. Sadaqat looked up and appeared troubled, albeit hardly intimidated. Blaylock had only the vaguest notion of how the young man might respond, and a far more pressing sense of the gamble he had taken in seeking to enlist Sadaqat as an advocate for his new dispensation.

At last Sadaqat spoke. 'I don't believe . . . that the mosques are so significant? Or that the problem you see is so much down to imams? But I think you're right, Mr Blaylock, that only Muslims can make the argument you want made. And that Muslims have to want to make it. As for what you, the state, should do? More regulation, more law enforcement . . . ? I can see why you talk about that. And – by your logic, if what you say is true – maybe that is the road you should go down . . .'

Sadaqat had not endeared himself to the room, and this only made Blaylock admire him more. He held up a hand as the silence left by Sadaqat now began to fill up with forceful disputation.

4

Though Adam Villiers and Brian Shoulder of the Yard awaited him for the regular Thursday session – itself to be truncated on account of his appointment in Cogwich – Blaylock was required to beg their patience, Roger Quarmby having finally trapped him on a phone line to vent his displeasure over the delayed publication of his report.

'*What exactly do you mean by "not yet ready for public announcement"? What part of the work I've done is in any sense unsuitable for consumption?*'

Quarmby had a high-in-the-nose Lancastrian accent that, together with his narrow hooded eyes and pursed lips, gave him a schoolmasterly aspect now being exacerbated by his obvious belief that he was being fed a load of dog-ate-my-homework excuses.

'We have queries and comments, Roger; these will be compiled and returned to you for your attention so that your final version is wholly accurate.'

'*Home Secretary, my submission was wholly accurate. You asked me to do what I took to be important work, for which I surveyed all the evidence. I do not draft "political" documents to endorse a preordained view, wishing things to be other than what they are – that is of no help to anyone, in fact it's harmful. If that's what you have in mind to engineer here, be assured it is not acceptable to me.*'

'Roger, I'm sure when you see our queries you will appreciate this is a fuss over nothing . . .' Having attained what felt to him like the height of disingenuousness, Blaylock pressed on.

*

Entering his sequestered session with Villiers and Shoulder, Blaylock knew at once, by Villiers's lowered solemn head, that there was bad news to be broken. Indeed, he was advised that one of the 'persons of interest' under risk certification had absconded from surveillance: a Pakistani baker's son from Birmingham named Haseeb Muthana, married father of two with a third on the way, believed to have studied bomb-making during an excursion to the Afghan borders.

Blaylock felt a prickling between his clothing and skin, knowing what he could be subjected to in the House for such sloppiness.

'The hopeful news, arguably, is that we strongly suspect Muthana has left the country.'

'How did he get out? Surely we were holding his passport?'

'We have formed the view that he got across the Channel Tunnel in the back of a lorry and picked up false documents in Belgium.'

'So, should I be relieved?'

'Muthana's a fairly shrewd individual. We've suspected him not of any driving urge to martyrdom but, rather, of playing an advisory, directorial role in the bomb-making ambitions of various small cells. That's a role he can continue to play so long as he has means of communication. So we must keep our ears open, and hope to pick up his voice somewhere out in the ether . . .'

Since conversation with Alex was proving fitful while they waited, Blaylock got out of the car, also to take the air and check his messages. He was booked on the evening's political TV talk-show, and he now learned that Madolyn Redpath had been drafted onto the panel at short notice. The thought of his inaction over her lobbying on behalf of Eve Mewengera was a splinter in his conscience. He preferred to focus on delivering Alex back home by 7 p.m. following a day of good filial relations that would pile up further credit for him in Jennie's eyes.

Peering through the car's smoky glass window he watched the boy cleaning his camera lens diligently with a soft cloth, unwinding tangled black leads, and methodically replacing items within the folds of a small black leather carry-case. It seemed a notable investment of effort in such a teensy piece of gear. Blaylock realised that Andy, too, was watching the boy. They exchanged looks.

'The passion of it, eh?' Andy remarked. 'Reminds me of my boy when he plays his American football on Sundays. All the padding and taping and putting on the war-paint. He goes into another world.'

The world Andy was describing was one in which Blaylock rather wished Alex would spend more time. Finally the boy slid out of the Jaguar, camera in fist, soft black bag of odds and ends over his shoulder.

'Okay, Spielberg,' Blaylock ventured, 'we're ready for our close-ups.' A withering look, though, told him he'd name-checked the wrong sort of film director.

They were in a car park tucked behind the redbrick high-rise of Cogwich Shopping City, and passers-by beyond the wall evinced no interest in the ministerial visit. But then barrelling toward them came their host for the afternoon, Bob Gaines of Panoptic Answers Ltd, a big enthused side of beef, red-faced under fair hair, who pointed up to CCTV cameras on the car park's nearest lamppost.

'Smile, you're on telly.'

Mr Gaines led them into the rear of Shopping City and to a lift in a stairwell, proselytising for his business every step of the way.

'These shops were dead for years, the rate-payers just couldn't see how to revive it when there was so much thieving and dossing about. The council knew what retailers wanted, they just couldn't afford to give it to them. Until we stepped in and made a viable offer.'

He bade them enter the CCTV control room, a plush suite where staff peered fixedly at a wall of real-time monitors offering angles on the streets outside, surrounding roads and the interiors of various shops.

'So, all the premises signed up with us have no bother letting us know if there's trouble. You see our rangers in the orange hi-vis jackets? They're discreet but everyone knows they're there. And they're in radio contact with us, and to the cop shop if it comes to it.'

Gazing at the grid of screens, its unblinking relay of mid-afternoon human traffic, Blaylock started to feel a throb between his eyes – perhaps just fatigue, or the want of some caffeine in the absence of adrenalin. He blinked and refocused on one particular screen, where a man was glancing up at the camera and seeming to glare. Blaylock looked aside to an image of two women ambling along with shopping bags. Weirdly, even they too seemed to risk a furtive look to the lens.

'Oh blimey, oh now that is just naughty . . .'

Blaylock looked now to where everyone else was looking, Camera Seven, a screen that captured a swaying man in an alleyway urinating a fulsome arc between two skips.

'Watch this,' muttered Bob Gaines. 'The great thing about our cameras is they talk . . .'

An operative killed all audio but for Camera Seven, and the room heard a nerve-straining klaxon followed by a calm clear automated female voice. '*Urinating in public is an offence. Please desist.*' The offender was already shambling away without having tucked himself in.

'SR-Six?' said Gaines into a fixed bendable mic. 'This is Control, will you have a wander over to Gowan Lane, we've an offender leaving a scene . . . Vectra, can you get a cleaners' team to Gower for wet-down?'

Gaines looked to Blaylock with quiet pride. Blaylock was momentarily lost for words.

'Your team must see all sorts.'

'Oh, that's a rarity these days. Anyone who's not half-cut knows the cameras are there. Some might say they don't want Big Brother on their shoulder but my view is, what are you hiding? Who's going to fight for anyone's right to piss in an alley after five pints . . . ? Sorry, I'm afraid you'll have to knock that off in here, young sir.'

Blaylock, aware that Gaines was frowning past his shoulder, turned and saw that Alex, camera in hand, had retreated to the furthest wall and crouched as if to obtain a floor-to-ceiling angle on proceedings. Gaines stepped past Blaylock and put his bulk fully before Alex's lens.

'Howay, maestro,' said Blaylock, seeking to leaven the mood. But Alex returned the camera to his bag and came forward to the control desk as if obediently. Then he turned to Gaines.

'All this footage you're generating – what happens to it?'

'Technical, eh? There's a cupboard full of drives in the back, it all goes down the pipe into storage.'

'And how long do you keep it for?'

Gaines looked newly serious. 'We've a strict retention and erasure policy. Six weeks tops.'

'Who's allowed to look at it apart from in this room?'

'Well, we'll share it with the police, if they make a request, or if we think there's something they need to see.'

'You'll have got me and my dad in the car park earlier, right? Can we see that?'

Gaines stiffened. 'We've a strict disclosure policy, too. Requests have to be put in writing.'

'The cameras record sound, too, right? What we were talking about?'

'Alex,' Blaylock eased in. 'Bob here is not under oath.'

'He's fine, Home Secretary. No, the sound recording is only triggered by volume level. So unless you were having a right go at your dad—'

'Not today, at least,' Blaylock butted in, with a faked laugh.

'You okay, Alex?' Blaylock enquired of his silent son in the car back to London.

'I'm fine. I was thinking you were narked with me.'

'No, no. You asked very pertinent questions. I was proud. Did you find it interesting?'

The boy let out a short laugh. 'I suppose the word I'd use is "appalling"? How, like, normal everyone was being. How we've sleepwalked into *that* being normal.'

'Give it some credit. Shopkeepers running their own businesses, responsible for their own bills and livelihoods – they like having that extra security. Where's the harm? In their shoes you'd be glad of it.'

'I pay my own bills, Dad,' Alex groaned.

'That's not what I mean, Alex, but obviously it's your mother and I who support you and your sisters while you're under our roof—'

'It's not "your" roof any more, is it, Dad?'

'What I mean is your mum and I made an arrangement, as is right and proper, so, howay, don't throw it in my face, eh?'

'Yeah well, things change, people move on.'

'I'm not going anywhere, Alex.'

'Don't feel obstructed on my account.'

'Alex,' Blaylock sighed, 'try as you might, you won't keep me from caring about you.'

'There are other people who care about us.'

'"Us" meaning?'

'Me, Cora, Molly, Mum.'

'Right. And that's supposed to mean . . . ?'

'Forget it.'

'No, why not say what you're insinuating?'

'You know, you talk like you still run the show, when you're a drop-in, you're not interested in what we do, in our lives, you just want to give us what for. So, y'know, don't confuse that with caring . . .'

Incensed by the steep descent into this miserable bickering, highly apprehensive that the boy owned some intelligence he wasn't sharing, Blaylock glared at the back of his hands for some moments.

'Is there something you want to tell me, Alex?'

'Just what I said.'

He had been half-minded to take the boy with him to the television studio for the evening, but now his only intent was to see Jennie. When they reached the door of the Islington house, however, it was the ill-humoured Radka who welcomed Alex over the threshold.

At the studios Deborah Kerner met and took charge of him, insisting that he sit properly for the hair-and-make-up girl. 'Don't be touchy, David. Under those freaking lights everyone's skin looks like shit without a good base.'

Thus caked and coiffeured he was led to the green room, where he was immediately face to face with Madolyn Redpath who looked as weary as he was feeling.

'No restraining devices this time?'

'I wouldn't waste a handshake on you,' she shot back. 'Did you not think you owed me some sort of response about Eve?'

'I looked at the file . . . all I can say is it's complicated.'

'So you'll do nothing? I'd just wait for you to get the boot if it weren't so dire for Eve. I see the papers are after you on domestic violence. I'm not surprised, frankly, given what you're prepared to tolerate in the places where you lock up innocent women.'

He took the lashes, feeling he more or less deserved them, and could accept them from her to the extent that she seemed to have cast herself in the role of his private mortifier. He fully intended to give a better account of himself, however, once they had an audience.

Half an hour later they were seated side by side and peering out past the hot lights toward a selection of the public that seemed to frown in unison. Madolyn had quickly found a questioner to agree with.

'This government seems committed to a steady assault on our freedoms – whether it's ID cards or cameras on every street or snooping on people's emails or giving the security services whatever powers they want in the name of national security. We are a big, brave, free country, we don't give in to people who want to attack our liberties, so why would we accept it from our government?'

Hearing the applause, weighing his reply, Blaylock considered saying that he wished he was in charge of anything so airtight as the surveillance state Madolyn imagined, given how many strays the system missed. But he thought better.

'Well, the work of the security services is shadowy, because the shadows are where the threats live. Threats to our security are launched in secret, so the means to fight have to be secret too. CCTV? I think the public get what it's for – deterring crime, solving crime – and they know it works. Emails? I mean, ours is a world where billions get sent every hour . . . Does anyone really imagine I want to read them all? But even where we collect bulk data, it hardly seems to me an invasion of privacy, if that word retains any meaning. The speed of our lives now, the convenience we expect, it depends on data flashing round the globe. And I think democratic societies are agreed on this, the world over. We say to retailers and big tech companies, "I want it now, so here's my data." And those companies are loved and trusted for the services they sell us, even if they retain and sell our data, even if they don't pay their taxes, even if they're not madly bothered what sort of bad guys are abusing those services, too. But if someone becomes a person of interest to our security services? You can be sure there's a reason, there's hard intelligence strongly suggesting they're a threat to public safety. In which case, I want to know who that person's talking to.'

Madolyn looked at him askance. 'Do you *ever* turn down an MI5 request for surveillance?'

'Yeah. Of course I do. It's a question of resources and sometimes my instinct is it's not right. But mainly the security services are very meticulous in identifying a threat, and I take it seriously because the public expect me to, and you would take it seriously, too, if you were in my chair.'

'Next he'll tell us that he walks the walls at night so the rest of us can sleep in our beds . . . Every Home Secretary tries that line, that only he really understands how big the terror threat is, so all us little people should just take his word for it and shut up.'

'It's not so simple. With the wisdom of hindsight, sure, every decision is clear. But when you have to assess developing situations . . . quite often every option is equally unappealing. The point is, we are obliged to act, otherwise people will rightly suppose we couldn't make a decision, didn't have the nerve for it. And nerve is what's expected of us. Now, I respect the integrity of civil liberties campaigners, but it seems to me that it leads by logic to a position where one can argue that the price of liberty could be a bomb going off on our streets. And let's not kid ourselves about what a hard ask that is. Do we ask the general public to pay that price? Would you or I?'

The room was subdued, a mere smattering of applause, but Blaylock was hopeful he had disconcerted at least a few among them.

Afterward, as they stood having their lapel mics unclipped, Madolyn showed every intention of extending the quarrel.

'It's tough for you, I see that, I don't know how we can build your Jerusalem until we've all got chips implanted under our skin, right?'

'Sure, that's what I dream of, Madolyn, the UK as one big infrared grid, like a web that twitches with every tremor.'

'And you at the centre like a big fat spider. Do you never feel like a fraud?'

'Say again?'

'Do you ever just feel like you're an actor on a stage? Do you actually understand what you say might have consequences? About more than just your career and keeping your party in power?'

'Oh Christ, now you're being offensive, you might as well have brought your bloody cuffs if you planned to dog me round all night.'

She thrust a torn envelope at me. 'Will you read this? It's a letter Eve wrote to me. She'd be appalled to think I'd shown it to you but, really, I don't know what else to do. She's due to be put on a flight at Heathrow on Sunday night, leaving 8 p.m. If it makes any difference to you.'

He shrugged resignedly. 'You can be sure I'll give it a look.'

'Care or don't care, just don't pretend you care.'

Back at home he extracted from the envelope and unfolded a curled and blotted sheet of lined paper written in a careful hand. He sat on the edge of his bed and read.

Dear Ms Redpath

I want to thank you for your efforts on my part. I understand I may be sent back in days. I am preparing, as you ask, to tell my story, the facts of my case, for one last time, one last try, and I do appreciate your advice.

It is true what they say of confinement – your senses get

stronger, but you wish they were weaker, since what is around you denies all senses anyway. You are just living inside your head, and your head is a wretched place.

But, be assured, this detention centre is still not the worst place I have been. There are women nearby me who cry out more. I am not diabetic, not pregnant, I am otherwise 'healthy'. The worst for me, as you know, was in prison in my homeland. I could have died and for some time I was unsure if anyone would have known or if my captors would have cared – not the guard who violated me, or his colleague who taped my mouth and held my arms. But since in the end they let me be a hospital case, and because I took my chance and ran I am here! Luck . . . I crossed borders, and the gravity of that has hit me only now in trying to see through the eyes – into the mind? – of the British state. I see now that in the Home Office I have a powerful opponent.

That my story was not quite believed by them? I have seen worse of human nature. Did I fail to tell my story well enough? I accept that I struggle to tell it clearly to myself, because it revives a pain in me that cuts like a knife.

I have accepted my treatment – 'the rules' that have been applied to me as to everyone. I only question the sincerity of the process. I do not believe my case has really been considered on its own terms, justly. I think I am being locked up and sent back because it is easier to treat me this way.

I suppose the guards think I would run. I might if I could. Some women are watched closer than me, for suicide risk. I have no such intention, life is all I have and it must be cherished, whatever. I know just beyond these walls is space and green and sunlight, something like the England I knew from books – at least I saw it from the vehicle that brought me here! But it seems I will not be so lucky as to know it better. And maybe, in any case, I was mistaken.

Blaylock stood, enveloped by gloom, and set the letter down carefully on top of his bed. He went to his bedroom window and gazed out at the square below. Though the glass was armoured, Andy's perennial advice was that Blaylock should not offer himself to the assassin's sights. There were times when he wanted to dare as much.

Rain streaked the pane, the square below was in darkness but for the halos of lamps, the streets sodden and deserted. The moon above was hopelessly muddied by the miserable night. He pressed his brow up against the chill glass, the bulletproof border separating him from the blackness.

He was required to be overseer and defender of a system that sorted and processed individuals in this way. The charges thrown at him of indifference – he understood them, he felt the reproof. But the price of a change of heart weighed heavy – easier, for sure, to look away, to 'hide behind procedure', even if there was no place to hide from himself.

5

He was en route to his constituency by the early train when Jennie called him, sounding untypically helpless, and his heart lifted. Overnight an unkempt wisteria tree had buckled and half-fallen outside the front door of her mother Bea's cottage in Barnard Castle, and Bea was struggling to cross her own doorstep, hoping the tree might yet be saved, but having no luck in stirring up a local tree surgeon.

Blaylock understood at once. Jennie's father had passed away five years before, her sister now lived in New Zealand, Bea's more helpful neighbours were ageing, too. The situation added up to a burden of guilt for Jennie, with her workload and the children. She needed someone with whom she could share it; and Blaylock was very content to be called upon. He anticipated an honest job of work that might amount to more than its own reward. He assured Jennie that he and Andy would call round to Bea's in the late afternoon and do the business.

Per Vaughan's demand, Blaylock gave the morning to escorting Jason Malahide round his patch. Together they visited the Port of Tees, donning high visibility jackets and hard-hats, peering respectfully around the premises of a maker of transoceanic fibre-optic cables, a biomass renewable energy producer and a colossal petrochemical cracker plant. Malahide was high-tempo, pointing and enquiring with the chief execs, managing both to speak quickly and ebulliently then to listen and nod with equal intensity. Amid the perpetual motion it was, Blaylock thought, quite impossible to guess what the man really thought.

Their respective bag-carriers made a buffer of sorts, and Malahide had to be on his way before lunch, but as they zipped to the train station *à deux* in Blaylock's car it was obvious they would have to converse, as much as Blaylock sought to distance himself by gazing out at the royal blue edifice of the Transporter Bridge over the Tees, rising above the drab industrial riverfront with a kind of penny-plain poetry.

'The northeast . . . It doesn't change, does it?'

'Excuse me?' Blaylock turned to see Malahide affecting ruefulness.

'I mean, that's a lovely old port we just saw, but what's it for? Shipping in bits of prefab kit to get screwed together. The trouble with this region, it's still looking to the same old ways of making its living. I get no feel up here of any respect for entrepreneurs, risk-takers? Just people thinking their money's in the taxpayer's pocket, when it's customers they need.'

'That's a partial view, I'd say.'

'Fine. But where's the digital quarter round here? Where's the university lab doing innovative stuff in life sciences? *That's* where you should have taken me, David. Less metal-bashing, more key-punching.'

'Next time, then, Jason.'

'Ha, right. But, listen, it was good to get a look at where you come from. What's made you the curious fellow you are. You're aware of your singularity, right?'

'As a northeast Tory? Yup. I couldn't miss it.'

'It's more than that. There are enough posh Northumbrians, still a few geriatric Thatcherites. But you have something else – that thing of being the people's man? This party always has a role for someone who sounds like they could be that. Right now it's you, David. Don't get me wrong, I know what you're really like, which is, clearly, a bit of a cunt.'

Blaylock nearly had to laugh at the heedlessness of it. Instead he said, 'That's not very collegiate of you, now is it?'

'Oh come on – you connive, you play the game, set people up, you've got your foot-soldiers. It's okay. You can be yourself with me.'

'You, of course, are a saint.'

'I don't say my hands are clean. But I don't pretend, not like you. I'm not in knots that way. It's why I don't really see you as competition.'

'I am not a threat to your . . . ambitions, Jason.'

'I know you're not, but I think you'd like to be. I don't see you in the frame, though, David. I get why you impress a few people, but I see your limitations. Where's your base support on the backbenches? Your so-called common touch maybe gets you a few admiring columns from the broadsheets and their readers, who'd never vote Tory in a million years . . . And ID cards are going to do for you with that lot, I'm afraid.'

They had pulled up into the station car park, and Malahide's entourage were already on the steps. Malahide shot Blaylock a look so well pleased that it nearly invited a sock to the jaw. Blaylock merely clapped his shoulder.

'Thanks for coming. I'm glad we had this talk.'

He and Andy stopped by the Maryburn house where they donned old clothes, Blaylock loaning his bodyguard a spare pair of denims and a shirt, since they were similarly sized; while from his neglected garage Blaylock retrieved wire and shears, bolts and a drill, and his dependable twelve-foot ladder. Then they drove up through sunlit Durham to Bea's pensioner's cottage in Barnard Castle, where, in the manner of the fairy tale, they cut a path through stooped and clinging boughs to her door. Bea let them know – in her reticent fashion, never knowingly in anyone's debt – that she was glad they had come. She made tea and when Blaylock asked after her health, she replied, 'I've been better.'

In Bea's company Blaylock was reminded that Jennie was the apple who fell not far from the tree. Bea had been marked for marriage and motherhood like every girl in her class of 1960 but instead had gone to college and carved a career for herself as a radio producer and Mother of Chapel. He had known her to be formidable, always good in a crisis: it was typical, in a way, that she had beaten cancer by chemotherapy and stoicism, then buried her husband the next year, without falling apart as Blaylock believed he would have done in her place. Now she managed alone, defiantly, still driving herself about, still dressing herself smartly. But she moved unsteadily now, her hair had grown back ash-grey, the once-taut lines of her square face appeared gaunt. Her eyes, still startlingly pale blue, had lost their old sense of fast mooring.

As she enquired politely about Westminster business he hastened to drain his tea. 'Better crack on while we have the light.'

He and Andy lopped the worst of the tangled branches, heaved up the tree and nestled it atop a privet; then they measured, drilled holes, sunk bolts, and clipped and twisted at long wires until the wisteria trunk was snugly re-fixed against the brickwork by the bay window. As they struggled to artistically 'train' a few straggly boughs Bea came to the doorstep with a critical look and issued a few directives.

In truth, she seemed as pleased as Blaylock had ever seen her. Back when he had courted Jennie, Bea had appeared to approve of him without fuss, by a nod of the head; ten years later she had disapproved of him, quite decisively, in much the same manner. After he had assured her it had been the simplest of errands and she had waved them away down Darlington Road, he was heartened to think that here was one sober judge who had ruled he was not such a bad man. From the road he called Jennie to confirm the job was done, and she, too, was unusually, gratifyingly effusive. He looked forward to seeing her.

*

Shortly after Sunday lunchtime Blaylock presented himself at Jennie's Islington door and was taken aback to have it opened to him by a strange girl with a long lick of vermilion hair half-obscuring her smoky eye. She wore a washed-out hoodie, torn jeans and boots, a ring high in her left ear and a stud in her right nostril. She seemed very much at home even as Blaylock gaped at her.

Jennie climbed the stairs from the basement, drying her hands on a tea towel. 'Hi David, this is Alex's friend Esther?'

Alex was behind Jennie, and he put a possessive hand on Esther's arm, whereupon they mounted the stairs together. As a pair they certainly had the proper conspiratorial air as Blaylock remembered it.

He followed Jennie into the sitting room.

'Are they an item?'

'I'd be glad of it. Think it's just friends for now. He met her at a gig? Nice girl, she's doing a photography diploma at the City College – she's twenty. So, she'd be a cradle-snatcher, to be fair.'

'My god. I hope he knows what he's doing.'

'Eh, he's got a lot going for him, whether you see it or not. Listen, do you mind if he stops in today? He's a bit besotted, to be honest.'

'Of course not.' Blaylock smiled, wanting to say that he was all for infatuation. Today, though, Jennie was all business. Then their daughters appeared, Molly in her favourite jacket and flowery leggings, Cora in a version of Esther's slacker duds, though on her they seemed purposely shapeless.

'Cora, love,' sighed her mother, 'would you not think to wear the new top I got you?'

Cora only yanked her hoodie top over her head such that her hair protruded scarecrow-fashion. 'What's your problem?'

'It's whatever makes her happy,' reasoned Blaylock.

'No, David, it's whatever makes me happy.' But the look she

threw him was pert, more in the way of the old routines that made Blaylock obscurely content.

It was a fair, blowy autumn afternoon and so they walked to the nearby park: Andy Grieve at the rear of the foot patrol, Molly trundling along on her bicycle, Blaylock swinging her fluorescent pink helmet by a strap, half-listening to the girl's report of her waning enthusiasm for violin lessons, mindful of how clammed up Cora seemed, her fists thrust into her hoodie pockets as she traipsed away in front.

At the park's pavilion café Cora frowned over the menu while Blaylock queried her fruitlessly about schoolwork and friends and then gave up. In the end she dipped carrot sticks into a tiny tub of hummus, listlessly so, even after Molly, having demolished a mound of chicken and chips, had secured Blaylock's permission to go off and ride her bike round the paved perimeter.

'Cora love, would you maybe take the hoodie off?'

'No, I'll be cold.'

'You're going to sit there like that?'

'What are you going to do, Dad?'

He didn't 'erupt', merely nodded, and stared out across the park at the perambulators and dog-walkers and Sunday footballers. There was something in Cora's determined solitariness that just reminded him of him. For that and for her flat rejoinders, he had to count himself responsible. Molly had been just a baby, had been spared. But when Cora and Alex were small children he had shouted at them terribly, inexcusably, and over time, even if only in their own reduced ways, they had begun to throw back at him the anger they had witnessed. 'If all you ever do is try and settle it by force,' Jennie had told him quietly, 'you never learn a better way.'

Unhappy at feeling the past so close at hand again, Blaylock allowed his thoughts to stray instead toward the thousand drear dilemmas of work. Though he managed to keep his phone inside his jacket, his thoughts were soon elsewhere. The letter from Eve had stayed with him, as had Madolyn Redpath's contempt. He wondered what on earth he could do to redeem himself, since every option was painful.

It was the guttural bark of the dog that made him look up sharply, in time to see the scene unfold on the concrete forecourt in front of the café – he saw the German Shepherd, free of its leash, bound toward Molly on her bike, he saw her swerve dramatically and come crashing off head-first and un-helmeted onto the concrete.

He was out of his chair in an instant and yet Andy Grieve had moved before him, and got there first. He waved away the dog-owner's flapping apologies and crouched by Andy, who was carefully elevating Molly's upper body. To Blaylock's alarm there were no tears, no blood, just a groggy, disoriented, awfully pale face.

'She wasn't out, was she, Andy?'

'No, boss.'

Blaylock took over the holding of her and stared into her helpless pupils. 'Get Martin, she needs the hospital.'

In the A&E waiting room he cradled Molly and buried his nose in her hair as fitful sobs finally came forth. He cursed himself for having let it happen – for all that he had suffered worse mortifications in front of a triage nurse. Gradually Molly consented to take small sips of water, spoke mournfully of a headache, but seemed to have come round.

Cora had been whisked home by the police vehicle before he had even reached Jennie on the phone, whereupon he had found her unusually calm. He was mildly surprised she had not chosen to join them, but then his reassurances, however guiltily, that all would be well had tended to ward off a mercy mission. He had wanted to do penance, and he was feeling fractionally better for it.

The A&E was fairly crowded with people, wearily accepting of the wait to varying degrees. The television was tuned to a drear afternoon soap for the grown-ups. The donated toys and games and injected plastic play-sets were heavily weathered and amputated of working parts, batteries long dead. Blaylock's phone had no games. But Molly disinterred a chapter-book and he read to her and she to him, and so they rubbed along until disturbed by the swish of the automatic doors, and a miserable mucus-ridden sob.

Blaylock looked up to see a woman in obvious distress, shuffling into the waiting space with the awkward assistance of a female companion who had a close hold of her shaking shoulders. The woman was large, ageless and sexless in sweatshirt and sweatpants, unidentifiable under a curtain of long dry dark hair. Once she had been helped to sit, the distress became clearer for she raised her head and took her hand away from where she had been pressing a handkerchief. There was blood on her fingers, blood on her forehead, blood on the handkerchief. One eye socket was bruised – even, Blaylock feared, depressed. He could not guess how many blows she had sustained about the head and face. But he folded Molly into his arms against the sight. He had no wish to stare himself, but he sensed the whole room was sharing the discomfort.

The woman's companion – of similar age but lean and better attired – had crouched by her yet wore a look of curious sternness.

'I can't stay, Gracie. But you'll be okay?'

After the briefest glance Gracie returned the hankie to her eye socket.

'This time, but, you have to do it. Right? It can't happen again. If it does I can't be helping you . . . You understand? If you don't do something it'll never change, you'll get no peace and nor will the rest of us neither . . .'

Gracie emitted a great shaking sob then was quiet, as if crushed.

Her friend got back to her feet, looking sorrowful and angry. Blaylock made eye contact and she shot him a hard look. Because he was nosy, he wondered? Or because he was a man? Or because she felt guilty over leaving? At any rate, with another swish of the doors she was gone.

It wasn't long before a black mother with a bag of mints sidled over. She sat for some moments before Gracie took a mint and uttered thanks in a voice thick with phlegm and embedded distress. But she only held the mint in her fist.

By 6 p.m. they were back to Islington with a clean bill of health and a sheet of instructions on monitoring head injuries. He carried his daughter to the door, where Jennie nodded at the sight of how deeply Molly had burrowed into her father's neck. Her sympathetic look seemed to encompass them both. She leaned in to nuzzle Molly, near enough for Blaylock to breathe the scent of her long hair.

'Is it okay if I take her up?' he asked. Jennie nodded.

Molly stirred. 'Can I go in your bed, Mummy?'

'Of course, sweetheart.'

Upstairs he held her steady as she undressed to vest and pants then slid under her mother's heavy down-filled duvet. Blaylock stroked her forehead, whispered his affections, and lay down next to her at a suitable remove, careful to keep his muddy-soled Oxfords over the edge of the bed.

In the dark his head swam somewhat – from the daze of the day, and the soothing maritime shades of the room, such that he could have believed they were alone together in a cabin on the ocean.

The room was an affable mess, an inversion of his own. Papers were piled on every flat space, not just the roll-top bureau but Jennie's vanity table and the long trunk at the foot of the iron bed-frame. A clutch of dry-cleaning bags hung from her Scandinavian wardrobe, though already removed was a sheer silvery dress that he thought stunning, evidently tried on and ready for use. He glanced to the bedside clock, to find his view obscured by a screwdriver atop a bag of metal screws. Then he heard a light rap on the door and eased himself off the bed.

Downstairs in the half-light of the hall he wanted to tell her about what he had seen and how well they had been seen to at the hospital; and yet he struggled for words.

'It was a . . . god, you know . . . you see some things. Misery.'

'God bless the NHS, eh? Listen, next week? I've a plan to maybe take the children off for the weekend. I wondered if we could shift things?'

'What you up to?'

'Just a couple of nights away. Camping.'

'You're kidding me?'

'There's a first time for everything, David. The site's just inside the M25 but it could mean we're back later on Sunday. Might you want to see them Friday day instead? Or have all the following weekend?'

'It's not the easiest. I'm in Brussels Thursday and Friday. Let's say sometime Sunday and I'll take what I get, eh?'

For the first time all weekend she seemed less pleased with him, but not, he hoped, vitally so. As she showed him to the door he hoped for some gesture of physical closeness, but he could read from her eyes that her mind was elsewhere.

Back home in his study he sat for some time staring at Eve Mewengera's letter, aware that the hour was getting late and that something in his heart was already resolved, such that to deny it would be the worst karma: the low repudiation of what one knew to be true, and at another's expense.

He made two phone calls, the first to Eric Manning, with apologies for the lateness of the hour, asking Eric to contact Immigration Control immediately. The second was to Madolyn Redpath.

'Madolyn, it's David Blaylock. I thought you should know, I've revoked the deportation order on Eve Mewengera. The concerns for her health and wellbeing, I believe, are correct, despite the assurances we've had. So she won't fly from Heathrow tonight, she'll be released from Blackwood, and her appeal can restart.'

'I, god . . . I'm amazed. Thank you . . . My god, Eve will thank you.'

'I'll consider it a favour if you don't look to make great hay out of this or tell the world I've belatedly seen sense. It's a delicate matter and I've weighed it carefully on its terms.'

'You mean you're afraid you'll have to do it again?'

'Just in this case, I saw sufficient grounds to reconsider.'

'Well, listen . . . I can't say all that will follow but "just in this case" you can be assured I think you're brilliant and I could kiss you.'

After the call ended he felt an overpowering oddness, as if he was himself newly discharged from hospital and taking tentative steps.

6

His regular Monday morning gatherings of the troops were bumped, for he had to prepare to head to Gravesend before 11 a.m. and first had some urgent business he hoped to transact. Thus he went to 11 Downing Street to see Caroline Tennant.

'I've been lobbied for some time about the grave situation of refuge services for women fleeing domestic violence? A shortage of beds and skilled people, the numbers turned away getting to be concerning ... I sourced figures on what it would cost to protect the beds we have, ensure they stay open. It's ten million. My view is we have to do it.'

Caroline was giving him a look he thought worryingly polite – pitying, even. 'How long have you been considering this, David?'

'Too long. A month or more.'

'You've not just buckled to pressure from the *Post*?'

'I believe that "pressure" is rightly applied. I think it was an oversight of mine that I want to remedy. Because it's an emergency.'

'Wouldn't you say the *Post* campaign, from what I've seen, has presented rather a uniform vision of the problem?'

'I'm not sure I follow.'

'The women on the front pages – the case studies? White, working women in the main, aren't they? Don't the services tend to deal with more ... intractable problems? Women without income, or drug and alcohol issues that they share with their abusers? Women with lots of children who speak no English? Obviously I can see how one could fill every bed, I just wonder what you do next to remedy the problem?'

'An emergency is an emergency, Caroline.'

'Yes, but there must be more than one way to tackle it? I'm just surprised, David, you're not more focused on a law enforcement solution – cracking down on the men, getting them out of the home and into custody. Whereupon, it surely follows, the refuges face less pressure?'

'As you know, Caroline, I'm not in a position to ask the police to do more than they're already doing.'

'So you want to stick a bandage on the problem?'

'To stop the bleeding. Yes.'

'For ten million – where would you propose to make the corresponding budget cuts?'

'Caroline,' he scowled, 'I've met my budget targets up to now, I'm cutting the police grant, counter-extremism monies . . . I came here to ask you for help from reserves.'

'In entirety? Not possible. Have you looked again lately at your Borders and Immigration budget . . . ?'

It was with a Pyrrhic sense of accomplishment that Blaylock returned to Shovell Street and summoned Mark Tallis.

'Okay, I have a deal with Caroline; once it's signed off we need to contact Marjorie Michaels and the *Post*. I'd like us to arrange some sort of meet-and-greet at a refuge, and the *Post* can be assured I've been happy to acknowledge the merits of their campaign and glad we share a view of this problem and what needs doing, et cetera.'

He noticed a text from Jennie – *David do you have a moment to speak? Jx.* – and he asked Mark for five minutes, hoping it might be more, their recent exchanges having offered so many moments that he had felt to be of real promise.

'David, I wanted to talk, it should have been sooner, something I've been meaning to tell you . . . and I didn't have the nerve in person, which is silly . . .'

Instantly Blaylock knew how this tune went, the mournful strains of *goodbye* and *so sorry*. He cursed himself for failing to see it, feeling abruptly like an adolescent in a hallway clutching the family's Bakelite handset as his heart got filleted.

'*I'm seeing someone. For a while. I didn't talk about it, didn't assume it was serious, but . . . it's gotten that way . . . . I mean . . . I'm part of a couple again, it seems. So I want to be straight about it with you.*'

Taking the blow, Blaylock weighed his response, harder yet on account of her god-awful decorum that never faltered.

'To be honest, Jennie . . . I mean, first of all, good for you, and second, you needn't be so shy. It's your life.'

'*That's good of you to say, David. It's because it's about our kids, too. This is someone I think is going to be part of my life – part of their lives, too.*'

'Okay. That does sound – serious. But good, that you feel that way about someone.'

'*Yeah.*' He heard her exhale. '*It is good, I think, David.*'

'Should I know anything about him? Anything you want to tell me? Not that you have to.'

'*No, his name's Nick. Nick Gilchrist? You might even have heard of him, he makes films, documentaries? He's well respect-ed.*'

Blaylock thought for a moment, tugging on memory's threads, for there was certainly something there at the far end. 'I think . . . I do. I might have seen something . . . Sorry, how long has it been? That you've been seeing him?'

'*Four months, maybe, we've been dating? We took it slow. The last couple, we've spent more time, done some things all together.*'

Since the summer, then: he thought anew about those months, his own emotional weather in that interim, and what Jennie's had been, quite independent of his imagining.

'Together as in with the children? They kept remarkably quiet.'

'*I didn't instruct them. Just asked them to go easy on me. I think the message got through. They're wiser than we think.*'

'Okay, well, what else can I say, Jen? It would be an odd thing, wouldn't it, if I didn't assume you were a grown woman? Yeah, maybe you could have told me sooner, since it's pertinent to the kids.'

'*Like I say, I didn't know myself for a while.*'

'Yes, but you just said, you wish it had been sooner. You can do that, you know. Tell me things, I won't break. Better that than any sort of subterfuge. The kids knowing things I don't.'

Her sigh travelled down the line. '*As you say, David, I'm a grown-up, we both are, we all need some kind of privacy. And in a house of children that's not easy to come by. I mean, as if relationships weren't hard enough, at our age – trying to make them, learning to trust someone and all of that. Trying to get over the inhibitions from the past ...*'

'You mean inhibitions I put in you by the way I behaved, et cetera.'

'*No, David, honestly, I'm not talking about you, I'm just talking about me and this man. Nick ... he has kids of his own from a marriage that failed. What I mean is, he gets that there's a sensitivity to this situation. As do I. But, I dunno, you maybe think that's all namby-pamby crap ...*'

'Of course not, Jennie. Just, don't think you ever have to handle me like porcelain ... Look, thank you for telling me, and if this is a good thing for you, then great.'

'*Thank you, David, I appreciate that.*'

'The children – they get on with him okay?'

'*They've spent some time, enough, they get on. Yeah, he's good with them. He's a good man.*'

'Good. I suppose I'll meet him.'

'*The camping trip I mentioned on Sunday. It's ... we're all going together, so ...*'

'Right, yeah, I knew there had to be a reason . . .' And he laughed, extending the laugh to fill the space, so that nothing in his manner might sound hollowed, emptied, or otherwise impaired.

Well before his arrival in Gravesend Blaylock had lost all savour for the day's business. En route he was advised that the National Statistics Office believed that the encouraging trends boasted by the day's official police crime figures were 'not credible'. Now he felt he was going through stage-managed motions. Even after collecting Richard Colls, who cheerily sported a lipstick-sized video camera affixed to his lapel – 'I wore it for you, David' – Blaylock's mood was not improved.

They drove to a new-build garden estate of identical two-toned family homes, and on the street's corner, in the estate community centre cum doctor's surgery, Colls introduced him to a pillar of the community, a plump and silvery sixty-four-year-old named Deirdre.

'When I was a girl this estate was a highly desirable address. Then it got so nobody wanted to be here. Oh, I tell you. It was bandit country. But the community decided they wouldn't stand for it no more, they rallied round and organised to get something done.'

'What made the difference?' Blaylock eyed Chief Constable Colls.

'Oh, the council deciding to knock the whole estate down. And build it back up good and proper. And, best of all, they didn't let any of the bad families back in. Told 'em to sling it.'

This was a more drastic, expensive remedy than Blaylock had been planning to endorse.

Deirdre then accompanied him and Colls on a tour of the locale, dictating their pace as she walked with a stick. Blaylock was invited to peer very intently down a deserted pedestrian cut-through, at some fiercely chopped bushes around a church hall, and at a shiny, deserted playground – all places where, according to Deirdre, 'the druggies used to loiter'.

Colls offered a commentary: 'We got CCTV on the playground, we lit up the alley, wherever the gangs hung around we moved them on.'

Moved them on where? was the nagging question in Blaylock's head.

Back at the centre they met Deirdre's husband Maurice, stooped and bald as an egg, a cheery follower of current affairs. 'You're the bloke gave that car thief a clout? Good on you, son. I wish I could do that. But they're not afraid of me . . .'

Patiently Blaylock began to extol his faith in restorative justice, keeping youths clear of the court system, offering offenders a way to repair misdeeds. Neither Maurice nor Deirdre were madly keen.

'That won't work for the real troublemakers, the hard nuts, the bad families. They can be very large families, see. And if you get into a quarrel with one then you've a quarrel with the lot of 'em.'

'Their parents go round sticking up for them, saying it's everyone else's fault . . . No, soft touch is the problem, bad parenting and that. I mean, you're a parent, aren't you, Mr Blaylock?'

Blaylock nodded and made a serious face, deciding not to offer himself as the acme of child-rearing virtue.

He and Colls drove on to 'The Avenues', a shabbier older estate of two-storey houses and staunchly maintained older person's bungalows, over the road from a stretch of barren gated parkland. They pulled up outside a squat whitewashed property hemmed by a low wall, metal grilles across its windows, and a hand-painted awning that announced AVENUES COMMUNITY HUB. A cherry-red mobility scooter was parked by a closed garage where a man stood vigorously whitewashing some aerosol graffiti from the expanse of the metal door. He was introduced to Blaylock as Terry Beggs, the administrator of the premises.

'What did it say on the wall?' Blaylock asked. 'You can tell me.'

Terry Beggs winced. 'Uh, "Fuck Paddy Vaughan"?'

'Right. Someone knew we were coming?'

In the snug main shop-space computer workstations were arranged round the walls. Terry explained carefully that the hub was a place to help the 'digitally underprivileged' get assistance with their searches for work and entitlements to benefit in the interim.

Out the back door where a young man was steering a grass strimmer round a scruffy square of lawn, Blaylock was introduced to Scott, who hadn't shaved and wore his baseball hat low, but had zipped up his tracksuit top.

'Scott got in bother, he did his service,' Terry explained. 'Now he runs our repairs team, it gets the young people involved in gardening and decorating and handy jobs round the community.'

Next in line was Roy, a lean white-haired sexagenarian who leaned on a metal-topped cane and whose handshake was exquisitely limp. Terry shouted to the strimmer – 'Chris!' – to down tools and come over.

'So, Chris, here? He got in bother, got himself under the influence, nicked Roy here's mobility scooter and pranged it. He didn't have form, there were . . . circumstances. He knew he'd offended. His parents came in, it was made clear it could be criminal proceedings or restorative justice. And he chose the latter. So, we talked to Roy here, as the victim, would the process work for him? And now this is where we are.'

After a cogitative moment Blaylock weighed in. 'So, Chris, how are you feeling now about this system and how you've been treated?'

'S'alright. S'good, yeah? Better than court. I know now, see, Roy had problems and stuff? If I'd known how things was for him – and he'd known how it was for me – reckon we'd have got on.'

'But you think it's a good system, a fair system?'

'Worked for me, mate. Not much else I can say.'

'Right. And how's your experience been, Roy?'

'Well, as a form of punishment I'm glad at least there's some disciplining aspect to it at the outset, that police are present and it gets thrashed out over a table . . .' The refined flow of Roy's speaking voice was interrupted by a barking cough that came out of Chris and made the older man grimace. 'Of course, it's hardly the Bloody Assizes. But, you have to try to get on with people in life is my credo. For a while I thought Chris's voice was being heard more loudly than mine, and even now I'm not sure . . .'

Ben Cotesworth appeared at Blaylock's shoulder. 'The press are all ready for you out front, David.'

They all trooped back out front where the media had gathered, Blaylock folding some notes away in his pocket before the cameras got a look. He took up a position cleared for him in front of the newly whitewashed garage door.

'Thank you for coming. Recorded crime is down once again, news for which we should be thankful, but I came here today to see for myself the reality of the street—'

Abruptly a great rumbling sound – the booming bass of dub reggae as from a big amplified system – rose up from the street.

'You can run but you can't hide,

You can run but you can't hide . . .'

Heads turned in great consternation seeking the source of the sound. Then came gasps and laughter, and Blaylock realised eyes and cameras were pointing behind him, his police team suddenly bothered. He turned and beheld the white door, upon which words were materialising from the air in the form of dripping paint, as if by magic:

LYING TORY SCUM!

Blaylock saw young Chris had clapped a hand over his mouth, though his eyes shone. It was indeed a stunning prank. He moved hastily out of shot, even as the first words on the door erased themselves to be replaced by others:

YOU WILL BE CORRECTED!

That evening, as he sat in his study in semi-darkness before a laptop, nursing three fingers of Macallan, Blaylock took a call from a chastened-sounding Richard Colls.

'*The perpetrators got away through the park, David, but they had to dump the kit they'd been using, and we retrieved it. Basically it was handheld laser projection – like a laser graffiti gun? It was wired up to a laptop in a canvas bag, and a computer program did the animation bit so it looked like paint.*'

'Ingenious,' muttered Blaylock, swilling his medicine round his glass tumbler.

'*So you know, there's a mob online have claimed credit for it through social media. They're called The Correctors, online is sort of where they seem to live. We've had some sight of them before at protests, demos and whatnot, that's what they do – pranks and stunts and flash mobs, with that sort of anti-capitalist, anti-establishment angle. There's a fair old archive of stuff related to them if you do a Google video search . . .*'

Within minutes Blaylock sat clicking through YouTube sidebars. It was remarkably easy to find traces of his alleged tormentors, and their repertoire of sound and image felt remarkably familiar to him.

The most substantial piece of work he found started sharply, backed by a doom-laden score, with a quick-cut montage of what an inter-title called 'callous, unfeeling elites' – world leaders, bankers, other forms of grinning well-heeled scum. His pulse hardly jumped when his own face jumped out at him amid the blink-editing. Was he entering the Carlton Club a few weeks previous? It was all too brief.

The imagery changed to tumultuous scenes of visible poverty, streets reeling from bomb-blasts, glaring lines of police in riot gear. Then, consonant with a fade to black, came the kick of dub reggae, ushering in scenes of placard protesters, vociferous marchers, the dancing and jigging and grinning of passionate youth. A *vox populi* offered snatches of affirmative speech by an interchangeable succession of students, some of them masked.

Then, finally, something Blaylock saw and heard made him sit up.

'*Define The Correctors? I can't do that . . . This is a movement, and that means – it moves, it doesn't stand still. The Correctors are just a vehicle for ideas, and no one person is driving. No one can get in its way, either.*'

The white translucent plastic mask had successfully anonymised the speaker's face, but the halting conviction of his voice, not to say his sculpted crest of hair, would have been known anywhere by his father.

'*But there's no logo, no platform, no tee-shirt . . . I just think what we'd say is that our ideas, our energies, are for the people, and against the neoliberal world order. The enemy is neoliberalism, and its ringleaders, and its apologists. We have to fight them. Their errors must be corrected.*'

The piece concluded with a sequence of title-cards.

CORRECTION: THE REMOVAL OF ERROR.
CORRECTION: PUNISHMENT, THEN
   REHABILITATION.
CORRECTION: HOW <u>SOCIETY</u> DEALS WITH
   OFFENDERS.
THE PEOPLE ARE THE POLICE!

Blaylock poured and knocked back a second, short whisky. A powerful instinct told him to get on the phone to Jennie. Some other force, fractionally more compelling, told him that her view would not be his view, the outcome nothing like what he rightly or wrongly wished for.

Keep your powder dry, he told himself, pouring once more.

7

Dominic Moorhouse was aggrieved. And if the Foreign Secretary was not an imposing figure – rather, with the look of an outsized school debater, frowning under his big specs and waves of hair – he was straining to make himself forcefully clear to Blaylock.

'The ambassador came to see me yesterday to express his extreme dissatisfaction over the revoking of this deportation order for Eve Mewengera? David, I'm struggling to understand what possessed you to undermine our position and cause us such a diplomatic embarrassment with a government whose friendship in the region is so significant to us. I mean . . . was somebody *getting* at you?'

'I received demonstrations, yes, Dom. After I reviewed them I formed the opinion, whatever the *realpolitik* of the thing, that this woman just shouldn't have to go back there.'

'Right, and should we be prepared for your taking any more of these kinds of unilateral decisions, now you've opened the door?'

'I really hope not, Dom. What I hope is that Ms Mewengera's case is the exception I believe it to be. If it's not, then what else would you expect from me?'

Patrick Vaughan, seated next to them in the position of adjudicator, was regarding Blaylock with one of his stock expressions of brow-creased botherment. 'It *is* a bloody odd thing for you to have done, David.'

But Blaylock simply didn't think the Captain cared enough. And for his own part he was growing weary of being hauled in early before Cabinet to account for himself like the errant schoolchild.

Diane Cleeve was due in to see him later, and the requirement of best behaviour weighed heavily enough on him already.

In Cabinet proper, Blaylock briefed colleagues by rote on his agenda for the bi-monthly Consilium in Brussels where he would meet with his European counterparts. He told the table he would be pressing for bilateral agreements on restricting free movement rights within the EU. No one believed he would achieve that. He told them he would push Germany to release advance passenger data from its airlines. He didn't even believe himself on that one. Everyone in the room knew that to make a fuss of principles in Europe was a mere performance. 'Serious concerns' were to be acknowledged, not addressed; a 'coherent European response' was a non sequitur; an 'action plan' was no such thing. A 'working party' was the best, dreariest option one could expect. Thus Blaylock went through the motions.

At Shovell Street Adam Villiers and Brian Shoulder came to see him, Villiers with an update on the absconded risk certificate Haseeb Muthana. 'We believe he's got as far as the North Waziristan borderland. He may have gravitated toward the village nearest to the training camp he attended five years ago.'

Blaylock merely nodded, hopeful that Muthana, having dragged himself so far from sight, might also be put out of mind.

'On the subject of the Free Briton Brigade . . . ? Something of note, perhaps. I had begun to wonder – in light of the sophisticated design of their website, their growing links to international organisations – who was paying for their paper-clips, as it were? Obviously they have some keen and voluble activists, this Gary Wardell for one . . . However, I wasn't persuaded it was adequate to keep their gravy train in motion. Then this man lately began to append his name to their public pronouncements.' Villiers slid a landscape ten-by-eight photo across the table. 'Do you recognise him by any chance?'

Blaylock peered closely at a fifty-ish man with crinkled features under a tweedy flat cap, dressed as for a football match in a Harrington jacket.

'His name is Duncan Scarth, he's a bit of a whiz in commercial property, a millionaire many times over. Has donated to the Conservative Party in years gone by. Keeps homes in Geneva and Oslo, but also in your constituency. He's from your neck of the woods . . .'

With an aperture thus prised open, Blaylock now felt the past flood in. 'Oh yeah. My god. We were at school together. He's got to be five years older than me, mind you. But, yeah – he was an entrepreneur alright, used to run his own tuck-shop at breaktimes. I don't remember him banging on about sending the buggers back, but that's not to say he didn't hold those views . . .'

'Has he tried to contact you lately?'

'Not that I know of. Do you expect him to?'

Villiers shrugged, reclaiming the photograph. 'No, no. Just a thought. Given that connection.'

Blaylock prompted Mark Tallis to his feet as Geraldine showed Diane Cleeve into the office, at her side the big shaven-headed man Blaylock remembered from the previous week's memorial service.

'Mr Blaylock, this is Pastor Ruddock. I joined his congregation recently and we've been working together on certain projects.'

Blaylock accepted the powerful handshake of the pastor, beside whom Mrs Cleeve was birdlike, his bulk packing out the seams of his dark suit. Yet Blaylock did sense some kind of mindful rapport between them, as he found himself a little guiltily picturing their running a pub together in some seaside town.

'Thank you for making time for me.'

'Always, Mrs Cleeve. Please, sit.'

She beheld him with the frowning directness he well knew.

'First thing you ought to know, as of this week I am quitting Remember the Victims, that association will be at an end.'

'I see. A big step. Can I ask, are you—?'

'It's time to move on. Other people will take it forward, I don't doubt, but from my side the work's done.'

'They'll miss your leadership.'

'I don't think so. It can go on being what it is, which is a victim support group. What I've come to feel is, if you're not careful then it keeps you a victim. Nothing changes. What I've observed, Mr Blaylock, is that years go by and people stay angry and bitter, and what they suffered just defines who they are. And that's stifling, I'd say. You need to find a way to breathe again . . .'

'Well, I certainly respect that—'

'The second thing I want to speak with you about is Jakub Reznik.'

'In what regard? Is it his minimum term?'

'A month back I got a letter from him, and the other week I went to visit him in prison.'

Blaylock had been startled. 'What – was in the letter?'

'An apology. Not his first. You'll recall he tried to cut his wrists last year, and the chaplain who saw him told me he was full of remorse. I didn't care, obviously. I'd heard he'd been violent since he went in. I'd thought, excuse me, but what can you do with a bastard like that?'

'It's a special problem of the life sentence,' Pastor Ruddock spoke up. 'Prisons got their own culture. As a lifer you carry that stigma, nothing you do means anything. So, what you get is worse violence.'

'This letter.' Mrs Cleeve paused, uncharacteristically. 'Reznik, he said he'd taken Jesus as his saviour – that he must have had the devil in him, when he done when he done to Lisa? And he'd been praying to God for forgiveness, but he didn't think that was "possible". So he'd started praying to Lisa instead.'

'I'm sorry?' said Blaylock, fearing he would lose the thread.

'He begun praying to my daughter? Being as how that's who he sinned against. And he said that one night, in his cell, he'd heard Lisa's voice speaking back to him. Saying he'd done a despicable thing, but it was in his hands to redeem himself. As a human being. Before God.'

'Does the prison have an opinion of his mental state?'

'Ah, you think he's barmy?' Mrs Cleeve looked to Pastor Ruddock, who cleared his throat sizably.

'You could see it another way, sir. Which is that he'd come to a proper view of his sins – a spiritual understanding, if you get me? There's a sentence on all of our souls, sir, then one day we die, and sentence is passed. Some men, they don't see that – or they see it too late. But them what sees it in time . . . ?'

Pastor Ruddock looked to Mrs Cleeve, who resumed. 'Yeah, like I say. I went to see him – Reznik. I felt driven to it, is what I'd say. I sat across from him like I'm sitting across from you now. And he sat there, sobbing, like his old man at the trial. Looked about as broken down as his old man, too, so he did. And, I tell you, I could believe he had the devil in him when he killed Lisa? 'Cos there's nothing there any more. Just this wretch of a man, all eaten up. I looked at him and I thought, what he's done to my life, how he lives with it, how I live with it . . . And part of me thought, how could he dare? And another part—'

Mrs Cleeve stopped, looked aside, exhaled heavily.

'You think of all you've been through – because you've only got this life, just this one – and what you do with it – I sat there and, I felt something *rise* inside me, almost lifting right out of me? As powerful as that. And I thought, "Is this what forgiveness is?" I'm all for punishment, see. He's been punished, Reznik, like he should. Most likely he'll die in prison. But I've got to thinking now – about forgiveness, what it can do?'

Blaylock saw that, as intently as Mrs Cleeve was looking at him, Pastor Ruddock's gaze was equally fixed. 'Just as repentance is a true Christian idea, Mr Blaylock, forgiveness is a gesture of true goodness. It has wonder-working power.'

'Forgiveness,' said Mrs Cleeve. 'I want to encourage it in people. I want to encourage it in me. And what the European Court's saying it wants? To give a life prisoner a chance of a review of their sentence? See if they've changed, if there's any good there? I want to support that. I want to say, okay, maybe a person can atone. So that's what I'm doing now. And I'd like your support.'

Blaylock had listened in a state of mounting discomfiture. 'Mrs Cleeve, first . . . I obviously respect the sentiments you express. But it's the settled view of this country that certain crimes merit whole-life orders, and that how long those who have killed should spend in prison is a matter for our Parliament and our courts. It's not possible for me to endorse your thinking as you ask.'

'Did I not hear you lately talking about, what – "restorative justice"? Respecting the victim's wishes? Thought you were all for that?'

'For petty crimes by kids who didn't know better. Not murder. A bereaved parent could be sat where you are, demanding I bring back hanging. I'd only say what I say to you, our courts administer justice.'

'You've got the power, haven't you, to review a life sentence? On compassionate grounds? You can pardon people if it came to it?'

Blaylock shook his head. 'I can allow a terminally ill prisoner to die at home, not inside. Pardons are for the innocent, Mrs Cleeve.'

'You know, that almost seems a waste to me.'

Blaylock felt a desperate need to shift the discussion onto ground where he might feel firmer. 'Have you considered that this decision of yours might impact on the valuable work you've done with Remember the Victims, the solace it's given people?'

'If people were consoled, they were consoled. This is something I'm doing for me. Who's to say it won't be just as valuable?'

'And, forgive me, but – have you considered the possibility Reznik was playing some sort of stratagem?'

'Of course. I'm not a fool. I made a judgement. And I can tell, Mr Blaylock, you ain't comfortable with it. You're rather my position stayed the same. Closer to your position, yeah? "Tough on crime" and that. So if we have our photo taken together it's like we're saying the same thing. Well, my position is what it is now, and it's up to you if you still want to stand beside me.'

As Blaylock groped for a response Mark Tallis leaned forward. 'It will be a tough position for the general public to accept, Mrs Cleeve. In fact, it could get quite tough on you.'

'Tough? Do me a favour. After all I been through? I've told my mum what I'm doing, my ex-husband – they're in bits about it. So what do I care what a load of strangers think? Is that all *you* care about?' She focused wholly on Blaylock. 'I'm talking about rehabilitation, the chances of that. Do you not believe in it? I'm appealing to you as a man.'

'I'm sorry to say, in this office I hold . . . I don't get the luxury of what you're describing – of just doing the things I happen to believe in that I might think are right and good.'

It seemed then to be Mrs Cleeve's turn to display incredulity. 'My god, don't say that. That's a desperate thing to say. How can you sit there and say that?'

'I'm not sure', Blaylock said quietly, 'what else we can discuss.'

'No, me neither.' She stood, deeply dissatisfied, and Pastor Ruddock stood too, albeit with a look that suggested he had truly expected no better.

'I'm sorry I can't do as you ask. I hope – you might yet think some more about this.'

'Are you serious? After all what I told you. No. It's interesting, but, the sense I get of how you make your decisions. What your priorities are? More people ought to know, I think.'

*

As Blaylock retook his seat Tallis looked up from absorption. 'Well, that was insane.'

Blaylock sighed. 'It's an unfortunate end to – an association.'

'I can't believe how she tried to box you in on the restorative justice thing.'

'She's . . . a tough character.'

'Not as tough as her minder. The so-called pastor? My guess would be that's a man with excellent reason to believe in forgiveness . . .'

'Listen, Mark – I don't totally disdain the view she's arrived at . . . I just don't think it will make sense to anyone but her.'

'That's her choice. My concern, *patrón*, is if she decides to make trouble for you. I just think possibly you said too much? Essentially you did tell her that you do a bunch of things you don't actually believe in. You think she wouldn't use that against you down the line?'

'Mark, howay, don't me make feel worse than I do already.'

Tallis only shrugged his shoulders as if to say it couldn't be helped.

Come 6 p.m. he was alone with his papers for the Brussels Consilium when Geraldine knocked and entered with a shy look of a kind he rarely saw.

'Um, David, some nice news, the *Criterion* magazine just mailed to say congratulations, they've chosen you as their "Politician of the Year".'

He managed a chuckle, and joined her by the door to take receipt of the citation as contained in an email she had printed out.

Blaylock's record as Home Secretary is looking heavyweight: crime and immigration down, also the Home Office's unwieldy budget. He routinely knocks Martin Pallister around at the despatch box, and we loved his message at Tory Conference: he reaches parts of the

Perusing what struck him as claptrap he wandered out into the corridor, feeling the familiar sense of desertion about the place – until he nearly collided with a security guard who nodded to him, somewhat fretful, in the manner of a new start.

'Where's Fusi got to?' Blaylock asked. 'You know Fusi?'

'*Przepraszam*, I, sorry . . .' The guard shrugged, sounded Polish.

'Never mind. At ease . . .'

8

On Thursday afternoon he was driven in full convoy out of Westminster and down the M4 to Heathrow, where red-suited and glossily made-up ladies conducted him to the VIP suite. Offered a glass of champagne, he requested water. Something about the superfluity of European excursions inclined Blaylock to frugality; but he had to concede his usual defeat once a limo was bearing him and his party a hundred yards across the tarmac to British Airways Flight 397.

Three hours later he was ensconced at the Brussels Plaza, splashing water on his face over a marble basin in which he felt a man could conceivably drown. There was a sumptuous beige-bronze blankness to the décor of the room; his emperor-sized bed struck him as pointlessly expansive.

After texting an update on his arrival to Sir Michael Roebuck, the UK's chief civil servant in these parts, he lay back atop the bedcovers, clicked on the television, and surfed idly through the hotel orientation package, CNN, News 24 and the global stations.

He dallied for a little over some breathless coverage of a film awards ceremony from London's South Bank: handsome types in evening wear parading down a red carpet lit up by camera flashes. Mildly diverted by the effort to recognise any of the talent, he then sat up from the bed as if shot, seeing Jennie – in the sheer dress he had so admired – standing at the side of Nick Gilchrist, he in black tie, nodding and absorbing the attention as though it had to be ruefully expected. Jennie looked lovely, and mildly abashed, then she was gone.

So it's official, he thought, feeling a coldness in his chest cavity.

Moments later he was in the grip of burning resentment, of hatred for a rival, of bewilderment over what in god's name Jennie saw in such a man over himself. The whole situation was demeaning, unmanning, infuriating. He pressed a hard palm to his temple and exhaled.

Watch yourself, pal. Just . . . watch it.

He shut off the TV and spent some dour moments staring at the big rococo gold-leaf mirror that showed him, marooned and morose, amid the redundant splendour. A sense of futility suffused him by a little and a little. He felt no relish for his work come the morning, and miserably little appetite for anything else besides.

His phone pulsed. His first instinct was to chuck it at the velveteen wastepaper basket. He lifted it and saw a text from Abigail Hassall. *Are you in Brussels? Me too. Might we meet? AH*

After considering for some minutes his options, his duties and his sense of what was prudent, he tapped out a reply. *Lovely idea. Let me get through tomorrow's hostilities and we'll see what can be done. DB*

'Our expectations are modest, of course,' Sir Michael murmured to Blaylock in his unreconstructed smoker's gravel. 'But who knows how the chips will fall when honest Lithuania's in the chair?'

Roebuck sat by him in the concentric charmed circle of the conference room, the multiple advisors and attachés confined to the outer ringside seats. Yet there was no position that struck Blaylock as one of executive authority – not even Lithuania's – for everything in the great Europa was pre-fixed and made frictionless, a sequence of scripted roundtables and conveyor-belt photo opportunities, a train, nonetheless, that some parties seemed never to want to get off.

He endured it by the company of Roebuck, ex-investment banker, and to Blaylock's eyes as effective an operator as any Cabinet

Minister he had known, rightly renowned for a pawky effectiveness in negotiating and horse-trading, above all for keeping up the desirable closeness with the Germans on a number of key policies. Alas for Blaylock, said policies were all about tight budgets and liberal markets, and nothing to do with borders, bodies or security.

Karl Giesler, Blaylock's German counterpart, at least offered his view with the grace of a sorrowful smile. 'The UK is not alone in wanting its welfare systems unmolested. But we must respect what we have made here by consensus, yes? No two-tier Europe.'

Lydia Schmit of Luxembourg was more waspish. 'Our rules are good rules. Yet Britain pleads exception, as if the rest of us are inadequate somehow . . .'

In the chair, Lithuania pondered. Wordings were tried out, typed and passed around. Ultimately all member states agreed that free movement was a 'core value' of their Europa, but that at some point in the next year a working party might report on how the rules, so very good, so very agreed, came to be abused. With that, the parade went by.

Blaylock's 'off-line', 'bilateral' conversations had a degree of candour, at least. The Spanish Minister, Gonzalez, balding and pugnacious, seemed as vexed as he by security in major transport hubs. Karl Giesler privately shared his woes about campus recruitment and radicalisation among German-born Muslims of foreign descent. 'Our great problem', Giesler sighed, 'is a conflict of systems from state to state, data not shared. If we had a total-system solution . . .'

'That's what I think ID cards can do,' Blaylock nodded fiercely.

But Giesler shook his head, with a look suggestive of wisdom dearly bought. 'In Germany? That notion is . . . no. Not acceptable.'

Before he could return to the hotel he was ushered toward a small gaggle of bored journalists to give a compulsory briefing. But he saw Abigail among them and felt his heart lift. She stood tall in strappy high-heeled sandals, svelte in a wrap-round red dress, her golden bob lustrous under light and her green eyes sending out their darkly amused allure. He sensed her eyes on him as he delivered boilerplate remarks.

'We are not alone in Europe. Anyone with eyes can see the shared concerns. Of course there are differences, but compromise is doable . . .'

He was meant to have dinner with Roebuck and the team. Excuses were unconscionable, and he made it through two of four courses, before affecting a look so profoundly dark in pleading the pressure of work that he managed to secure an 'early night'. Once inside his room he texted her again, telling himself that he was only flesh and blood, however aged and non-vintage.

Would you like to meet for a drink?

I suppose we could get round to that :) Where do I find you!?

Room 237, just knock. Is 10 p.m. okay?

There remained a ticklish matter to negotiate, and so he rapped on the partition door. Andy Grieve admitted him to the adjoining bedroom. On previous excursions they had shared a late whisky around this hour, and Blaylock felt a vague embarrassment in explaining that he would shortly have a social visitor.

'Happy to stand down, boss,' said Andy with a little mischief in his grin. 'I reckon you'll be in safe hands.'

'Here we are again,' she said, slipping out of her smart jacket and setting her bag down on the table. 'We must stop meeting in fancy hotel rooms.'

'Slightly more illustrious than Birmingham,' he said, pouring wine for her and whisky for him, sitting opposite her. 'Though, as ever, be aware there's a man with a gun next door.'

'Yes, I do find that strangely heightening.'

They exchanged looks and took sips.

'What should we talk about?' she said finally.

'There's not a great deal to bite on here, I admit. Sir Michael grinds the organ, I'm just the monkey. Do you absolutely need a story?'

'It's not really why I came.' She put her face in her hand and gave him a sending look. 'Cards on the table, I've been thinking about you.'

He returned her gaze with what he thought to be gravitas and raised his whisky to his lips, but somehow missed them, thus spattering his chin and shirtfront.

'Christ, forgive me,' he muttered as he dabbed at himself with his tie. 'I must just be feeling a little . . . over-stimulated.'

Her look hardly changed, only softened by amusement. 'I knew you weren't the usual politician, but I am starting to wonder if you're actually some kind of a monk?'

This did feel to him, gallingly, like one more cap that fitted, albeit at this given moment more regrettably than ever. 'You'd be amazed', he managed, 'the things you can conquer by not thinking about them.'

'Yes, they call it denial.' She straightened and set down her glass. 'Look, I will probably find it a little . . . awkward, if I have to extend myself too much further in your direction? Maybe I should withdraw – sensible girl that I am. If I hurry out now I might still get a decent look at the statue of the Peeing Boy.'

She picked up her bag and stood. He stood too, quickly, and moved to intercept her, then, anxious that he was showing all the delicacy of a nightclub doorman, took some care in gently prising her bag from her hands and returning it to the table. Then he put his hands round her waist and bent to kiss her mouth and saw her mirroring him, lips parting, eyes closing.

Though their kiss had urgency, he sensed that she felt as he did – still somehow constricted by something other than mere clothing, as though they were actually clad in opposing armours. He led her by the hand to the bed then hastened to whisk the long curtains together, though the pulley system fought him for some vexing moments. When he turned back she had sat herself on the bed and begun to undress, efficiently. He turned aside to strip off himself, struggling only to think of where to put his trousers.

Turning back he saw her laughing lightly, already down to bra and knickers, and then, rising, she unclasped the bra and threw it lightly to the floor, a gesture he found hugely helpful to his mood. He realised now how stylishly she adorned herself in what she wore since, unclad, her broad hips, curved biceps and shallow breasts had an athletic, gym-honed solidity. Still, the aureate flush on her from head to toe was heavily arousing as she swayed across the parquet toward him.

'The undies are all new, just so you know . . .'

This, said in a girlish murmur, also went straight to his blood, likewise her light touch of his chest and the longing brush of her cheek against his. As they made love he felt sure the urgency on her face mirrored his own, echoed his urge to make good, that their coupling would prove the flirtation had been worth the candle. She crossed her ankles at his back and he exulted in the sensation of being high inside her, snugly sheathed, welcomed home again.

They must have drifted off together, and such was the expanse of the bed that when Blaylock stirred with a start just after 2 a.m. he needed some moments to locate her shape more than a body's length away from him beneath the cotton sheets. But he had no intention of sending her out into the night, whatever was her preference. Fumblingly he set the bedside alarm for 5 a.m.

Waking first, he shifted up onto a crooked elbow and studied her honeyed shoulders, the nape of her neck, her hair on the pillow. Abruptly, oddly, he remembered times when Cora had crept into his and Jennie's bed, Jennie quite often clearing out to fall onto

Cora's narrow cot. He had always loved to watch his daughter awaken – innocent, in a way it seemed to him that no one could be so innocent again. He peered closely now at Abigail's auburn roots, until she rolled over, wincing slightly, stirring. Blaylock was keenly aware he would keep the memory to himself, since he also divined what Abigail was about to say before she opened her mouth.

'What are you thinking?'

'Just how lovely you are.'

She dressed while he shaved, and as she made to go he looked at her fondly from head to toe, superbly assembled, if just a tad more tousled than usual. *Will I see you again?* was what he thought he might say, but he judged it unwise. He stepped forward, embraced her strongly, kissed the top of her head, stepped back and smiled.

'Will I see you again?' she said.

'I'd like that. If you like, this weekend, I could show you Tees-side.'

9

The humdrum assignations of Blaylock's constituency Friday had a fresh appeal to him in anticipation of what the evening promised. After lunch he busied approvingly through a local school, previously under special measures, now sorted out by a new head. He chatted freely with A-level history students, listened to a brass instrument recital, posed with a school football shirt.

By dusk he was in his constituency office being taken through the order of the next day's surgery by Chloe, the intern, who seemed to be slowly mastering the rudiments of the job. Bob Cropper, plotting his larger media grid, impressed on him the need to accept an invitation to an upcoming 'citizenship ceremony' at Thornfield Town Hall, where he would present certificates to newly confirmed British citizens.

'They'll all have passed their language test', said Bob, 'plus their little history exam on what it means to be British. And I'm not sure all our constituents could do the same. Not always certain I could, frankly.'

Blaylock didn't think twice. He knew he ought to be there, though he could imagine not everyone would be pleased to see him.

'We done?' he asked, slapping his thighs.

On the way back to Maryburn he mulled over the hopeful stir he felt inside, uniquely odd to him given the time of year – the true autumn of All Hallows and Bonfire Night, in its fecundity and decay, its slow-stripped branches and slatternly leaves. Usually these put him in mind of the sand in the hourglass. Now the quickening possibilities of a new relationship had changed the picture.

The Maryburn house had come to feel like a lair, the dwelling of a private creature with rough manners. In the time he had before Abigail's arrival Blaylock tried some remedial work. He raked wet leaves, slashed the hedges into shape, changed his bedsheets and mopped his bathroom floor, then called on the grocer and the butcher and filled a box with best silverside, aromatic herbs and spicy Syrah.

Not long after 9 p.m. he saw headlights flare on the driveway and she purred up in her purplish Lexus cabriolet. He padded out into the dark to steer her into a berth within his garage and as he drew down the door he had the feeling of a mission accomplished.

Their hello kiss was long; he felt the soft impress of her tongue, and the warmth of her body through her black trouser suit. He finished off the meal while she read an old paperback entitled *The Anatomy of Human Destructiveness*, her legs curled cosily beneath her. To his delight she ate red meat with brio, mopped bleeding juices with bread, and knocked back red wine without a jot of demurral.

Over coffee, his red box open between them on the low table, he took care to say little of its contents, considering her not yet fully cleared for such confidences. Still, he found himself describing at length his unsettling encounter with Diane Cleeve. Abigail listened intently, with a studious tilt of her head and the odd thoughtful pull on her earring.

He felt easier drawing some family background out of her. She referred to a younger sister, married to some charmless hedge funder and raising twins in a Twickenham house 'like a vicarage'. Her college contemporaries, as she evoked them, were increasingly married with children, 'boring on about school catchments and house prices'. She assured him that she, conversely, had a driving need to meet new people and new ideas, to play in larger playgrounds.

He asked her politely what she was working on. She described a longish piece in the works about predictive science. 'That's more interesting to me than trying to tap MPs for quotes.'

She rises above it, he thought, *she can take it or leave it, she knows there's more to this world.*

'Someday soon you'll have to tell me who told you all these mean things in the piece you did on me.'

'Nuh-uh,' she smiled. 'Impossible. Then I'd have to kill you. Or, sorry, have you killed.'

When his phone pulsed on the table he meant to give it only the most cursory look in light of the hour. But it was Adam Villiers. He excused himself and went into the kitchen.

'David, it's a matter of some urgency. Haseeb Muthana's wife gave birth this morning, an hour ago he spoke to her by a satellite phone, and we have a fix on his whereabouts. We have it thanks to Washington. Where Muthana is, whether by coincidence or design, is in a compound in Babur Ghar being used by a leading Pakistani Taliban commander whose name is Gul Sayid. It's clear from what I understand that the Americans are not about to hesitate now they have such a high-value target in sight.'

'They're planning to hit the compound from the air?'

'That's right.'

Blaylock stared out into the darkness beyond the floor-to-ceiling glass of his kitchen. He thought about Haseeb Muthana, his wife and newborn child, the revolving eye in the sky now trained dispassionately upon him, the power to kill in the joystick-grasping hand of an operative somewhere in the Nevada desert.

'David . . . ?'

'I mean, there's nothing to be done at our side, is there, Adam?'

'That's my view. But I wanted you to be aware, David. Also I believe Caleb Aldrich may call you shortly.'

Sure enough, Blaylock was still tapping his phone ruminatively when it pulsed again.

'David, you're briefed on Sayid? I'm aware you got a pass-

port holder in the mix of this, but the window's closing on these co-ordinates and I gotta say we can't guarantee anyone in the vicinity's gonna be walking out of there . . .'

It seemed a long way back to the room. In the event Abigail came down the hallway toward him.

'David . . . ? Are you okay?'

He thought for some moments, abruptly recalling that she had once been keen to know if he had ever killed a man.

'Sorry, it's not really discussable.'

She nodded, seeming to understand. He was comparing her to Jennie, without wishing to. And Jennie was a sort of living reprimand. With Abigail, though, he chose to believe there was a shared sense of the world's moral murk.

They embraced under the cool clean sheets and he could have settled for that, troubled as he was and with wine taken, but she clambered on top of him, made the running, and he was carried along and energetically worked. Finally she fell on him, and he stroked her head and let her fine hair pour through his fingers.

In the night he awoke sharply and in fright from an obscurely menacing dream, feeling as though the bed were shaking violently beneath him. He slammed back against the mattress as if to evade his fate; but in an instant the silence and darkness all around him reasserted their sway.

Saturday morning surgery was at the office, and as his last-but-one appointment failed to show he slipped out to the caff to stretch his legs and wolf down a bacon roll. On his return young Chloe advised that his 11 a.m., Mr Peter Ayrton, was already seated in the meeting room.

The gentleman at the scuffed round table was fiftyish, in a smart tweedy coat, blue jeans, scarf and flat cap, like a veteran rock 'n' roller turned country squire. He stood as Blaylock entered, hand outstretched.

'Mr Ayrton?'

'Pete's my mate, actually, David. Forgive me, I gave his name. But I'm Duncan Scarth, pleased to meet you, we very nearly met before?'

Blaylock, digesting this information, elected not to take Scarth's hand, debating instead how badly he should react.

'I take it, but, that you know who I am? My job's in bricks and mortar but I'm also the co-executive director of the Free Briton Brigade.'

'It's not on, this. Coming in here under false pretences.'

'Well, I doubt you'd have seen me otherwise, would you, David? For all that you're my MP.'

'Come off it, round here's not home to you.'

'I bounce about a bit, but this is where I'm from, and I've a place in Maryburn just like you. Now look, I'm not here to cause you bother. Otherwise I'd have gate-crashed one of your little sessions at the shopping centre. I've got some concerns, but. About how the policies of your government are affecting ordinary folk round these parts.'

'You're a spokesman for them, are you?'

'I've a little bit of a following behind me, yes, David. I know we're easily scorned. I'm aware it gets said we're a racist party? Point of fact, we judge no man on the colour of his skin. What we want is a decent democratic society, everyone respecting its laws and its freedoms. They say we're anti-Muslim? Not a bit of it. But we oppose Islamism, because it's anti-democratic. Now, is that so bad? Does that mean ye and me can't have us a civil conversation, as MP and constituent?'

Blaylock lowered himself into a seat. Scarth did likewise, loosening his scarf, his cap jauntily in place.

'Go on then. You've got fifteen minutes.'

Scarth sniffed. 'Fair do's. So, I listen closely to all what you say, David. I don't see we're so far apart.'

'Your FBB leaflets say different.'

'Eh, I don't sign off every draft. There's a range of opinion in our group. Listen, I cheered every word you said at Tory Conference. And on the telly the other week, with that daft little girl, the civil liberties gasbag? Trying to make out like you're a relic in your own country . . . I get that, too. It baffles me. I don't want the bloody 1950s back, I wasn't around, man. It's the future what bothers me. How do we live together? Make things fair? So we happily pay wor taxes for all what we need?'

Blaylock listened fretfully, wanting not common ground but clear blue water between himself and this man. He saw, though, as Scarth leaned forward, that a 'but' was on its way.

'Thing is, David, then we see them immigration figures, rising all the time, and we have to ask, is it not just talk? When nothing ever changes? Answer me this, how did you get on in Brussels this week? Did you do anything to stop the flow of foreigners into this country?'

'I had good exchanges with our European counterparts. My commitment is clear, they agree we need to work together to—'

'Howay man, spare us that politician's talk. Did you or did you not get owt out of them?'

'My sense, Mr Scarth, is that nothing would be adequate for you. I don't get the feeling you want us to have anything to do with Europe?'

'You're such a big fan of it, are you?'

'I believe this country has a place in Europe, whatever the shortcomings of the arrangement. And you?'

'Free Briton Brigade's not anti-Europe, David. We're a pan-European organisation, we've good comrades in Holland, Austria, the Baltics, in France. They don't mess about, the French. They know they're a nation, proud of their identity, their heritage, their culture. What we have in common is, one, we's believe in our own sovereignty and, two, we're not buying any fake idea of a greater

Europe. As you well know, Europe is only the start of the bloody problem . . . Why have you got all the African lads piling up at Calais to cross into us, not stopping in Germany and Norway? Plenty jobs there, decent wages . . .' Scarth had been patting his pockets a while and now produced a tobacco pouch.

'No smoking in here,' Blaylock snapped.

'Fair do's. But you'll not mind me rolling one for when I'm outside . . . Where was I?'

'You were telling me what a problem immigration is round these parts? When we've got maybe two thousand immigrants, in a population of a quarter-million?'

'Those numbers are on the up, and you pretend you've a grip on them, and you don't. Makes a difference up here, David. Don't tell me you've not had people in your surgery saying they can't see a doctor, can't find a place to rent, nursery for their kids.'

'That's not on account of two thousand immigrants, Mr Scarth.'

'They see how it is in the waiting rooms. They see the ethnic shops. They're on the bus and they can't hear English spoken. Or they've lost work on the building site because some blow-in has quoted cheaper. You're telling them not to believe their lying eyes?'

Blaylock could not take Scarth for an affable man, and yet his features were perpetually contorting into the look of patient amiability.

'I know the facts don't support that analysis. What I accept is people are having to deal with certain changes in the society.'

'Changes, yes. Change can be disturbing. We're not London, see, not got that exciting diversity you like down there, the Ethiopian food and the Polish brickies and Mary Poppins from Budapest. In my view it's not a badness that's in people, we just know what it means to be native British. You know what it means.'

'Do I?'

'Howay. You know. A like-minded sort of people, living in the same place, talking the same language, believing the same things, respectful of the laws and traditions of the land. As I heard you at your conference, them who were here first have first claim, and them what come later, as guests, need to be good guests. Right? And if they've come to claim benefits 'cos here's nicer than wherever they've been? Nah, forget it. If they've come to take jobs where we've got wor own people? Not needed, thank you. If they've come to wreak havoc on the streets of our cities? Howay, either respect the law or hop off to some Muslim country, right? I mean, what's the United Kingdom for, David? To safeguard our island nation, isn't it? We're a bloody island and we can't nail down who gets to cross our borders?'

It had not taken much, Blaylock observed, for the canny veneer to wear thin. Having had the pleased demeanour of a man with a lunchtime pint set up before him, Scarth now wore the glare of one who had six beers under his belt already.

'I'm sure you think you sound very reasonable. But what me and the public see of your group is hordes of young men, full of drink in the middle of the day, swarming into areas where Muslims live without bother, chanting a lot of hateful things and challenging the police when they're told off. Or are you not aware of that impression you make?'

Scarth raised two palms in concession. 'Fair play, some of our members are lads who've been asked to leave football grounds in their time. Some, I'd admit, never even got through the turnstiles, right? And, god forbid, one or two of 'em might have thrown a punch at a man. But then so have you, haven't you, David?'

Blaylock returned Scarth's grin with a scathing look. Scarth leaned in, serious again. 'This is a young movement. Some of them who are drawn to us? Okay, they mightn't cover us in glory. I might not love their company. But, see, our best recruiting sergeant is you, David. Because you talk and talk, and it doesn't match up to what they see, and they're sick of it. And they don't reckon you're bothered.'

'My record is clear, what I've said and done, I believe in a fair immigration system, one that we control sensibly—'

'David, David, I am always ready to hear a man plain about what he believes. You'll always hear me say, "Speak up, that man! Tell us your truth!" But when I hear weasel talk from a so-called Conservative, like you . . . I mean, howay. You represent Teesside, not Tanzania. Forget what's the done thing in Westminster or bloody Brussels. You owe loyalty to the people you represent. There's you in power and you want to sit back and wash your hands while our country lets in any colour of toe-rag and all their filthy backward practices from the worst cesspits in the bloody world. And they're just allowed to get away with it, with the blinds pulled down, funded by the fucking taxpayer—'

'Mind your language,' Blaylock snapped. 'Where do you think you are, man?'

Scarth's face had reddened and he had begun to sound as if he needed to spit. Clearly he didn't take well to a telling-off.

'I've sat and heard you out, Mr Scarth. I can't satisfy you, and that's okay by me. I know what I stand for and who I represent, which is the basically decent, tolerant people of this region. And I know what I'm opposed to, which is thugs and bullies, wherever they're from.'

'If you think you know people round here so much better than me, let's ye and me have a proper debate in public, see who comes out on top.'

Blaylock shook his head. 'Get away. You've not earned that. If you want a platform, if you love democracy so much, get yourself some policies and stand some candidates. No one's stopping you.'

'"No one's stopping . . . "? That's a bloody laugh, what with the time you put into suppressing us. We've abided by your rules to now, but I tell you what, we might have to look at that, Mr Blaylock. We're sick of these confrontations with police, every bloody time we try to gather. Like east London? Where we're penned in next to that shower of shit that want to crow and goad and give us stick – the commie anarchists, fucking wasters, students thinking it's big to shout "Fascist scum!" into a megaphone? Not one of them has done a brave thing in all their born days but they rant on like it was them fought the Battle of Britain.'

'That, too, is free speech. I'm sorry you've such scorn for people who disagree with you.'

'Howay, even you can see! The glee on their faces, knowing we're the ones who've been silenced – there's something not right there. Naw, I'm past weary of our getting kettled. A movement has to make long strides, activists have to feel active – we need to break our cage. And, listen – if I really fancied it, if I'd a serious mind to, I could bring fifty coaches of lads right down your street, nee bother. I'd not tell the police about it neither. And I wouldn't smile about that if I was you.'

Blaylock could not restrain his contempt. 'Y'know, you sound just like them, all the tin-pot *jihadis*. It all has to end in threats, doesn't it?'

'Not a threat. Just a fact. I'll not be talked down to in my country. Not by you or anyone. It is a war we've got on here. And – talking straight, like? – I see you as my enemy's friend, Mr Blaylock.'

Blaylock pushed back from the table and stood up sharply. 'Right. You've had a good slot, you've been listened to. I know who you are now. Come see me again, any time. Just have the guts to give your own name at the door. And if you feel you've got to bring an army with you, well, I'd not be at all surprised.'

He opened the door and held it open. Scarth made quite a performance of tying his scarf and lodging his roll-up behind his ear, without taking his eyes off Blaylock's. Blaylock watched him walk out, then went to the foyer to check the CCTV. Andy Grieve came to his side. On the black and white monitor Scarth turned and looked up to the lens, ebullient again, sweeping off his flat cap in farewell.

10

7 a.m., and Blaylock was wet-shaving with one ear cocked to the review of news and papers on the radio. Distractedly he nicked himself, saw blood through the foam and was about the staunching when he heard Andy's light rap on the bathroom door.

'Ms Hassall has to be getting on her way, sir.'

Andy grinned as Blaylock passed him heading down the stairs. The illicit air of the situation seemed to amuse him still.

She was waiting by the drawn blinds of the living room window, tapping on a small tablet-and-keyboard contraption, wearing a short zip-festooned jacket of soft black leather over a belted dress. She looked up and smiled slightly to see him, bare-chested with a bloodied old towel round his neck, in the style of a nearly finished fighter.

'It's a big old property you've got on your hands here. Just a bit of loving care could do wonders.'

He looked about him and saw the décor anew: if clean and tidy, the place was spartan and tired, its appearance minded by hired hands in his absence. He had missed another weekend's window to rescue his autumn garden from dereliction.

'There's never the time, it was bought as a family home. "Bought for happy people, therefore standing empty", like the poet said.'

He failed to resist a glance to the mantelpiece and the picture of his children, a copy of which he kept on his desk at Shovell Street. She followed his gaze – maybe a little ruefully, he thought.

'You'll be seeing your family later today?'

He nodded, not wishing to elaborate on the prospect of Jennie's new partner, the novelty of the camping trip, his unease over it all.

They embraced, and it felt to him a lovers' embrace, but equally that both of them were quite ready to get on with their respective days.

'Off I go,' she laughed lightly. 'The thief in the night.'

He led her down the step into the chilly and gloomy garage, disreputably disordered with its odour of cold concrete, exhaust fumes and unwiped tools. He lifted the garage door on a view that was a *sfumato* of drizzle and fog.

'I didn't get to see much of Teesside, then. Shame.'

'Next time, eh?'

He couldn't see her green eyes through the gloom but the whiteness of her smile was strangely clear and she pressed her scented lips to his. Then she was into the driver's seat, revving up, off and away.

On the train from Darlington Blaylock inspected the morning's red-tops. What jarred him on a look inside the *People* was a splashy piece dedicated to exposing the apparent folly of Diane Cleeve's 'bizarre quest for mercy for her daughter's killer'. The better part of a page explored her apparent 'close relations' with a 'self-styled pastor' who had previous convictions for armed robbery and GBH. The tone could hardly have been more pitying and dismissive.

Disturbed, Blaylock stepped out to the juddering vestibule of the carriage and got on the phone to Mark Tallis.

'Mark, I'm a little curious to see the papers going after Diane Cleeve. Any idea how that's happened?'

A sigh came down the line. '*Well, full disclosure, I might have had a word there*, patrón . . .'

The train lurched with speed and Blaylock had to steady himself momentarily. 'You know, had you raised this with me, Mark, I'm not sure I would have approved.'

'I know, I know, I'm sorry, David, but I felt I had to make some enquiries. There was a sanctimony in that room that I just wasn't having. And what I found out . . . well, it's not made up. You're a good man and I won't sit back and see you get grief for no good reason.'

Blaylock knew he could not upbraid his spad for such praetorian zeal. Mark was a born crisis manager – always prepared for the worst, ever watchful for tides in the affairs of men that might carry certain unfortunates out to sea unless defences were packed and stacked high. He let the matter drop.

He was waiting outside the Islington house when he received a text from Jennie: *Running a shade late but on way, 5mins? Pls wait. Jx*

The black Cherokee duly swept up to the gates. As he ambled toward them in greeting, Blaylock found it somehow stunning to see Jennie in jeans again, indeed to see the whole clan so jumbled and besmirched and yet cheerful – even Alex cheerfully ruddy-faced and dishevelled. He had not seen this coming. That they should have enjoyed themselves so was unfathomable to him.

'How was that?' he asked Molly as she jumped from the back-seat.

'Great!' she said, veritably breezing past him.

Behind them, quietly amused, came his surrogate. Gilchrist was a big unit in the flesh, clad in a good outdoorsman's shirt and jeans, his mane of thick silvery hair agreeably unkempt, his gold-rimmed spectacles clearly not those of a bookworm. He looked worryingly capable, not easily intimidated. They shook hands.

Blaylock felt a strong, chastened need to pitch in with the hard labour, however belatedly. He offered to help shift indoors some gear, tents and holdalls and boxes of provisions. Upstairs, water was already thundering steamily into the claw-foot tub. It was wash-up time for the children. He had rarely felt so spare as he lumped Alex's gear along the landing to the threshold of his bedroom wherein, predictably, the boy had already fired up his laptop and now peered at the screen.

Blaylock leaned against the door jamb. 'Hey, so did you see your dad get pranked in front of the cameras this week?'

'Aw, yeah . . . Uh, sorry that happened, Dad. Embarrassing for you, I bet. Mum said it shouldn't have happened.'

'I thought it might have amused you . . . The mob who did it, they're called The Correctors?'

'Yeah. I've heard of them.'

'What's it all about? The politics of it?'

'I don't know. I think that's sort of the point? It's just a banner people sort of gather under. To protest with a bit of, y'know – humour.'

'Against the likes of me. I admit, I didn't find it quite so funny.'

'Yeah, well, like I say. I thought it was out of order.'

Blaylock thought for a moment, then thought better. 'Okay. Cheers for that, son.'

He came down the stairs and, seeing Gilchrist stood waiting formidably by the newel, prepared a tight smile.

'David, I'm just going to brew up before I shoot off – can I make you a brew?'

And so he followed Gilchrist down to the basement, welcomed at last into the forbidden kitchen, and watched Gilchrist's broad-shirted back as he busied with kettle and cups.

'Yorkshire Tea okay?'

'Sure. Glad to have it. Jennie used to say it was too strong for her.'

Gilchrist turned and looked about, momentarily baffled. Then his eyes brightened and he stooped and opened the dishwasher, whereupon he retrieved the ceramic teapot he had clearly sought.

'I find it so hard to work without order,' he murmured, in the manner of a man clearly content to think aloud in company. 'Then you realise, there's so much we can't control . . . you might as well go for it.'

'Yeah. I've never lost the unfortunate tendency to run my house like a barracks.'

Gilchrist spun round again, properly thoughtful this time, or so it seemed to Blaylock. 'Am I right you soldiered in Belfast?'

'Just one tour. Not the height of things. But a pretty torrid year for ambushes, as I remember.'

'I cut my teeth in documentary over there, while it was still in a fair bit of turmoil. I've nothing but respect for that job.'

Blaylock chose to glide over what struck him as a strategic courtesy. 'Alex is very into his documentaries.'

Gilchrist poured the tea. 'He is. He has good taste. And a good eye, I'd say.'

'You can offer him some guidance, I expect.'

'Yeah, well, he has his own ideas. Which is good. Having the passion is the main part. I suppose my big thing is to advise him that if you want to do it then there's more important things than lenses and lights and kit? Which is going to people and places themselves. Getting your hands dirty in the stuff of life.'

'Are you working on anything at the moment?'

'I'm, uh, reading, as my agent would say. Looking at fiction possibilities, actually. Just speculatively. But I find when I'm interested in something . . . I don't know what I think. You ever find that?'

'Very often. But when I finally make up my mind I realise it was what I thought all along.'

Gilchrist had been leaning by the kitchen counter while nursing his mug but now he pulled a chair and sat next to Blaylock.

'Listen, David, I want to be direct, that's my way. I appreciate this is a strange situation. I'm a divorced man myself. I've two grown boys of my own . . . I've seen all sides of it. I know what kids mean, however things are between parents. And I just want you to know I respect that.'

[285]

Blaylock nodded, seeking to keep his expression judicious, before he saw from Gilchrist's look past his shoulder that they had company.

'There's tea in the pot, Jen, or shall I brew coffee?'

'Oh, I don't mind . . .' To Blaylock's eye Jennie, clutching herself as she yawned, epitomised the term 'tired but happy'.

'C'mon, what do I always say? Between any two things you always have a preference.'

'Tea's fine. David, the kids are . . . shattered. I mean, I don't know that they're good for any more than flopping in front of the telly.'

Blaylock stood up. 'Look, let me go fetch you in some takeout.'

He waved away her enervated gratitude and trudged back up the staircase and out of doors. Andy climbed out of the Jag and came toward him, quizzical. Blaylock explained the mission. He turned in time to glimpse Jennie and Gilchrist as darkened shapes in the hall past the front door – his kiss on her forehead, their shared embrace.

Blaylock looked away, knowing nonetheless there were things he had to acknowledge and not seek to dodge. Yes, he had begun to picture a path to reconciliation with Jennie, allowed a seed to germinate within him. That hope had suffered a setback and now he would have to hold fire, review the unwelcome turn, practise tolerance. In his heart, though, he knew full well, he was uttering a kind of curse upon their union.

Then Gilchrist bounded out to his Cherokee and they exchanged cheery waves. Blaylock stood watching his rival reverse and rev away down the street.

'Are we heading then, boss?'

He realised Andy was watching him closely – realised he had been gnawing absently at a knuckle – pondering, more deeply, he knew, than he ought, Gilchrist's surely throwaway remark about preferences.

COMMONS SELECT COMMITTEE ON
HOME AFFAIRS

Minutes of Evidence re: The Identity Documents Bill, November 4
Chair: Rt Hon. Gervaise Hawley MP
Witnesses: Professor Malcolm Wringham, representing the
  UK Institute of Computing Technologies; Mr Graham Petrie,
  representing the Home Office Delivery Unit.

GERVAISE HAWLEY MP: . . . *Reviewing your evidence, then,*
  Professor, is it fair of me to characterise your view of the
  Home Secretary's plans as 'sceptical'?
PROF. WRINGHAM: *Oh, in the end I'd only say, why do*
  this unless you absolutely need to, unless you're sure the
  benefits outweigh the costs? It seems to me there are several
  hundred things that could go very seriously wrong and I'm
  not convinced the Home Office has imagined even half of
  them. But, just for starters, on the technology – if you want
  one database that has to function twenty-four-seven then
  your software contractor has got you by the short hairs. And
  meanwhile you've made a huge target for the hackers to hit –
MR PETRIE: *May I interrupt the Professor, can we be clear? It's*
  not 'one database', the ID card is just a passkey to a variety of
  government databases. And what we pledge is that the issuing
  of cards to individuals will be done according to the highest
  standard of security checks. After that it's pure biometrics –
  your card has your iris code and fingerprints, and no one else
  can use that card without triggering a massive alarm.
PROF. WRINGHAM: *Forgive me, but if you think the global*
  crime cartels won't be working from day one to subvert the
  biometrics – fake contact lenses, fingertips, all sorts – then you
  must have been born last night. On card issuing I agree, the
  highest standards of enrolment and processing will be crucial

to the security of the system. You need top-drawer staff. Has the Home Office got such people? I doubt it.

GERVAISE HAWLEY MP: So, it's as much the Home Office as the ID cards themselves that warrant your, forgive me, scepticism?

PROF. WRINGHAM: To be fair, most government departments rarely know what they're getting on big procurements – they don't understand software, they fall for the hype, so they just nod dumbly and hope. Some are okay, but the Home Office? No. That's before we get to the crucial issue of how the cards are to be checked, the card readers, what they cost, who gets to have a reader and gets to access this Identity Register—

MR PETRIE: Professor, you're just loosing off shots now—

PROF. WRINGHAM: Well, because you've set up this huge target . . . I mean, I have asked myself, genuinely, what are these cards really for? Improving public services? Fighting terrorism? The bill is about all these issues, but I can't see why the card is actually a solution to any one problem. It feels closer to a sort of sinister idea of a perfect system . . . and mankind does not tend to perfection.

GERVAISE HAWLEY MP: I'm sure the Home Secretary would recoil from your describing his idea as 'sinister' when he has always sought to characterise these cards as working hard for the public good.

PROF. WRINGHAM: I'm afraid it's possible there are any number of things the Home Secretary might say are for the good that could tend, in fact, to disaster. I don't automatically accept that the Home Secretary's motives are honourable. Who knows?

MR PETRIE: Sorry, I think that's an out-of-order remark.

GERVAISE HAWLEY MP: Mr Blaylock will get his say here in due course.

PROF. WRINGHAM: Well, to return to the question, ID cards

are not the worst idea in the world, but it would be worth as long as it took to get the specification right. It's certainly not right yet, in my opinion.

MR PETRIE: And meanwhile we just let our problems rumble on, leave our underperforming systems in place . . . Is that your idea?

GERVAISE HAWLEY MP: Do you have an answer to that, Professor?

PROF. WRINGHAM: Well, I'm all for passports. People understand them, and passports have chips and biometrics in them, right? So why not make the holding of a passport compulsory? I mean, we know – this is the unpleasantly coercive thing – we know there's this date when ID cards are meant to become compulsory, so UK residents of a certain age who go for a new passport will have to get an ID card, and go on the register, and pay the fee or else pay a fine. I don't think the British public will take to that kindly and I wouldn't be surprised . . . well, frankly I would just advise the general public to get out and renew their passports now. I mean, tomorrow.

PART V

1

Pacing out of Kennington Park Blaylock was gladdened by the thump of his heart behind his ribs like a good and faithful engine. Andy, his double in black, ran abreast but not ahead, a companion, not a rival, and together they bombed along the usual stretch.

As Georgian white stucco came into view Blaylock eased down, but today he couldn't be bothered with his usual paddle through the papers at Dev's Corner News. The headlines spelt trouble, as ever, but he had been through it all with Mark Tallis past 10 p.m. the night before, during which he had, little by little, suppressed the urge he felt to summon Professor Malcolm Wringham and slap him all around Shovell Street. In a short while, instead, he would go on the *Today* programme with his paws up.

Now he unhooked his iPod, checked his watch, watched his breath condense and glanced around and about. The run had begun in dark but now at 7.30, despite the cold, there was some stunning fire in the sky, an orange-pink efflorescence bronzing all the stucco facades. He rubbed at his calf tendons, absently observing Andy's more rigorous warm-down, until he realised his bodyguard was looking intently at him.

'This lark you've got planned for the weekend, in North Yorkshire? With the Asian lads from Stapletree?'

'Sadaqat's group. Yeah?'

'I've talked to the police team, they've been and had a look. This cave you'll be heading into? It's not for novices, boss. Seventy foot down a black hole. You ever done this spelunking thing before?'

'Once or twice. In college.'

'Right. Back when you were a promising heavyweight?'

Blaylock waved a hand as if to say Andy could scoff all he liked.

'Well,' Andy sighed, 'I'd a go at that malarkey myself maybe seven or eight years back. I expect it'll all come back to me once I'm suited up.'

'Nah, you're not coming down the cave with me, Andy.'

'Boss, I'm gonna have to—'

'No, no. Just me and them. That was the invitation. It's the whole point of the exercise, Andy. That I don't show up with the heavy mob.'

'With respect, boss—'

'It's not negotiable. Now let's be getting back, eh?'

They began the jog home, still side by side, if now at odds. Blaylock knew Andy's wariness was eminently sensible and, as such, he found it intolerable. What he was doing, he had long since resolved, was something only he could do, *ergo* he had to do it alone. If it was an eccentric endeavour, he had nonetheless formed such a good impression of Sadaqat Osman – of the young man's initiative, uprightness and pragmatism – that he was resolved to honour his word. He had phoned Sadaqat personally to confirm his participation, feeling just a mite apprehensive on account of some of the headlines he had garnered lately. But Sadaqat had sounded blithe, indeed contrite, as he explained that his travelling party would be smaller than he had hoped.

'Yeah, it'll just be myself and Javed, and Nasser Jakhrani and Mo Abidi who you met at the Centre?'

'I thought the plan was to get a load of young guys into out-ward-bounding . . . ?'

Sadaqat chuckled softly. 'Between our dreams and what is real, Mr Blaylock . . . Subs just weren't so high this time, what can I say?'

Blaylock was undeterred. If he was not making the legion of new young associates he had hoped for, he had found at least a decent platoon.

An hour later, suited up for the day's labours, Blaylock leaned back in his ergonomic chair, swivelled to give himself a sober panorama of grey London through the window of the study, and readied to take incoming fire from *Today*. Laura Hampshire's preamble came down the line with chilly clarity, unsullied by any audible shuffle of crib-sheets.

'*Now, a fortnight ago CIA drone operators launched a night-time missile strike on a private residence in Babur Ghar near the Afghan–Pakistani border, their target the Taliban commander Gul Sayid, who was killed. What has since been confirmed is that at least seven other people died in the drone attack, among them three women, and a British citizen, Haseeb Muthana, who had recently absconded from risk certificate restrictions. We're joined on the line by the Home Secretary, David Blaylock. Mr Blaylock, were you aware in advance that this drone strike would happen and that Haseeb Muthana's life would be in danger?*'

'First, Laura, let me be clear, I know that great care is taken over attacks launched by unmanned planes, great precautions are taken, but still, it is sadly the case that people are killed accidentally – it is rare, but it happens, it happened here, and it's taken very seriously.'

'*Did you know Haseeb Muthana was at this address in Babur Ghar?*'

'I did not. I wish I had known his whereabouts, he was as you say under risk certificate, we had reason to suspect he was seeking to recruit for and orchestrate a terror attack on British soil . . .'

What Blaylock heard issuing easily enough from his mouth was, he felt, more or less the appropriate political veil to be pulled across what he actually believed. Examining his conscience, he felt no armour-piercing remorse, just as there had been nothing vindictive in his head at the time. He felt some pity for what Muthana's life had amounted to – the terrible waste, the violent

wrong-headedness of it. But soon enough he felt sterner sentiments rise and settle on him like the cap of the hanging judge.
Thus didst thou. Thus are thy deeds repaid.

'*While we have you, Home Secretary, perhaps a word on the
current chaos in the passport system . . . ?*'

Mentally Blaylock closed one heavy set of accounts, hefted up
another, and girded himself anew for the task of being clear.

'The surge in passport applications and renewals this past month
has been just . . . flabbergasting.' Eric Manning shook his head
and offered his sorriest wince round the table. 'About a hundred
thousand over the average for the time of year?'

'Panic buying,' muttered Mark Tallis.

'Right,' Eric nodded. 'But just you try to stop a stampede.'

'Have we not got any kind of legal case against this Professor
Wringham? You know, for shouting "Fire!" in a crowded room?'

Tallis was flailing, Blaylock knew. Personally he was bothered
more by an aura of illicit smugness from his familiar adversaries in
the weekly meeting. He rapped the table. 'As usual, the real problem is not the apparent problem – it's not the Professor's helpful
contribution. The real problem is, yes, stuff happens to screw up
our plans, so have we got the right contingency measures in place?'
Blaylock raked the table with his gaze. 'So, have we?'

Eric pushed up his spectacles and consulted his notes. 'We've
instigated mass overtime, cancelled all existing leave. We're re-
deploying a fair number of experienced officers off the kiosks at
the airports and putting them onto application checks – temps can
stand in at the airports. Plus we've hired another three hundred
temps just to do processing, and by Monday I think we'll even
have desks for them.'

Blaylock had noticed Phyllida Cox sitting utterly upright and
wearing her most critical mien. Now she passed comment. 'Do we
think it very likely that agency staff will be competent to assess

whole box-loads of passport applications with the necessary rig-our?'

'If they err on the side of caution we'll be fine,' said Eric. 'The risk is that we'll go at snail's pace. But if they just stamp and move on—'

'Then the risk is greater.' Phyllida's nod was brisk, her brow dark. 'And the staff on extra hours, with their holidays cancelled . . . how is morale, do you know?'

'Well,' – Eric whistled through his teeth – 'you might say sui-cidal.'

Blaylock leaned forward sharply. 'Eric, unless people are throw-ing themselves off buildings let's not use that expression, eh? It's cheapening. Yes, we've had an unwelcome surprise but, come on – Christmas is round the corner. Right now we need everyone to hold the fort and do their job.'

Round the table there were a few nodding heads but more pursed lips. *'Bastard', right?* Blaylock thought. *That's what you all reckon to me. Well, who the cap fits must wear it.*

A last piece of business nagged at him with the customary sense of chaos being held at bay by way of fingers in dykes: Roger Quarmby's Immigration Services Report, stuck for some weeks in the long grass.

'We need the Quarmby report out there. It's time to admit what needs admitting. Is the work on it nearly done?'

Some reticence in the room told him that, quite possibly, said 'work' had been awaiting his further instruction. Eric spoke up. 'We have been awaiting your guidance on that, through Mark. Obviously we all agree it should be released before Christmas.'

'I've been waiting on a suitable bad-news day,' offered Mark.

'Take the next one,' said Blaylock, wincing, keen to wrap up.

Afterward he conferred with the spads, weighing up the evidence that had been heard already by the Identity Documents Bill Committee. His own performance, scheduled for eight days' time, would have to be of the highest calibre.

'Come on, Ben,' Blaylock chided. 'You got us into this mess, tell me how we're going to win the day.'

Ben looked bothered. 'Let's leave aside what you feel about Wringham. His whole case that ID cards just need more thought – that's actually the lowest bar to clear. Because *you* believe, right, we can't waste one more day, that the risks of not acting are too big?'

'Yes. *We* believe that, right?'

Still Ben didn't smile. 'In my view the stronger objection is still the one Madolyn Redpath made in her evidence – people are just not happy about the state handling so much of their personal data.'

'Not bothered,' Blaylock sniffed. 'We point to other countries. We point to the whole way everybody lives their life online these days.'

'Well, then maybe your biggest problem is Bannerman having come out to say he doesn't believe ID cards will reduce crime.'

'That was vindictive of him. But plenty other cops agree with me.'

'Most of the public aren't aware that you and Bannerman don't get along. They just hear the top cop in the land saying there's new toys on offer to him and he doesn't want them.'

Blaylock was pulled from dark thoughts by Geraldine flagging an urgent call – unusually, from his electoral agent Bob Cropper.

'*David, we've just had word that the F-bloody-B-B have called a big march in Thornfield. Guess what date? The same bloody Saturday you're meant to host the citizenship ceremony in the Town Hall.*'

'So ten days from now?' Frowning, Blaylock waved the spads from the room.

'*Saturday week, aye.*'

'Lovely timing.'

'I'll send all the nonsense through to you but what they're basically saying is it'll be "a peaceful demonstration in the name of British values".'

'Yeah, I heard that on *Jackanory*. I'll need to meet the Chief Constable on the weekend.' Blaylock tapped his pen on the desk, irked that Duncan Scarth had been just as bullish as his word. He was brooding still when Geraldine knocked and entered, demure in a blue floral dress, spotless as a china plate in her father's vicarage. She handed him a windowed envelope.

'You'd better take your theatre tickets for this evening.'

'Right. *Coriolanus*. I don't know it, do you? Any good?'

'It's never been one of my favourites.'

'Oh, afterward, and overnight? I will be at Miss Hassall's.'

Geraldine nodded, smiled tightly, and left him to it.

'Miss Hassall' had been the official parlance since the start of his and Abigail's relations, in which time he had spent several nights at her mews flat in Holland Park. It still sounded absurdly decorous to his ears, yet Geraldine seemed disinclined to lighten it. He sensed, sadly, that she did not approve of his choice of partner – that for the first time he had properly disappointed her – and he was disconcerted. Mark Tallis, alone among his spads in being taken into confidence, had sounded unenthused, too.

Andy Grieve, by contrast, had given Abigail another cheery thumbs-up after an hour spent security-proofing the mews flat. On those evenings when Martin had dropped him nearby and he strode forth toward the light in her window, Andy vigilant at his back, Blaylock had rather liked the idea that his girlfriend was some covert affair of state. If in daytime he found it no big chore to resist the distraction of thinking about her, by night the rigmarole of being smuggled into her bedchamber brought a definite frisson.

The question that ran rings round his head, though, was that of when he would tell Jennie of his changed circumstances. He had worried that the news might sound tacky – a calculated reprisal, born of hurt feelings. Worse, in worrying so he had to ask himself why he dwelled on such rather juvenile concerns. True, Nick Gilchrist's growing presence in Blaylock's former household had begun to loan it the alarming look of a functional family, and Blaylock felt that as a blow. Still, by any reckoning it seemed unfair that he could not, in turn, permit himself to form one half of a presentable couple.

Thus he had decided he should call Jennie and come clean; then, to his dismay, he had decided he shouldn't. The urge had simply drained away and left him to wonder whether a veil of secrecy was something he now felt obliged to throw up around as much of his life as it could cover. As a man who liked to believe he valued outward-facing candour, Blaylock's own reticence bothered him.

At bottom, he knew, he hated to imagine Jennie mirroring Geraldine in disapproval of Abigail – that she would consider the courting of a glamorous blonde journalist crass and predictable, a standard politician's after-hours lunge. And what pained him just as much was the implied disrespect – his own – for the woman he was actually sleeping with. Abigail was a prize, by any standard. Wasn't she more than that? Oughtn't she to be?

Thus did his thoughts turn in their gyre. He was disturbed by a commotion at his doorway and looked up to see Mark and Ben, both breathless.

'David, some bloody bomb's gone off at a mosque in Dudley.'

As Blaylock rose from seated Mark was already switching on the BBC News channel.

'What do we know?'

Ben gestured hopelessly to the screen.

' . . . *what is already being described on the scene as a suspected terror incident, a huge blast felt half a mile away, from an incendiary device we think planted in a car, we've seen police helicopters over Wellesley Street where the mosque is located and which is now cordoned, debris has been thrown wide and I myself have spotted nails strewn across a pretty wide area . . .'*

'*Catherine, has anyone been hurt?*'

'*Ambulances have attended, James, and what I'm hearing is that a father and his two daughters have been taken to hospital having suffered injuries . . .*'

Blaylock swallowed, and felt a shiver wrack through him.

For the car ride up to Dudley Blaylock was joined by Paul Payne, Ben Cotesworth and Becky Maynard, though Becky's eyes stayed fixed throughout on the refreshing screen of her phone. Reports from the scene had levelled out, at least, in their sense of panic. The situation, though lamentable, was under control – no one had died, shrapnel injuries were few, the blast zone and surrounding streets had been evacuated, fears of further explosions had receded and forensic examination had begun.

Nodding at each improved assessment, Blaylock remained subdued, badly wanting good news on the situation of the children reported injured.

'*Gaffer, I think you should get up there.*' More than simple duty, Blaylock had thought he heard some element of reproof in Ben's advice, something he might not have accepted from another party. Ben now sat with a ring-bound pad on his knee, scribbling the outline of a statement for his gaffer. Digesting the outrage, weighing some of his past statements and positions, and how these might have been perceived – in all, Blaylock wanted Ben to find the words for him today.

Paul Payne's presence was a gesture Blaylock had known he would make within moments of deciding to go, and yet he knew Payne was someone he could bring himself neither to like nor to trust, a feeling he took to be mutual if unvoiced, and unlikely to be relieved until one or other of them sought alternative employment.

As they edged toward Wellesley Street, a drab residential area, the foreboding marks of police presence were everywhere, plastic barriers and tape strung across roads, human traffic being managed, officers still doing a job of 'Get back, stay back!' In the course of some hours, though, shock and alarm looked to have turned largely into curiosity and unrest. Most onlookers stood pensively, arms folded, starved of news.

Blaylock's group parked and approached police lines, past which the locus of concern was clear: a foursquare redbrick building topped by rotund grey minarets against a grey sky. By the mosque's iron gates forensics officers in all-over whites huddled near to the torn and blackened back-end of a saloon car. Windows down the street were boarded up, an acrid smell hung in the air. Glancing upward Blaylock noticed – was gladdened – by a CCTV camera set high on a lamppost pasted with a sign declaring ALCO-HOL-FREE ZONE.

A constable took charge of them – 'Sir, the mosque has just had the all-clear by Counter-Terror, we can debrief in there.' Blaylock followed where he was led, removed his shoes and placed them in the orderly row, padded across an emerald-green shag carpet and was introduced to Assistant Chief Constable Gavin Ball.

'Without doubt the intent was to cause serious harm to the patrons of the mosque. The blessing is that the bomber seems to have gone by an outdated calendar – he didn't clock that mid-morning prayers were an hour earlier as of last week. The other good news is, I expect we'll have good CCTV.'

Blaylock nodded. 'I thought so.'

'But, we're treating it as a terrorist incident, no question.'

'Tell me about the little girls who got hurt.'

'A man and his daughters, the only people on the street, about a hundred yards from the blast? The fact none of them were very tall was a big help, but . . . one of the little girls got a nail lodged in her head.'

'Aw god,' Blaylock winced.

'God willing it'll come out clean and, well . . . we'll see.'

They agreed to speak to the media jointly, then Blaylock let himself be led and introduced to one of the mosque's trustees and its imam, solemn in *kurta* and *topi* and flanked by a translator, plus a younger Asian man in jeans and windcheater who looked at Blaylock – or so he felt it – distinctly critically.

'Thank you for coming,' said the trustee.

'I wanted to show my support, on behalf of the government, and let you know we abhor this outrage, and we'll find the perpetrator.'

'We are lucky, so lucky,' sighed the trustee. 'So many people we have here usually, two hundred maybe? If the hour had been different . . .'

The imam, nodding, unleashed a stream of words from which Blaylock made out '*Al-ḥamdu lillāh.*'

'May Almighty Allah protect us,' offered the translator.

The trustee introduced the younger man as 'Haroon, from our association of shopkeepers on the street, he saw it all.'

Haroon shrugged off the introduction. 'I heard a bang, felt the heat, but all I saw was my windows going in.'

'The police got here quickly?'

'Could have been quicker. How serious they take it, I dunno . . .'

Blaylock was oddly relieved to find Gavin Ball was at his side. 'The light's going outside, we should do this.'

In the street Blaylock checked his script discreetly, memorised what he had to, and took his turn before the assembled media.

'This was a mindless and vicious act . . . Mercifully, injuries are fewer than they might have been, but our prayers are with those who were hurt . . . We will not allow thugs and terrorists to hide among us and inflict these cowardly acts upon innocents . . . I urge all mosques to be vigilant, and to contact the police with any suspicion. Those who seek to inflict terror on peaceful communities in this country are despicable criminals, and they will be caught, they will be prosecuted, they will be defeated.'

As he delivered the words to shoulder-mounted cameras, flashing lens and thrusting recorders, Blaylock did wonder whom he was truly addressing, or who, indeed, was listening. The 'community', the desired audience, were behind him, behind cordons. Before him he mainly saw Paul Payne, his lip slightly curled, and Ben, contemplating his shoes.

Afterward Blaylock moved directly to the Jaguar, feeling that no connection had been made – that he had blown in and now was blowing out. Police were clearing the street for Martin to reverse, and Blaylock observed a big pasty-faced bloke with a boy hugging his side as he remonstrated immovably with police blocking his path.

'Sir, I'm afraid I can't say exactly when but some streets may have to stay shut, you can get a tea over there—'

'We don't *need* tea, we need to get *home*.'

Blaylock couldn't stop himself from pacing round the vehicle to where the disputants stood. 'Sir, what you need to do is to listen to the police? And do what you need to do to keep your kids safe.'

He regretted it even as he said it, yet the bloke gaped at him long enough for Ben to take Blaylock's arm and urge him back to the car.

Blaylock was sitting restless and dissatisfied, the Jaguar hardly back on the M1, when he took a call from Geraldine in which she referred bewilderingly to 'disturbances in central London'. *Hell's teeth*, he thought as she patched him through to Sir James Bannerman.

'*First off, you needn't panic, David, it's nothing we can't handle. However, it's needed a range of deployments. We've mustered some armed officers and dogs and there are kettling manoeuvres going on in the shopping streets.*'

'Sorry, what the blue blazes is going on?'

'*What we seem to have on our hands is a co-ordinated action in the centre of town, on quite a scale – maybe ten thousand bodies or so, mainly students, young crowd, that's the profile.*'

'No warning? Unannounced?'

'*Correct. It's clear there was some kind of plan enacted, so around two this afternoon students just walked off campuses around London and began heading to the centre on foot, a few cohorts of sixth-formers bunking off, too. A lot converged on St James's Park but then they fanned out in umpteen directions, some to Oxford Street, some to Westminster. We moved directly to get some lines established round Parliament, but it's the shopping precincts where we've had trouble – shop windows smashed, attacks on CCTVs, a bit of bother in an Audi showroom. Our lines are holding, but a few likely lads have had a go at pushing through.*'

'Has it got any kind of leadership to it?'

'*There's an anarchist element, I'd say, a few balaclavas. But it doesn't look like it has any centre. More as if it started from a shout in the street.*'

'How's it looking round Parliament?'

'*Peaceable. Odd sort of atmosphere, like a carnival. Banners and chants. It's all being broadcast simultaneously online, that outfit calling themselves The Correctors are claiming credit.*'

Blaylock felt a twinge of disquiet. 'Any criminal damage?'

'*Other than that someone's had a go at Tory HQ, I'm afraid, a bit of spray-paint damage, graffiti . . .*'

'What did they spray?'

'*Well, "Lying Tory Scum" was the phrase, I believe . . .*'

As they headed down the darkening motorway, zipping under concrete flyovers, Blaylock slumped into the gloom of the backseat and tapped out a text to Jennie: *Hi J, do you know is Alex at home? D*

2

Nearing London on the A4, for all that Martin sucked his teeth and exhaled displeasure, Blaylock insisted that they press on toward the centre of town rather than to Westminster.

London had always seemed to Blaylock a tough place to sow disorder, so well did it organise its chaos; but in the thick of the commuter hours it was eerily clear to him that pandemonium had indeed occurred and left marks. Past Grosvenor Square and marooned in traffic, Blaylock found himself, perforce, staring through his window at PAY YOUR TAX! sprayed across a smoked-glass storefront; a shattered window three doors down; and a banner strung high across the office of Citibank, proclaiming WE THE PEOPLE ARE EVERYWHERE. At length, feeling intolerably caged, Blaylock decided he had stared long enough.

'Martin? Pull over. Andy, howay, we're walking.'

'Aw boss . . .'

Blaylock got out on Brook Street into a November dark that felt uncommonly heady. As Andy moved swiftly to his side, Blaylock saw, twenty feet ahead of him, a metal canister arcing and falling to the pavement then skittering across the concrete.

Even as Andy seized his arm, Blaylock for one instant felt the world's motion slow to a crawl before his eyes. Then the canister disgorged a great jetting plume of red smoke, fast-blooming clouds of which began to billow into Hanover Square.

The two of them hustled and dodged down Regent Street, against a tide of bodies, amid an air of directionless flurry, proof that misrule had been declared. Glancing down a side street Blaylock saw a gaggle of agile youthful figures hopping over some now abandoned plastic barriers, walking with a swagger as though they might roam as they pleased, chanting, *'We! The People! Everywhere! Now!'* He could tell from their vigour – this, too, was 'politics', of a sort, nothing he had known personally and yet at close quarters its appeal seemed clear.

By the time he and Andy paced down Whitehall Blaylock could hear vuvuzelas, thumping drums, the bass signature of sound-system reggae – the curious carnival feel over which Bannerman had puzzled. Then Parliament Square opened up to his view, densely crowded with vociferous youths in jackets and jeans, some holding placards aloft, floodlit by the face of Big Ben. Stopping at a safe remove behind police lines Blaylock clocked the parked paddy wagons and the perimeters of yellow-jacketed cops, their preoccupied stares sending out from under their visors. But there were no riot shields, no batons – it was, even now, a peaceable demonstration.

A stocky young man, bespectacled and with a bobbing ponytail, paced back and forth in a narrow strip five yards before one cordon of officers, speechifying confidently through a loudhailer.

'. . .'cos what this government wants is to turn us all into little Americans, yeah? Load us all up with mountains of debt before we're even voting age, man! So we spend our whole lives like indentured slaves in their dirty fucking neoliberal system!'

Finishing with this roundly cheered flourish, the speaker fell to leading a chant, rousingly adopted. *'We! The People! Everywhere! Now!'*

A police constable stepped forward, with a loudhailer of his own. *'Okay, you've been warned, so understand, you have five more minutes to leave the square in an orderly fashion, otherwise you will be liable to arrest . . .'*

This was met by raucous jeers and boos. Nonetheless Blaylock noticed a few individuals drifting off, perhaps having made an early withdrawal to the periphery for just that purpose.

And then his eye was grabbed by one young retreating couple who turned back briefly, raising their clasped hands together in defiance. Both wore white masks, but what sang out to him was the long lick of reddened hair drooping down the left of the girl's mask, and the sculpted crown of jet-black atop the boy's. Blaylock knew as sure as the back of his hand that he was looking at his son – and the boy's lately acquired, slightly older love interest.

He started to press forward, only to feel Andy's cautionary grip.

'Boss, please, you've gotta keep clear of this.'

Blaylock, frustrated, knew Andy was right – for the police cordon now began to advance upon the remaining demonstrators in shuffling formation from all four sides, a slow and steady pressure. The demonstrators stuck doggedly to their own formation of linked arms, but the kettle was soon closing and pressing, forcing the decision to stand or retreat.

Hoarse cries drew Blaylock's eyes to a full-blown altercation, two officers engaged in push, pull and shove with one demonstrator – bearded, muscular but outmanned – whose comrades jostled in for support as if they might free him from his inevitable arrest. His long hair lashed the air as he struggled.

'Everybody mind yourselves, people!' Blaylock heard a youthful shout. *'The cops are wearing cameras! Just remember your rights!'*

But in the next instant the long-haired demonstrator was on the ground – Blaylock winced to hear the clash of head against pavement – then officers were dragging protesters aside while phones were held aloft in witness. Blaylock watched a tearful copper-headed girl remonstrating with the officers who crowded round the fallen man.

'Shame on you! Shame on you!'

The strangest image had formed in Blaylock's head – a deposition scene, a battered Christ, the solemn hoods of John and Nicodemus, a grievous redhead Magdalene. Again he felt Andy's urging grip, and at length he turned away and headed for sanctuary through the carriage gates of New Palace Yard.

'I'm sorry I missed your text . . .'

To Blaylock's impatient eye Jennie appeared fully briefed, as ever – unfazed by this surprise appearance, but clearly fatigued by another day's work and disinclined to offer him a chair, much less a drink. He stood in silence in her living room, watching her drape her black silken jacket over a chair before launching into her case for the defence.

'I've talked to Radka and, yes, Alex did go down to Westminster after school finished so, yes, he was at the demo.'

'I know, Jennie. I saw him there. Him and the girl. Esther?'

She pursed her lips at the prosecution's springing of surprise evidence. When she resumed, her tone had acquired measure.

'That's right. Alex told me they met up and went together, and then left together, and he walked Esther home.'

'That's my boy. Where is he now?'

'Upstairs.' She must have detected his urge to go directly, for she added, 'Nick's up there too.'

Blaylock fought the urge to check his watch. Coming here had been risky. He had heard radio rumours of a West End theatre blackout given the day's disturbances, but it seemed his own show was going ahead, and Abby even now would be awaiting him at the National Theatre.

'So do I take it all this is okay with you then?'

'David, I don't see that Alex did anything wrong. He didn't break any law. He attended a peaceful demo.'

'An unauthorised demo, in Parliament Square, where the cops had to kettle the crowd to clear it.'

'What tactics the police stoop to isn't really the issue, is it?'

'C'mon, what are the coppers supposed to do? They had bloody mayhem to contend with round Oxford Street and all.'

'Don't tar everyone with the same brush, David. I knew what Alex was protesting, they all are, it's the cost of education, low pay, public spending cuts—'

'Protesting against my government, yes.'

Jennie shrugged as if to say this was a corollary, be it as it may. 'He feels passionately. On principle. I know you remember what that's like.'

'Look, I don't have a quarrel with his rights or his passions, but I do need to know he understands that actions have consequences. I'm concerned for his welfare, I'm his father, I'm saying he needs to cut this out.'

'David, you can't march into this house and lay down the law like that.'

'My voice is superseded now, is it? Other voices count more?'

Jennie's eyes narrowed. 'It's my house, David. My rules. Since you ask, as a matter of fact, Nick agrees with me. Why you have to bring him into it . . . though I should have known it was coming.'

'That's a cheap shot, isn't it? The point is Alex. I don't dispute you're with who you want to be with. So am I. We're grown-ups, right? The point is Alex.'

He had seen a flicker in her eye, and he held her gaze, but when she spoke she sounded nothing but impatient. 'Obviously the point is Alex. But also, your usual view that you always know best.'

'C'mon, can you not see he needs to pack it in, Jennie? He can engage with politics without ruining his future before he's even got going. You know what'll happen down this road, he'll end up with a criminal record, and for what?'

'Alex is sensible.' Jennie sighed deeply. 'Are you sure it's not your own future you're fretting about, David?'

Blaylock felt the blow as only this woman knew how to land them. 'That's a rotten thing to say, Jennie. How can you say that?'

'Because it's a wicked world, as you've never tired of saying.'

'Well, it is that. And I tell you what, if Alex gets dragged into the spotlight – arrested or whatever? Yeah, the press will love having a big old stick to beat me with, but do you not think I'm fucking well used to that by now? And it'll not hurt me nearly as much as it will him, Jennie. So don't act like you can just turn a blind eye.'

'David, there's no "blind eye" here. *Please* don't try and raise the spectre of neglect, okay? Because there will never, ever be a right time for that, not from you.'

'I want to speak to Alex,' he said firmly.

'I'm here . . .' The voice issued from behind the wall of the arch between front and rear living rooms. Now Alex stepped into sight, still in the dark garb of the demonstration, his features clenched but exuding a clear resolve.

Blaylock recovered himself. 'Son . . . you know what? Smashing windows, graffiti . . . it might get you an easy cheer off of certain types but you need to realise all you're helping is the status quo. You'll not change a damn thing like that – not in a democracy, no chance.'

Alex was shaking his head. 'I didn't smash anything, Dad. I didn't do anything wrong.'

'Why wear a mask, then? What are you afraid of?'

'I'm not afraid of anything.'

You can say it, Blaylock thought instantly. *You're afraid of me.* He shook his head, looked to Jennie, felt the hopelessness, the distance in the silence between them.

Finally, quietly, he said, 'Well, son. This road you're on? Be sure you understand where it's headed. Don't start what you can't finish. Because there are some things, you know . . . a late apology won't cut it.'

Alex stared back at him. 'I hear you,' he said, insouciant.

Blaylock looked again at Jennie – who looked aside – then at his watch, a gesture he regretted in an instant.

[311]

He reached the National in the nick of time, having fired off a text to assure Abby as much, but as he bolted from the car his temples were still pulsing, he thirsted for a strong drink, and wondered scratchily how long he could endure an evening of unfamiliar Shakespeare without medication. Still he pressed on through the Olivier Theatre's doors at 7.29 into a darkening auditorium of murmurs and coughs, and he and Andy performed their merry dance as pre-arranged, Abby rising from the last seat of the back row to let Andy in, then bumping along one such that Blaylock could slump in on the end beside her. He took a moment to survey the crowd – an ageing, well-tended lot, it seemed, an inherited audience propping up a moribund form. But as the stage lights sprang up across the great Olivier stage he felt Abby's cool hand slip into his, and his spirits lifted.

Minutes later he was vexed anew – thirst returning, head newly sore – as the stage was thronged by a thespian approximation of an angry placard-waving mob, their querulous voices damning some hateful politician. Soon enough a smooth-talker was trying to calm them down, but Blaylock sensed what was coming. Presently the object of their opprobrium marched into the fray in a matt-black breastplate, evidently a soldier–statesman, just as vividly a blowhard, beet-red in the face, veins bulging in his neck, hair tossing about his forehead.

Blaylock felt Abby stroke his arm lightly, sensing something meant in the gesture. The play, after all, had been her choice.

Unengaged, unable to recline or relax, Blaylock let his mind slip into work matters, and his attention to the play was fitful. He gleaned, though, that the fortunes of the black-clad Coriolanus constituted the whole of the piece, the drama arising from the degree of the warrior's willingness to address popular grievances and grease his way past politicians more facile than he. The odd bit of fluent verse-speaking pulled Blaylock in – but he groaned as Coriolanus feigned to capture a city single-handed with a great deal of silly choreographed sword-waving.

Still, when the mob reappeared to pontificate on their victorious general's virtues, Blaylock felt the sore temptation to stand up and berate them for a shower of cowards – and chastened himself for the degree that he knew he was being manipulated. Abby, he felt sure, had known all of this was coming. And by now, having steeled himself not to glance her way admiringly too often, he found himself not greatly caring to.

They made their separate ways back to her apartment under cover of dark. He exited the Jaguar lugging his red box, knowing Andy would keep watch outside until around midnight, by which time he expected to be curled around Abigail beneath her cool bed-sheets, his face pressed into the bergamot-scented softness of her hair.

First, though, came what he felt to be a curious mime of domesticity, as he sat on a tall stool in her tiny but immaculate kitchen, perusing papers from the red box and nursing a large glass of white wine that she poured for him before turning to the griddling of scallops and the mixing of a dressing for salad leaves. Mark Tallis had drafted some remarks for him to deliver at the *Criterion* Westminster Awards tomorrow night, and he read them with growing dismay. A forced jocularity was the spirit of the thing, and gags were not Mark's forte.

She asked after his day. He gave her fragments, as no part of it had been anything he cared to revisit. Offering some impressions of the ruckus in Parliament Square he withheld any reference to Alex and the reason for his late arrival to the theatre, telling her instead of the injured youth he had seen being so fiercely defended from the clutches of police by his pious girlfriend.

'It did strike me', he said, after a big gulp of wine that made his eyes water, 'how easy it is for people to get badly hurt at these things. The cops have plenty of barriers on hand, but really they could do with a few more medics.'

He was thinking of Alex, weighing the resentment he felt toward the boy against the natural desire to prevent any harm ever befalling him. Lately, he couldn't deny, he had wanted Alex to suffer some rude awakening, some pointed encounter with the sharp end of reality. Yet to imagine his son in any real distress was a plaintive thing that clutched at his innards.

Abigail wiped a sharp knife clean then wiped her hands on a cloth. 'I hadn't pictured you as so much the bleeding heart.'

He grunted. 'Yeah, well. When people are hurt you have to help them, even if they're the enemy. Especially if they're the enemy. That's how the British Army's made its name the world over.'

'One way it's made its name.' She smiled without giving him the favour of her gaze.

'I'm serious. I saw it umpteen times. Early on in Belfast we got into a gun battle in Andersonstown – spotted a bunch of Provos holed up with guns trained on us, we fired first, went into the building after them and found them bleeding all over the place. And you wouldn't *believe* the pains we took to patch them into shape. We shot 'em up, yeah, but then we shipped 'em out.'

'"Shot 'em up" . . . ?'

She was still immersed in plating for two, yet her manner seemed to him as one whose windbag boss had come over for supper, to be indulged and politely suffered. It took another moment or two for him to feel his disapproval tick up to the familiar register.

'Yes, "shot 'em up". It was their plan to shoot holes in us so I – we, my men and I – we fucking shot them up instead.'

She turned to him, bearing two identical servings on ivory dishes. 'Okay, David. Okay? They're not here now.'

After they had eaten – the work of mere minutes – she sat in an armchair across from him in her smart low-lit living space, the programme from the theatre in her lap, a small smile round her lips that rather maddened him, reminding him as it did of her interviewing mode. He gestured to the full bottle of wine between him, successor to one that he seemed to have polished off by himself.

'Am I going to drink all of that?'

'I don't know, are you?' She leaned and poured a splash into her glass. 'I was quite struck by the play. Were you?'

Blaylock shrugged. 'Mixed bag.'

'How did you rate his political acumen? Coriolanus? Do you suppose a fellow like that could function in Westminster today?'

Blaylock swigged wine and shook his head. 'He wouldn't last five minutes. His own man and all that, but . . . a politician can't be that badly divorced from the mass of the people. Even though the play takes them all for bloody fools.'

'Ah, then you agree with the guy writing in the programme notes.' She read aloud. '"While ostensibly proposing a debate between authoritarianism and the democratic will of the people, Shakespeare contrives to make the case against democracy near irrefutable. He has Coriolanus embody a standard the plebs can't get close to: the great man whose word must be heeded, since he knows for a fact, by bloody experience, what the proles can't possibly imagine from the purview of their meagre little lives. This is a devilish contention, but then in writing *Coriolanus* Shakespeare was of the devil's party, and probably knew it . . . "'

'Who said that?'

'Nick Gilchrist. The filmmaker?'

Blaylock sniffed, feeling his foot tap the carpet as though it were his tail.

'Yeah, I interviewed him once. He lives just a few streets from here, on Elgin Crescent? Quite a fascinating man. Fairly political.'

'You mean "political" as someone who has a bunch of opinions? As opposed to a disposition to try and do politics.'

Abby's eyes narrowed amusedly. 'So you know his work?'

'He's actually my ex-wife's current . . . partner.'

'No! Really?'

'You sure you didn't know that?'

'How would I? It's not general knowledge, is it?' She sat up with a new keenness, so making Blaylock conscious of how he had rather slumped into his chair, wine glass to his chest. 'It's not like you tell me anything, David. Or do you think I've been "research-ing" you?'

'C'mon. You did a bit of research, right? It's your livelihood.'

'I'd have said things have developed a bit between us since. To a point, anyway. No, in terms of your, oh, "private life" – I've just been assuming there are things I'm not to know.'

'I've told you,' he said with a sigh, 'a fair old bit about myself, Abby.'

'Yes. Things you might tell a journalist, if only to put them off.'

'Well,' he gestured, vexed, 'how much do I know about you?'

'David, you could ask me anything. I'm not ashamed. The fact is you've hardly asked me a thing since the first night we met.'

'You've been counting? Look – I've thought we have a pretty good understanding of one another. But maybe not.'

She sat back with a rueful head-shake, supporting her chin in her hand. 'I don't know, David . . . What's going on?'

'What do you mean?'

'What have we got, you and me?'

He met her gaze while casting around inwardly for some rejoin-der. She was right, of course. He had entered this romance with barricades carefully erected around the area nearest to his heart. Now she was only pressing him for the closeness any lover would expect. He remained resistant. And yet now, quite suddenly, he sensed a familiar kind of crumbling-unto-collapse in their rela-tions, and the idea that a dismal day might now conclude in such fashion was abruptly, unutterably depressing to him.

'Listen . . . I'm sorry. Really. The disturbances today, in town? My son Alex was there, I saw him, in the thick of it. I went to see him and Jennie tonight, it's why I was late . . . The whole thing's bloody awkward and it's just . . . preying on my mind.'

'Good lord.' She looked at him closely, clearly computing. Finally she said, 'Was Alex hurt? Or arrested?'

'No, god no. He made a sharp exit at just about the right time. But he's . . . he's drawn to that kind of, y'know, protest politics? And I'm not sure he knows what he's getting into.'

'What does his mother think?'

'Oh, she's big into fighting for rights, Jennie. And she doesn't think Alex should suffer – I mean, be deterred from things – just because I'm his father. The thing is, but, it could be trouble for him.'

'Trouble for you, too.'

'Yeah, that's what his mother reckons and all. But it's not the issue.'

'A factor, though. People love a dysfunctional family in politics. The higher the better. Like Reagan and his kids? This would have those elements. The only thing would top it is if Alex became a ballet dancer . . .'

Blaylock was mildly amazed to note her new animation, how she now took a keen sip of wine, with a rapt look on her face for which he didn't much care.

'Have you thought it through? Worst-case scenarios? Say, if he got nicked swinging off the statue of Churchill?'

'It's not something I want to . . . brainstorm. This isn't my idea of useful speculation. It's not *helping*, Abby.'

'Sorry, I'm just trying to get my head round it. Your problem.'

'Yeah, well, you sound almost curious to see it happen. I mean, Jesus.' He lurched from his chair, realising he had nowhere particular to go in the small space, so finding himself looming over her. 'Jennie doesn't see a problem, it's true, but you, you appear to relish it.'

She closed her eyes and turned her head away as if abruptly tired of seeing him before her. 'Oh David, c'mon. It's like you just want a fight tonight, any old fight, and I'm here so I'll do.'

'I don't want a fucking fight.'

'Sure about that?'

She was correct insofar as he felt little now beyond the twinges of irritation, the tenseness of his brow, the desire to prolong the storm.

'Would you rather I left?'

She rolled her eyes, her shoulders slumped. 'It's your decision, David.'

'Okay. Fine.' He paced to the kitchen, collected his jacket, hefted his red box. She did not move from her chair. He looked at her from across the kitchen island. She looked back at him and said nothing. She was – he had known it from the start – a tough customer.

Outside Andy was clearly surprised to see the boss stomping back across the street, but he made the call to Martin, and Blaylock then endured a chastening drive back across the river to Kennington.

He was aware he was wincing reflexively, muttering to himself, cursing under his breath, putting his hand to his face. He was aware, too, that Andy watched him silently from the corner of one eye, and Blaylock sensed some unacceptable pity there, and so tried to pull himself round, contemplating some light remark to relieve the gloom of the car. But nothing came, nor by effort of will could he seem to stop the physical tics afflicting him.

The squabble he had found himself in was nothing new – indeed it was starting to seem like his fate. What was novel was the loss of face he felt this time round. A line was running round his head – Nietzsche, if he remembered right, some of whose sayings had been hits with his Sandhurst contemporaries, especially the one about near-death experience somehow making one 'stronger' rather than massively debilitated. The one Blaylock had in mind was more slippery. *If a man has character, he has also his typical experience, which recurs.*

'Character' – he associated it with virtue, constancy. But increasingly it seemed to him a cage. *I have a Problem*, he said to himself. *A Problem.* 'When will you do something about your Problem, David?'

He had never cared to talk about it. There had been times when he felt he had more or less psychoanalysed himself, and not unsatisfactorily, either. Yet still his typical experience recurred, and he did nothing else to ward it away. He had to ask himself: was it fear? Faintheartedness, for sure. For when he conjured the thought of 'seeking help' it was accompanied immediately by thoughts of the House – gossip round the House, insinuation in the House. That prospect, he realised, did raise an alarm in him – and to be so conscious of his spinelessness was to realise, too, however belatedly, that he would now do something about it.

The request was put simply and casually to Geraldine, that she secure him an appointment around 11 a.m. at his local surgery, but with a female GP – preferably Dr Quayle, whom he remembered to be reliably detached, even semi-distracted. He told himself it was a decision from which he might still retreat if the day's business turned bad.

In fact the morning brought heartening news from Gavin Ball up in Dudley. The little girl who had suffered the nail in her temple was recovering from a successful surgical removal; meanwhile the manhunt had narrowed to a single individual, his face reconstructed in photo-fit from CCTV. *'We've put it out there and we hope for help from the public.'*

He repaired to one of Level Three's soundproofed 'study pods' and closed the door, resolved to phone Abigail and try to repair the damage. He had the words prepared. His call, however, went straight to voicemail and so he recited into a void. 'Abby, it's David. Last night . . . I want to apologise, I was out of order. I got out of hand. The things on my mind, they are what they are but I . . . obviously should not have lost my temper like that. Please call me when you can.'

After checking into the doctors' surgery he loitered awhile in the vestibule on his phone, returning a call from his constituency office with regard to a local Labour councillor – one Akhtar Chopra, holder of the portfolio for 'community cohesion' – who had been ringing insistently with demands that the FBB's planned march through Thornfield be banned.

'I'm seeing the cops directly when I'm up tomorrow, he can see me directly after that,' Blaylock told Bob Cropper, idly kicking the wall with the toe of his shoe. Through the glass door he heard his name over the tannoy, and hoped that it sounded thoroughly anonymous to the coughers and sniffers huddled in the waiting area.

Dr Quayle was dependably unsmiling, wearing her usual hunted look as he took the hard-backed chair opposite her.

'It's a personal matter, a wellbeing issue . . . For a while now I've been conscious of an issue in terms of controlling my temper. It's been observed, pointed out to me, by people close to me. And it may have had an effect, on my relations . . . it, I don't know, could be colouring my judgements on things.'

'You're saying you're prone to temper tantrums?'

Hating the sound of that, while wanting to make progress, Blaylock nodded. Dr Quayle was visibly relieved.

'It's nothing to be ashamed of. It's a common enough part of life.'

'I wonder if I would benefit, if there's someone I could see, talk to, about ways to manage anger?'

'That would be cognitive behaviour therapy.' Quayle nodded, clearly yet more convinced she could kick this can down the road. 'I can offer you a referral, there are a number of providers.'

He nodded and she turned to her computer and clicked her way into a database – then seemed to think again and, rather fearful, swivelled back to him. 'We're talking regular weekly two-hour sessions, that's something you could commit to?'

'I'd take it seriously, yes, of course.'

She returned to her screen and, biting her lip, hit a key to print.

'The suspect's name is Kristian Vollan,' Gavin Ball updated. *'Norwegian, late twenties, works in a foam rubber factory on an industrial estate outside Birmingham. An employee clocked him from the CCTV we put out, it wasn't the cleanest image but the fellow had had his suspicions, funnily.'*

Blaylock whistled down the line in appreciation. The Dudley investigation was moving with truly gratifying speed.

'He was alone?'

'*We're making enquiries with the Norwegian authorities. But, we have his computer, it's all there, his interests. The pieces. So probably alone, yes, but he's plugged into Norwegian far-right groups plus a bit more of a wider web clan opposed to "the geno-cide of whites" and the "Islamic conquest of Europe".*'

'Dear god.'

'*He seems to be a fan of the Free Briton Brigade? Attended some convention they were at. His Facebook page is full of praise for them.*'

'That ought to widely known, I'd say. Come the time.'

Feeling strangely buoyed he repaired again to a quiet sound-proofed pod, took paper from pocket and, before he could stop himself, tapped out the Hampstead number for Dr Amanda Scott-Stokes, Chartered Clinical Psychologist, BSc, MClinPsych, DPsych.

The voice that answered was owlishly posh, slightly lisping, but business-like. '*Yes, yes. Not next Monday but the Monday after? Good, good.*'

Marking off his accomplishment, feeling himself worthy of merit, he tried Abigail again.

'*Hello, David . . .*'

'You got my message?'

'*I did. Yes . . .*'

'But, you didn't call.'

'*I didn't know what to say to you . . . I still don't, really. But I think there's something we need to talk about. And I'm sorry to have to say it . . .*'

He sat down, as if he had been told to, feeling like a much younger and less assured man.

'What's on your mind?'

'I think ... things have happened and ... I've thought about it and I don't feel things are right between us. For either of us. If it wasn't for the jobs we're in it might be different. But because of that I think maybe we need to ... just say it's a thing that isn't really in the stars ...'

Some moments later, the line dead, Blaylock was still muttering to himself, replaying the tape in his head, formulating a position, as he held the door handle and readied a face with which to face the world. He knew, no question, that he was processing an abrupt reversal of fortune, a rejection he had just not seen coming.

And his chief feeling was humiliation, sticking to him unpleasantly as if tipped out over his head. His warm feelings for Abby – narrow as they had been – had turned in a trice to loathing. For, whatever his efforts at self-persuasion, she had remained a trifle in his eyes, without a jot of Jennie's substance. He should have been the one to decide when the game was done. Instead he had been left feeling done up.

Then a darker thought fell on him, as he recalled Mark Tallis's dim view of her all the way along. Had Abby really been playing him? Could he have been so mistaken? The thought was too terrible, so he pushed it away and pushed out through the door.

Feeling so hollowed, Blaylock was in no mood to plaster on a fake smile and take a bow at a meaningless awards ceremony. And yet he knew the 'Politician of the Year' could not possibly send apologies: there would be no hiding place from the low-level bitchery he would set on himself. And so he made the effort to brush up, get robust, appear unfazed. He told himself it was no crime to take, for one night only, some validation in the praise of Westminster's insular press corps.

Within minutes of stepping inside the venue's plushness – its walnut panels, damask drapes and dripping chandelier – he wanted to be gone. Near enough his first sight was Abigail in the midst of a press table, unimpressive male specimens at either side of her. After the briefest of eye contacts he made sure to look elsewhere.

He was seated by Caroline Tennant, the *Criterion*'s 'Minister of the Year', with whom small talk was, as ever, futile; though she did ask him with an authentic perplexity if he could explain the distinction between their respective awards.

'It means you're considered competent and I'm considered "colourful",' Blaylock replied, topping up their glasses.

Once proceedings were under way, though, there was nothing that could dissolve his dislike of every aspect of the awful spectacle, from the piped music that heralded each speaker to the heavy-handed light-heartedness of every speech: fake esteem, fake conviviality, it seemed to Blaylock, when the sum of petty hatreds and envies in the room, suitably refined, would be enough fuel to fire a rocket into space.

'You're not enjoying it, David,' Caroline murmured after he had absently missed a prompt to applaud.

'How did you guess?'

'Something to do with the way you claw at your face, I suppose.'

He did sit to attention, however, for Madolyn Redpath, winner of 'Campaigner of the Year', in a black dress less schoolgirlish than her usual preference. He hadn't seen her for a while and felt, with some sort of a pang, that he had rather missed her. In these surroundings she did cut a notably unspoilt figure.

Then came his own turn, and after generous applause he hefted his plaque and stood at the dais blinking into the lights.

'I feel a bit unworthy, like perhaps I've been given this just for thumping somebody. And that's not politics, as we know. Though it can be great fun. If you don't believe me, just think for a minute, what it would be like to thump the person you're sitting next to.'

The room, previously so generous, now seemed put off.

'Forgive me. My jokes are often misunderstood. Even by me.

But I won't cry, won't go live in self-pity city. That would go against the image I've so carefully cultivated . . . and for which I expect you've bestowed on me this honour – so, thank you and goodnight.'

Proceedings done, the room began to empty, Caroline saying her cool goodbyes to him before hastening out to her carriage. Clocking Andy at the door, Blaylock poured a last bumper from the full-ish burgundy on the table, and looked up to see Madolyn standing over him, glass in hand, plaque under her arm, further encumbered by a large clutch bag.

'Congratulations.'

'Back at you.' He held out his hand and she shook, smiled and sat down beside him. He was yet more admiring of her dress, a structured number with buttons down the front that fastened across the collarbone. She fixed him with her direct and gleaming gaze.

'I've owed you a call for a while, actually. To say well done on what you did on women's refuges. The stand you took.'

'I was lobbied very hard. As you know, I'm not impervious to a case well made. But, thank you.'

'You know,' she ventured, 'if I gave the impression I thought you were the worst there ever was – I mean, I expect you think I'm awfully sanctimonious – but, so you know, I do believe you're a decent man.'

'That does actually mean a lot to me.'

Looking at her intent eyes he feared he might blush, even if the ruby-redness were largely the work of the burgundy.

'I have something for you,' she said, lifting her bag to her lap.

True, he had thought her highly priggish from the off. Yet he couldn't deny he was pleased she had identified virtue in him. Unease pulled at him, though, as he watched her rummage in the clutch – for one, a discomfiting awareness of how badly he sought to see himself reflected favourably in a woman's eyes; for another, the surety that he would disappoint this woman again soon enough, since the world, through it all, remained wicked.

The candle on the table was burning low, the last stragglers leaving, wearied waiters poised to sweep the tables. Peering past the small flame Blaylock saw Abigail glance his way as she left. For a moment he wondered hopefully if perhaps she was singeing a little.

Madolyn had produced a grey bundle and she put it in his hands. He unfolded a cotton tee-shirt bearing the decal legend FEMINIST, and below that, smaller, GOT A PROBLEM WITH IT?

He smiled. 'Nice. A little snug for me. Maybe I'll frame it?'

'You wouldn't wear it?'

'Oh, I'd feel a bit . . . phoney.'

'You wouldn't call yourself a feminist?'

'Well, I mean – do I have to?'

'If you believe in basic equality for women, then yeah.'

'I do. I just don't want to have to swallow a definition you can fit into fifty characters . . . I mean, I'd rather just be judged on my actions and have it known I'm not a prick about this stuff than have to declare it across my chest. Sorry if that's a let-down.'

She was indeed giving him a sceptical look, albeit slightly smiling. 'Yeah well. If we're doing regrets, I'm sorry I had to mullah you over your fucking ID cards the other week. The fight goes on, right?'

Blaylock rolled his eyes and lifted his glass. 'Take care of yourself, Maddy.'

He watched her sashay away, feeling a little lifted out of the day's gloom, some sense of *amour propre* restored.

4

Though Blaylock's weekend had a challenging look about it, Friday at least offered a sooner than usual escape from the office to the Darlington train. From the comfort of his berth in First Class he studied the morning's papers, their widespread and gratifying coverage of the capture of Kristian Vollan in Dudley.

Leaving Andy to mind their goods he pin-balled his way through the carriage toward the toilets. Beside the door to the vestibule was a man alone at a table of four, reading his evening paper held upright and stretched stiff over what looked to be the remnants of a full English breakfast. But as Blaylock neared, the newspaper came down to reveal the face of Duncan Scarth, a study in self-satisfaction.

'Afternoon, David?'

Blaylock's instinct was to walk on, yet he felt the provocation.

'Mr Scarth. Where are you headed?'

'Home for the weekend. Like yourself, eh? A bit business, a bit pleasure.' He folded his paper and tossed it to the table. 'Yeah, as you'll be aware, we expect to be in your neck of the woods in a week's time. The response on Teesside has been very encouraging.'

'I doubt that very much.'

'Well, I trust you'll respect the rights of ordinary working-class people to meet and express their opinions. You'll not be running off scared as seems to be your wont.'

Andy had come down the aisle, to Blaylock's dismay.

'Yeah, I've no fears where that's concerned. As to your little pub crawl, Cleveland Police will decide if it's viable.'

'What, you'll not have a say? Tsk. Typical politician. Always ducking the issue.'

It was foolish, he knew, to squabble with such a man in such a public space. If he did so with Scarth, why not a thousand more? Glowering, he pushed on through the door, leaving Andy to give Scarth a little more of the evil eye.

From Darlington Blaylock was driven directly to the campus-like headquarters of Cleveland Police, there to discuss the FBB's Thornfield march with the Chief Constable – a lean and unprepossessing man, anxiously furrowed of brow yet given, in Blaylock's experience, to a notable bluffness that might have been calculated to remind folk he was from Leeds, and not just some sort of pencil-pusher.

'I take it the key factor at your side is the citizenship ceremony scheduled that day at the Town Hall, yes?'

'Right. Obviously that goes ahead, we're not stopping that. I'm sure it's not escaped the FBB's notice. The guy in charge of them—'

'Gary Wardell?'

'No, their bankroller, Duncan Scarth? He has implied to me heavily that he wants to cause me bother in my own constituency.'

'You've had – dialogue with him?'

'He keeps following me around. Like the proverbial smell.'

'Well. Look. We can police this demo, no bother. For starters there's no football on. We've a provisional route mapped out that's a good mile away from the Town Hall, they'll not get near any hot-spots. Plenty of barriers, good visible presence of officers, we'll get the community support out and about, and a few wagons of riot boys on standby.'

'You seem very confident.'

'Confident, yes. Not complacent. So am I reassuring you here? Or have you still got concerns?'

'The Met have given me some grounds to think there's more

badness in this lot than meets the eye. You'll be aware the bomber in Dudley had . . . affinities with them. Of some sort.'

'Yes. Awful business, that. But a load of clicks on the internet doesn't add up to a movement, does it? I'd say we have a pretty good intelligence picture ourselves. People like your man in Dudley, they're lone wolves. They don't mix in too well with football hooligans. And hooligans, really, are what we're looking at here. Wouldn't you say?'

Within the hour Blaylock was sitting in his constituency office over mugs of tea with Councillor Chopra, having attained the settled mind he had sought; but having settled, too – given Mr Chopra's evident disgruntlement – into the role of bad guy that seemed to be his lot. Blaylock wondered anew if he didn't somehow wish it for himself, or consider that no scenario was otherwise complete.

'The view of councillors is unanimous. The community, unanimous! Business, unanimous! There will be trouble in the streets, shops will stay shut for fear. We don't *want* them here.'

'The march can't be banned unless the police recommend it, and they do not. The Chief Constable is sure they have the resources to deal with the thing properly.'

'Why should taxpayers foot that bill? For such people?'

'It's not my view that affordability should be paramount where you're talking about the right to demonstrate.'

'Excuse me, Mr Blaylock, your type of politics is all about telling us what our taxes can and can't afford.'

Blaylock acknowledged the insult by meeting Chopra's incensed eye. 'This is a one-off cost that is manageable. But I'd ask you to set aside the idea it's about politics. There's no ignoring the free speech issue. So I'd suggest you try to imagine the logic of the ban you're proposing being applied to speech that you're in favour of.'

'These people, they talk free speech but on social media it is "Muslims are terrorists", "Muslims are paedophiles". All they want is a cover for their racism. So they can strut around parading their Islamophobia.'

'I totally understand your wish to have them silenced. But as distasteful as some of their views are—'

'*Some* of their views—?'

'Yes, "some". There is a line, in all public speech, between the sort of thing any decent person should deplore, and the sort of thing one may just disagree with or not want to hear.'

'You are *defending* them?'

'Not a bit. But nor do I see why you need to feel so protective of your religion.'

'Mr Blaylock – our community is fearful, right now, with great reason. It is besieged, and you seem oblivious.'

In that Blaylock planned to spend his Saturday afternoon tramping through a dank cave with a group of young Muslim men, he felt his ties to the community were as tight as they had ever been. And yet the thought of those exertions ahead was already giving him phantomic twinges in his back and knees, and having sworn himself off the whisky for the night he wanted his bed.

'I don't downplay that. I ask us all to stand together. Not to be cowed. There is a provocation I'm well aware of. It's our citizenship ceremony being targeted, on a day to celebrate diversity. I believe the correct approach is to show these people they have the right to speak, let them speak, and let them shame themselves.'

'To me, a politician must say when things are not tolerable.'

'Words bother me less than deeds, Councillor. Now I've got a very early start tomorrow, will you forgive me?'

5

Blaylock was on the roads by 11 a.m. and did the hour's journey to the North York Moors in gauzy November sunlight that broke through the clouds and gave the bracken slopes a burnished glow as the Jaguar ripped along country lanes. From his backseat Blaylock silently admired the broad grassy moorland, the dry-stone walls and grazing sheep and secluded whitewashed pubs, behind whose wooden doors he felt a wistful urge to vanish for the afternoon.

Martin had for some time been scowling at the sat-nav when their joining party came abruptly into view on the horizon, congregated by a parked minibus on a gravelly hard shoulder ahead – four young men ready for action in neoprene and over-suits, helmets on, harnesses with belay plates and Prusik loops dangling.

Climbing from the Jaguar Blaylock was uncommonly aware of his police team parking up behind, though he could read little reaction to them from the expressions of Sadaqat's group. Sensing he needed to pitch in big he exchanged hardy greetings and handshakes with them, though there were not the jokey spirits he had expected, more of a subdued pre-match feel in the air, not so far from Blaylock's own mood. Sadaqat's quiet authority was clear, his gaze intent under the dark line of his brow. Javed continued to exude the vague discontent of the perennial wingman. Muhammad, 'Mo', he of the tonsured lightning flash, seemed tightly wound, nodding his head to some internal beat. Bespectacled Nasser was the only one who smiled, albeit in a sickly manner that spoke of nerves.

Sadaqat beckoned Blaylock to the minibus bonnet, spread out a map and pinned it against the breeze with his elbows. Blaylock was aware of Andy sidling across to peer over his shoulder.

'Looks like we've plenty to see down there?'

'All the trouble you've gone to, I didn't think you'd want to just climb inside a hatch and poke round some grotty passageways. It's a long-ish cave but no big surprises. We abseil in, okay by you?'

Blaylock nodded, imagining Andy's expression at his back.

'We go along some vadose canyons. The water disperses a few different ways but we'll keep clear, mainly we're just hacking along phreatic passages that used to be streamways, and finally we get back to the light through a sump. Not too hairy but we're gonna get wet, yeah?'

'Got it,' replied Blaylock, more or less nonplussed.

There was gear awaiting him in the back of the minibus and he climbed in, stripped off and suited up with some awkwardness, relieved that no smartphone-wielding Instagrammer was around to snap him in his jockey shorts. Moments later it struck him with a vexing pang that this whole outing was a notable photo opportunity to which no one, it seemed, had thought to invite an official photographer.

A shuddering bang on the door of the van made him start. It was Sadaqat. 'We ready?'

They clambered over a stone wall and picked their way along a beaten track in silence, Sadaqat very much the point-man, Blaylock glad to feel the exertion and the good air and the grass under his boots, his mood only partially clouded by imaginings of the challenge ahead. Not far into a nondescript field Sadaqat stopped by a small manhole cover, and he and Javed stooped and heaved it aside. As Blaylock stood somewhat apart watching Javed unravel an abseil rope and Sadaqat fasten himself up in readiness, Andy moved to his shoulder.

'Boss, you sure you don't want me to say you've been urgently summoned to Downing Street?'

Blaylock feigned a chuckle and moved toward the manhole where Sadaqat was evincing a notable zeal to push off.

'Don't you want your helmet light on?'

'Nah, my friend. I like to just – plunge into the void, yeah?'

Then, with a good seize of the rope, he was backing away down into the blackness. Blaylock waited, clocking the blank expressions on the faces of his comrades for the day as Sadaqat vanished.

'Rope free!' The cry echoed up from the depths.

'You, sir?' Nasser indicated to Blaylock, somewhat bashful.

Blaylock clicked on his own helmet light, clipped and fastened himself and, with a little local difficulty, heaved himself to the brink of the drop. He gripped the rope and, gingerly, put his weight to it, intensely conscious of the eyes upon him. Then he leaned back with his legs apart and sought the happiest distribution of his bulk, taking the judder and scrape of the shaft's surface under his boots. *Howay!*, he goaded himself, and began to let the rope release through his hands.

He took the descent gently, peering about the gloom as the faces and the rope above him receded from view. Soon he could make out the shape of Sadaqat below, then he felt his soles settle on a balcony of rock, and he set to unclamping himself.

'Okay?' Sadaqat's voice seemed eerily disembodied.

'No bother,' Blaylock replied, breathless. 'Rope free!'

Now Blaylock knocked off his own lamplight and watched the others come down one by one, their torch beams swivelling wildly round the shaft. Mo, rather as Blaylock had expected, flew downward with one or two cavalier thrusts of his boot-sole away from the rock. And then they were five, the darkness making it a little difficult to truly discern one from another.

'Okay,' Sadaqat spoke from the stillness. 'No rules down here but do as I say.'

'And, look after each other, right?' offered Blaylock. In the silence that met him he was conscious of sound reverberating off rock, a distant dulled rush of water, his own heartbeat – all the strange music of the underworld.

Sadaqat led and they followed, sploshing into a watery passage of stooping height. As the torch beams darted about, insect-like, Blaylock saw the walls were red clay. Peering closer he made out crude markings scratched by cavers past – 'Pickering FC', 'Kill Nothing But Time!', 'Lost! Dave's Bollocks! Please Return!' – as rough as the odour of damp and fetid cave air.

'Why do I think some animal died here fairly recently?' he uttered into the dark.

'What you're smelling', Sadaqat shot over his shoulder, 'is Nasser.'

For all that Blaylock felt heavy-footed he could tell that Nasser, to his rear, was more so, judging by the rhythm of his steps and frequent muttered exclamations.

They passed into a clean-washed canyon where Blaylock's hopes for a head-height ceiling were dashed. Rather, it gradually decreased to a gap of merely a few feet from the ground. 'Time to grovel, boys,' grunted Sadaqat. Crawling on hands and knees, his nose grazing mud and gravel, elbows periodically immersed in water, Blaylock had to ask himself why he wasn't slumped in an armchair at home, with tea and toast and the football on the radio.

The next cave, however, enlarged gradually such that they could all walk erect. Up ahead Sadaqat's long figure and ridged backpack loaned him the appearance of a winged messenger, and past his questing figure Blaylock could see two passages cleaved by a rocky obelisk, one carrying the water's slow-flowing course. They took the other, so entering a tube-like tunnel, its walls evidently smoothed clean by centuries of erosion. Sadaqat paused at the head of a chamber and beckoned them with a hand.

Blaylock looked up and about, his helmet's beam vying with the others, glancing in reflected colours off the crystalline calcite spar that appeared to have petrified the cave surfaces. And he felt wonder fall upon him – felt himself, momentarily, to have entered some great and ancient catacombs – for on all sides were shelf-like rock formations, large petrifactions of humanoid proportions, suggestive of bodies laid upon bodies, conceivably not dead but merely dormant. Looking up Blaylock saw that the ceiling had assumed, to his eye, more fantastical, grotesque shapes – clusters of swollen bulbous stalactites that appeared, amid the subterranean dankness, like markers of a creature's lair.

'Amazing,' he muttered. No response issued from the silence, until Sadaqat called out, 'We've got a squeeze coming up.'

They came to a narrow, slimy gap between rocks, the exertion of passage through it causing Blaylock to feel for a fleeting instance that he was somehow birthing himself. The passage they entered was teardrop-shaped, a stream running down its middle in a trough, its walls, floor and ceiling all decorated by water action. There, looking up and about, he was newly stunned – for the walls had been scalloped, their surfaces ridged and fibrous, folds upon folds glistening and pearly-pink in the flicker of the helmet lamps.

Bracing himself with his fingers splayed against mucid rock, Blaylock had the strongest urge to throw back his head and laugh from his gut at the sheer flesh-like, feminised beauty of what he was seeing – so removed from the necrotic chamber through which they had just come. He would have liked even more to share the laugh with his companions, and the towering inappropriateness of that notion on near enough every level struck him as a laugh all of its own.

Then he heard Sadaqat from behind him. 'Headlamps off.'

The others obeyed. Blaylock, perplexed, nonetheless did likewise. The darkness was complete. The silence settled.

Inside his neoprene shell Blaylock began to feel simultaneously clammy and chilly. Then he could hear feet shuffling around him, and had the strangest sense that he was being encircled. Unease reared up in him with a prickling rapidity.

'Listen . . .' he heard Sadaqat say.

Then Nasser laughed – his sickly, uneasy laugh. 'Nah, this is just weird, man. I mean, crazy.' The laugh strangulated into a cough. 'Fuck sake, can't be doing this.'

'Nasser, be quiet.' It was Sadaqat, sharp. 'Man up, yeah? No one lose their head. I am in charge, you listen.'

Blaylock, wanting to speak, found his lips had gone dry.

Nasser, though, could not stop. 'Naw, can't *take* it, you fucking *hear* me? I cannot take it, *I'm not fucking kidding around*!'

Blaylock reached and turned on his helmet lamp, suddenly seeing Nasser's panicked features under white light. The other dimmer faces appeared motionless. He stepped forward and took Nasser by the shoulders.

'You're fine, Nasser, okay? There's nothing to fear. Tell me you're fine.'

'I'm not—' he stammered, still dazed.

'It's just your mind. Alright? Trust the ground under your feet. We're all here with you, there's nothing to fear. Just breathe, let it go through you, the panic – it's nothing.'

Nasser's eyes met his at last, somehow guiltily, but attentive. Blaylock swung round, his light swiping round the group.

'Let's move, right? Right? Sadaqat? Get the lights on.'

The moment seemed to stretch until he heard a low exhalation and, once more, multiple light beams riddled the black murk.

A quarter of an hour later, after one final slosh through a freezing cold sump, they scrabbled up over rocks and back into the daylight, where Blaylock was struck to see Andy Grieve looking so plainly relieved. The group retraced their path back to the vehicles, Blaylock deciding to walk with Nasser, who still wore the demeanour of a mistreated hound. Remembering Sadaqat's introduction he asked after the young man's ambitions in medicine. Nasser spoke fretfully of his need to attain a biology A-level, since chemistry was all he really knew.

By the van, while the others peeled off their neoprene skins,

Blaylock approached Sadaqat. 'Listen, the lights-out routine back there, what was that about?'

Sadaqat stood up tall yet looked abashed. 'I want to apologise. It was . . . the wrong move. See, my thing is, in the cave I like to find a way to take a moment? Just to be quiet, in the dark, and just listen to the cave, and the ambience, and your heart in your chest . . . that silence, yeah?' He shrugged. 'Nasser, I think maybe he just thought he could hear things crawling about.'

Part of Blaylock wanted to be on his way, but another part, dissatisfied, wished to round off the day's activity with some gesture of companionability. And so in fading light the Jaguar tailed the minibus to the site of an outdoor centre, a converted barn with outdoor burners where the group were booked among others to camp overnight.

Blaylock accepted a glass mug of hot sweet tea, a samosa of spiced vegetables and an invitation to sit with the group round a burner. Lowering himself with a wince, he was glad of the heat on his face and the relief for his swollen knees and aching back, more conscious than ever of the senior figure he cut in this company.

'I don't think I've had such a workout since the army.'

'How come you joined the army? Back in the day?' It was Mo who spoke. Blaylock realised he had rather hoped for such a show of interest.

'I had some idea about serving my country. Not that I achieved it as a soldier . . . But, you know, that idea has carried on to other areas.'

'You weren't, like, into the idea of being a soldier? 'Cos of the excitement and that?'

'Oh . . . there was maybe a bit of thrill-seeking to it. It was a different time – I never saw real war, thank god. Not like Afghanistan or Iraq. Not so many war stories . . . But, we all lived. So I should be thankful.'

'You were in Bosnia,' Sadaqat stated, with an assertive calm.

[337]

'That's right. Part of the UN peacekeepers. No, what I was going to say – the reason you join up, the appeal of it, the principle of it – is that your character gets forged. And you do get tested, there's no escape. But the worth of it? Arguably you have to decide for yourself. If you're going to die – or worse – then what is it for? It's certainly easier if you're sure you're on the right side. And where I was, we were facing some pretty bad sorts.'

'Bosnia, that was a bad scene for them Bosnian Muslims, yeah?' Mo picked up the baton. 'They was getting it real bad?'

'Yep,' Blaylock sighed, setting his tea down on the grass. 'The regular Bosnian army, it wasn't much cop. They really needed help. But we had limits on what we could do. What changed the game, really, was *mujahedin* coming in, proper fighters, proper gear, fiercer, more committed. I mean . . . you saw them and you weren't in any doubt they were ready to fight and kill and maybe die. It had an effect, you could tell. Even the regular Bosnian guys at checkpoints, they stopped hitting on their hipflasks and started saying their prayers.'

'You had respect for *mujahedin*?'

Blaylock studied his shoe and pondered Mo's question. He was holding a circle and being listened to respectfully, like the wise elder. It seemed a useful position – flattering, to a degree, and possibly one Sadaqat had bargained for. Still, he was obliged to be honest.

'Some of those fighters were – problematic,' he said finally. 'I had a bad time at a checkpoint once . . . Some bad things happened, not always black and white . . . But, I saw stuff that troubled me.'

'Stuff like what?'

'There was a thing . . . Some aid workers from Norway setting up a refugee camp east of us, they sent a message that they were worried about a *mujahedin* training camp there. Asked for our assistance. I took some of my platoon out to this field and we arrived in the middle of . . . quite a scene. Fifty-odd fighters all clamouring round in a semi-circle, and we shoved our way through into the midst of it and found this guy there, on his knees with his wrists bound and his head down, next to a fresh-dug hole in the ground. They had knives, the *mujahedin* – they always had knives. And there was a guy with a Koran and I had the weirdest sense he'd been praying for the condemned. The prisoner, we got him off his knees – he was Croat but he wasn't a soldier, he was a schoolteacher. So we saved his life, I suppose. We could do that much – summary execution, that wasn't on. But it was something the *mujahedin* brought to the party. And it disturbed me. They'd been invited, sure, they were drawn to the fight, they made a difference. But they couldn't be commanded, as far as I could see. You couldn't put the genie back in the lamp.'

Blaylock had been staring aside. He heard a low, grave yet indistinct mutter and looked up to see Javed, unhappy.

'Sorry, say again, Javed?'

'I said what's with the Ali Baba bullshit?' He shook his head. 'Genies and lamps. These were flesh-and-blood men. Come to help their suffering brothers, right?'

'I don't mean anything by it. My point is – the violence I saw in them, it was – notable. And I don't think that helped Bosnian Muslims.'

'Why *you* feel so strongly about Bosnian Muslims?'

Javed was sounding yet surlier. Blaylock, perplexed, gestured with open hands. 'Because of . . . the injustice. What they were subjected to.'

'Injustice is everywhere, man. It wasn't because they was *white* Muslims? That didn't mean more to you? Their lives and not—?'

'Javed, leave it.' Sadaqat's voice cut through. 'You're out of order, man.'

After some moments, Javed's eyes flicked back up to meet Blaylock's. 'I apologise. I shouldn't put words in your mouth, thoughts in your head and that. What do I know? I'm sorry.'

'We should speak freely,' Blaylock replied. 'That way we know what we're thinking.' He smiled as broadly as he could, drained his tea and got up, less steadily than he had hoped.

On the darkened journey back to Maryburn Blaylock was deject-ed, counting up what the day had cost him in physical capital – he felt it in his bones. Once back at home, melancholy settled on him like some fine, constricting web. Yet again he was alone with his work, the numbing constant in his life – indeed life seemed little but. In front of him lay a huge week: his identity cards plan in the balance, the Free Briton Brigade to be confronted. He could not say what it would amount to, but for sure the work dwarfed the cramped canvas of his 'private life', where privacy had resumed a look of barrenness and disuse.

He had done a decent job of expelling Abigail Hassall from his headspace but now, in the physical space that had briefly been their weekend retreat, he could not shut out the haunt of sexual loneliness. As he sat, absently, he set about worsening things for himself, imagining what Jennie and his children were doing with their Saturday evening, since there was no surer self-flagellation.

Fatigue darkened his eyes in the bathroom mirror, his spine felt as heavily knotted as vines round a listing tree. Undressing for bed he was dog-tired, bruised blue in patches down both arms, unable to raise either above his head. He wondered now if he would really keep his appointment with Dr Scott-Stokes in just over a week's time. Some part of him resisted it still, refused to see the need of it. What did he really need? It seemed obvious – a respite, a holiday, to which he was not entitled. As he tugged off his socks wincingly and saw dried blood between his toes, he was reminded that Christmas, at least – his least favourite time of year – was in reach. He began to murmur an old Sinatra tune, his voice so risibly croaky that he cackled.

He was awakened in evening darkness by the phone, and realised he had slept atop the covers. It was Mark Tallis calling, and given the hour Blaylock knew instantly it could only be trouble.

'Patrón, *I'm sorry, you're going to need to get your eye onto this because the papers are all over it and it's heavy.*'

'Go on.'

'*A woman called Sally Duffett was found murdered yesterday in Harlow. Essex Police have a witness, they've let it out that their only suspect is her ex-partner, he's an ex-con, ex-illegal immigrant and they're saying he flew into the UK first thing yesterday, went to this woman's place, killed her, then flew straight back to Latvia out of Stansted.*'

'Hold on, what – what about his immigration status?'

'*I know, how did he get in and out of the UK? When he's done prison time here and, the word is, he had form in fucking Latvia, too.*'

'Was he on a fake passport?'

'*We wish. The papers already got the nod it was his own legit passport, he just got waved through. The theory they've got their teeth into is that some new joiner at border control, one of our temps who'd just had a day's training, didn't know any better and waved him through.*'

'Aw fuck it, *fuck* it.' Blaylock stood, feeling a powerful urge to dash his handset to bits against the wall.

'*This is what I had read down the line at me, allegedly a regular border guy at Heathrow, "A proper Borders officer would have had this guy's number, that's what happens when the Home Secretary lays off a thousand passport control workers." Et cetera ...*'

Blaylock rubbed his face, feeling cold beneath his feet and, creeping up his back, the flush of calamity.

'Okay. Okay. I'll have to put my paws up. Statement to the House on Monday.'

'*Number Ten are asking what's the line? We've got to be clear.*'

Blaylock stared ahead at the wall, conscious of his brain still trying to engage with his mouth through the fug. But it wasn't clear. Nothing was clear other than that he would sleep no more for the night.

6

The first train to King's Cross gave Blaylock ample time in which to review the story's utter misery. In black and white it was perfectly grim and run by all outlets: 'UK LET IN FOREIGN FLY-BY KILLER'.

As ever, the photographs said too much and not enough. The victim, Sally Duffett – a florist's assistant, lively, outgoing, said to do a good turn for anyone – surely could not have been involved with such a violent man. But the suspect, Viktor Karlov, was a figure of mystery: Latvian passport, resident in Poland when he received a British work permit, believed to be Russian on the building sites where he had laboured. Burly in cement-caked jeans and tee-shirt he grinned from his photo like one far too friendly to ever be found in a police line-up. Yet in Latvia, unknown to UK authorities, he had been imprisoned for causing a man's death in a bar fight. And at Snaresbrook Crown Court he had been sentenced to three years for assaulting Sally Duffett, a year of which he served before release on the condition that he left the UK never to return. Such was his hatred of Sally that he had risked just such a return to attack her and beat her until she died.

That Karlov had not been stopped pointed to a tiny yet acute flaw in oversight, and there were innumerable reasons why that chink had opened – but Blaylock knew that none of this mattered, for he was alive and Sally Duffett was dead, and the gloom in which he had gone to bed the previous night now seemed to him a culpable puddle of self-pity.

Sally Duffett's parents had given a lancing statement to the papers through a lawyer. '*It is very hard to accept that a danger-*

ous criminal could come and go unbeknown to authorities. The system has failed us.' There was no answer to it, though Blaylock knew he had to send his condolences, in what form he could not say. For the part of the account that was causing a true ache between his eyes was the family's allegation that a threatening letter from Karlov to Sally had been passed by her to police, who forwarded it to the Home Office, Shovell Street.

The existence of such a letter – and whether it was received and logged and replied to – and if so, whether it was replied to adequately – were questions nearly sufficient to make Blaylock hope Monday would not come. His Sunday was already determined for him. He was resisting all media requests but he needed working hours to prepare his defence in light of the week ahead. Nearing London he called Jennie with an apology to say he would be unable to take the children for the afternoon.

'No, I understand, you'll have a day on your hands,' she replied, sounding uncommonly low. He asked if she was okay. She admitted that her mother was in worsening health, due to undergo a bone marrow biopsy. He felt the cold hand of his news: Bea, he knew, had made plain that if cancer returned she would have no stomach for a second ordeal. Offering his felt sympathy, he knew Jennie would be wracked, that the children would be loving and supportive, and that he needed to press on alone with his own share of woes.

Sunday afternoon, as he worked behind drawn blinds with media loitering across the road, was wretched. Taking a break to check through a pile of recent correspondence, he was further dispirited to find a letter from Diane Cleeve, rebuking him as the source of her recent troubles in the press – as well she might, in Blaylock's opinion.

On Sunday night Mark Tallis called and things worsened immeasurably.

'This is bad, patrón. Someone's leaked Quarmby's immigration report to the Correspondent.'

'His draft? Or the one with our redactions?'

'His. They seem to know all the internal arguments. I said we don't comment on leaks, but, this, Jesus . . . This is the lead: "The Home Office has been sitting on and censoring an independent report that shows a damning record of failure and neglect in immigration services." Obviously they're going to town on the delays and the dumping grounds and all the limbos and the legal failures but – this whole thing of foreign offenders we haven't deported and people refused who we've lost track of, it just—'

'Yeah,' Blaylock filled in, quietly. 'It would be bad any week. This week it's murder.' His mind still reeled uselessly at the implications.

'Thing is, patrón, I have to say, it's your girlfriend's paper, it's the fucking Correspondent.'

'She's not my girlfriend. Abby and I are done.'

If thrown momentarily, Tallis pressed on regardless. 'Well, she must have known, she must, it can't be an accident, David.'

Blaylock knew Abby had known of the report – of its suppressed status, too. She could have had no sense of its contents unless she had snaffled it from his red box. Was it possible she had crept from their bed to carry out espionage while he slept? The image was too awful.

'So, we're in for a week of fucking misery, a week if it goes well, we need to get ramped up for it . . . David? David, are you there? Have I lost you?'

Blaylock had shut his eyes and the blackness in his head was suddenly so huge and suffocating he thought he would be over-whelmed by it – even wished it might be so.

'Mark, this is not the greatest time for clarity in my mind . . .'

'I know, patrón, but you're got to hear the signal on this. Some-one's out to get you. I don't mean a conspiracy. But you know the media, there has to be one politician in the stocks at any given time, and all of a sudden you fit a lot of descriptions. So, someone's had a push, and given you a knock, and now they're all queuing up to give you a shove that'll knock you right off.'

Blaylock listened, conscious at the end of a hard weekend notably short on collegiate phone calls that Tallis was probably the truest ally he had. He rang off with the assurance that he would act.

First, he called Roger Quarmby.

'Roger, I have to ask if you knew your report was going to reach the public in the way it has?'

'Obviously, I don't know the full range of tactics you consider respectable for your ends, Home Secretary, but I would never resort to such a thing as you imply. So, no, I am not your leaker. May I now suggest you put your own house in order? I have been saying something similar for a while now, have I not? And for the future – if we can speak of futures – my further advice would be that when you ask for a report, then just publish the report you asked for.'

Having taken a scratch sufficient to get his back up, Blaylock then dialled Abby's number. She answered sounding breathless, like some parody of their former close relations.

'David, I guess you heard.'

'You couldn't have given me some warning of this?'

'Truly, I had no idea. It's just happened very fast, it was all fixed up between one journalist, and the editor and the news editor, and . . . I heard about it probably when you did.'

'That's bullshit, Abby.'

'David, come on. Don't act now like you don't know how it works. Look, I'm sorry, obviously, I realise it's trouble for you.'

'Thank you.'

'But . . . I mean, you knew it would be trouble, yes? You must have seen this coming. It's not like the story's wrong—'

'It's a leak of a draft containing errors and information that oughtn't to be in the public domain, so don't rush to the high ground, okay? There's sensitive information there, are you the judge of that?'

'*It's not my story, David.*'

'Right, you just work there. Who leaked it to you?'

'*To the paper? Come on. I just told you, I've no idea.*'

'Not convincing, Abby.'

'*Sorry, are you actually asking was it me, David?*'

'Yes.'

The long exhale down the line was also oddly reminiscent to Blaylock of time shared. '*Surely you see, there is someone in your operation who's done this, and . . . I'm trying to understand why you've got on the line to grind your teeth at me about it. The problem is in your own ranks, David. Forgive me but I'd have thought that's where you need to go shout at people.*'

'Thanks for your advice.'

The silence was searing to him, and again familiar, and he realised he should have known it would come.

'Do you have any interest in helping me out on this? For old time's sake?'

'*I'd be in an impossible position.*'

'Fair enough. The position's always been impossible, hasn't it, Abby?'

It was a dead rejoinder. He hung up, shaking his head slowly at the pure dismay of it – the connection he had briefly imagined between them, one that had wound up as entirely of the lower sort.

'*You're unusual.*' Hadn't she said that? He had certainly believed it, and that credulity seemed now the most damning thing he had to accept as his crime. In fact – certainly in this case – he was nothing of the sort. It was indeed stunning to him just how much he had turned out to be like all the rest; and how much so – a blow of its own to the spirit – had she.

November 15

Dear Mr Blaylock

I felt I had to write to you, though Pastor Ruddock was less keen on the idea, and he and I have discussed for some time now what is the proper Christian thing to do in a situation like this.

The first thing to say is that of course I know very well that it was you and your office that tried to plant stories in the press concerning me and the Pastor. That was of course a very cowardly thing, that you could not face me to make your own point, and instead connived and schemed to try to undermine mine. I suppose some will say 'that is politics'!

But if the plan was that I should be belittled by all of that, then you should just know that I feel nothing of the sort. The fact is I feel great kinship on this with Saint Paul when he said, 'For the which cause I also suffer these things: nevertheless I am not ashamed: for I know whom I have believed, and am persuaded that he is able to keep that which I have committed unto him against that day.'

With tricks of your sort you really do injure yourself more than you do me. And you would be amazed how much the stronger I feel by my faith and how it allows me to see these things such as you engage in as basically low, small and not worth bothering with.

For all that, I would like you to know that you are forgiven by me.

I do believe there is a better person inside you, as God knows of all of us. I have spoken to you on this matter and I know you choose not to listen, but I hope and trust that you will, finally, see reason.

Yours sincerely,
Diane Cleeve

PART VI

1

First light on Monday required the call to the Captain. Vaughan offered Blaylock no surprises: just the grave, not wholly unsympathetic manner of a headmaster who expected him to do better forthwith, and would cast only dark looks his way until Blaylock proposed a viable solution to the trouble he had caused.

An hour after that sobering discussion Blaylock was then required to speak to Al Ramsay, and to hold his tongue throughout.

'David, you'll not be shocked to know you were the hot topic of the PM's morning meeting. You and your department have got a pincer movement coming down on it – what are we supposed to say?'

'As I told the Prime Minister, I take responsibility, we will get to the bottom of all of this, and it will not happen again.'

Ramsay – from whom Blaylock had never heard a single word that he took for the honest truth – only grunted as if to suggest he put no great faith in Blaylock's current efforts either.

At 8.30 a.m. he closed his office door, as he expected he would be doing for the foreseeable, and huddled at the table with his spads.

'Okay, as of now no one says anything on my behalf but Mark. This room is my golden circle.'

'David, you can trust us, and the private office, you've got that much,' said Tallis, so much the company second-in-command that Blaylock was touched.

'Thanks. As for the rest, though, we have a serious mole here,' he said, then added, despite himself, 'a major fucking rat.'

'We need to look at who's resentful,' offered Deborah, looking relatively dishevelled for once in a shirt and trousers, also more pensive than usual. Blaylock wondered if she and indeed the other two were suddenly mulling the possible loss of their jobs, too. 'I just wonder, has someone done this alone or are they being worked by the other side?'

'I've not got time to call in Sherlock Holmes,' said Blaylock. 'We need to do our own digging. Ben, any ideas?'

Ben seemed as subdued as Deborah. 'I've a few thoughts. One or two ministers' private secretaries. They might have been up to this.'

'Paul Payne's gone on air this morning and said something not terribly helpful,' Tallis offered moodily. 'Some bollocks about accountability being clear, going to the top?'

'The trouble is, that's not bollocks,' Blaylock groaned.

'Who's your biggest enemy in the building?' Deborah was abruptly reanimated. 'Who's given you the absolute biggest grief?'

Blaylock thought for a moment, then nearly laughed. 'Phyllida. I mean, if I had to name one . . .'

The morning's regular departmental meeting was devoted entirely to crisis management, though Blaylock didn't detect a crushing sense of criticality in the air.

'In respect of the Quarmby leak I have spoken to the Cabinet Secretary,' Phyllida Cox announced assuredly. 'The Cabinet Office's investigative panel will convene and look into it forthwith.'

That's going nowhere, Blaylock thought. 'My main concern today', he spoke with care, 'is that Sally Duffett's family say she passed a letter along to us, via police – a threatening letter. What are our records? Have we established that we got the letter? Did we reply?'

He watched pens scribble all around the table. When the room emptied Phyllida Cox remained in her seat, studying him, scarf sharply pinned at her throat, and what he read as a gleam in her eye.

'You're remarkably serene, Phyllida,' he said finally.

'These things happen. I gave my view at the time, you might recall, on the wisdom of cover-ups? I don't see government as a game, David, but if others persist in doing so then they will be played in turn.'

He settled his elbows in the table, as if to tighten himself against raising his voice. 'Someone in this building has leaked a classified document. Someone we hired failed to correctly check a passport . . . I always like how responsibility falls here. There is a mountain of things in this department where I was assured that action would be taken—'

'How odd,' she butted in with uncommon boldness. 'To hear you resort to the passive voice? I appreciate decisions are lonely in leadership, but you have taken them, very firmly, and let people know it was your view. The fact that miracles can't be worked—'

'I've never asked for miracles,' he butted back. 'Only that we all be judged. Now, the calm round here is stunning to me. Is that because no one feels their position is remotely compromised?'

'David, need I remind, you said the buck stopped with you? Another thing on which you were advised?'

'As I recall, I took that view because I sensed I was alone in all this, and on that score I think I was correct, judging by the size of the mess.'

'It couldn't have happened to a nicer guy.'

Well, well, Blaylock thought, disarmed to a degree in the face of the combative glow she exuded. At length he stood up and forced a smile, keen that she see his teeth.

'I can see, at any rate, that no one round here is inclined to the Roman way of contrition.'

Phyllida also stood, and with a bearing he could only call imperial, as one who had let slip war from the folds of that Liberty print scarf. 'I'm sorry, you want me to fall on my sword? Like the noble Cato? You might consider that option yourself, martial type that you are.'

Geraldine rapped and entered simultaneously, a reminder to Blaylock that urgency was not entirely missing from Level Three. 'David, after your statement Martin Pallister's been granted an Urgent Question? "To ask the Home Secretary about the security of UK borders and the absconding of violent criminals."'

Blaylock nodded, straining to stay self-contained. 'Of course he has.'

'Also, Gervaise Hawley's being quoted by the news, he says, "Today's reports make dismaying reading. We must have the Home Secretary, his Permanent Secretary and Immigration team before us without delay, as clearly there are many questions they must answer."'

'A date for you and me then, Phyllida?' offered Blaylock, as his Permanent Secretary moved to the door.

Before that day Blaylock would have said he had never truly feared the House. He had been called worse names in school playgrounds, had heard far more daunting levels of din, and had never known the complete ignominy of being the baited bear in the bear-pit, guts all on the floor. But that day reset all records.

He delivered his contrite statement. 'The error was profoundly regrettable – the public will, rightly, be angered and dismayed. I give my undertaking that the lapse will not be repeated. The unprecedented difficulties we have had with the passport system have happened. But they are already in the past, and we will move forward and make right.'

He heard himself clearly, knew he had been heard out. Martin Pallister, however, rose to the despatch box with an assurance

Blaylock had rarely seen even in one so proud.

'Today we see the scale of the incompetence under this government, the shambolic state of border controls – for all the Home
Secretary's past pledges. The government talks tough on immigration and in private it flounders. It's all just talk. Who gets in and
out of Britain? The Home Secretary should stop pretending he is
in charge of our borders, he should stop sending out his troops
on pointless dawn raids. Because now we learn the truth hurts so
much he decides it must be suppressed, sat upon for weeks – *he*
decides it's too hot for the public to hear. Does he not now think
that honesty was the best policy? Wasn't it his own convenience
he had uppermost in mind? An easy life for the Home Office,
keeping the government out of the headlines, instead of the truth
that's owed to the British public?'

There was huge and hearty support from the Opposition benches. Blaylock knew he had to get a rise in turn from his own side.

'It is a fact that we inherited a broken immigration system—'

Instantly he was assailed by jeers.

'And, *and*, we have battled hard to fix it. The deportation system remains clogged by years of mishandled cases and unreliable records, and the conditions that permitted the current state to
come about were not engineered on our watch—'

The jeers intensified – as, in truth, he had expected.

'*However*, we take responsibility for our own failings and for
setting the failings of the past right.'

Pallister came to the box and leaned, insouciant. 'Can the Minister tell us how many people are currently in the United Kingdom illegally?'

'There are no official estimates of the number of illegal immigrants in the UK' – *jeers!* – '*because* by its very nature illegal immigration is hard to measure, any estimates would be speculative.'

Jeers! Pallister now had the high-nosed look of the emperor
wielding say-so over outcomes in the Circus Maximus. 'Oh, but

surely the Minister could make a fair guess based on data he has at his disposal? Isn't it the case that he knows very well? He just has no clue what to do about it?'

Blaylock felt his face burn much as if it had been slapped. 'My position, the case I have made, as the Right Honourable Gentleman well knows, is that so many of the needless obstacles we have faced will be avoided with the introduction of identity cards.'

Jeers!

'The *fact*, the *fact* is that the law requires employers to determine if people they hire have permission to work in the UK. Likewise banks accepting new customers, likewise private landlords renting properties . . . But once we have identity cards and the national register I believe we will be where we need to be to see the end of this sort of farrago.'

Pallister shook his head, commanding the high tide behind him. 'A farrago indeed, Mr Speaker – when people have suffered tragedies they might have been spared. When it could have been avoided by simple competence within a government department. This demands action. How many foreign national offenders are currently in the country? How many dangerous individuals have gone missing since this government took office? The Minister tells us often enough his number one priority is to protect our society and citizens. When he has failed so clearly, does he not feel his position is untenable?'

Blaylock got to his feet, aware he was flailing, aware of the subdued mood at his back, hating the sound of his own voice. The clamour in the Chamber was exceptional, his sense of sinking worsened by knowing there was no hole to swallow him. As he prepared to tell the House that he was the man to sort out the problem, he realised his own view was that he was nothing of the sort.

The battering done, he peeled himself off the canvas and retreated to his Commons office, where his PPS Trevor Parry – another ally appearing visibly queasy about his own fortunes – made a show of a ringside exhortation.

'That was a poor effort in there by our side. I am going to bloody well get onto some people and tell them support is needed.'

Blaylock sent Parry on his way in time to receive the Prime Minister, a drop-in for which he had prepared the painful words that seemed necessary.

'Patrick, I want you to know that if you think it's right then I'm ready to resign. I said the buck stops with me, and I will sort it out. I am fully focused on rectifying the situation. However, I appreciate public confidence is vital, and I've no wish to harm the government.'

Vaughan looked thoughtful. 'We don't throw in the towel in round one. What I need to know is, what's actually going to make the difference here, David?'

Blaylock opened his mouth to speak then closed it. The difference would be the public having heard his apology, believing what had not been done before would be done now; the agenda moving on, no more front pages; and nobody else losing their lives as a result of bureaucratic failure. In all, it was a tall order. And it occurred to Blaylock that, even if he could pull it off, he would not survive if Vaughan had someone in mind to fill his shoes.

Back at Shovell Street he found that Eric Manning had been swift in uncovering the fate of the document trail. However, the outcome was yet more dismal. 'Yes, the letter sent to Sally Duffett came to us from the police. We replied to the police that he "was no longer of interest to us".'

'Because we were just happy he was gone.'

Eric nodded. 'However, it's not clear the police had relayed that message to Ms Duffett before . . . what happened last week.'

Mark Tallis entered, cheerlessly bearing updates. 'Quarmby has given a press conference saying he stands by all his figures in the original report. Pallister's reiterated the call for your resignation on the BBC. "If the standards to which we hold ministers have any meaning then the Home Secretary needs to consider his position."'

Blaylock shrugged.

'What irks me is this, from some mouthy anonymous. "Someone has to get a grip at the Home Office. Whether that person should be David Blaylock is debatable. If it's such a long-term problem then let someone else try." See, I reckon that's Paul Payne.'

Blaylock's mobile pulsed. He saw that it was Abby, but decided not to wave Mark away.

'*David, is this an okay time?*'

'There won't be one of those for a little while, I don't think.'

He heard her exhale. '*Listen, I haven't felt great over how things have . . . come to pass. I wanted you to know that.*'

'I . . . appreciate that.' He saw Mark watching him, evidently wishing he was listening in on an extension.

'*So I wanted to let you know, so you understand, so you're ready. There's more to come. The* Correspondent *will be running more.*'

'Look, I know Quarmby's report, obviously. They haven't held anything back I can see.'

'*It's not just the report, David. There's other stuff. About your department. About you. You'd just better get your tin hat on, okay?*'

He cast a baleful eye over the nightly news and saw Jason Malahide, on his way out of the Palace of Westminster, yet allowing himself to be flagged down by a microphone-waving reporter: '*David Blaylock is an honourable man, he can be trusted to do the honourable thing.*'

The innuendo was typical, Blaylock thought. He checked his watch, 10.35 p.m., and regular as the school bell Mark Tallis called with what he had gleaned of tomorrow's papers, starting with the *Correspondent*'s line of attack.

'*"A blind eye has been turned to illegal immigrants cleared to work in sensitive Whitehall security jobs, including at David Blaylock's under-fire Home Office. One such employee, subsequently dismissed, is 25-year-old Nigerian national Fusi Solaragu, who was on such friendly terms with Blaylock that the blundering Home Secretary gifted him a gratis hospitality package to a top Premier League football match."*'

'My god. I'd wondered what had happened to that guy.'

'*So, you didn't declare those tickets,* patrón*?*'

'No, Mark, I forgot all the fuck about them.'

'*To be fair,*' Tallis coughed, '*people might say it was decent of you.*'

'Come on, Mark, I just told the House every employer in the land has a duty not to hire illegals. This is just cutting me off at the knees.'

'*Yeah, I've talked to the guy who wrote the story, I told him, "You and me are going to seriously fall out." He said, "That's politics, Mark," like he was my fucking dad or something. Then he tells me, "My boss said your boss has a target on his back and we'd not be doing our job if we didn't keep firing."*'

Blaylock's eye was drawn back to the muted TV screen where the presenter was showing off tomorrow's headlines. 'BLAYLOCK'S BLUNDERS.' 'KNIVES OUT FOR BLAYLOCK.' It was as if they wished to bury him under a welter of alliterative crisis-cliché. He could see that a study of disarray was being painted in thick strokes, with him in the centre as an ad hoc, skin-saving, trouble-dodging chancer. Worse, the longer he looked at the story, the more he seemed to recognise himself.

2

On the second morning of the debacle Blaylock disturbed Phyllida Cox bright and early, seeking to arm himself with some clarity in advance of a live interrogation he had agreed to undergo on *Today*.

'*Yes, David, some weeks ago we were alerted to some problems with our subcontractor of security services, I ordered a recheck of all credentials, Mr Solaragu had a professional licence, what he didn't have was leave to remain – his documents were false. Obviously he had to be dismissed and deported.*'

'Nobody thought to tell me this?'

'*There was a desire not to bother you, a concern for what would be your reaction—*'

'You're saying it was my fault?'

'*Of course not, what I mean—*'

'Forget it, I see where we're going.'

Mere minutes after his ramparts had been reduced to smoking ruins by Laura Hampshire he stepped out of his front door to be met by a jostle of shouting press. 'Are you going to resign, Home Secretary . . . !?'

Arriving at the Cabinet Room antechamber close to the wire for the start of proceedings he observed his fellow holders of the great offices of state, Tennant and Moorhouse, in a tight conference with the Captain and Sir Alan Ruthven. He had a sudden, paining premonition of his removal from the top table – and sidling up to this group revived in him some adolescent sense of trying to fit in with a set of indifferent peers. Belatedly he realised they had been discussing the planned gathering of ministers on Sunday at Vaughan's rural fastness in Dorset. Only when Vaughan made eye contact did Blaylock have any sense that his presence was still expected or required.

In Cabinet he directed a grimace at the table for the four-item forty-five-minute agenda, aware that at the bottom of a slough it was a forlorn hope to find company. What was clear was that for the moment he was leprous, radioactive; and he could imagine that some round the table would happily put a hundred quid on his being gone by the weekend, and uncap a good bottle of something in the event.

The evening paper piled onto his predicament with reports that his 'closest allies' were apparently as frantic and accident-prone as Blaylock himself had been painted. 'YOU DON'T WANT TO MAKE HIM ANGRY!' was the headline splash. Their reporter had recorded a call in which Mark Tallis had warned the hack away from further incurring Blaylock's wrath. The paper had also obtained verbatim accounts of texts sent to backbenchers by Trevor Parry, urging loyalty and claiming Blaylock was being witch-hunted. Blaylock winced at the terms used. 'For god's sake ask yourselves why DB being targeted!? You think certain jealous parties aren't out to get him?' The implication that these loyal foot-soldiers were ventriloquist dummies for their boss was clear.

Tallis was excruciatingly contrite. 'I know, *patrón*, if I become the story it's the worst outcome, I mean I feel I'm the cause of all this—'

'Oh, lay off, Mark, it's a venial sin in the scheme of things.'

A text pinged to Blaylock's phone: *David can you talk? If so please call. J.* Fully expecting Jennie to add to his pains he went out and found a vacant soundproofed pod.

*

'How's Bea?' he asked her, and knew at once that he had touched the exquisite point.

'The cancer's back. And it's spreading, rapidly. The oncologist said even an aggressive treatment might only give her a few months . . .'

'I'm so sorry, Jennie. What will she do?'

'Well, you know her view. We're just talking about . . . managing it.'

'If I can help in any way.'

'Thank you.'

They were silent for some moments.

'David . . . why I really got in touch, a journalist tried to reach me at chambers today, by false pretences I might add. And when I called them back they just wanted to ask me about you, and our marriage. I'm sorry to say they must have got to a few other people who may have, I don't know, hinted at stuff . . . about your temper and the police getting called that time. I told them it was all beneath contempt and I had no comment.'

'That was . . . good of you, Jennie. I mean . . .'

'Oh, it makes me sick. This hack has the nerve to say to me, "If that sort of thing went on don't you owe it to your kids to be honest about it?"'

'Well, I mean, it's not for me to say he hasn't maybe got a point.'

'David, I honestly don't think it's any other bugger's business. Not now.'

At 11.36 Tallis phoned him with the news that the *Correspondent*'s morning offensive would focus on passport chaos: 'FRESH BLOW LEAVES HOME OFFICE POLICY IN TATTERS.'

'Yeah, they managed to find the one fucking border agent on a passport kiosk who's an illegal immigrant.'

'That's a pretty good one,' Blaylock sighed. 'I have to admit.'

'Yeah, well, the rest of it is just the most abject sniffing about.

They put a hotline up for people's stories and you've got people talking rot about all the times they arrived into airports to find deserted customs halls and empty desks.'

'We know that happens, it's not us, but, hey – what can we do?'

'Not just take it, is what, patrón. *The thing that's out of order, they've hashed up a sort of a sidebar on you with stuff about your divorce, your kids—'*

'Yeah, I know. Whatever. There are no skeletons there. There were only two people in my marriage, and Jennie will not be talking.'

Tallis, seeming to feel the sudden bite in Blaylock's tone, was pacified.

On the third day of the debacle he began to wonder if he was paranoid, or whether, in spite of his freefall, his department had actually acquired a collective spring in its step. He kept seeing slight smiles on people's faces as if, in the teeth of catastrophe, their day had been made.

There was no tremendous hurry, the size of the current crisis seemed to defeat urgency. Rather, the die was cast, the Fates had chosen and the Minister was about to get hanged. Such urgency as there was, he felt, could easily be about how to cleanly show him to the door, what to get him as a light-hearted leaving gift. Who would buy the card, who would arrange the covert collection?

He was grateful when Geraldine put Lord Orchard through on the phone, with an offer of dinner at the nearby Spice of Life on Vauxhall Bridge Road. Blaylock fancied he might ask Jim for his advice on the possibilities of life after politics.

Duty told him he needed to keep focused on departmental work: after all, it still mattered. And yet it was absurd to him that he should act as though there was not a massive chance he would be out of the job by Friday. Preparing for Select Committee he found himself silent when asked for his thoughts. *I could say any number of things, but so what?*

Afterward he convened the spads. He felt physically diminished, and they looked etiolated themselves.

'I hate to sound a wimp but I'm not sure how much of this attrition I can handle. Outside our little circle, who really thinks I should stay? Maybe we're outside reality. In our bunker. "The last days." Maybe I should keep the cyanide capsule close at hand.'

Deborah shot a withering look, more like her old self. 'Forgive me, *mein Führer*, this ain't Berlin, okay? And I'm not fucken Eva Braun.'

Tallis seemed to rise to the grim spirit. 'Nor am I Goebbels, if that's the typecasting. And I don't see any Russian tanks rolling up the Mall.'

Blaylock felt a helpless hissing laugh escape him, the laughter that awfulness encouraged. 'Who are you in this role-play then, Ben?'

Ben, though, was subdued. 'I don't much care for the tone of it.'

Poor Scarecrow, he'll miss me most of all, Blaylock thought.

He took his seat for Prime Minister's Questions to the Captain's right, between Caroline Tennant and Dominic Moorhouse, who shrunk from him such as to give him rather more room on the bench than he needed. Then came the onslaught.

'*Isn't it clear that the Home Secretary cannot give his department the leadership it's crying out for?*'

'*I will take no lessons on leadership from the Right Honourable Gentleman. The Home Secretary has my complete confidence ...*'

Vaughan's declaration roused the Opposition to jocose heights. Blaylock smiled, arranged his features condescendingly, trusting that the whole government bench were doing likewise in solidarity. In his heart, though, the Prime Minister's words felt like the serving of the proverbial cup of hemlock. *It can't go on like this. It has to stop.*

He headed for his Commons office with the first sentence of a resignation letter having formed an ineluctable shape in his head. The Chief Whip lay in wait by his door.

'David, a word, the chair of the backbench committee has been to see me . . .'

Blaylock nodded. Trevor Parry was also drawing near, undeterred even by the Chief Whip. At close quarters Blaylock realised the alarm on Parry's face. 'David, it's urgent, there's a gunman on the loose up in your part of the world.'

Inside his office the challenge was to power up the small television and locate its remote control. The scene on the small too-bluish monitor was a live unfolding story, the TV news image presented split-screen, and still Blaylock knew at once that he was watching RAF helicopters in the air over Sedgefield and Trimdon in County Durham, evidently vying for airspace with TV choppers.

'Police are reporting a number of fatalities, at least two people feared dead, the same suspect in each case, currently in a vehicle.'

'Carol,' Blaylock uttered without looking to his secretary, 'please can you get me the Durham Chief Constable on the phone?'

'What we know – he's been identified, his name's Billy Darrow, he's in a Ford Mondeo armed with a twelve-bore sawn-off and a twenty-two rifle. We've got multiple crime scenes. It looks very likely that he's targeted certain individuals he's borne a grudge against. Mind you, he's shot at least one totally innocent bystander. So the message is out for people to stay indoors.'

'Where's it all begun?'

'We got our first call about eleven, the neighbour of a woman named Joyce Fairlove, who's Mr Darrow's ex-missus. This neigh-

bour was away out to her car from her front door and saw Darrow shoot Mrs Fairlove on her own doorstep. Mrs Fairlove had her daughter with her, her and Billy Darrow's kid, and the child runs screaming to the neighbour who locks them both in and calls us. Darrow, he legs it, he's off.'

'The daughter's safe now?'

'Aye, safe, but Mrs Fairlove was gone by the time the ambulance got there. From there Darrow's drove into the village – we get a call about shots fired, he'd shot Mrs Fairlove's solicitor dead then shot someone who just got in his way as he's driving off. A constable who'd heard the radio call was near enough to get after him, but he got in a collision with another of our cars arriving to the scene. The latest I've just heard is Darrow's brother's been found dead in Trimdon. Talk is there's a lot of bad blood in that family.'

'How close are you? To snagging him?'

'We've had officers in pursuit since the first call, we've just not been lucky yet. But I've every armed officer out, choppers supporting us, support from every neighbouring force – we'll get this man, Mr Blaylock.'

'I'll take no more of your time, Chief.'

He watched the TV screen as a photograph filled it, the snapped face immediately if vaguely familiar – Blaylock felt the shock of recognition.

'And this just in, Cleveland Police have named the gunman they are hunting as William Darrow, forty-six, from Port Clarence, and they have issued this photograph . . .'

Now he felt faintness creeping down his legs, as he realised that William Darrow had once sat before him in his surgery at the Arndale Shopping Centre in Thornfield. But whatever he had said, Blaylock had no recall, and no appetite for phoning the Thornfield office to find out.

*

Mark Tallis was instructed to come and get him out of Select Committee in the event of major developments in Durham. He met Phyllida Cox with a nod outside Committee Room Three, his grave demeanour seeming to ward away the truculence that had lately become her signature. Since she was off-guard, he attacked.

'Anything to report on the hunt for our leaker?'

'There is . . . no news.'

'Why am I not surprised?'

They took their seats and Blaylock surveyed the familiar panel: relatively youthful Labour Members, reliably troublesome Tories, none of them ever to be counted sympathetic, with the possible exception of Nigel Rhodes, a Tory whose career had been entirely expended in committees and who occasionally sought favour by this route.

Centre-stage at top table Gervaise Hawley had a prim, exquisite air as he sifted his pages. Blaylock found it hard to see past the immaculate bulging knot of the man's salmon tie. An aide came to pour a hushed briefing into his ear – regarding Durham, Blaylock assumed – and Hawley's brow and the set of his mouth assumed consternation.

'Good afternoon, Home Secretary. I gather there are urgent matters that have required your attention today. Thank you for joining us. We shall aim to be brisk. The Home Office seems suddenly to be coming apart under your stewardship, as a consequence of regrettable decisions on your part. Now there is the case of Mr Quarmby's report, and the disreputable delay of its release. You seem to have tried to sit on it and rewrite its conclusions?'

'Chairman, I respect Mr Quarmby's expertise. His report had issues and needed work before publication. I don't see that the leaking of it to the press is a minor concern. I don't see that the problems the report discusses are greater than that of releasing misleading data.'

'Well, Home Secretary, if you would let us see a *little* data now

[367]

and then it would surely be appreciated.' Hawley put down a page. 'Dame Phyllida, was the delay of this report necessary in your eyes?'

'Obviously the point of having an Independent Inspector is that he will shed light where there has been darkness. Where there are problems it is better we know about them . . . We are charged with serious duties, things do go wrong but there must be accountability . . .'

'And where, in your view, does the buck stop?'

Phyllida glanced at Blaylock. He felt only irritation now. *Go on, strike the fucking blow, it's what you've waited for.*

Tallis re-entered the room with the clerk, who approached Hawley just as Tallis went to Blaylock's side, there to whisper hotly in his ear. 'David, a police officer's been killed.'

Hawley was nodding gravely. He snapped his folder shut.

Out in the corridor he walked abreast with Phyllida, since they would share a car back to Shovell Street. Once they were together as two in the lift to ground, he addressed her without looking at her.

'Whenever this business is done – whichever way it falls out – it's clear, isn't it? One of us must go.'

'Yes. For once we are in complete agreement.'

'You agree, if, by whatever miracle, I'm still here next week – then you would need some very compelling reason to be here too?'

'It would be impossible for me to continue, given my opinion of you.'

Nodding, he invited her to exit the lift first.

He reached Shovell Street to be told the havoc was over, the damage done, for Billy Darrow, too, was dead, his body en route by emergency ambulance under police escort to University Hospital

North Tees. It was all now just a reckoning of the cost of the rampage.

Blaylock listened gravely to the account of what he had missed. Darrow had gone to the gated rural home of an ex-boss of his, a building contractor, but found him not at home. Police Constable Christopher Tweddle had then arrived at the scene in response to radio reports. Unarmed, he had been shot fatally by Darrow through the windscreen of his vehicle. Darrow again fled but shortly thereafter an armed response vehicle was on his tail, whereupon he dumped his car and went on foot into woodland, carrying his shotgun. The police formed a hasty cordon, got marksmen into position, and made forlorn shouted efforts at dialogue with Darrow before he put the shotgun barrel in his mouth and fired.

The BBC's anoraked live reporter stood summarising on Blaylock's office screen. *'I'm sure the officers are relieved it's over, the whole community will be. But the deep sadness, the tragedy that innocent people have died and a police officer has fallen . . . And the questions will begin – how could this have happened and could it have been avoided?'*

Blaylock sat at his desk, paralysed. In a moment he would get on to the Chief Constable, offer his condolences, thank him and ask him to thank his men. His conscience sat uneasy. But he was already resolving to think no more of it, never to speak of it – otherwise he would never hear the end of it, it would surely be the end of him, after so many thwarted attempts. Still, the idea that anything in his own livelihood was truly 'at stake' now felt accusingly emptied of meaning.

'Well,' Lord Orchard offered with a heavy, practised sigh, 'I am the devil on your shoulder but tomorrow you will be off the front page.'

Such were the manners Blaylock expected from his old associate as they passed around the chutneys and sipped their lagers with a near-ceremonial solemnity. They had both been of the view that Andy Grieve should sit and eat with them, but Andy was tucking in like one who only ever permitted himself ten minutes to pack away a feed.

'What if I'm back on the front pages come Friday?'

'No matter how big the fuss, it is forgotten as soon as the public move on. Usually within a week. You've had a bad, what, three days?'

'I'm still getting hammered. And I can't change the channel.'

'I know, it's like the weather, isn't it? You have the PM's support?'

'Who knows? I'm supposed to go to his place on Sunday, I still don't know if I'm welcome.'

'I agree if it dragged into the weekend . . . you may need to think hard.'

'If I could just – get my hands on the leaker. Draw a line. Stop the flow. But I don't know who it is that's bleeding me.'

'You've really got no useful intelligence?'

'All I can think is I just haven't ever made enough friends.'

'Don't rule out the possibility that people you thought were your friends became disaffected. People you didn't give enough hugs to. Or people you may have hugged too close, when they were never really with you?' Orchard set down his lager with a look of hangdog emphasis. 'Could it be your mistake was of that larger order?'

He lay on top of his bed and watched Billy Darrow's life unpicked on the nightly news: his form for assault, the alienation of his former friends, the gun licence he held on account of his ten-year membership of a rifle and pistol club. A member of the public told the BBC's man in an anorak that she had been nearby when the police were bawling for him to drop his gun, and she had heard 'animal-like' wails. The tragedy, Blaylock knew, was going to be turned over and wrung endlessly.

At 10.37 Mark called, sounding almost medicated in his heaviness.

'*They've got emails of yours, patrón. Emails that I typed, obviously. The ones where you, I, we, say that you're afraid of negative media coverage. The public shouldn't know about this, it'll be "open season" on the Home Office . . .*'

Blaylock no longer knew what to think. Overhearing his name on the television he turned the sound back up.

'*. . . and the Home Secretary did make clear in a statement that gun licence laws will be looked at in light of this but that he didn't think the arming of police needed review. Now, how long this will be David Blaylock's concern . . . ?*'

'*Indeed, Tom, what's the latest, will he go?*'

'*Nick, one backbencher told me tonight that he is* amazed *David Blaylock is still there. There are three reasons I think he* may *stay. He seems – I stress "seems" – still to have the Prime Minister's support. Two, as bad as things look at the Home Office right now, some will say he needs to stay to sort the mess out. And, three, the Home Secretary himself is known to be a fairly robust character. However, I just wonder – it may be that David Blaylock himself, reflecting on the pressure he's facing, which tonight shows no sign of abating – he himself may decide that the right course is to walk.*'

3

The crispness of the morning and its lukewarm sun made plain the turn of autumn into winter: Blaylock skidded on the frost-coated pavement on his way into Downing Street by the back entrance. He found Vaughan awaiting him in the Cabinet Room, and kept his coat on.

'I've not stopped feeling concerned that my continuing in this job has gotten to be a distraction from the government's work. I remain willing to see it through, but if you feel I should leave . . .'

Vaughan was either deeply thoughtful or giving his politician's impersonation of thoughtfulness. He stood up, went to the window, pondered the cluster of hardy red roses.

'No Prime Minister wants to lose a Home Secretary. People told me I should have had a more pragmatic sort in the job. But I've had cause to be glad of your . . . grit. The trouble now – part of it, anyway – is that you don't quite seem yourself to me, David.'

Blaylock considered this. 'I have . . . yeah . . . felt the strain.'

Vaughan returned to sit by him. 'Look, we want the same thing. And I believe it's what the public want. Properly enforced borders. Proper vigilance. Deporting every illegal who's deportable. Right?'

'If we call ourselves a nation, yes.'

'If you stay, do you believe you can turn things round?'

'Can we power through some great revamp of immigration systems? No, Patrick. We've not got the resources. The costs are too high – for the times we're in, anyway.'

'We have no other.' Vaughan smiled slightly. 'So, can we call it the devil's share? Do some other things that are a bit cheaper but still effective? By legislation?'

'We can make it harder for immigrants to get a job, rent a flat
. . . We can make Britain seem a grimmer place to live, sure, yeah.
Arguably, over time, you'll see a deterrent to people coming here.
What Caroline and Jason feel about that, of course . . . And then,
ID cards . . . not cheap, but I do believe they will help.'

'Okay. If you still believe you can win that argument, fine. If
you think you can't, maybe we should cut our losses.'

The Captain stood again, evidently finished with this particular
piece of captaincy. 'You need a hard think. You need the fight back
in you – the old David, eh? Otherwise it's pointless. I'll give you
two hours. I have to make a statement to the House at 11.30 about
the awful business in Durham. If you're ready to fight on then I
need you to have given me the nod before then, okay?'

He repaired to his office, sat at his desk, pushed aside a pile of the
morning's sorry press cuttings, and stared sightlessly at Geraldine's trusty A4 page of engagements by his muted computer. He
contemplated the impotence of backbench life; and what Thornfield would think of him as 'just' their MP. He wondered, for what
seemed to him the first time since the army, what he ought to be
doing with his life. The sense of emptiness amazed him.

He plucked a sheet of letterhead from a sheaf in a tray, took up
a pen, and mentally rehearsed an opening gambit – *'Dear Prime
Minister: It has been my privilege to serve . . .'* – then set down
the pen again, oppressed by the moment and all that would follow
if he simply succumbed to it.

The top of the cuttings pile caught his eye – another *Correspondent* sidebar to his woes, for which they had dug up some more of his
private and personal failings. If one rat had made trouble for him
initially, more of them, clearly, had followed in its stead.

*Once a leading light of the 'modernising' Tory left, Blaylock's
behaviour in office has caused old allies to wonder whether*

his true opinions weren't always more to the right. A history
graduate, he is known to enjoy making bizarre allusions to
incidents in the lives of Hitler and Mussolini, which have
struck some staffers as deeply inappropriate.

He had to laugh at the sheer dullard pettiness – as if he were at it all the time. Wasn't a man permitted a sewer-level gag at certain low moments, among friends who knew him better? He could remember perfectly well the trifling instances that some humourless berk had seen fit to make a song and dance about.

It was then he felt the curious childlike sensation of a puzzle solved silently in his head. It was almost elating.

'I've got him,' he said aloud, feeling himself suddenly flooded by the charged possibilities of deceit and connivance, a state in which he took up the pen again and absently etched 'FUCK YOU' in big neat blocky capitals across the letterhead page.

Suppressing a chuckle, his brain now fully a-whirr, he folded the sheet of foolscap into a Conqueror envelope, then dialled the nearby Hilton and reserved a room, and then called Abigail Hassall, who answered with an exquisite wariness.

'Listen, I saw the Prime Minister this morning.'

'*So . . . I hear. You were snapped leaving by the back onto Horse Guards Street.*'

'Of course. He's going to make a statement later this morning. I'd like to talk to someone first. Someone I can talk straight to. Tell my side. All things considered I'd prefer it to be you. If you can keep a secret.'

'*Gosh . . .*' She went silent, her instinctive caution clearly not so easily bought off.

'Bring your tape recorder, eh?'

She duly placed her recording device on the low glass table between them and smiled wanly. 'Okay, so we agree you won't have me shot for this?'

He merely tossed the Conqueror envelope onto the table beside the digital recorder.

'That is . . . ?'

'This morning the PM and I agreed I ought to write a letter. That's what I wrote.'

'You've resigned?'

'I am resigned – to my fate.'

'I'm sorry.'

'I can't really blame you, you understand. But you must have known it was coming. It was the point of the whole pursuit, right? For your paper?'

She shrugged. 'Maybe I'm still a bit green on these things. Obviously I was kind of hoping you would, y'know . . . muddle through.'

'Within the department, the atmosphere is . . .' He shook his head. 'I know now how many bitter enemies I've got. The leak was so calculated. At least I figured it out. Who the leaker is?'

Abby twitched slightly, though her eyes invited him to continue.

'My Security Minister, Paul Payne? Ever since he got that job he's been totally brazen about his disagreements with me. Over this whole crisis he's been open about wanting me out. Maybe I've earned it, but . . . the way he's gone about it has been bang out of order. And I'll be telling him that to his face before today's done, quite forcibly, I expect. So there's another story for you, okay?'

Abby winced. 'David. It wasn't that guy. Don't waste your time.'

'You know better?'

'Yeah. I do.' Her eyes flicked downward. 'It was Ben, your special advisor.'

'You what . . . ?' Privately Blaylock had expected some grim satisfaction, yet to hear it now confirmed was to feel there were worse things than heartbreak. 'You're sure? I thought it wasn't your story?'

'It wasn't but . . . I guess I helped it to happen. Back when I wrote that profile of you? I'd asked around, and I got introduced to Ben. He was an interesting guy, clearly conscience-stricken. He said the smartest things out of everyone, I thought. Then, later, he got in touch with me, said he'd just . . . oh, got disillusioned with you, the more he knew you? He didn't know about you and me . . . and I didn't want to be in that position, but I agreed to make the connection for him, to a colleague.'

Blaylock studied her composure, finding at long last that he disliked her deeply. 'He wasn't the only one disillusioned? It seems like I don't inspire much loyalty . . .'

She sighed. 'I had to be objective. It was a story . . . Look, a spark is a spark, David. I was very drawn to you, at the start. You were definitely different. Hard to get, my god. Most men in your position, even the worst nerds, they do rather take it as their due that women find them irresistible. I had thought about you, a lot. I wanted to know what you were like.'

'But you didn't like what you found?'

'Oh . . . some of it was just having to watch you going about all the petty deceits of politics . . . But, look, you can be, I have to say, pretty disagreeable. Being with you in a real way is – a challenge. I sort of imagined myself up in Teesside every weekend, being shouted at. Made me wonder how it was for your wife. Forgive me if that's . . . too far?'

'It's alright, Abigail. You're entitled to your opinion.'

She leaned back assuredly in the low sofa. 'See, the anthropologist in me – I've never believed humans are innately aggressive, it's socially learned, I'm sure of it. I think aggression is mainly a predictable reaction to frustration. What's problematic is if it never brings any catharsis . . . You're a damaged person, I think, David.'

'Aren't we all?' It sounded a lame riposte to him, but unimportant, as he was now simply playing with time, despite the ticking clock. Perhaps she was right. And if he had given her insufficient room to talk when they were together, she was extracting some recompense now.

'The fact your father died when you were young . . . I've had a few thoughts about that. Do you want to talk about it?'

This much he rated unacceptable, but he feigned a chuckle. 'I intend to, one day soon. But, that's another engagement.' He stood up, offered his hand. All her wariness resurfaced instantly.

'Where are you going?'

'Back to work. Much to do. People to see.'

His trap was sprung, and he had clearly succeeding in stunning her, though it felt to him now like a small-time move.

'What about your letter?'

'Just one more petty deceit, Abigail. No, the letter's for you.'

He noted her perplexity with minor satisfaction, then turned and made for the door.

From the Shovell Street atrium he took the stairs, not the lift, and as he hurdled two at a time he felt his breathing grow irregular but his body get set for confrontation, adrenalin coursing.

On Level Three he strode past the offices, past some curious looks, to the open plan area where Deborah sat with her hand on her brow, espresso by her side. She, too, beheld him with some surprise.

'Where's Ben?'

'Uh, he went to one of the work pods?'

Blaylock spun and strode off around the central lifts to the long side aisle where the pods were lined up. He could feel his fists, indeed his whole person, clench and unclench. *Keep a lid on*, he muttered to himself.

The first two pods were occupied by studious seated females. The third stood empty, door wide, to Blaylock's massive frustration – and then he saw Ben come round the other side of the lifts from the kitchen, bearing his pint mug of tea. Blaylock advanced and saw alarm spike in Ben's eyes, the spad setting his mug aside as if to protect it.

Blaylock jerked a thumb at the empty pod. 'In there, now.'

Ben stood his ground and raised a pacifying hand that Blaylock found incensing. 'Take it easy, David, alright? Let's—'

He grabbed Ben by both lapels and swung him about and through the pod door, advanced and shoved him against the black inner wall of the pod, then pulled the door behind them with a shuddering slam. Turning in the tight space he saw Ben was chewing his lip, breathing hard, clearly frightened. Blaylock cautioned himself to get a grip.

'You've gotta calm down, okay?' Ben ventured.

'Aye, sure, first you tell me this. Why did you do it? Eh? Tell me. Why'd you go and do this pointless fucking thing?'

'Not pointless. There was a point. I'd had enough.'

'Enough of what, Ben? What?'

'Of just doing the easiest fucking thing and talking tough about it, and dodging out of the consequences when it went wrong. Kidding yourself everybody else is incompetent . . . It's just a job to you, David, but people's *lives* are affected, man.'

'You think I don't know that? Who d'you think you're *talking* to?'

'I don't know. Really, I don't. Not a clue who you are any more. I just know what goes on here isn't good enough and I was sick of being part of it.'

'Sick of working for me? Why didn't you fuck off somewhere else then? Was it because I'm your *patrón*? No one else would have you? Or did you get a bit soft on Abby Hassall? Don't be bashful, bonny lad, so did I. How bad is my judgement of people, eh?'

Blaylock felt calmer now by degrees, the confrontation done, as he saw it – though Ben, as if emboldened, stared back at him hotly.

'Nothing more to say for yourself, Judas? You could try "Sorry". Eh? How about that?'

'No one gave us thirty bits of silver, David. I never got *nowt*. That's not what it was about. It's about how much goes on round here is bullshit. You think you're some sort of reformer, you don't change a *thing*—'

'Alright, that'll do,' Blaylock snapped. 'Howay with me to see Phyllida and let's get this done.'

Ben didn't move. Blaylock seized his arm.

'Don't put your hand on me or I'll make a proper complaint.'

Blaylock studied his erstwhile protégé with real scorn. 'Oh, now that would be a *good* one, son.'

He swung open Phyllida's office door, to her clear consternation, and bade Ben enter.

'Right, Phyllida, you can call off the master spies, Ben here is our leaker, he's freely admitted it. No need for the police. Just a straight sacking, gross professional misconduct.'

He left them to it and strode round to the open plan area where Deborah and Mark, having stood in stunned conference, now peered at him somewhat aghast. He pulled a chair, sat down and looked straight back at them.

'Then there were two.'

Mark looked about him, anxious. '*Patrón*, you know, in glass houses . . .'

'Yeah yeah. Deborah, I need to speak to your pal Gavin Blount. I've a job for him.'

Blaylock reached the Commons Chamber by 11.27, just in time to take his seat on the frontbench between Caroline Tennant and Dominic Moorhouse, who moved aside smartly as he bore down. The Captain glanced up from his notes in respect of Police Constable Tweddle, saw Blaylock and raised his eyebrows over the top of his reading glasses, an enquiry Blaylock answered with a nod.

4

'Home Secretary, do you appreciate why the public fear you can't be trusted to make them carry identity cards?'

Chairman Hawley looked, as ever, as though he meant nothing by it but was merely curious on behalf of the rest of the world. Blaylock glanced down to his briefing before meeting Hawley's eye.

'You mean me personally? And by the public do you mean the forty-eight per cent who support the cards or the forty-one who don't?'

'Well, if you steer by such polls, let's take the two-thirds who don't expect you can keep their private data safe. Didn't the merest rumour you would use the passport system as a form of coercion lead to a wild upsurge in passport applications?'

'That rumour was put about irresponsibly.'

'Ah, you think it's better people don't know what you're up to, Home Secretary?'

Blaylock let that one roll off him. 'My view on privacy is that nowadays it's something all of us give away a little in return for fast and convenient services. We all more or less happily give out our bank details, health details, work details online. And we trust private providers to look after it . . . In terms of the services offered by the state, for which you routinely have to prove your identity, what we will guarantee is a gold standard of proof. Yes, we'll put people to some inconvenience at first – they have to come and give a biometric scan and pay a fee, and after that we'll ask them to keep their data current. But that's because they are the custodians of their data. The card, it's not so vital. It's the register, the scan that's tied to the person. The records have no meaning without the physical person. You are your identity.'

'And this register will be used by . . .'

'HMRC, the NHS, certain government departments, accredited private sector organisations. But never without the individual's permission. Other than to investigate or stop a crime.'

'Have you priced in the legal challenges you're going to get from people who feel more entitled than yourself to some sort of private life?'

'We have. It's not a reason to shirk from the thing in fear. We can't be making policy out of fear.'

'And the total cost of this experiment? You don't really know what that will be, do you?'

'Our first estimate was five and a half billion, it crept to nearer six. The point is we don't lack for bidders here. I believe it will come in as currently budgeted, around eight-point-five.'

'We've heard sober estimates of twelve, one as high as eighteen.'

'No. I don't believe it. The Permanent Secretary and I will take a strong line in the procurement.'

'Really? And what else could you buy with those billions? A great many passport inspectors. An awful lot of anti-terror police. We have heard James Bannerman's grave doubts that your plan will do anything much to assist the police.'

'You will have heard differing things from other senior police-men. I respect all those opinions. My view, obviously, is on one side.'

'You choose to discount Commissioner Bannerman's views on counter-terrorism?'

Blaylock paused, folded his arms and squared himself to deliver the hardest blow he had in his armoury. 'I can only speak from my own experience. I really wish our existing systems were rigorous enough to deter terrorists. But they're not. I was a British Army officer in Belfast, in the days before photographic driving licences became standard on the mainland. But every driver in Northern Ireland had a photograph on their driving licence. And nobody felt that was a great bother, other than those individuals who were plotting acts of violence – ferrying guns and explosives about and so forth. So I have to say, for me and my men? That small onus on the public to be able to prove they were who they said they were was very useful. And there's an analogy, I think, to how these cards and this register will serve to impede the free movement of individuals who mean to do us harm.'

Hawley had looked increasingly displeased as Blaylock's remarks wore on, and now he sounded so, too. 'It is remarkable to me, Home Secretary, how, whatever compelling objection is put up, you weave to one side and dig up some new rebuttal as to why we need these cards.'

'Well, yes, and I note, too, how you duck my rebuttals and go off to dig up some compelling new objection. It's not a game, Chairman. I'm not jousting, it's not "sport", when I say the purpose is to defend the realm and uphold the law and better serve our citizens in terms of what they're entitled to. We are asking the people to take a stake in making the state function better. It requires faith – just as much but no more than we would have in a search engine. I'm asking our citizens to trust in their representatives – to have faith in the state, if you like.'

'"Faith", Home Secretary . . . ?' Hawley, evidently, did not like that. His wintry half-smile sang of half-suppressed scorn.

'Faith, Chairman. Yes. I'm sorry you find the idea so amusing.'

As Blaylock stepped into the corridor a waiting Mark Tallis gave him a nod, as if this were now the *omertà* of the family. But past the crowd of heads departing the public gallery he saw Madolyn Redpath, alone and turning a very acute look on him. She moved off, and he followed her into the stairwell, where their footfalls echoed crisply off the concrete and inclined them both to hushed tones.

'How are you, Madolyn?' he ventured.

'I feel pretty sick from what I just heard. I must have gone soft, getting pally with you.'

'I'm sorry you feel that way.'

'Just answer me this. What you did for Eve, stopping the deportation – you didn't do that just for me, did you?'

'Well, yes, for you. Since that's how things work. By association. And that's why Eve and not someone else. Because you chose her case and made it to me.'

'So, basically, it's still just all about contacts, right?'

'What, as opposed to binding principles? Yes, it is. It's still a way to get good things done. You should be proud of yourself. But, I see, I'm the world's worst person again.'

'No, but all your tricks and "tough" positions just to keep yourself in a job . . . Trading on what you call "public opinion". You bloody *do* act out of fear, you know. Don't ever kid yourself it's honourable.'

'I'm no saint. But I don't kid myself.'

'God, can you not see, if you would just . . . stop the bullshit, stop the wheel and get off, start telling the truth?'

'No. It's you who doesn't see, Madolyn. I really do believe the things I say I believe. So we'll just have to agree to disagree.'

He put out a hand. She looked at it so witheringly he was taken aback. He had wanted her to think well of him. There had been no complications to do with attraction, no designs on her. Just a rather paternal urge to show a bright young mind of a different persuasion that he was not such an ogre. Clearly, however, the peace talks had run into a ditch and they would just have to resume hostilities.

'Okay, so be it,' he said quietly, then headed past her and down the stairs, the sound of his footfalls sharp as tacks.

In the quiet seclusion of a Shovell Street basement room he was joined by Gavin Blount from the Northern Ireland office, whom he thanked for making the time.

'I'm interested in your authoring a report for me. First I'd like your opinion on a few issues. What do you think about arming our police? Routinely, in greater numbers?'

'After the awful business in Durham?'

'That, but there's also a broader context. Their being better armed for self-defence in the face of an armed attacker, an Islamist, say.'

Blount sighed. 'Well, it's not our tradition, is it? If the police are routinely walking around with guns, it changes things. Officers believe it would be daunting to the public, I know that. I rather think it raises public fears, too, when they see armed police.'

'They may have very good reason to fear. They might get used to the reassurance the firearms bring.'

Blount smiled. 'Officers, too, will be concerned for what's put on them. That they become targets.'

'Okay. I know that argument, that officers don't want it. The public seem to, though. Myself, I don't know. Belfast may have warped my view.'

'We have armed response, maybe not enough of it. But London's fine, the Midlands are fine . . . Okay, once you're in Durham, Northumberland? Less so. People are rightly appalled. But these incidents are still so rare.'

'What if the decision were down to you?'

Blount smiled wryly, looked aside for some moments, then back. 'I was in Paris last summer? I did feel a certain assurance looking at the gendarmerie and their semi-automatics. Where policing has arisen from those paramilitary functions . . . ? I could see the sense in a number of officers routinely carrying side-arms on patrol. Even just a Glock. But I sense the equipping and training will cost more than we have spare. Forgive me, than *you* have. I speak hypothetically.'

'Maybe not so much. If a vacancy arose around here? For a permanent secretary? Would that interest you?'

Blount raised his eyebrows, pursed his lips, then slowly nodded.

That night at home Blaylock stood by his bedroom window, nursing a tumbler of whisky, gazing out onto the eerily serene square. The halos of the street-lamps cast light onto the Georgian brick terrace opposite, and put an illumined frame round the square, its long carpet of leaves hemmed by tall, gaunt sycamores and a low perimeter of chain-linked black iron bollards.

Blaylock felt that his prospects were renewed. He had not been killed, made a little stronger – maybe old Nietzsche had a point. Yet his spark was low.

The whisky he had poured he no longer fancied. Despite its allure he knew it to be a vulnerable anaesthetic, medicine to be taken, first in hope of an instant cure, then with a dull surety that the operation would take more time than one had factored for.

Madolyn Redpath had stung him again: *'You bloody do act out of fear . . .'* He was certainly not confident – not unfearful – of the effectiveness of the machine he controlled. All he could see now was the monolithic rigidity, and curious inadequacy, of his habits of thought. Security, liberty – what did they mean, and how could he arbitrate over them? He had never understood liberty, for he had never believed in what freedom might achieve as much as what bondage prevented.

He heard the pulse of his phone from its place on the bedside table and went to retrieve it. It was Mark Tallis, earlier than usual.

'Can you believe Gervaise Hawley? This is what the fucker has just tweeted. "The Home Secretary is looking tired, fraught, on edge after his recent strains. Genuinely worried for him."'

'Not a bad needle. Killing me with kindness.'

'It's out of order.'

'Off, but not unexpected. I told you, Mark, don't waste your time hunting down my critics on Twitter . . .'

He went back to the window, and instantly felt his breath catch. Under the trees near a bench was a man, hooded, leaning against a sycamore, looking up at him, albeit shadowy and out of the light cast from the lamppost. Something about the dark beard and trails of hair snaking from out of the hood registered – that, and the man's dulled, distressed, demo-ready urban combat-wear.

Then the man turned and was moving at pace, across the square toward a narrow pedestrian-only outlet to the main road. It didn't strike Blaylock as coincidence. This man had taken flight, for he had been watching, and had not cared to be seen.

5

He sat in the back of the parked car and studied the scene through the glass, at a decent remove from the fray, in the company of policemen and feeling himself to be not so unlike a policeman either. The focus of his gaze, a hundred or so feet ahead, was a close-penned sea of close-cut white heads: all male, mainly in bomber jackets and jeans, shuffling and smoking, a grim liveliness about them on a greyed-over Saturday afternoon. The gathering snaked away from sight but it consisted, Blaylock reckoned, of between three and four hundred bodies.

He had grown a tad fixated on one fellow at the periphery of the throng, clad in a fishtail parka and wraparound shades, phone pressed to his ear, as sour-faced as a secret service detail while his mates larked around him. A couple of mounted policemen sat high up on restive horses, looking down sternly on proceedings, a police car in front of them, a cordon of officers on foot at their back.

Then Blaylock shook his head sharply and blinked as if to sharpen his middle-aged vision – for he thought he had half-glimpsed, weaving amid the pack, a familiar figure in tweedy cap and coat. But finding his view obstructed he reached for the door handle.

'Aw, now you musn't leave the car, sir,' said the Cleveland Police constable seated beside him. 'Sorry, but – please.'

Andy grinned from his berth at the officer's other flank. 'Quite right.'

Blaylock sat back. 'What would you do, arrest me?'

The officer grinned, touching the brim of his hat. 'If I had to, sir.'

A raucous cheer from without reached the car and Blaylock looked to see a union flag being unfurled and raised above the demonstrators, just as the toll of a clock-tower bell rang through the air.

'Okey-doke, that's gone one,' sighed the sergeant in the front passenger seat. 'Take 'em to Missouri, Matt.'

The police car was moving off, the horses geed up behind, the cordon of officers following, and in their wake the congregation.

The sergeant leaned back to Blaylock. 'Right, so they're off down Pinstone Road, left on Neville Street and up Coulson Parade to the war memorial. And that's where they're stopping.'

Chants, which had risen from stray pockets of demonstrators before, now resounded clearly, born of football fandom in their blunt repetition, one slogan in quintuple time.

'*Eff-Bee, Eff-Bee-Bee! Eff-Bee, Eff-Bee-Bee!*'

'*Eng-land! 'Til I die! Eng-land! 'Til I die!*'

'*Our country! Our streets! Our country! Our streets!*'

'Let's be getting you to the Town Hall, sir,' murmured the sergeant.

Thornfield, if not a beauty spot, was nonetheless to Blaylock's eye a perfectly presentable northern town. But he knew he might think different were it not for the Town Hall. Set amid the depredations of the high street, but on a central island serenely apart from the haberdashers and the credit union and the takeaway pasty shops, this Georgian redbrick building projected just enough residual civic pride – just enough faded grace in its clock tower and belfry, its pantiled roofs and leaded windows – to improve all else in the environs.

Within the council chamber Blaylock found a big union flag had been fastened across the wood-panelled back wall and Pachelbel's *Canon* was being piped at sufficient volume to echo round the space. A queue of applicants – some sober-suited, some in florid national dress – were having their names ticked off by a registrar then adjourning to be snapped by camera phones as they stood by an easel holding up a pleasant photo of the Queen. But Blaylock's eyes were drawn to a pint-sized Indian girl-child in a sari, whose big watchful eyes and mop of dark curls delighted him. He made conversation with the child's mother – a nurse named Aparna – largely so that he had an excuse to lift little Gitti up into his arms.

Presently the Mayor called proceedings to order: Blaylock hoped he would be the soul of brevity, having never, ever, in all his days heard a mayor speak well. After seven or eight minutes in paean to the welcoming environment of Thornfield, and the obvious virtues of Pakistan, India, Bangladesh, Thailand, Sudan and the Democratic Republic of Congo, and how much he, as Mayor, personally loved to eat the fiery native cuisines of all of these places – he at last invited Blaylock to make ready for the handing out of framed certificates of naturalisation.

The inductees followed the registrar in solemn recitation: '*I will give my loyalty / To the United Kingdom / and respect its rights and freedoms / I will uphold its democratic values . . .*'

Names were called, people moved forward, Blaylock shook their hands and murmured pleasantries – with Mr Elmadi from Sudan, and Mr Diatezua from the DRC. After a brisk bellow through the national anthem the business was done, and Blaylock accepted a cup of tea and a sandwich, posing cheerily with his new fellow citizens in front of the Queen and the flag.

'So we have a nice letter from you,' Aparna smiled at him, and Gitti thrust a page upward for his inspection. Nonplussed for a moment, he then saw his passport-size portrait next to his Home Office letterhead and remembered approving this 'Welcome to the UK' boilerplate. If these things had seemed perfunctory before, he was feeling buoyed by the unfussy pleasantness of this occasion. It occurred to him that his native northeast of England probably needed all the highly motivated and well-mannered newcomers it could get.

His ear picked up on the crackle of a police radio and some *sotto voce* exchanges; then he watched the grave constable draw nigh.

'Sir, could I possibly have a private word in the corridor?'

Blaylock had guessed the matter and beckoned Andy Grieve to come out with him.

'We've had a bit of bother with the FBB march? Some of the marchers, they've splintered off and got past our cordons, it looks like they're making in this direction. Actually looks to have been planned like that . . .'

Blaylock nodded and let himself be led to a stairwell with a long-window hundred-and-eighty-degree view of the surrounding streets. The first sight he clocked was that of yellow-jacketed police, regrouped for action in riot gear, helmets with visors and sticks in hand.

Then he saw white heads, a posse of bomber jackets and jeans, all barrelling out of a narrow alleyway into the lower end of the square and stomping across the piazza toward the Town Hall. A bottle was tossed, and it shattered in the dead space of the paving; and then another, as the marauders pressed forward.

'We'll have to hold tight,' muttered the constable.

'What, like Fort Apache?' Blaylock shot back.

Dozens upon dozens were thickening into a crowd, all truculence and tattoos and branded tee-shirts, a sea of pointing and chanting, some with arms spread wide as if declaring their love of a ruck, others with phones aloft, capturing the moment.

'*Eff-Bee, Eff-Bee-Bee!*'

Those on the frontline before the riot police made challenges with stuck-out chests, some adorned by three lions. Cameramen ducked and weaved between them as if in a war zone.

'*The country's full! Fuck off home! The country's full! Fuck off home!*'

'This is deteriorating fast, boss.' Andy took Blaylock's arm. 'We need to get you out of here.'

Indeed Blaylock saw yellow jackets jogging up the stairs toward them. He looked back to the door of the oblivious council chamber.

'We go all together, that's the only way. We need paddy wagons fronted up here and we need to get these people safely out, right?'

'Sir, I can't say we can—'

'It's what we're doing. Tell your Chief Constable if you like. But get in the chamber and tell our new citizens calm as you can that we're all going to make an emergency exit under police guard.'

He stayed by the window until he saw the chequered vans back up as close as they could to the officers manning the hall's rear exit, whereupon he joined the small group of inductees in the corridor, and noted with a pang just how much panic was in their eyes. He felt purpose, and rising adrenals. The yellow jackets formed up in a protective wedge around them.

'Everyone ready?'

He heard a thin wail and turned to see Aparna stooped and holding Gitti's face in her hands. He made an executive decision and, for the second time in the day, scooped the girl up into his arms.

The door into daylight was thrown open and they made the big push, Blaylock near the rear but aware Andy and Aparna were behind him. The mob was alarmingly close, barely cordoned by officers with sticks, but the sanctuary of the vans was only forty feet away.

'*Move back! Stay back!*' the officers shouted at the mob. But there was hard jostling, jeering and spittle in the air, and Blaylock was met by red-faced close-quarter exhortations to a fight.

'*Blaylock! You fuckin' disgrace!*'

'*Be a fuckin' man and come owa here, ye!*'

'*Cunt! You cunt!*'

He heard a cry and turned to see Aparna stumble, but Andy had her. He turned back to see a great bullet-headed lump of a man who had bullied through the police line and was now lunging at him. With the hand not clasping Gitti he gave his attacker a stiff-armed fend-off straight to the face. In the next instant he was lifting Gitti into the van, Aparna was being shoved into his back, and Andy slammed the door.

'We're clear, go, go, go!'

The van was being pilloried from all sides but it grumbled and lurched and at last they were away and off the piazza at speed. Blaylock looked behind him – at officers using both hands to shove back the protesters, some bare-chested in November, and yet still they came. One was strutting across the square in some alcoholic rapture, his narrow chest swathed by the flimsiest flag of St George, but evidently savouring the sweetest of afternoons.

He heard Gitti calmly tell her sobbing mother that she was okay. And so, clearly, were they all.

'*The coverage is pretty good, I'd say, patrón. After the week you've had, I guess the sum of it is – there's nobody quite like you . . .*'

Blaylock was back in the Jaguar, having travelled back to London on a late train the previous night, now en route to the Captain's rural summit – policy, direction, prospects for the next election – hosted at his Dorset home. Jaded and pensive, he was content to listen to Mark Tallis exulting over the papers.

'*Even the fucking* Correspondent *has gone all "He-said, She-said". "Is Blaylock a liability? Or do we need more of his sort in politics?" I mean, a poll in* The Times *says thirty-one per cent still think you should quit but there's an* Observer *op-ed saying you ought to be leader.*'

'At least it's only them . . .'

He had made some front pages, but the various messy snaps of his mercy dash from Thornfield Town Hall all seemed to catch him in a fair light. His high praise for Cleveland Police was widely reported. The *Mirror* liked the scathing judgement he had delivered on the FBB. ('*What do this shower have to say to the honest, hard-working local people of this area?*') It seemed to him one of the better things he had done lately. Again he could not but feel that hitting someone – so long as it was the right one – was something he ought to do more often.

They reached Corfe, a grey stone village under a blue-wash sky, replete with church and market square, nestled under the watch of a ruined medieval castle and a whaleback ridge of hills. The Jaguar zipped past a row of ceramic shops and a pub that, at lunch-hour, spilled out with a discernible mix of locals and Londoners.

It was unmistakably Sunday, steeped in the special torpor of rural life and England's upper middle class. He had come to a corner of England that was true blue – just as the Prime Minister was, just as Blaylock was not.

Stepping over the threshold into the Captain's country kitchen Blaylock was met by an aroma of fresh-ground coffee and by Vaughan, in the midst of slathering two legs of lamb with a gloop of garlic and rosemary, wiping hands slippery with olive oil onto a black apron as he came over.

'David, how often is it that I'm shaking your hand like you've just returned from battle?'

Glancing past the Captain Blaylock clocked the cohort for the afternoon – just him, Dominic Moorhouse, Caroline Tennant, and the Captain's usual coterie, the Etonian–Oxonian clan who direct-ed the daily Downing Street meetings Blaylock never attended.

His out-of-place-ness was underscored by the others' casual dress code of denims and good shirts. Even the indefatigably soignée Caroline Tennant wore jeans with her white silk blouse. Blaylock – suited, though tieless – cringed at how programmatic his life had become, that the suit was simply what he had pulled, unthinking, out of his wardrobe.

They sat round a long, heavy oak table across from the kitchen island, set with blue glass bottles of fizzy water and pots of that potent coffee. Blaylock decided to slough off his discomfort: he had earned his place at the table, he could call himself a survivor.

Al Ramsay presented the latest polls: the government ahead on providing leadership and a strong economy, trailing on protecting the NHS and knowing the price of a pint of milk. '"Out of touch", I don't buy it,' Vaughan muttered. Blaylock feared the whole session might be a brow-furrowed stare at this set of numbers. But it wasn't long before Vaughan steered them to his personal reading of them.

'The big theme', Vaughan asserted, 'just needs to be security, no? Trust us. Competence. Yes, we don't want to neglect transforming people's life chances and all of that stuff. But things are a bit dicey, so for a while at least we need people to be a bit more hard-headed.'

Today Blaylock was unusually conscious of Vaughan's remarkable calm, perhaps because all week long he'd had reason to be glad of it. The Captain seemed never truly to agonise: he made a decision, guided by the heads he trusted, then he moved on, however unsteadily. His confidence didn't appear feigned; it came from some real place, not merely the offspring of privilege. For all that life had been good to him, Vaughan, though not pronouncedly churchy, seemed to exude some Anglican conviction that life was not all – that 'all', in fact, was vanity and vexation of spirit, the world far from perfect, but a Tory government, at least, was the world turned right side up, and so the job was to keep winning and stumble onward. It was not the 'radicalism' Deborah Kerner urged upon Blaylock; yet it seemed altogether more effective.

'David,' said Vaughan, turning fully to Blaylock. 'What do you think are the odds of our pinching a seat or two in the north?'

'Well,' he sighed, sitting back. 'There are plenty of voters without the ideological baggage their parents had, just wanting to get on, used to shopping around. As long as we're a vehicle for good ideas, and we're competent . . .' Blaylock heard himself falling into rote, and decided he didn't like it. 'But, look, you can govern without the north. It might be too much work. I honestly don't think the gap in ideologies is why you get the hate, it's more of a gut sentiment.'

He was being peered at, and sought to clarify.

'I mean, there'll always be a proportion of northerners who hate you because they've never met you or anyone like you, and they think you're a load of posh moneyed tosspots.'

'"You"?' Caroline Tennant sounded amused. 'I'm sorry, are you not one of us, David?'

Blaylock realised he was more tired than he had thought, and that no amount of piping hot coffee would relieve that.

'David, would you join me for a stroll?'

The injunction was plain. Blaylock was perfectly fond of hacking around hills in the north. This 'stroll', though, seemed clearly an extension of the day's agenda. Vaughan thrust a pair of green Hunter wellies at him and went off on a hunt for his own gear, rummaging the coat rack and the boot rack that had their own tidy room next to the kitchen door.

Pulling on the boots Blaylock was struck for the first time by how Elspeth Vaughan resembled Caroline Tennant – though her smile was toothier, her flaxen locks longer and untamed. She and the Captain had the look of a family firm. He watched them confer in hushed tones, saw him stroke his wife's cheek then address his ten-year-old daughter Tabitha, shyly at their side, as 'darling one'. At this, Blaylock felt a twinge in his breast.

The afternoon had clouded over as they headed up the wide escarpment to the hills above Corfe Castle, their security guards twenty paces behind. They climbed over stiles and through kissing gates to follow a muddy pathway skirting the hill on the low side.

'You seem very much at home here,' Blaylock offered.

'As opposed to Downing Street? Our "fake" home, as Tabby calls it. Yeah. I don't know that it does me any good but . . . this is where I'm from, what I am. I can't change it. I don't have your grit.'

If not emollient, it could have sounded patronising. But Blaylock had to admit Vaughan was good that way. 'If you'd grown up on a council estate you'd still be getting it in the neck. It's the job. If it was me in your place I'd be "out of touch", too.'

The pathway had come to an enmired end, and what beckoned them now was a near-vertical trudge up to the heights of the ridge by a well-trodden grassy track.

'To the sunlit uplands, eh?' Vaughan smiled.

Halfway up Blaylock felt a deep post-prandial torpor, his blood sluggish, like cream in his veins, and the wind resistance further wearied him and his calves. The Captain, though, had colour in his cheeks. As they reached the top a splendid panorama opened up – behind them the resilient limestone ruins of the castle, around them a mosaic of fields, woods and nestled villages, and before them hills rolling away to the horizon and Poole Harbour. This was England, too, no doubt. Blaylock so easily forgot this part.

The sky was all fire and muzz, the cloud formations had become starkly luxurious swirls. The wind on his face was cool and it refreshed like water. Up here, it was clear and poignant to him – the world was a perfect creation, not even counting all the lives and the love in it. And yet he was lanced by the feeling that it was perfectly full without him – his contribution superfluous, other than, perhaps, the degree to which he had helped others have their share of it.

He had the strangest urge to take off and race down the slope, to let the gradient carry him, and run until his chest erupted – until he was a blur, mere ether, transformed into energy and made to vanish. Something deep inside him was telling him, *Begone!*

'It's good, isn't it? The view.'

'Great. Really great, Patrick.'

'How are you feeling about things?'

'It's been a week. But, we're through it, I suppose.'

'I know. Some of the scraps you get into . . . I know I've said, but you don't need to get into so many.'

'I've appreciated your support.'

'Not at all. The only thing that ever worries me, David . . . just at times, you can seem detached, somehow, from our fortunes? When really that's all there is, isn't it? Power is what it's all for. Government's the only place to be. I need to know you're with us.'

'After this week, please don't ever doubt my loyalty.'

'Fine, fine. But what we do from here isn't about me being re-elected. My time's nearly up. "It has been written." We all of us need to be thinking of our futures. The jobs we can still do.'

Vaughan's look was so sincere, so pregnant, that for one hallucinatory moment Blaylock saw himself stooping to one knee, bowing his head. *The altitude*, he thought.

A raucous *ruff!* broke the peace, and they looked to see a woman struggling with a big hairy hound on a lead, both being warily scoped out by the bodyguards. *It's their hill, too*, Blaylock reasoned – a useful reminder, lest he and the Captain had been dreaming that all the kingdoms of the world were theirs to dispose of.

He made it to Islington for 5.30 p.m. as he had pledged, in time to take his children out to tea. To his surprise, from the moment Jennie answered the door with mildness in her eyes, it seemed that he had done something right. He got a long hug from Molly. Cora said gruffly that it was 'quite a cool thing' he had done in Thornfield. Even Alex appeared very nearly impressed by the old man.

'I trust you see, son, how we deal with the right to protest and the duty of public order.'

He requested access to the upstairs bathroom and was still a little surprised when Jennie assented.

'Nick's not here?'

'He has a project and he's running around. He always is . . .'

As he washed his hands he could not avoid the sight of the big black masculine toilet-bag by the sink, akin to his own, yet glaringly other, spilling over with Vitamin D, herbal embrocation, a topical remedy for bleeding gums and – painfully – a square pack of Skyn condoms, 'ultra-thin and ultra-soft'.

He came downstairs and watched his children putting on their coats. Jennie had her fingers pressed to her lips, her gaze sightless.

'You okay? Any news on Bea?'

'Not good.' She shook her head. 'She's going to move to a hospice.'

'Aw god. I'm sorry.'

He studied Jennie's face, her holding of emotion in check; and he absorbed the news for himself. He had genuinely admired Bea, and always wished for her approval. He couldn't imagine her gone.

Jennie's fingers had strayed back to her face. 'Oh, I'm worried, David. I'm really worried . . .'

It seemed very vital to him that they had this much to share. He laid his hand on her arm. 'Of course you are. The people we love, we've got to hold onto them. Nothing else matters.'

She nodded, managed a smile at the gesture he had made. In that moment he wanted so badly to do more for her. For all it was worth, his hand stayed on her arm.

7

He got into Shovell Street early and fixed himself a full cafetière, intending to take an hour before Monday meetings to find some words fit to be said at the funeral of PC Tweddle. He had hardly got settled, though, before Phyllida Cox knocked and entered.

'You should be the first to know, I am resigning and moving on. A position at English Heritage. I've been talking to them a while.'

He was taken aback somewhat, never quite prepared to trust the sensation of being given the thing he wanted, since it seemed to call for some sort of check on the state of one's spiritual worthiness.

'So be it. I'm sure you'll make an impact wherever you go.'

'Will you consider it difficult of me if I'm gone by Christmas?'

'No. I can live with it. Someone can act up.'

She stood, wavering, seemingly unsatisfied herself. 'Irrespective of our differences, and what you may think to my opinion, I would urge you for one last time to consider the issue of your . . . personal volatility.'

'Thank you. I have taken it under advisement. For my part I'd advise you in future to always bear in mind who you're working for.'

Once she was gone he turned back to the lines in front of him: *'The men and women of our police service go to work every day to protect the public, and we ask them to be ready, if the need arises, to put their lives on the line. Christopher Tweddle was an officer who bravely answered that need.'*

It had been real everyday courage, no doubt, to go forth against a man blinded by a killing rage, blind to the pain he might inflict, who had come to put such a paltry value on life, including his own. Still, Blaylock had to imagine what it would mean to say these words in a church full of rank-and-file officers, in the presence of the man's coffin, his widow, and his two sons, left fatherless by the deranged act.

He tried to imagine himself in PC Tweddle's shoes, the last moment, the crack of the glass and the searing blackness into oblivion. He wanted the police adequately protected, yet he needed them, still, to be brave enough to go first through that door into the unknown.

He sat back and surveyed his screed. He had written what he meant to say. And still it wasn't good enough.

He left his post before midday and Martin drove him to Hampstead, on what felt like a covert errand, for which he had to steel himself. He did, at least, feel anonymous and reassured to enter a quiet, private, prosperous enclave of London. It was the sense that some vintage, cultured, serene version of central Europe had settled amid rows of orderly double-fronted redbrick English homes, all with manicured front gardens.

Amanda Scott-Stokes met him diffidently at the door and led him upstairs to her consulting room. He studied her as she poured them two glasses of water. She looked sixty-ish, with a dark bowl haircut, lined and glaucous eyes behind black-rimmed spectacles. She wore black tights and roll-neck, a grey woollen skirt, altogether an ageing bluestocking with a notable bust. Lisping and diminutive, she was nonetheless possessed of an undeniable learned assurance, her disconcerting smile suggesting to Blaylock reserves of private and arcane knowledge.

Was it because her built bookcases dominated every wall? Diverse scholarly journals were strewn across her coffee table. Over the fireplace was a framed sketch that Blaylock hazarded might be a Picasso. Watching from the next wall was a photograph of Marilyn Monroe reading a chunky Russian novel.

He lowered himself into a white leather Mies van der Rohe chair. It was she who took the sofa, crossed her legs and rested a yellow legal pad in her lap.

'We should talk a little first, yes?'

'Sure ... Talking is the greater part of it, I understood?'

'Well, quite.'

'There were children in your marriage? Were you angry toward them?'

Having waited for her questioning to reach this point, Blaylock felt an obligation to reach deeper for his answers than he had done hitherto.

'My wife, my ex-wife, would say that my temper made a climate in the house. So, the children couldn't escape it. Like the weather, I suppose ... It's hard to escape from anger in politics. The work demands so much of you. And you get uncomprehending moments because no one round you can possibly comprehend. That would frustrate anyone, I think. All the petty battles ... So, it could be that way at home, too.'

'Just a "climate"? Or were there – outbursts? Incidents?'

'Oh ...' He exhaled, suddenly feeling himself flag under the burden of miserable memories. 'There was a time I started shouting at my daughter Cora and I just couldn't stop.'

'Did you ever raise a hand? To your wife or the children?'

He took a deeper breath yet. 'Yes. One time I grabbed my wife quite heavily ... wanting her to understand ... I mean, utterly stupid and cowardly of me. She ran upstairs and locked the door and I broke it ... I calmed down but she called the police, rightly. I ... she didn't pursue it, though she certainly could have. But ... I always think that was the end, effectively. Of our marriage.'

'Are you in a relationship currently?'

'Not at present.'

'You've had relationships since your divorce?'

'Vanishingly few, but, yes.'

'Were any of these . . . coloured, or marked, by the anger issues?'

'Not so much. In my view. Some cross words. But my feelings probably weren't engaged to the degree they'd been in my marriage.'

'No subsequent relationship has been as serious to you as the one with the woman you were married to?'

'No . . . How could it?'

She seemed to weigh this. 'Why do you suppose you've been moved to take these steps now? Not sooner?'

'Because in my personal life I screwed up and I paid a price. My work life is what I have now, I can't screw that up.' Blaylock paused, appalled at what he had just said. 'And my job is a big responsibility. I need to know that won't be . . . adversely affected, beyond repair.'

'At work are you ever physical in expressing anger?'

'I had – an incident, a few days ago, raised my hand to a colleague. It wasn't typical, you don't get a rise out of me that easy now.'

'Can you say a little more of this incident for me?'

He sighed. 'I trusted a young man who was working closely with me, and he betrayed my trust and when I found out – he owned up, but he didn't apologise . . . I was so vexed just looking at him . . . But I calmed down. I didn't hit him, much as I wanted to. I mean, it's fine to disagree with me but not to lie and dissemble. You have to do things honestly. Even in politics, much as that may astound people. Be honest, or go do something else.'

She looked at him – so he thought – rather sceptically. The look lasted. She looked again at her notes, as if myopically, then shook her head. 'Heavens. I do thank you for telling me what you've told me. I appreciate this is an unusual situation. You would be an uncommon patient.' She was visibly in thought. 'And, I'm so sorry, David, but I'm afraid I don't think it will be possible for me to take you on. Forgive me. I hope you'll understand?'

Blaylock had the sudden sensation of having failed a test, of being informed with regret that his application had been unsuccessful.

'Fine . . . Why not? What is it?'

'You talk of honesty . . . I'm not certain you're ready to look at yourself with sufficient self-awareness. It has to be done that way, or not at all. Then, to be absolutely candid for my own part, there's also a political matter.'

'Political?'

'Yes, and that does pertain when someone comes to see me privately. I need to have a sympathy for that patient. You are a public figure, and you are associated with a government of whose policies I disapprove. In that sense there will always be a sort of impediment, do you follow?'

'Yeah. Ha. Fine, whatever.'

'You see my predicament?'

'Sure, Jesus. Obviously. If you think I'm so corrupt . . . Okay, yes, I get it. This was a strange waste of time, wasn't it?'

He stood and gathered his coat. She was still peering at him, spectacles shining, in a manner he now thought grossly patronising.

'But, just so you know, I'm a human being, too. I'm not just a set of headlines. Moreover, can I just say, you're full of shit? Sitting there in judgement. You disapprove, fine. Do you judge a government's policies by their outcomes? Or is it just the intentions? Anyhow, your position is ridiculous. Pathetic. You follow that?' He felt the tension released from him, and took a purposeful breath. 'Okay, so what do I do for this? Do I write you a cheque?'

She crossed her hands on her lap. 'Oh David, do forgive me, please. I angered you purposely.'

'Excuse me?'

'It must seem like a low sort of a ploy. But I'm afraid I needed to . . . see a "rise" out of you, as you put it? Really, I'm sorry. Of course I have no such objections to seeing you as a patient – as you say, it would be ridiculous. Really the only question is whether you feel able to talk to me. And that you wish to proceed, even after my little subterfuge. I do understand if you don't.'

He considered – then put down his raincoat on the chair and lowered himself back into the Mies van der Rohe chair, uneasily, as he felt it give anew under his weight.

She carefully tore a sheet from her legal pad, set it beside her, looked at him, blinked, and smiled – that encouraging smile, as if reserved for a slow learner.

'Let's begin again, shall we?'

J118: It's not long, uncle, not long to go now.

KU2: That – yeah. (muffled) Yes?

*J118: I should tell you . . . I have concerns. For arrangements.
And other parties . . . If I was to say about the trust I have
in—*

*KU2: I don't need to know. It's not necessary. Other than when,
so I can do my part. But the where and the who, I don't want
to know. I will not be where you are, so . . . Just understand, I
send you my blessings.*

*J118: No, but what I'm saying, uncle, I'm not certain the
marriage will happen . . . there are so many different things to
be organised, that have to all work together . . . If it will work.*

KU2: Tell me. Tell me what you're thinking.

*J118: Uncle, you've always said to study, and I know marriages
that have worked, that were all that everyone hoped – there
was so much care taken to do it right. I wonder if we have
done this right . . . It only takes one thing to go wrong and
everything could just be . . . disaster . . .*

*KU2: Listen, everybody must be sure. You cannot . . . it cannot be
done by half measures. All must enter the marriage of their
own choice and be committed to its success.*

J118: If it isn't a mistake . . .

*KU2: You have to know. When the gifts have been bought, the
places have been hired . . .*

J118: I'm sorry, uncle, it's hard to make myself clear . . .

*KU2: Don't agonise, brother. Think. The decision is yours.
Remember, time is not meaningful. The right things in life are
ordained. Once you have decided it has already happened, it is
God's will and you are on a path to be free.*

J118: *I met a woman I've been talking to.*

KU2: *Talked to her of what?*

J118: *No, not marriage, but she—*

KU2: *No, I can't – you have to take a view. If you thought you'd be a happier creature in the world, cuddled up with your face between a woman's thighs . . . Fine. But you have to want to challenge that weakness in yourself if you want to do something with your life, yeah? You've got to want to cleanse it from your heart. If you don't . . . well, then you are better out of this thing.*

J118: *You, you're sure yourself?*

KU2: *I will go through with my intention, yes, I will be married.*

PART VII

1

The usher from whom they collected orders of service studied Blaylock with a rather unseasonal asperity.

'May I remind you, sir, of the custom concerning hats?'

Blaylock had genuinely forgotten the hound's-tooth cap, a recent purchase, atop his head. He removed it and thrust it into his coat pocket.

'Heathen,' whispered Gavin Blount amusedly.

Thus corrected, they filed in among the shuffling hundreds whose frozen breath and holiday chit-chat faded into some form of reverent abashment upon crossing the threshold into Westminster Abbey. Within was the pipe-organ eloquence of Bach and the abbey's gloomy majesty of stone and shadow, dressed up with seasonal effulgence. This was Whitehall's Christmas Carol Service; Westminster was demob happy and cheerily observant.

In past years Blaylock had come up with excuses, but tonight attendance seemed, for a change, to be the right and improving thing to do. Dr Scott-Stokes had been advising him to address his solitary tendencies, to seek out simple shared experiences. Asking Blount to accompany him as Permanent Secretary-elect was a further act of will.

What Blaylock couldn't muster was good cheer: never in his born days had he managed to maintain for any stretch the jocular face that Christmas called for. Even pre-divorce it became the settled view of his family that 'the season' posed a challenge, for reasons all to do with him.

He watched the choir proceed, singing 'Once in Royal David's City'. The mild-eyed, lisping Dean of Westminster stood and welcomed all 'to celebrate the great festival of Christmas'. The idea of a winter festival, at least, Blaylock endorsed – wine uncorked wherever one went, tables groaning with baked meats. The victuals he expected for his Christmas lunch up in Thornfield did not look nearly so promising.

The Bible passages were allotted to ministers. He watched Caroline Tennant read with tuneless emphasis about tax revenues under Caesar Augustus; then Jason Malahide declaimed of 'The mighty God, The everlasting Father, The Prince of Peace' as if referring to himself.

The Dean, sermonising, addressed himself seriously to all sinners. 'The message of Christmas should inspire us to work together for love, justice and the betterment of all – the sick and the lame, the fearful and lonely, the wounded, the bereaved. May the hope of the Christ-child bring solace to all in darkness, and remind us we are one family.'

Blaylock grunted to himself. It was a decent idea – the child born to redeem the wicked world. Who had not looked down at their own newborn in wonder, believing that perfection, at last, had been achieved on earth? He liked less the Dean's social-working extrapolations. Christmas seemed to him irreducibly a time for lurching to the end of another year and weighing the balance of forces in one's own life: how much or little money was in the bank, how much goodwill remained stored in one's family – or how little enmity, at least.

He suddenly recalled that in his first school nativity he had played the Bethlehem innkeeper, in a towelling robe with a tea towel on his head, regretfully advising the visitors from Nazareth that there were many with business and need of lodging in the City of David that night. The memory succeeded in amusing him.

'May the blessing of God almighty, the Father, the Son, and the

Holy Spirit, come down upon you, and remain with you always, amen.'

He watched the choir move off, then, retrieving his cap from his coat, joined the crowd to shuffle back out of doors. Mark Tallis was moving purposefully toward him between bodies, and Blaylock said his goodnight to Gavin Blount.

'I had a word with Nigel Rhodes,' Tallis whispered. 'The committee's definitely minded to approve the Identity Documents Bill. He told me there's a "consensus" that the cards "can make a significant contribution in a number of areas". It's on, I think, *patrón*. First reading in the New Year.'

'Ben's gift to us,' Blaylock smiled. 'Another plan of his that came unstuck.' But his true feelings were merely that the boat remained afloat, and soon the battle would be rejoined.

He felt the throb of his phone, then saw Jennie's number, but out on the Sanctuary it was much too thick with bodies to respond. He had been quietly aggrieved by her in recent weeks, she having travelled with Gilchrist and the children for a long weekend in California that Blaylock had thought utterly gratuitous, negligent on a number of counts, and intolerably swaggering on Gilchrist's part. But he remained ready to receive an apology. He hastened to find a spot on the green of Storey's Gate and called back while Andy loitered.

'Jennie?'

'*David. Is this okay? Can you speak?*'

'Of course.'

'*David, I'm on a train heading up north, with the kids. My mum's carer called from the hospice this afternoon – she's deteriorating, quite rapidly, they think – it's days, at best, they don't reckon she'll see it through this weekend.*'

'Aw god – I'm so sorry, Jennie, truly.'

'*I know. Listen, she can't say too much, she's in and out of consciousness, but . . . she's saying her goodbyes, now. That's why*'

I'm taking the kids, she asked for them, she should see them, it's what I want and what they want. Nick's in the States for work, so . . . but why I'm calling, the thing of it is . . . Mam mentioned you, too?'

'She . . . ?'

'She said something to the carer about you. My feeling was, I think she'd probably, if you were able, it would mean something to her to see you, too.'

Blaylock swallowed, caught off-guard.

'I mean, I know it won't be the easiest thing but, I obviously had to ask.'

'Of course I'll come. Of course.'

They spoke in concerned, responsible tones about the shifting of commitments, train times, directions. Under the motions of the conversation he felt a little light-headed – struck by the proximity of death, by all the memories that attended his relationship with Jennie's family, and by the prospective force of this unexpected errand.

Not for a single second had he imagined Bea might act to bring them together again – least of all in circumstances of this kind. And yet, for all its sobering aspects, he now found himself anticipating the journey, the experience. It was to be a family Christmas, of sorts, after all.

2

Martin collected Blaylock and Andy at Newcastle Central Station and they headed out on the Hexham Road, twenty or so miles to the old Roman garrison town of Corbridge, past the august grey stone dwellings and shopfronts of the well-tended village, before arriving at the western outskirts that offered stirring views across open fields. Such was the vantage point of the Hygieia Hospice, a handsome new-build construction. Climbing out, Blaylock admired its stone gable end, its facings of render and timber and big tinted windows. Within he noted the carers in blue uniforms busying about, the natural light streaming down corridors, the side-tables laden with floral arrangements and handcrafted items. A café was fairly full of older women chatting over lattes. It was only as Blaylock made way for a stooped old gentleman making crab-like progress on two sticks that he caught the truly terminal aura of the place.

Given a kindly steer down one sun-dappled corridor, he instantly saw his ex-wife standing by a closed door, tapping at her phone, casual in jeans and tee-shirt and a long cable-knit cardigan he had always loved her in. She gave him a smile and a snatched hug.

'She's asleep, but . . . oh, she's not sounding good at all.'

A piano sonata played softly from a small black docking station. Bea lay propped up, eyes shut, her breathing as laboured as Jennie had intimated. The absence of machines and tubes took Blaylock aback for the moments he needed to remember that this was a place where painkilling was continual, treatment otherwise withdrawn.

The room was dressed with cards, framed photos, pinned-up pictures, several vases of flowers, and Blaylock's three children who greeted him with rueful eyes. The stoicism of Alex and Cora did not surprise him, but Molly's quiet calm surely did.

Unsure of what tone was best, he enquired softly after their bed-and-breakfast lodging twenty minutes' drive away, then asked Molly what she would like as a gift for her birthday in nine days' time. Unusually she shrugged, and made no special requests.

'What plans for the big day?' he asked of Jennie.

'Oh, we're thinking small, maybe a sleepover with a couple of schoolmates? We'd half a mind to take her away for the night.'

'Just let me know when I can drop by with a gift.'

Jennie was not looking at him. She was looking at her mother, whose eyes had opened and now surveyed the room exhaustedly.

'Eee, well, look at this . . .' she murmured.

Blaylock went forward and took a chair by the head of the bed. 'How are you, Bea?'

Her eyes narrowed in the way they always had when she addressed herself to the slow-witted. 'I've been better.'

Jennie came, moistened a cloth in a metal dish, and gently wiped her mother's lips.

'I manage. If I wake in the night, I'm not so good. But I'm ready, David.'

Bea gestured limply toward the long window looking out to the hospice's back garden.

'This is good, but. I see the sky, birds, a bit green . . . Alex, bonny lad, would you open that . . . ?'

Bea meant the window. Alex obliged. They sat and stared awhile through the glass, at birds bickering at a table. In the hush Bea's breath came rasping from her open mouth. And yet Blaylock could hear the birdsong from out of doors, a cheery, repeated two-note peep.

'What is that, Bea? What bird?'

She looked at him with slow, wan mirth. 'A great tit.'

Blaylock smiled, sensing without looking that others in the room were doing likewise. Bea gestured again, murmured something he could not catch and he had to lean close to her parched lips.

'Starling. Up in that tree. Lonesome one. He's like you.'

Her eyelids fluttered, and Blaylock had the sharp sense of sand running fine through the glass. Her hand, the skin of it blotched perilously dark, lay palm open on the bedcovers. He took it in his, finding it dry and cold, feeling for the life in it. She studied him, her eyes grey and mild, and he felt the hard duty to say why he had come.

'Bea . . . I wanted you to know my great regard for you. How glad I've been to know you.'

She nodded, perhaps approving. 'It was a great shame . . . how it fell out between you and Jennie, but . . .'

Blaylock weighed his reply, conscious of the other presences in the room, yet feeling the heavy onus to be truthful with one so near her end.

'It was. I'll always feel bad about it.'

Bea managed almost to shrug. 'Eh . . . it happened that way . . . At least, now, things are settled.'

Jennie leaned in and spoke with some urgency. 'Mam? David and I had happy times together, and three beautiful children came of it, so I just think that's the thing we should remember.'

'These children . . .' – Bea's grey head shook slightly toward Blaylock – '. . . are a great credit to you both.' She squeezed on his hand with a strength that surprised him. He felt a sudden tautness in his face, feared he would cry. Knowing it to be so much the wrong thing to do he rallied and suppressed the emotion.

Jennie took her mother's other hand. Bea's eyelids fluttered again.

'I'm sorry, Jennie . . . Sorry, pet . . . I need to sleep.'

Again Jennie applied the cloth. 'You sleep, Mam, you sleep.'

In the corridor Blaylock felt impelled to run a stroking hand on the arms and shoulders of the children, who seemed disconsolate but not unappreciative of his touch. They dawdled toward the café but Blaylock excused himself to step into the administrator's office, where he enquired after the policy in respect of donations and wrote out a cheque for two hundred pounds.

When he entered the cafeteria Jennie asked the kids to take themselves and their cans of fizzy pop outside awhile.

'How are you feeling?'

'Aw, you know, David. Just the things we all feel. It's not enough, is it? Life? So much we take for granted.'

Blaylock was glad of the excuse to look at her and feel that his gaze was welcome. Today she seemed younger somehow – a daughter again, and yet notably like her mother round the eyes. He resisted an urge to reach and blend her foundation, applied somewhat slapdash round her jaw-line. Abruptly in his mind's eye he had a picture of her in the early months of their marriage – damp from the shower, absently chewing her lip as she brushed her hair, fixed herself into her bra, sorted the inky blacks and crisp whites of her professional uniform.

A broad window gave them a good vantage on the children. Cora had sat on a bench with a paperback; Alex had produced his camera and was practising pans across the hilly vista looking south into the sun. Molly was visibly pleading that he look her way, whereupon she turned a cartwheel.

'They're proper people, aren't they?' Blaylock murmured. 'What did we do?'

'Oh, they're their own inventions, I think. They make up their own minds. I could say Cora's like me, with her books and her bit feminism. But I can't tell her a thing, really. As for Molly the gymnast, mind . . . that must be your side.'

'Oh, I think they've all successfully escaped my influence.'

She shot him a searching look. 'I think it would mean something to Alex if you'd give him a bit more credit, for the person he is.'

Somewhat stung, he wanted to tell her, *Look, sometimes kids remind us of bits of ourselves we don't like. Or things we never liked about anyone.*

Instead he said, 'I know, I missed a chance there . . . Listen, I'm feeling full well reminded of a person I used to be. I know you won't want any reminding of it.'

'Howay, David,' Jennie replied with eyes narrow as her mother's. 'Don't go to self-pity city. I meant what I said in the room. Times like these . . . I think you remember it's better not to judge one another too harshly.'

'You mean our happy times together . . . ?'

'Well, "together" we were fine. The trouble was when we got detached. Doing our own things.' She cupped her coffee mug. 'I think back now, how lonely motherhood was for me. I just got the hang of it when you, oh, found your mission and started haring around constituencies . . . And, you know, you sort of made me feel the kids were my department, and had to be kept in line and the house run to order while you were off. Then when you *were* home – I sort of stopped recognising you. It was like a mask starting to grow on your face. That bloody politician's face . . .'

'Bloody Tory politician, you mean.'

'Listen, we just had divergent views, don't pretend you were so even-handed . . . Until we were married you'd never let on how much you thought that everything I believed was bullshit . . . Anyhow, as you know, that's not the reason things became impossible for you and me . . .'

There was such a familiar pity in her look at him that he felt an idea move forward sharply from the back of his mind to the tip of his tongue: he should tell her he was seeking professional help. It would surely be a significant admission. He took a breath.

'I do. And I want you to know, just lately, I've . . . tried to have a hard look at myself. I took your advice. I appreciate I've used anger, resorted to it, out of . . . fear . . . Out of not being able to admit error.'

She was studying him with interest, eyebrows slightly raised.

'I know I'd have been a better husband – better father, better man – if I'd faced up to some things sooner. I can't apologise for everything. No more than I can undo it. The world's not made for that. But I do want to apologise, properly, for what I did to spoil what we had – you and me and the children. I just . . . I will just always regret it, Jennie.'

He put a hand to his brow, having managed to affect himself. Though he felt improved by having made the confession, some faint shame seemed to lurk in his motive. Still, he was able to measure the success of his words by the moist glint in Jennie's eye.

'Oh David, you're going to set me off . . .'

He reached and took her hand, and she enclosed their joined hands with hers in a way that seemed to him heartfelt. He realised he could not stop himself.

'I love you, Jennie. I always will. It just, it can't be helped.'

The line of her mouth creased, he saw real pain there. 'David . . . I'll always, always . . . have love for you. And I'm sorry, too, how things turned. If I could have seen . . . it wasn't just you, okay? You know that. And what we shared . . . you never forget.' Then she released his hand, looked down sharply. 'The kids . . .'

He touched her arm. 'Will you think about what I've said?'

'David, I'll not be able to stop thinking about it,' she said, rubbing a corner of a reddened eye, her face brightening as Molly came near.

*

He struggled to feel that he was fully present at his final constituency surgery of the year. The matter was certainly sobering: people coming to see him on the last Saturday before Christmas clearly had no hope of a restful holiday. Eventually a woman in clear despair over the state of her family finances broke down in tears and Blaylock had to get his case worker in to take her outside for air. Feeling glum for her and at a loss, Blaylock got out his wallet, found three tenners and thrust them into the depths of the woman's handbag.

With the team he reviewed his schedule for Christmas Day over a pot of tea and a packet of supermarket mince pies, then headed for the car. On the journey to Maryburn, belatedly realising he had forgotten to un-mute his phone, he saw that he had missed Jennie's call.

'Late last night she went right downhill. I dashed over at two in the morning, she was propped up but her breathing was, oh, awful, she couldn't get words out. She knew she was going. I just stroked her and mopped her brow. She went away for a bit, then came back. Then the breaths got further apart ... then there was just one that was, oh ... it was like all the life leaving her.'

Jennie's voice on the line seemed to him deeply saddened but impressively composed; he realised that in some way he wished he could hear notes of helplessness.

'Is there anything I can do for you?'

'We're good, David, thanks. Nick just got here on the redeye. I did the groundwork, so we'll have a cremation on Tuesday, then I'm sending the children home on the train that afternoon, Radka's going to meet them at King's Cross, Nick and I will finish a few things up here and come back on Wednesday.'

He had ceased to hear after the mention of Nick Gilchrist, but the funeral arrangements were important, on account of what he knew was his unavoidable self-exclusion. Tuesday would see him in Hampshire to observe preparatory exercises for the policing of the G20 summit set to convene in London early in the New Year.

'I wish I could join you for the funeral, I've just . . . I've got to be at Longmoor army base and I don't think I can get out of it . . .'

'*I wouldn't have thought you could . . . Honestly, David, I know you'd like to, but you came and that meant a lot.*'

He completed the sentence in his head: *And Nick is here, and all's well.*

'Well, okay. Please just say, if there's anything. I'd do it gladly.'

'*I know you would, David. We'll manage.*'

'I'll see you on the other side then? For Molly's birthday? You'll let me know?'

'*I'll be in touch, yes.*'

In the silence of the house he had to acknowledge that he let a little hopefulness kindle in him, against all good sense, and that this had now quite properly guttered out. The emotion of the occasion had swayed him, he could see that. Still he chastised himself inwardly for having fallen into wishful fancy when he knew full well he simply had not earned the thing his heart sought. He had not yet made a proper confession, not truly renounced the devil and all his works.

3

MONDAY, DECEMBER 21

'Forgive me, David, but you seem out of sorts.'

'It's a miserable time of year.'

'That is a point of view, I suppose . . .'

He had indeed spent some time staring fixedly and gloomily at the walls. He had wondered all morning about the worth of showing up. But here he was, mainly struck anew by the arrangement of Amanda Scott-Stokes's room and its many testimonials to high culture, as if this were a sufficient force to keep a man right-minded.

'Talking, as you gathered, David, is the greater part of it. I can't help you unless you can say what concerns you.'

But Blaylock couldn't bear to describe his weekend in Thornfield, the wound of his dashed feelings for Jennie, the low hostility he harboured toward her new life, from which his exclusion seemed to be assuming a finality.

'I had wondered, when you were a child . . .'

'Oh Christ . . .'

'Was it a strict household? How were your parents on discipline?'

Blaylock sighed. 'My dad was in charge of it. Never let me get away with much. But, he never raised a hand. It would be a sharp word or a hard look. That was all it took. I hated to get wrong off him. Because generally I knew he was right whether I liked it or not.'

'He never lashed out?'

'Not at me. Nor my mother, before you ask. He'll not have been a saint all his life. But you're on the wrong horse going on about my dad.'

He shifted in his seat, feeling familiar tempos beating in his brow and through his shoulders, a storm of irritation.

'Truth is, I maybe took the wrong example off my dad. I avoided physical conflicts as a young person, I would go to any lengths to tamp it all down instead.'

'You never "lashed out"?'

'No, what I'd say is that I lashed in. Things that angered me . . . I used them, like a whip, to push myself harder. I didn't want to be angry, aggressive, I associated all that with . . . weakness.'

Having thought it and said it, he felt the word hang there between them. Dr Scott-Stokes looked at him with her slight, encouraging smile.

'However,' he resumed quietly, 'I would say, in retrospect, that I was avoiding certain kinds of necessary confrontation.'

'But then you joined the army. You ran toward confrontation.'

'I don't know any more what I did there. I've talked so much about it, I get accused of embellishing it and god knows what. I don't know why I joined the army. Except that it was a mistake.'

'Did the army make you a more aggressive person?'

'Look, I've no regrets about any violence I was part of as a soldier, there was always a reason for it. The only things that live with me, that haunt me, are things I failed to do. In the face of violence. Failures of moral courage. Bad decisions I made as a leader, decisions other people paid the price for – yeah, those, they do . . . plague me.'

She was looking at him closely, concernedly, but silently. After long resistant stumbles down a path he was acutely conscious of the threshold they had come to. He looked away and past her to the grey of the window. It seemed to him he could open the door, or else leave it and walk away, live to fight another day, for what it was worth.

'There's no day I don't think about things that happened . . . in Bosnia? There was something . . . I've never been able to bear the memory of . . . I stop myself thinking of it when it comes.'

Still she was silent. He felt light-headed, weak around his limbs. So much had to happen to bring him to this fork.

'It was near the end of our tour. We were so nearly out of it. I led my platoon to a village, mainly Croat village, under siege by the Bosnian Muslims. Because the shoe was on the other foot, right?

'We'd been told the villagers needed help, might need evacuating. There were mortars coming in, heavy fire, sniping . . . and a lot of terror. So we went in, and we found some very frightened, sorry-looking villagers holed up in a church – fifty or so. Handsome old place. But it had become just a refugee bedlam. With that creature smell . . . everything overturned, shot up, broken windows, coats laid out like skins, no light or heat.

'We parked our vehicles round like a shield, ran a UN flag up the belfry. But the incoming just intensified. We fired back, but there was . . . real terror round us, and we, me and my men, we were right in it now. It was a big choice, if we got them out that was it, they became displaced peoples. But to leave them to the mercies of the Bosnian army . . .'

He shook his head. 'So, I called for reinforcements, all the vehicles we could muster to evacuate. I explained, through my interpreter, how we'd do it, forming them into lines, running the gauntlet, women and children first, dozen or so in the back of each vehicle and no looking back. They were scared but they seemed to know they had to do it. Except for one girl who wouldn't come out, literally curled up cowering in the confession box while her mother pleaded with her. Asked me would I get her out. She'd big wide eyes, buck teeth, looked malnourished. Her name was Rozi. What I did, I'd told the men not to hand out stuff but I had a roll of peppermints and I offered her them, said they were hers, and

[425]

she came, I got her to come out of the dark and join us.

'Then we had to crack on. Our vehicles, three Warriors, got through and up the hill and backed up to the monastery. We got them all in a sort of order. But I wanted them sorted by size, not family, so we got everyone in for the space we had. We started shepherding. There had to be covering fire. We filled one vehicle, off it went. Then the next was all but done, and we'd room for one child, I thought. I was by the Warrior and I looked, Rozi was by the door of the church, I shouted for her to come. Just her, not her mother. I said, "Come on, don't be scared!"

'She *was* scared. I should have gone and got her. Why I thought it was job done and I'd saved the day . . . I just should have gone and got her.

'She must have believed me – she got this purposeful face on, she ran out, stumbled, dropped the sweets I gave her. She got on her feet, looked at me, and at the sweets – like should she pick them up? Then she was hit. Sniper bullet. Direct to the head. And that was that. That was that. She just dropped like a stone to the grass and I knew.'

Dr Scott-Stokes put fingers to her lips. 'Oh,' she whispered.

'I looked at her mother, and . . . as long as I live I'll never not be seeing that woman's face. Hearing the sound that came out of her.'

The doctor's lined and lugubrious face seemed a mirror for the torment Blaylock had revived in himself. He felt tremors rise through his chest and succumbed, getting the back of his hand to his face to stifle a sob, then burying his face into his fingers as his upper body shook.

'Aw god . . . I'm sorry.'

'Please don't say sorry, David . . .'

For some moments he could hear nothing but his own sobs and snuffles.

'I understand, the cruelty of it . . . But the girl's death was caused by the sniper. It wasn't your—'

He looked up sharply. 'No, no. I can't let myself off like that. I don't need to be told what my job was. I should have gone and got her. You have to do the thing you said you would the way you said you'd do it.'

'Were you able to discuss this with anyone? Superiors? A counsellor?'

'There wasn't the time. Never the time. Listen, any number of men saw worse than me on that tour. I knew the pain some of them were in. You just had to live with it. For me it was going back after the war, volunteering. Before I . . . before Jennie and I got together.'

'You told Jennie about this?'

'No. No way. What could she do about it? It would have . . . impaired me, too much. I needed to be someone else with her.'

'What do you mean?'

'She admired me as an ex-soldier who'd done noble things. Not some fuck-up. I liked that she thought that – I needed her to keep thinking that. Of course, in the end, I bloody showed her I wasn't. I showed our children. In abundance.'

He rubbed at his eyes, looked up and blinked, shook his head and stared aside – miserable, depleted, unrelieved.

'It seems to me in some ways you blame your ex-wife for not understanding you. But how much has she really known?'

'Well . . . it's done now, Amanda, so . . .'

'David, the things we can't forgive ourselves for – they're far more damaging than things inflicted on us by others. Because there's no escape from the offender. The anger turned inward, the "lashing-in" you describe . . . I think you need to give some thought as to how you could forgive yourself.'

He could not keep derision out of his deep sigh. 'Sorry, that seems to me . . . impossible. Selfish. A religious thing, like going to a priest. I'm surprised you'd even suggest it.'

She looked stern. 'I don't mean to load it with connotations of virtue. That is wholly secondary, the question is what serves a patient's needs, what might relieve the mental and physical stress of chronic anger. Which is why I propose we discuss it.'

'Amanda, I just wish to god it hadn't happened. To her, and, utterly selfishly, to me. Yeah, one side of my head could say it forgives the other. But the other's not going to be fooled. It's not for me to forgive myself. I don't have the right, it's too late. The only person who could forgive me is dead.'

'Oh David, but to see it that way is hopeless.'

'Yes. You're right. Yes.'

He stood up.

'I'm sorry, I realise how it seems . . . and I think we just need to conclude our business here. Thank you for listening.'

She did not move from her seat yet seemed very sombre. 'If you leave this now, David, what have you achieved?'

'I talked, you listened. It wasn't nothing . . . We agree, I've done some regrettable things. But I believe I can change, things happen that change you, people, events . . .'

'David, I'm sorry, forgive me, my fear is you will just continue to bury your problems. You say "regrettable things". I'm afraid I could all too easily see you do worse—'

'Goodbye, Amanda,' Blaylock snapped, shaking his head and heading directly for the door.

4

He stood exposed, bracing himself against a squalling wind that seemed to want to blow him sideways to the tarmac. If there was no dream day to be visiting a windswept parade ground, Blaylock thought this one notably bleak – a sorry way to spend the year's last day of work and the last of its daylight hours. Even the shelter of the corrugated iron hangars and outbuildings of Longmoor Military Base was off-limits, for Blaylock was required to be beside Commissioner Bannerman at the perimeter of the ground, ready to inspect the troops performing for his benefit. Blaylock didn't care for the view, or the company, or for anything much about the shape of his life, but he was aware that others gathered for the session were about to have it tougher.

Some of the officers looked less assured than others hefting their long shields, clad in the full anti-riot dress of black-visored helmets and ballistic body armour. But their opposition for the day, loitering at the opposite end of the ground, were not offering a hugely intimidating prospect, in their ill-fitting vests and caps and hoodies, clutching beer-can props – either, Blaylock assumed, warranted officers having a lark or some underemployed spear-carriers from the National.

A moaning klaxon broke out on the air. Armoured Land Rovers moved forward, lights ablaze, sirens going, then pulled up, allowing more officers to disembark, urged on by the hoarse cries of their drill supervisor, a squat Ulsterman with a thick moustache. '*Move! Move yerselves forward! And get beating on them shields!*'

Close behind the officers trundled the six-wheeled water cannon, a blank-eyed beast of a vehicle copiously bolstered by cameras, speakers, barrels and searchlights.

'I generally think just the look of these things is worth the cost of them!' Bannerman shouted to Blaylock over the wind.

'Yeah, we had 'em in Belfast!' Blaylock shouted back. 'They tended to get you running the other way!'

A heavily amplified warning blared from the cannon's tannoy. *'Attention, this is a police message, disperse at once or water jets will be fired.'*

The roof-mounted barrels were moving, a siren kicked in, and the water jets started to soak the ground in front of the vehicle's wheels. Then the pressure was jacked up, and the officers on foot hastily shifted to wider, warier positions. The cannons began to strafe directly before the pack of pretend demonstrators, who took to their heels in a manner Blaylock thought highly convincing as a mist came off the tarmac from the formidable measured sweep of the jets.

'What's the optimum pressure?' Blaylock shouted.

'No higher than what you're seeing!' Bannerman shouted back. 'Obviously if someone got it in the head they'd be in trouble!'

Now Blaylock saw one of the faux anarchists take a hit from the cannon directly to the small of his fleeing back, pitching him forward to the ground where he scrabbled with both hands in hapless disarray.

'How much does it hurt, do you think?' Blaylock shouted.

Bannerman grinned. 'Do you fancy finding out, David? We can loan you a spare hoodie . . . !'

'I appreciate you might be minded to direct the operation yourself, Home Secretary, and it's not to say we can't use a good wingman on the scene, but be assured, this time round you can stand yourself down.'

Bannerman seemed to be amusing himself. They were back inside the hangar, served with steaming tea, and the Commissioner, flanked by a stern Deputy Chief Constable with publications on civil disorder to his name, briefed Blaylock formally on their intelligence and operational plans.

'All leave has been cancelled for City of London officers, and we'll have men stationed with Land Rovers at all of these points where property's most likely at risk. You're going to be treated to the virtuous sight of big police numbers, David . . .'

Blaylock let the jibe run off. 'Tell me how you're prepared for smaller threats – splinter groups, surprise tactics and that.'

'Of course, you got blindsided on Mr Colls' patch in Kent,' Bannerman murmured over his mug. 'But that was a mere media stunt. Capitalising on inexperience.'

The DCC took over. 'We know protesters have prepared for months – we've had good sight of what's being shared. Obviously we expect factions, blocs within the protest, with divergent aims and tactics. Some of it will be non-violent protest, tactical frivolity—'

'Excuse me?' said Blaylock.

'Pranks,' Bannerman grunted. 'Like what happened to you in Kent. There are always these little mobs. But we don't anticipate the storming of the Winter Palace. Certainly not by a horde of adolescents and undergraduates.'

Blaylock sat back, sceptical. 'One thing I've observed from recent melees – I think you need more emergency first aid on site.'

'Your concern is touching, and noted. Obviously our duty as a police service is to enable peaceful protest. But if we have to scoop up any youngsters they'll all be treated as well as the rest.'

Blaylock began to pack up, mindful of the time, the trail back to London, and the last chores outstanding – mindful, too, of Bannerman keeping an eye on him as he nursed his mug of tea.

'What's it all about, eh? Young people, their whole lives ahead of them, so far out of their depth in this protesting lark . . . It's the parents I feel for.'

Blaylock could not escape the sense that Bannerman was jibing him again, somehow. But then the Commissioner's momentarily penetrative gaze gave way to the condescending tolerance he knew of old.

Two hours later he was squaring away his desk for the year, moodily drawing some red lines down a budget report, when Geraldine entered, bearing the familiar folder, the ritual despatch from MI5. 'Some urgent warrants just came in, David . . .'

Blaylock opened the folder with a strong disinclination to his usual close inspection or token query, intending just to append his signature and be done. The clutch of warrants, however, was thicker than he had anticipated. He was on the point of picking up the hotline to Adam Villiers when his main desk phone rang and Geraldine advised him that the Foreign Secretary was calling.

'*David, I thought you should know, MI5 has just sent me a surveillance warrant to authorise, the grounds being that it concerns an individual you're acquainted with, so can't sign for. Is that right?*'

'I've no idea, Dom, who are we talking about?'

'*Sorry, just one moment . . . A Mr Sadaqat Osman?*'

Blaylock went directly on foot to Thames House, where Adam Villiers received him in his fifth-floor office.

'Mr Osman lit up the radar a while back, it's true, we knew him to be an associate of an associate of a person of interest . . . a college classmate of his from ten years ago? But overnight we heard something to concern us. He was, we established, the other party in a conversation with a separate individual under watch.'

Villiers hit PLAY on his black tablet. Blaylock listened to two voices discussing a 'marriage' in fraught tones, one of them clearly quite young, the other clearly Sadaqat.

' . . . But you have to want to challenge that weakness in yourself if you want to do something with your life, yeah? You've got to want to cleanse it from your heart. If you don't . . . well, then you are better out of this thing.'

'You, you're sure yourself?'

'I will go through with my intention, yes, I will be married.'

When the room was silent Villiers studied Blaylock's disquieted face. 'Mr Osman is, in fact, already a married man?'

'He is.'

'Of course. The handset on which he received the call is his wife's. So the covertness, the obvious use of code that, I hasten to add, we have been hearing in other places – these are concerns.'

'Who's the other man on the tape?'

'Said al-Allam, a young cousin of an old college friend of Mr Osman's – Abul Rahman, whom we've had on warranted surveillance in recent months.'

'They're in league?'

'Mr Osman and Mr Rahman are not thought to have been close since they both graduated from SOAS nearly a decade ago. But they seem to have rediscovered some shared enthusiasm. Said al-Allam and Mr Osman we don't believe have ever met in person. But that's part of the trouble.'

Blaylock recognised Villiers's habit, whenever their business took on a notable gravity, to start to speak in riddles.

'Are you aware Sadaqat's line of work for some years has meant dealings with a lot of troubled young men – men who'll have likely come to your attention at one time or another?'

'That he has been thought to be good with young men? Relating to them, the issues they have? Yes. Mr Osman was employed by the Hardy Street Mosque? We've established that he left under something of a cloud. He was given rooms in the basement that the trustees felt he put to dubious uses. Weightlifting, not pious discussion. Even before he turned to his good works in the third sector some of his previous endeavours were a little more offbeat. Three years ago he visited family in Peshawar; I'm not convinced it was family he spent his time with . . .'

Blaylock felt himself back in the cave – in the darkness, insecure, footing unsure, his good senses disabled. The concern that he could have been so badly wrong thrummed through him. The notion that others might yet rescue him from folly was a lifeline – but a demeaning, debilitating one.

'I appreciate you may resist the deduction from this.'

'I do. I met this man, talked with him, spent time with him . . . I made a judgement about him, Adam.'

'Of course. As, now, have we. You should not chastise yourself. You would not be the first to have been fooled. I do appreciate these matters are testing. However, it is important to me that you have faith in us, our judgement, as you say.'

'It's Dominic Moorhouse who'll decide.'

'He already has, David.'

Villiers' arms had been folded, but now he pressed his hands together at his chin – not worshipful but, rather, judgemental. Blaylock understood: he was meant to be examining his conscience, making a good act of contrition, pledging to sin no more.

'In which case,' Blaylock said finally, 'there are, probably, some other associates of Mr Osman's you ought to be looking at.'

5

Andy and he were slumped into facing train seats, rumbling northward, both with steaming teas and bacon rolls before them, and Blaylock could nearly believe he saw his reflection in front of him, too. For Andy looked as beset and out of sorts as Blaylock felt – certainly not his usual ramrod-straight, taciturn self. In response to the simplest of cordial enquiries, perplexity poured out of him: the object of worry his college-age son, whom he'd had to stay for an unsatisfactory few days before the young man went to spend Christmas with his mother.

'The effort he puts into being a bloody shirker. It's not just slackness, boss, it's insolence.' Andy leaned in with an agitated confiding look, speaking *sotto voce*. 'He smokes draw and thinks I don't know. The girlfriend's been over, they have it off in his room then she's out the door, not a word. He just lets on like the rules don't *apply*.'

Blaylock had every sympathy, but no answer. He had heard worse things, no doubt. But it seemed to him that if the boy did not respect Andy then he surely respected no one.

They lapsed into silence and Blaylock gazed out at the flat expanse of Cambridgeshire, the dull and dispensable first hour of the journey. To be heading north had always felt to him a boon – hurtling up the length of the land, through Grantham and Newark to Doncaster, York, Darlington, the view a source of pleasure where others likely saw just fast-fleeting dullness. This was his England, the north his great good place to which he had

[435]

unerringly homed – to restart his life after the army, then to scout a place where he and Jennie could be wed, then to take newborn Alexander to see his grandparents, then the speculative treks of his quest to be adopted as parliamentary candidate. Where his old family ties had come loose he had made new ones, seemingly robust. Today, though, he had an unhappy sense of being twice estranged.

He hoisted himself from his seat. 'Khazi,' he told a distracted Andy, who looked for a moment as if he might get up and come along.

'Easy, Andy, you know you don't have to hold it for me.'

'I'd have to find it first, boss.'

That was more like it, in Blaylock's opinion. He grunted, steadied himself and lurched down the carriage to the swaying vestibule.

Up ahead he saw a figure rise from seated in the next carriage, parting the doors, and seeming suddenly to be coming straight for him – a strapping male, grave-faced, dressed for urban war in black combats and denims, yet Christ-like of beard and dark matted hair. Blaylock tensed up – but the man only ducked ahead of him and through the sliding door of the men's cubicle.

As Blaylock turned and paced, rapping his knuckles absently on the vestibule wall, it dawned on him quite suddenly that he had seen this man before. Simultaneously, to his surprise, the man re-emerged, shot him a look of glaring intensity then lumbered off into the next carriage whence he had come, not stopping at his seat.

Warily Blaylock stepped into the cubicle, seeing at once that something was awry. A sheet of printed A4 had been plastered by its dampened corners onto the mirror over the sink.

Blaylock stepped closer and squinted to read the type.

You don't know me but you need to trust me. Your son Alex is in trouble. Tonight he'll go to a meeting in E5 for anarchist

protesters who have <u>major</u> plans to disrupt the G20. The
meeting is at 5 p.m., police know all about it – it will be raided
– your son will get lifted. You can stop this if you act <u>now</u>.

Blaylock's pulse rose. Something nagged in his throat as he swallowed. He clawed the wet page off the mirror, turned and felt his feet move him forward, out of the cubicle, through sliding doors to the next carriage, blindly following the path his messenger had taken.

He clocked every seated face as he passed, bored faces, some flickering into recognition of him. But he could not find his man, not in that carriage nor the next.

He reached the last vestibule, the front of the shuddering train, where chained bicycles were slumped in a shadowy nook before the driver's cab. Then he spun sharply, sensing rightly that his messenger had emerged from gloom by the door.

'You got it, right?'

'Who are you, what do you—?'

The messenger dug into his black denim coat. Blaylock felt a lurch in his chest. What was produced and flashed unwaveringly for a few seconds was a Met Police badge and warrant card.

As Blaylock absorbed the disclosure and the messenger re-pocketed his ID, they both heard the crackle of a guard's announcement. *'We are approaching Peterborough, if you are leaving the train . . .'* The queasy odour of the brakes filled the cramped space. The messenger stepped nearer to Blaylock.

'Your boy's getting put in a fit-up, right? The raid, it's going to happen, and stuff's gonna get found, bet your life on it. Everyone in that place is getting nicked.'

Blaylock heard himself stammer. 'No. Can't be, I don't buy it, Alex can't be that deep in this—'

'He's not. He's being led into it. Like a prize pig.'

'Who's leading him? You?'

[437]

'Nope. You work it out.' And he scoffed. '*Cherchez la femme*, yeah?'

'Not the girl. Don't tell me she's a copper, too?'

He shook his head. 'Snitch. She'll walk away from it tonight, you can bet on that too. Not your boy, though. And by midnight the world's gonna know.'

'He's only seventeen.'

'Wise up. It's not about him. It's about you.'

Blaylock put a hand to his head as if he might still it. Through the window he could see the train easing down, rushing toward a sparsely populated platform. The messenger was clearly desperate to escape his confinement.

'Why are you telling me this?'

'You got people don't like you, Mr Blaylock. But it's not your boy's fault you're his dad. Listen, do what you want, you can wait for the call from the station or hear it on the news. But they're meeting tonight, five o'clock.'

He stabbed the release on the door and bailed out.

Blaylock turned, punchy, his feet unsteady under him, and started to run back the way he had come – only to see Andy coming powerfully down the aisle, visibly agitated, as if wanting to see past him.

'Boss, you alright?'

'No. Look, change of plan. Grab the stuff, we're getting off.'

Blaylock was caged by the return journey, head pulsing, trapped in his chair and kicking the upright, feeling hemmed and harried by undesirable options on all sides. He could not decide what to do or whom to trust. Worse, Andy wanted to understand, and Blaylock could offer only tortuous half-truths.

'I just have to see my son, it's just . . . it's as simple as that.'

'But I don't get it, boss. Can't you call him?'

'No, I – just, listen, I have to go fetch him, myself.'

Andy got on the phone and arranged a car at King's Cross. Blaylock checked his watch, 3.37. As the train zipped through the environs of the Arsenal stadium he called the Islington house. Radka picked up, her wariness of him clear down the line.

'Radka, do you know where Alex is?'

'He is with his friend? They have gone for coffee, to hang out? He said he will be home seven, seven-thirty I think, when Mrs Kirkbride is home?'

'Do you've any idea where they'll have gone? I've something for him, you see, for Christmas . . .'

'He said the Nomad café? Near City College?'

They surged out of the car on the Holloway Road and strode into the café, bringing the cold of the street with them. Andy pulled his badge and went directly to the bleach-blonde barista while Blaylock stood scanning the moodily lit space with darting eyes.

'Have you seen a boy, about seventeen? With a girl, a girl with long red hair? Red like scarlet?'

'Uh, they paid and left like five minutes ago?'

Blaylock shoved at the door, Andy already on his heels.

He broke into a jog in the direction of the nearest underground stop. It was hopeless. Before them in the dark and the cold was a pre-Christmas pavement throng, a heedless mass of bodies blindly in their way.

And then ahead, under the yellowy illumination spilling out of a newsagent's by Holloway Road station, Blaylock could make out two figures, their shapeless duds fringed with light, that mane of scarlet hair. He began to run, hearing Andy's strides fall harder behind him.

Through the threshold of the station they saw, beyond the ticket barriers, lift doors closing. Andy held aloft his warrant card, flashed it all around and, without hesitation, vaulted across the barrier and headed for the stairwell. Blaylock, borne forward by momentum, did likewise, jarring his knee against metal but clearing the hurdle.

Two steps at a time they leapt down the staircase, into the bowels of the station, skittering onto the tube platform in time to see a southbound train, its doors open. Blaylock looked both ways frantically, but the platform was deserted from end to end. A beep sounded to indicate the imminent closure of the doors.

'Boss, it's got to be this one!' Andy shouted and lurched aboard the train. Blaylock followed, wrenching his coat-tails free of the doors.

On the tube, perspiring, adrenalin coursing through his body, he felt curious eyes on him and looked down and left and right and then at Andy, trying to bring his breathing and agitation under control.

The train pulled into Caledonian Road and they both bustled off, Blaylock's gaze searching twenty yards down the platform – and finding his son's familiar frame and Esther's siren-like head as the pair headed to the exit. For the first time in two hours Blaylock felt his breath coming easily again.

They kept their targets discreetly in sight on the dim-lit pavement up ahead; Andy had summoned the driver; and now all that pulsed through Blaylock was the desire to finish the exercise. For Alex and Esther had now linked hands, and the surpassing strangeness of the pursuit had begun to make Blaylock feel vaguely disreputable, even as he resisted the thought of the greater unpleasantness that surely had to follow.

They had entered a deserted street. Just as Blaylock felt it was the moment to strike he saw the young pair pause. Esther, on tiptoe, craned her vermilion head so as to kiss Alex's willing mouth.

Blaylock felt sick. Perhaps something of his discomfort was borne in the air for, as the kiss concluded, Alex turned and finally saw his father and Andy Grieve together ten yards hence. The alarm on his face was all Blaylock needed for a cue, and he strode toward them.

'Alex, you have to come with me.'

'Dad – what the actual *fuck*—?'

'You're not going to this meeting. Not tonight, not any night, this ends now.' He bit off the words, keeping them low.

'What fucking meeting?'

For a cold instant Blaylock truly wondered if he was not, in fact, colossally mistaken, thoroughly played. 'C'mon. I know where you're going, what you're up to. You'll not go. I'm taking you home.'

'You're not taking me anywhere, I don't know what you're talking about.' But then Alex looked to Esther, and in his searching eyes and her visible horror Blaylock was sure he knew the gospel truth.

'I could take you straight to a police station. Cut out the middleman? I'd rather that than have you walk into a trap.' He rounded on Esther. 'You, tell him! Is everything going to be okay? It's not, is it?'

Esther turned and ran. Andy lurched as to pursue her but Blaylock laid a staying hand on him. 'Leave her, Andy.'

Alex, however, was moving, too, and Blaylock instinctively grabbed a handful of his chambray shirt. 'Alex, I know it seems—'

There was stunning enmity in the boy's eyes. He shrugged himself free and started to run, too, but now Andy caught his arm and Blaylock seized him by the shoulders, the boy writhing and shoving back with every sinew.

'I can't *believe* this! You fucking *spy* on me?'

'Alex, stop it.'

'You're a sick bastard, I fucking *loathe* you!'

Blaylock grabbed the back of his son's head and jabbed a finger at his face. 'Alright, that's *enough*, I *warned* you, didn't I? You think you know better than me? You've no clue, son, you don't know you're *born*, so shut your bloody mouth.'

Belatedly – after all the accumulated tension and anxiety of the day, now seeing his son's fury turn to alarm before his eyes – Blaylock began to comprehend the size of the hole he was in.

On the ride back to Islington he ignored successive calls but as the Jaguar turned into Alwynne Road he saw Gilchrist's Cherokee on the gravel. Before they had parked Alex launched himself out of the door.

'Keep him away from me!' he shouted as he stomped into the light and warmth of the house, past Radka and his mother.

Now Jennie came toward Blaylock, visibly beside herself. 'David, what the hell's been going on?'

'I had to see Alex and I had to talk to him, urgently. My hope is he'll tell you himself what he was up to.'

'Why the hell can't you?'

'Because I just can't, okay? What I can tell you is he was about to get himself in serious bother, like I said he would. He's not to see that girl again either, that's a fact.'

Jennie was looking at him with sorely aggrieved eyes, a look he had so dearly hoped to have seen the back of. 'Oh David, for Christ's sake, what is going on with you? I so, *so* do not need this. Not now. I mean, can you not understand that?'

'Of course I understand, can we not talk inside like normal people?'

'There's nothing normal about this! Are you mad?'

'I told you, he's just been going blindly down this road, it fell to me to step in—'

'Oh bloody nonsense, you tell me what in god's name you mean.'

'I *can't* tell you, Jennie, there are just some things where you and every other bugger just has to trust me—'

'David, don't give me that—'

'Will you ever try to see it from my side? You don't even have to know, you just need to believe that my judgement of things is basically honourable. I know that's hard, you disapprove of me that much, nothing I do could ever be really right.'

'I know that's *your* story, David, that I should just assume you're on the side of the gods and I just labour under some permanent delusion. That's it, isn't it?'

'Aw no, that'll never happen, not when your instincts are so fucking fine on everything and mine are in the gutter like dogshit.'

'Will you *please* stop clenching your fists and talking to me through your teeth? For crying out loud, David, look at yourself!'

Nick Gilchrist now came forward from the porch. 'David, look, are you—?'

Blaylock snarled. 'Nobody's *talking* to you, man.'

Jennie snapped. 'Okay, just get the hell out of here, David, I've had enough. Enough!'

'Aw yeah, that's right, Jennie, you decide—' But he was addressing her back now, and he saw enough of a look in Gilchrist's eyes – a shaming look – before his rival put a consoling arm on her shoulder and the front door slammed.

In the cold, under the stars, he could hear himself mutter. 'I knew it, I just knew it would be like this, I saw it before it happened.'

Miserably he kicked at a mound of stones, then turned, to see Andy standing by the car with his head in his hands – a dependable mirror still.

6

On a sullen Christmas morning beneath a grimy sky he trudged four hundred yards from his door down the road to Maryburn Parish Church, flanked by Andy and a back-up car full of police officers. The absurdity of the formality had never felt so mortifying or unmanning to him – the consciousness of his minders having Christmases of their own, families to be with, and yet here they were, shackled to his side, keeping watch over his forlorn ceremonials, for no good reason he could name.

Christmas Eve had required observance, too – another bloody carol service, another Toccata and Fugue, another juvenile organist and sheepish Year One nativity, one more lost hour gazing round panelled walls with their memorials to Victorian philanthropists and the Durham Light Infantry, worn and faded tributes – yet still more convinced and convincing to Blaylock than the lame testaments offered from the pulpit to the Lord Emmanuel.

That morning he had counted himself fortunate to be permitted to speak to his daughters when he called, though Alex would not come to the phone. Jennie spoke with a controlled antipathy. *'I hope you're satisfied with your handiwork, David, you've done your usual damage.'*

Up ahead he saw the church vestibule where Bob Cropper waited for him loyally in car coat and driving gloves. Blaylock removed his cap, and stepped over another threshold.

*

When the service was done and he had shaken every hand he made the short walk down a gravel path to the Fellowship Hall where he had agreed to take lunch in the company of those for whom the church provided, lest they otherwise be alone and unserved at Christmas. *The elderly, the Mayor, the homeless and me*, thought Blaylock, surveying the huddled gathering from the doorway, hearing the same old seasonal pop tunes echoing round the sparsely appointed space.

He and Bob took their places in the queue to get served at the hot food counter where a row of volunteer ladlers stood over steaming metal vats. Having received his slice of turkey Blaylock glanced to the man beside him, unkempt of beard and woolly-hatted, with the battered look of someone sleeping rough. They made eye contact and the man smiled, showing ruined teeth that made Blaylock worry for him.

'Good spread, eh?' Blaylock offered.

'Aw aye. Makes you feel a human being, like.'

Belatedly Blaylock realised the man was having his turkey dinner ladled not onto a plate but into a Styrofoam container.

'You're not stopping? It's bloody freezing out, man '

'Aw, I'm just, I'm not, I can't always, like . . .' The man stammered, gestured, his smile now looking stricken. Blaylock had to look down at his shoes, then focus anew on his choice of sprouts and parsnip.

At his Formica table of eight senior citizens Blaylock pulled crackers, passed salt, listened and did his best to hear, assisted by Bob, who gave a passable account of knowing everyone already. After the Queen's Speech Blaylock did his duty by kicking off the singalong and leading all assembled, shakily, through 'O Little Town of Bethlehem'.

Back at home, with the dark closing in, Blaylock asked his police team politely to stand down, offering each a decent bottle of red and wishing them a merrier Christmas than they had enjoyed to that point.

Finally it was just him and Andy Grieve. Taking a notion, he lit a fire in the hearth, the first of the winter. Then he switched off all the lights but for one standing lamp and watched the flames develop, until orange effulgence was flickering up the bland magnolia walls, and the room had assumed the pleasing snugness of a den.

He fetched an ashtray and invited Andy to smoke his red Marlboros freely, then went out to the garage, retrieved and uncapped a bottle of Glenlivet. He poured a tumbler for each of them and requested a smoke of his own. For a while, then, they sat and smoked and sipped.

'Boss,' said Andy eventually. 'I wanted to say about the other day, the train – when I told you about my son and all that? I'm sorry, I was out of order – laying it on you, and you having, y'know, more than plenty on your plate.'

'Howay, Andy,' said Blaylock, bemused. 'Don't be daft. You can tell me whatever you like. Y'know? I consider you a mate.'

'I wouldn't just assume that much, boss.'

'We're not strangers, are we?'

'Nah, nah. Just . . . I mean, you're not the easiest fella to know. I just, I understand, all that you've got on . . . that it's a tough job for you.'

'Well . . . I asked for it.'

Blaylock watched the fire awhile, feeling that Andy, after his own fashion, could tolerate a silence as sociable. After a pull on the Glenlivet, though, he felt some impulsion to talk.

'The thing of it is . . . you realise, you accept, you're not able to do good? Not really, not by choice, anyhow – if you do then it's by accident. Sometimes I think I can see it, "the right thing to do", it's so near I could touch it. But those are the times when I find out I was totally wrong. I mean, like a million miles off.'

'That's got to hurt,' Andy nodded.

'Oh, it's the devil's work.'

Blaylock took another gulp of the spirit and felt it make its burning way through his gullet.

'And you think, "Could I just retreat and say, 'Well, if nothing else, what I'll do is, I will do no harm?'" But, I don't even know what harm I've done when I've done it, most of the time . . .'

He glanced at Andy, who seemed so disquieted that Blaylock felt he ought to finish the maudlin and one-sided conversation he had begun, since it was he who now felt sure he had misspoken.

'No, I've realised, I just have to live on the other side.'

'What's that, boss?'

'From where I ought to be. Across the water.'

Blaylock stood to poke the fire. The first radiant warmth of the whisky had turned sour, the cigarette's aftertaste was petrochemical, his throat dry and brackish. Excusing himself he went upstairs to the bathroom. There, rinsing his hands he made the mistake of looking at his reflection in the mirror too long, and suffered a jarring moment of self-alienation, seeing a blank-faced stranger. He had to grip the edges of the basin and grasp about in his head for some anchoring reality.

Thus he found himself imagining others in the house, busy life and real presence under its roof – his wife in the bedroom, idly brushing out her hair, his son playing music down the hall, his elder girl with her friends gossiping behind a closed door, his youngest humming a tune as she lay on the floor and drew pictures of her family.

This spectral arrangement felt so close to him and yet aeons away. Above all, he knew there was no place in the tableau for himself.

The house is haunted, he thought. *No one here but me. Me. I'm the ghost.*

*

Blaylock had only just returned downstairs when his phone pulsed in the silence. For an instant he was obscurely hopeful. Then he saw the ident for Adam Villiers.

'David, my apologies, I don't mean to say Christmas is cancelled, but there's a matter of some gravity.'

'Yeah, I – knew it had to be.'

'We've seen some alarming patterns in our surveillance, supported by a number of intercepts, plus some information that's been volunteered to us. We have a sense of convergence, a plot – quite likely meant for Boxing Day? The evidence is sufficient, SO15 needs to move tonight. There's one highly urgent additional warrant we need you to endorse, it's coming through to you as we speak.'

Newly alert, phone cocked between ear and shoulder, Blaylock moved directly to the room he called his office and tore from the fax machine what Villiers had sent.

'I never saw a warrant on this guy before?'

'You did. You refused to sign. Your view at that time was that his web browsing habits weren't such a concern.'

'And you didn't know the company he was keeping?'

'That has since become all too clear.'

'Right. Okay. I'm going to leave for London now.'

'That I would not advise.'

'I might as well be there – from what you're saying we could be in COBRA tomorrow.'

'That is a case of "Not if we can help it". I would urge, David, that for the moment you are best where you are until this operation is completed.'

'What are we talking about? The operation?'

'There are a dozen men we need to lift, across five locations, three different constabularies. Birmingham, Grantham, Tooting, Wood Green and Stapletree.'

'Adam, is Sadaqat Osman among these suspects?'

'*He is.*'

'Will you say what he's suspected of?'

'*We suspect a plan for a number of co-ordinated attacks on a range of targets. In the case of Osman, we believe the target is you, David . . .*'

Blaylock felt sobriety reclaim him, coldly and completely.

'*. . . another reason why you're good where you are. Since we're sure where he is. Your security team's all in place?*'

'I'll need to . . . summon a few of them back, actually.'

'*Maybe you need a back-up team?*'

'No, no, look – my protection is more than adequate.'

Within minutes the lights of police vehicles flared and whirred from the threshold of Blaylock's drive through his drawn blinds. Andy returned from conference with the officers to find Blaylock back in the grasp of his armchair, disinclined to look out into the darkness.

'What do you want to do, boss?'

'Just sit here. Wait. See what occurs.'

Blaylock looked to the bottle, lifted his emptied whisky tumbler, then thought better and turned it upside down.

7

The streets of Stapletree were as he recalled them, but in the grey of early light they were sombre with a palpable sense of woundedness. At the junction giving onto the blocked road, officers redirected traffic and sought to stop onlookers from loitering near the cordon – most of them, clearly, journalists and TV crews. Across the way were men stood solemnly texting outside a pub that had opened early. Climbing from the car, Blaylock could feel a heavy aura of catastrophe narrowly averted, the urgent motion of a set of coping mechanisms all around.

Followed by Andy, he was bidden through the police tape to the cleared area – the blast zone. More police cars were parked forbiddingly across the far end of the road ahead.

Though his destination was clear – a tent of blue tarpaulin pitched across a big swathe of pavement – Blaylock stopped momentarily and surveyed the suburban scene in all its uncanny muted magnitude, turning three hundred and sixty degrees on his heels. He looked up and saw officers conferring on the roof of a nearby garage, and blinds and curtains flapping through blown-out windows of terraced houses. Across the way was the entrance to the communal park, where white-suited forensics teams steadily paced out their hunt for the terrible fragments of the explosion. Amid such a drab, unassuming environment it seemed all the clearer – the power of violence to shatter. Between him and the tarpaulin a car stood abandoned, its doors flung open, its windows spattered with blood and bone. Staring at it Blaylock had a vision of ruination so intense that a shiver went through him.

He stepped under the tarpaulin and saw a stretch of pavement saturated dark red, over which stood a uniformed officer of the Essex Police and a face he knew, the shaven-headed Detective Neil Hill of SO15, who nodded to him gravely.

'So, this is where he fell, sir. When our team raided his flat he got out over a roof at the back, tried to make an escape through the streets. He was carrying a knife, that was clear, and he didn't heed any of the verbal warnings. The armed officer had a clear shot, and there was no other member of the public in view, so he took it – obviously, not to know the suspect had the suicide belt on under his coat. And, yeah, so the shot triggered the belt. Blew him right in half. He was still speaking when they got to him, as I understand, spoke a few words but, you can imagine, everything below the ribcage was . . .' Neil Hill waved a hand levelly through the air to indicate annihilation.

Blaylock stared down at the bloodstain, broad and tall as a man. He wondered if this visit had been a wise choice, or a helpless gesture. It was a closing of accounts, perhaps, but one that brought no relief.

'If he's the sole casualty of the day', Neil Hill intoned, 'then we've been blessed. When you think what he might have gone and done.'

'He wanted to be a doctor,' Blaylock murmured.

'This world, there's nothing true in it – nothing honourable, nothing that's truly held sacred. It's a pretend culture, a plastic culture, but it demands our obedience, it demands we make ourselves dead inside.'

In Cabinet Office Briefing Room A the assembled – Blaylock, Patrick Vaughan, Adam Villiers, Brian Shoulder, James Bannerman, Rory Inglis – sat and watched Nasser's last testament, projected large across the master screen at the end of the room and on the touch-screens built into each seated place.

'*I just shudder, when I think that Islam might ever be as weak as the Christian faith – just accepting society's depravity, powerless to change anything. So that this should never be, I am making my stand – taking my part in this action, this demonstration, against a corrupt society, its filthy politics, its evil economy that robs from the poor and slaughters the weak ... I believe our action will be a cleansing action. My* shahadah *will be grievous, yes, but it will be repaid a hundredfold by wise and all-merciful Allah ...*'

Blaylock watched tensely, his hand clenched tight across his mouth. He felt certain in his bones that Nasser must have been, even to the last, trying to persuade himself.

Adam Villiers clicked the file closed. Patrick Vaughan nodded to him as if to say he still had the floor.

'Mr Nasser Jakhrani represents, arguably, our one security failure today. That said, he is the reason we moved when we moved, owing to contact made with police yesterday evening by a female friend of his, a fellow medical student of Palestinian origin, whom he had asked to meet with him at a London hotel. She found the request uncharacteristic, and the meeting disconcerting – she formed the impression he was trying to say a sort of farewell. We must be thankful for her powers of intuition and the duty she felt to take her suspicions to the authorities.'

Blaylock found something so pitiable in Villiers's account that he shook his head sharply, wanting to dispel the strange sympathy he felt for the wounded creature.

'Though we failed to take Mr Jakhrani into custody, the search of his flat yielded not only incendiary materials but computer evidence of a plan to attack the branch of an Israeli bank near Liverpool Street.'

Villiers looked to Brian Shoulder, who took over. 'To confirm, at the Birmingham address where West Midlands arrested three men, they found chemicals and electrics for the making of explosive devices, also protective clothing and evidence of preparation. Same sort of materials were found in Tooting, where two arrests were made. In Grantham, where two men were picked up, they found plasticised acetone peroxide, cut pipe, electrics – same in Wood Green where there were three arrests. In Stapletree we also arrested a man in possession of a Baikal handgun with silencer and ammo. All suspects have now been handed over into the custody of the Met and we're holding them at Paddington. We anticipate a range of charges under the Terrorism Act.'

Villiers nodded. 'In summary we believe we have foiled a hydra-headed plan to carry out a range of outrages across a number of sites, within a narrow window of time so as to compound the chaos.'

The faces and names of the plotters appeared as a grid on the screen. Not wishing to look at those he recognised, Blaylock glanced down to his briefing papers.

'There's a broadly familiar subject profile here – home-grown, second generation South Asian males, the youngest, Mr al-Allam, just twenty, the oldest, Mr Rahman and Mr Osman, both thirty-two. Essentially clean skins, other than Mr Hamayoon and Mr Rahman. Several college-educated. Few trained abroad. Mr Ali is a married father of three, Mr bin Ara's wife is five months pregnant. All the relatives claim "incomprehension", though of course we're questioning then closely. The plotters buried their exchanges well: instant messaging, peer-to-peer cloud email, non-standard operating systems. Still, co-ordination was clearly a challenge. As we know, the need for steel guts in a group situation like this is very strong. And this effort suffered a certain amount of . . . splintering. For instance, Mr Ali, perhaps the most vulnerable link in the chain, broke it so as to contact Mr Osman.'

Patrick Vaughan spoke up. 'What do we know of the other targets, Adam?'

'What we surmise is that the Tooting group were targeting Brimsdown Substation. The Grantham group would attack the sales at Greenlake Shopping Centre. The Birmingham group were looking at the Strathearn Hotel by Hyde Park. Wood Green, we think, had in mind an assault on several cafés in Golders Green. As for Stapletree, Mr Jakhrani had designs on the Israeli bank as mentioned. Mr Osman, we suspect, was contemplating an attack on the Home Secretary . . .'

All faces, sober and discomfited, turned toward Blaylock, who lowered his eyes to the table.

'David had had some personal contact with Mr Osman through Rory's office and this didn't escape the notice of Mr Rahman at the point where he sought to bring his old college friend into the circle. Clearly there was a suggestion that Mr Osman should exploit that proximity. Among Rahman's notes we found . . .' Villiers consulted his papers. '"The *mujahid* undertakes to eliminate target at point-blank range. No escape plan. *Mujahid* cannot survive." That said, certain other communications lead us to wonder whether Mr Osman considered this course of action but ultimately rejected it.'

Blaylock wanted very badly to speak for himself yet could not find the words. Patrick Vaughan moved swiftly into the silence. 'Well, in any case, we can but count our blessings. I'm really heartened by the response, Adam, and I congratulate the team on their tremendous work . . .'

'I want to second that,' said Blaylock.

Retaking the chair of the session Vaughan drove the agenda on – the ring of steel, the agreed advice to the general public and to VIPs, the increased deployment of armed officers, transport police and CCTV vigilance, the necessary reassurance of the three-million-strong Muslim community. Preoccupied, unsettled, Blaylock merely indicated his approval of procedures. When matters were wrapped and he exited to the corridor Brian Shoulder drew near with some urgency, indicating his wish for a private word.

'Sadaqat Osman, Home Secretary? He's at Paddington and he's not said a word to the interrogators but apparently he's asked through his lawyer to see you. He wants to "address his remarks to you". I mean, it's ridiculous—'

'Okay, fine,' snapped Blaylock. 'Let's go.'

He went through the steel door into the silence of the drab interrogation suite, to meet the sight of Sadaqat, high and straight in his chair across a scuffed table, his eyebrows a black line, his mouth straight as a blade. His presence seemed to defy the indignity of his standard-issue white forensic suit and the brow-furrowed solicitor at his side. The two police detectives across the table leaned back in their mismatched chairs, determinedly laconic, eyes raised to the small skylight above. It was, for a moment, a tableau – then one officer rose to greet Blaylock and the other asked the solicitor if his client was ready.

Blaylock planted himself before the table and stared at Sadaqat, who stared unblinkingly back, and then spoke.

'I understand, that you might feel some . . . grievance, with me? I'd only say, I never asked for your attention, or your friendship, or any such thing. It was put upon me. That was misfortune, for us both. It's a fact I became involved in some plans, to do with the taking of life. I accept the gravity of that. Those plans were terrible. But, in my view, necessary. I'll explain.

'You, you were part of those plans. I decided in the end to spare you. By talking to you I realised, you don't mean evil. You just can't see past your horizon. Ignorant that way. I take no pride in what I was party to, I will not list any Koranic justifications, I can't, there is no justification. But there is a reason. The reason is injustice.

'Had I been responsible for taking life, I would not have said the victims were lesser humans than me, whoever they were. But their victimhood would not be greater than that of innocents who

[455]

die because of your constant bombings and invasions and occupations of Muslim countries – murder by drone, death raining down on innocent people whose names you'd rather not know. By "you" I mean the West. But that includes you, Mr Blaylock. Because, whatever you tell yourself, I do believe – I'm sure – you think that your lives are more precious than our lives. If a bomb falls on a school, what you call an accident? And dark-skinned children die? You might claim remorse, but I don't believe you really feel it. It's too much of an old habit for you that way.

'You're too accustomed to your . . . fiefdoms, and your spheres of influence. Drawing lines on maps of places you've never been, where real people live and breathe. As if, the world is still really your world, to go round and administer? You have a stake, you've got your local clients that you've bribed, outposts you've built . . . But just for that, you still believe you get to say how it should be – you know what's best, you want to dictate things by force. Sometimes you dress it up with all anguish and sorrow. You say, "What should we do? What should we do in 'the Middle East'?" Listen, what you should do is *disappear*.

'You say there can be no accommodation? It must be our way, nothing can be done, you won't shift a hair? Understand, that's a worn-out excuse, and a grievous insult. Okay, so drones will kill, IDF will kill, settlers will bulldoze, mothers in Gaza will keep burying their children, the game of nations over our heads . . . Since this is not acceptable, and you will never change, I had to ask myself, "What is an honourable thing you can do? To demonstrate to these authorities how wrong is their authority?" And I believe that thing is terror – I see nothing else that gets through to you. Correct bombs, in correct places. So as to remind you, so you understand what it means to live in fear – that your life or the lives of those you love could be ripped away from you. Yes, it is terror, it is terrible. But, just know, it's by your own deeds that you're repaid. And that is all, yeah? The end.'

Blaylock had stood there, impressed all over again by the young man's composure and fluency. It was only that the quality of conviction he had once admired was now purest poison. In any case he had ceased to truly listen from an early point, once he had been advised that he was 'spared'. *I was spared? Or you got scared?* That others, ultimately, had been spared seemed to him the only thing of relevance, for which he was nearly ready to thank the lord.

He turned to the camera fixed high in the corner of the room behind him.

'Got all that, yeah?'

Then, with a nod to the detectives, he departed.

8

Ignoring all calls, he stuck by the terse statement Mark Tallis drafted in his name, giving assurance that 'all appropriate security measures' were in place for the public's protection while asking for their special vigilance. He further ignored Mark's clear urge to discuss with him the angles of the foiled plot in light of possible advantages to the case for identity cards. He saw only new flaws.

He had asked Gavin Blount to call on him. First, though, Martin drove him to an artist's suppliers where he bought an expensive set of oil pastels as a gift for Molly. Back at home he called the Islington number, at half-hour intervals, but got no answer, nor from Jennie's mobile, on which he left a terse message: 'If you think it's right, Jennie, that I don't get to see my daughter on her birthday then . . . I don't know how you expect me not to take that badly.' He did expect a response, however unfriendly, and yet gradually it became clear to him that no such call would be forthcoming.

A little after that, it further dawned on Blaylock that the boiler in the house had expired; it proved utterly resistant to manipulation. He paced around in the frigid air, feeling like a cold-blooded creature with no option but to keep in motion. When Blount arrived they sat in the kitchen over steaming teas; though Blount, to Blaylock's quiet satisfaction, appeared not to feel the chill.

'About the report I asked from you – I want you to broaden your thinking on what's appropriate to the problem, security-wise. Consider the matter up for grabs. What's the best joint deploy-

[458]

ment of army and police? The best positioning for the military in the event of a crisis? Is there a case for a small permanent armed forces command as "homeland security", say? What's the capacity for armed response round the country, not just the Met and Manchester?'

Blount smiled into his chest, stirring his tea. 'I get you. People will still recoil from some of this. It's just not the British way.'

Blaylock shrugged. 'We live in challenging times. If anyone's in any doubt about what's needed to counter extremism in this country, I have to say it's perfectly clear to me what we really depend on – surveillance, legislation, detainment, armed officers . . . and luck.'

Blaylock watched the house darken and his breath begin to condense in the air. Still no call came from Jennie. At 4.30 p.m. he pulled on his topcoat, snatched up the carrier bag from the artist's shop and told Andy they were going. Martin drove them to Islington, but the Alwynne Road house was darkened and silent.

Martin drove on to Upper Street, where Blaylock jumped out on foot and stalked down the pavement, peering through the glowing windows of pizzerias and upscale chicken shacks, familiar family-friendly haunts. But there was no joy. He sensed from the large presence at his shoulder that Andy's silence was of a concerned, not wholly approving nature – that his bodyguard was somehow apprehensive over how things were tending – but this only irked Blaylock further.

He lurched back into the Jaguar's backseat and slammed the door.

'Martin, we're for Notting Hill . . . Elgin Crescent?'

As grimly resolved as he was, he had anticipated more of a challenge once they reached the row of fine stuccoed townhouses. But his target was clear nearly at once, for a cluster of coloured balloons was fastened to one big black door between Doric columns. He felt a sense of victory, however crabbed, and a confidence he would make his point, shame his opponents unostentatiously, show to his youngest how shabby had been the whole charade put up falsely in her name.

'Okay, I will be ten minutes,' he told Andy. 'If I'm not out by then, you're welcome to bust in with all guns blazing and pull me out.'

Andy looked at him pensively, nodded. 'Sure, boss.'

It was only as he rapped on the door, an agreeable hubbub emanating from within, and imagined how the surprise of his face would be met that Blaylock felt some pang of regret. But it was burning in his chest now – the old familiar, heedless urge, pressing him on to the act from which sober contemplation would have steered him clear. The most urgent part of him believed rightness had to suffice, and no other self was strong enough to lay a staying hand on him.

A tall, solidly built youth in jeans and tee-shirt swung open the door with a mild smile that faded at once.

'I'm Molly's father,' said Blaylock.

'Sure, I know who you are,' the youth nodded, and called back down the hallway. 'Dad?'

Nick Gilchrist appeared from down a subtly lit hallway of framed pictures, looking solemn, his billowing white shirt spotted with fingerprints.

'Ah, hello, David.'

'Jennie and the children are here?'

'Yeah, and a few others. You'd best come in.'

He came past and saw Jennie standing in subfusc at the threshold of a bright and busy kitchen, a long-stemmed wine glass uselessly in her hand, her face a picture of disquiet, he felt. Blaylock had the strangest sense that everything was perhaps a little worse than even he had imagined.

'Not doing anything then, Jennie? So who are all these?'

She spoke in a tense hush. 'Nick's friends, the kids' friends . . . You won't know them.'

'You want to show me around?'

'How did you know where to come?'

'Oh, I've my spies everywhere. Didn't Alex tell you?'

She kept unhappily silent, and so, unwelcome, he glanced about him. The elegant splendour of the house was clear. Even from the hall Blaylock could appreciate the great gleaming kitchen ahead, busy with the keen chatter of adults and the splashy cries of kids, its floor-to-ceiling sliding glass looking out to a darkened expanse of garden. He realised abruptly that fixed to the wall by his head was a painting by Molly, a colourful collage of the type she favoured, organised around the word HOLLYWOOD.

Blaylock exhaled slowly, keeping himself together. 'Okay. I don't want a scene, I know the state of things, I just want to see Molly, give her my present, and my love. Obviously if you want to explain to me why all the subterfuge I'd say I'm entitled, maybe?'

Jennie and Gilchrist exchanged glances. Blaylock saw he had chosen 'subterfuge' correctly.

'Nick, would you give us a moment?' Jennie said heavily.

Gilchrist, clearly uneasy, nodded and retreated to the kitchen.

Jennie gestured up the stairs. 'Will you . . . ?'

'David, we had a set of circumstances to consider, me and Nick and the kids, we've been mulling for a while . . . but we've come to a . . . quite a big decision, together.'

'Yes?' Standing in a tastefully lit and appointed bedroom with an expanse of snow-white duvet between him and Jennie, Blaylock felt a driving need to break the barricades that seemed to have been erected against him all around this house.

'Okay. Nick is going to be in Los Angeles for some time, teaching at one of the film schools, and working on a movie, a big studio drama thing.'

'Good for Nick.' *Lonely for you*, he thought instantly.

'It's going to be two years at least. We all talked it over and worked it through and . . . we're all going to LA. Me and the children.'

Blaylock had never heard anything quite so offensive or impossible. 'You what? How'll that work? I mean, the kids, Jennie . . . ?'

'Alex has a place at Cal Arts to do film. There's a good high school for Cora, a good elementary school for Molly.'

'C'mon, the cost, but—'

'Nick's got a good deal, I've been asked to lecture at Stanford, I may take the California bar. We've got a good rented house to start with, in Santa Monica, the children like it.'

'Jennie . . . you can't *abide* America, you never have.'

'David,' she shook her head, 'that's not true. Los Angeles is a much more cultured city than people think. The children are excited. I think they see a big adventure. I do, too.'

The preposterousness of the idea was only affirmed in Blaylock's mind by Jennie's shifty, muted seriousness, a marker to him of how bad ideas, without proper vigilance, could take on a worrying solidity.

'Change is important, David, you have to do things while you can, seize them. The one life's all we have. I know the timing may feel hard to you, I realise it's a shock, but we didn't intend secrecy, and it's not been done lightly, it was a choice we had to make as a unit . . .'

'Oh yeah? Molly and Cora got votes, did they? But not me?' Now her deluded earnestness struck him as outright provocation. 'When were you going to raise it with me, then?'

'Not tonight . . .' Her expression betrayed further discomfort. 'But we're going back out for New Year, and to sort out the house. My plan was to speak to you tomorrow, honestly.'

'So this,' Blaylock slashed a finger through the air, 'this is a kind of a farewell party, am I right?'

Jennie suddenly looked more resolved. 'It's been a stressful time all round. But the kids and I want to keep this relationship together. This is who we are now. They're happy and comfortable, and I'm heeding them as much as myself.'

He had ceased to hear. He felt heat rising in his face, his heart restive in his chest. 'No, no. I don't agree to this, Jennie.'

'I know you're upset but please don't be blinded, don't just blow—'

'Aw fuck off. What do you expect me to do? Eh?'

He felt clenched all over. There was a knock on the door; unthinkingly Blaylock stalked across and flung it open, to see Cora looking at him with what he recognised as an awfully familiar unease.

'Cora, it's alright, love.' In Jennie's voice Blaylock heard far too much assumption of command. Cora looked a little too long before turning and fleeing back down the stairs.

Blaylock put a hand to his temple, mortally offended, a sense of entitlement beginning to burn there. 'Okay, I want to see Molly.'

'I don't think it's the time, David. I can see it on your face.'

'Don't fucking talk to me like that, how do you dare?'

'*Please*, David, just . . . why not take yourself out of here for now and let's meet tomorrow and talk then – I promise, we can reason this through.'

'Yeah, we'll do that then, now I want to see Molly.'

And he was off, moving down the stairs two at a time, feeling himself a force moving forward, parting the air in his wake. He ducked a head into Gilchrist's double reception, noting a cherry-red guitar on a stand, laden bookcases, some heavy gilded trophies over a fireplace – and his son looking up at him warily from a velvet sofa where he had been engaged in conversation with some professorial adult.

As he powered on through the kitchen the eyes upon him were warier still and people stepped aside, some not quite as swiftly as was best for them – he was barging a path, but he didn't care, being so much the unbidden guest, the unsightly beast off its leash. He wrenched aside the sliding glass door and saw, past the red coals of a cast-iron kettle barbecue, Molly and Gilchrist together in close conference out on the darkened lawn – Gilchrist down on his haunches, Molly grave and nodding silently.

Blaylock bore down upon them, trying to shift his features into a smile. But when Gilchrist, noting his approach, stood and stepped aside, Molly could not have looked more forlorn.

Blaylock stood before her, irritably aware that he was breathing heavily, and thrust out his unwrapped gift in its bag.

'Hey, my darling, Happy Birthday.'

Molly's face crumpled utterly, she lowered her head and ran past him toward the house. Spinning to look after her, Blaylock felt a paining bewilderment that, within an instant, felt vertiginous. When he recovered his head he could see Gilchrist staring at him with what looked very much like pity, and felt his last restraints snap.

'Proud of yourself, are you?'

'Listen, David, all I can—'

Blaylock advanced – Gilchrist anticipating enough to raise a hand – and threw a right hook through the defence, hitting his enemy awkwardly in the mouth, feeling his knuckles graze on teeth. Gilchrist reeled and crashed down heavily against the kettle barbecue, which toppled and spilled out its coals onto the grass by Gilchrist where he fell.

There was a frozen moment of shock, broken by Gilchrist's heavy cries of pain, then people were coming at Blaylock from the lights of the house. Feeling himself deranged he grabbed a wooden garden chair and hurled it aside such that it crashed against a trellis.

And then he saw Jennie running toward him, flanked by dauntless men, and he was being surrounded and grabbed at, Jennie shrieking and stabbing a finger into his face before darting to the side of the fallen Gilchrist. For a moment he was still, consumed by the towering grotesqueness of the events he had caused, then a hand fell heavily upon him and he slapped it away, whereupon he truly found himself being seized and held fast at all sides.

More people were coming, Gilchrist was being helped to his feet, having restraint urged upon him, too, for Blaylock at last read true matching animosity in the man's eyes. The air was thick with cries. 'What's happened?' 'He's thumped Nick!' 'Someone get the police!' 'I've called them!'

'Yeah, go fetch the fucking police,' Blaylock snarled. 'They're right outside.' It was then that he saw Andy Grieve coming through the glass door, his appalled face a clear sign of the sky having fallen.

By the time beat officers arrived to the scene, Blaylock had been penned to one corner of the garden by Andy and his Met protection team, who told him it was for his own good, whose eyes told Blaylock this was irretrievable. The beat officers' hurried consultations with guests were audible to Blaylock above the hubbub, as was Gilchrist's fiercely muttered 'I'm okay, the bastard didn't hurt me.'

Blaylock watched the officers listen, nod and nod again, then confer. Then one approached him. 'Sir, I'm arresting you on suspicion of assault and battery. You do not have to say anything. However, it may harm your defence if you do not mention when questioned—'

Blaylock shrugged off a second officer's custodial arm.

'Sir, if we need to restrain you we will.'

'You'll not put your hands on me, son.'

'I should remind you, sir, not to make this any worse for yourself, you're on camera.'

Blind to this point, Blaylock now saw the lipstick-size cameras affixed to the officers' lapels. The sudden sense of his own mindlessness was nearly enough to make his jaw drop.

'Yeah, you got it now,' said the arresting officer. 'Not such a big boy after all, eh?'

'*What* did you say to me?' Blaylock bridled, and this time it was Andy who took him by the shoulders, evidently wishing to forestall further disaster. Blaylock inhaled deeply of the cold night air and looked up to the black glass of the starless sky. His furies had been and gone, and he was left now to survey his own startling vandalism, the axe he had taken to his own trunk, the livid senselessness with which he had whacked and hacked and managed, at last, to fell himself.

Shamed Blaylock quits after assault charge follows brawl
By Jane Grey, Post Online

PUBLISHED: 02:34, December 29 | UPDATED: 07:48, December 29

Disgraced David Blaylock yesterday resigned his office as Home Secretary, after being charged with assaulting the partner of his ex-wife in a much publicised brawl on December 27. A tumultuous ministerial career, never far from controversy, has ended amid the turmoil of an altercation with officers of the Metropolitan Police, a body with whom Blaylock often had tense relations.

Forty-seven-year-old Blaylock, the MP for Teesside South and a former British Army captain, tendered his resignation to the Prime Minister with an apology for his behaviour, saying that this had 'fallen lamentably below what is expected of a Minister, MP or, indeed, any responsible and self-respecting individual'.

In his letter to Patrick Vaughan Blaylock further wrote that it was 'with great regret, also shame and remorse' that he left office, and thanked the Prime Minister for having 'very often had cause to rely on and be thankful for [his] support and loyalty'.

Blaylock pledged, however, to carry on as an MP. In his letter he referred to having taken soundings in his Teesside constituency, and promised to 'focus now on better serving the people who elected me'.

By the end of the day Downing Street had confirmed that Paul Payne, the well-regarded Minister of State for Security at the Home Office, would replace Blaylock as Home Secretary, a recognition of Payne's talents that also saves the Prime Minister the difficulties of a wider reshuffle.

At Hammersmith Magistrates Court yesterday morning Blaylock admitted the charge of attacking documentary filmmaker Nick Gilchrist during a private party at Mr Gilchrist's west London home

[467]

attended by Blaylock's ex-wife, human rights barrister Jennifer Kirkbride QC, and the three children from their ten-year marriage. Blaylock was granted bail and told to return for sentence in three weeks' time, where he may be liable to a fine and a community service order, on top of a possible order to compensate Mr Gilchrist. Blaylock admitted before the court that he had 'a number of personal issues to address'. It is reported that he recently underwent a course of 'anger management' treatment at a private Hampstead clinic . . .

EPILOGUE

Early light was seeping into the hallway through the transom window as Blaylock laced up his running shoes and sought to flex his obdurate calf muscles. Bent double like so, his eyes met the letter on his console table that he had been ignoring all week. *Get it over with*, he now thought, ripping open the envelope.

> *Dear Mr Blaylock*
>   *You will not mind my writing, I hope. Naturally I read about the comeuppance you suffered, and it did make me think, having the history with you that I do and knowing a thing or two about reverses of fortune. I would like you to know you have my sympathy, honestly. God knows we are all human, we all have our weaknesses, we all fail sometimes. I only hope you have learned something from your experience, by which you will profit, since that is what God wants.*
>   *If it is of help I would say I have taken a lot of encouragement from the words of Saint Francis of Sales, who says, 'Our dear imperfections that force us to acknowledge our deficiencies give us practice in humility.'*
>   *Yours sincerely,*
>   *Diane Cleeve*

Blaylock had begun to be irked by Mrs Cleeve's periodic postal admonishments, and yet he couldn't but feel she was entitled. If he ever sat down to respond one day, he would have a good deal to tell her.

He had to grant her, moreover, that Jennie had told him very much the same in one of their few conversations unmediated by a lawyer prior to her departure for Los Angeles. *'You've put quite a curse on the venture, David. But you've hurt yourself most of all. I'm sorry for you, but maybe this is what you needed.'* If he believed himself wrongly accused to some extent, certain charges stuck nonetheless. Jennie judged him correctly in many ways – he could hardly deny the evidence.

He went out to his doorstep where Andy Grieve awaited him, already limbered up and taking the air. Together they jogged out into the bleary south London street. It was a chill late February morning but the skies were pleasingly blue, and to Blaylock's view there was a measure of promise in that.

He had not assumed that Andy's assignment would survive his resignation – that close protection would still be offered him as a humble backbencher. 'Just the assumption you'll have a guard could be effective,' Caroline Tennant told him at first, scarily frugal as ever. But in the end she had come through, signing off Adam Villiers's risk assessment that advised extreme caution in the case of such a visible and recently threatened ex-Home Secretary. For his own part Blaylock was quietly grateful that Andy had volunteered to remain in the post.

Now they pounded onward, shoulder to shoulder, past the Peabody Estate, Toni's Caff and the Georgian white stucco. Blaylock cast barely a glance at the newspaper bins outside Dev's corner shop: the great affairs of state were no longer his bailiwick. That the Identity Documents Bill was now being throttled in the Lords was Paul Payne's concern, if concern his successor truly felt. The government would absorb the blow and move on – such was Patrick Vaughan's way, perennially grateful that Her Majesty's Opposition caused him a lot less bother than Their Lordships. The Payne Home Office retained hardly a trace of Blaylock's tenure, Mark Tallis having departed for a lobbying job, Deborah Kerner now prominent in a briskly right-wing think-tank, though Gavin Blount soldiered on thanklessly. If Blaylock missed anyone, it was Geraldine Bell, who had taught him that manners were not nothing but, rather, quite possibly the only thing.

Blaylock wondered, still, if politics were enough to sustain him now. His demotion was a manageable thing: he still knew how to make himself useful in the House, and didn't care greatly that colleagues considered him a diminished figure. Jim Orchard, possibly more upset by his fall than anyone, still took pleasure in ribbing him about his newly modest place on 'the roll of the public servants of England, hur-hur'. There was a degree of freedom in being out of office; yet he was newly shackled by his penitent pledge to serve his Teesside constituents, leaving him to ponder just how far he should sacrifice his judgement to the sorts of opinions he heard in the Arndale Shopping Centre every other Saturday.

What he took to be the angel on his shoulder told him he was better to focus awhile on being a good listener, to cultivate a modest notion of himself. By any reckoning his judgements had been profoundly flawed for far too long – he believed he had clung to fruitless desires that had been mere symbols, that promised no actual part of the desired thing in itself. What he had thought to be Jennie's gradual softening toward him, for instance, he felt he had ruinously misread. It would have been better had she been tougher on him, since no good deed went unpunished and all that.

The first and obvious objective of his penance was to see his family again, in circumstances free as far as possible from recrimination. A visit to Los Angeles at Easter did not seem so implausible, if he continued to conduct himself inoffensively.

Humility was hard to him, though – a tough middle path that you could only keep hewing, given how much you had to bite off, how tight you had to muzzle yourself. He felt older atavistic instincts always worryingly close at hand. And yet the cost of his rages was abundantly clear to him. He had long known, by bitter experience, that life didn't always give a second chance. *The one life's all we have,* Jennie had said, needlessly, and yet he managed so well and often to forget. He accepted now that he would just have to find a different way of living, effect a slow business of repair in the time that he had. But he had resumed weekly sessions with Amanda Scott-Stokes, and what was that, he told himself, if not humility?

He and Andy ran on into Kennington Park, taking their dependable daily route down a long straight asphalt path between muddy grass and stooping denuded magnolias.

It had become their custom to finish the run on a headlong sprint back to Blaylock's front door. Today, though, Blaylock had a notion to get ahead of schedule. The way forward looked to him like a decent hundred-yard dash, in the distance a row of green benches hemming the path, a man sitting pensively on the furthest of these seeming to propose a sort of finish-line.

And so he took off at a sprint, planting his feet firmly, driving forward cleanly. Andy was a tad slow to see the sport of it, by which time Blaylock had opened a lead, and was feeling all the good vital signs in place – the thump of his heart, heat in his face, his calf muscles taking the strain.

As he pelted to the finish, the man on the bench got to his feet and Blaylock felt sudden irritation, since he seemed to saunter obstructively toward the middle of the path. *You stay in your lane, kidder.*

It was yards away that he fully clocked the *taqiyah* on the man's head, the tunic under his long leather coat, the luxurious red beard. And in that instant he suddenly recognised a properly unforgettable face from the recent regrettable past – Finn, the maladjusted young man from Sadaqat's centre in Stapletree – Finn who now pulled a kitchen knife from within his coat and – as Blaylock belatedly sought to feint aside – rammed into him and brought him down onto the asphalt path.

Blaylock was pinned under considerable weight, and as he fought back he felt the knife plunging into his side, then withdrawn and plunged again – savage, invasive thrusts that caused him blinding pain.

'You see me, eh? See me now?' Finn barked.

Blaylock groped and thumped hopelessly, trapped in this awful embrace – and then Andy was yanking away Finn's striking arm, stamping on the hand, dragging the attacker off and aside. Blaylock tried to sit up only to slump back onto the path, faint-headed. It was from supine that he heard the thumping report of Andy's Glock pistol, once, twice, rhymed by cries of pain.

He felt sick and dizzy. *Don't panic*, he thought, and put his hand to his wound tremulously. But what he felt there was truly a tear, a great gape in his left side, and when he lifted his fingers shakily in front of his eyes he saw they were appallingly bloody.

A dreadful intelligence suffused him, and he felt fear. Andy, he could hear, was on his phone. 'Ambulance!'

He was conscious of shouts and footfalls coming from afar. Andy was suddenly crouched by his side, frantic.

'David, you'll make it, you'll make it. They're coming . . .'

But now he found himself fighting for breath: there was an unbearable constriction behind his ribs. Andy was touching his face, he could feel his friend's breath there. But nothing was so vivid to him as the stone-cold of the path underneath him, seeping through him, consuming all his conscious thoughts while his shocked higher functions seemed to recede.

'They're coming, David. Just hold on . . .'

He was losing his grip, something within was saying *Begone!* His head lolled back and he stared upward. The morning sky was a rippling blue veil, vast and unbelievable, filling his vision. Now it seemed to be descending, falling onto him, and in his mind he was racing to meet it.

ACKNOWLEDGEMENTS

In researching this novel I had the benefit of a number of conversations with MPs and civil servants both current and former, as well as individuals who have done time in various capacities within the Home Office and in Downing Street. These conversations were conducted under the Chatham House Rule, and were of immeasurable value to me in conceiving this fiction. It need hardly be said that I alone am responsible for the fanciful use I made of all the information, reminiscences and reflections that I gleaned.

Debts that must be acknowledged by name are to the transcripts of the proceedings of the International Criminal Tribunal for the former Yugoslavia and to Major Vaughan Kent-Payne's excellent memoir *Bosnia Warriors* (Robert Hale Ltd, 1998) – in particular Major Kent-Payne's accounts of the Prince of Wales's Own Regiment of Yorkshire's dealings with *mujahedin* and with the siege of Guča-Gora, incidents which inspired the account of my fictional David Blaylock's military service in Bosnia.

At Faber I am indebted as ever to my editor Lee Brackstone, the man who knows how and why; also to Kate McQuaid, Luke Bird and Kate Ward; to Tamsin Shelton and Hamish Ironside for first-rate copy-editing and proofreading; at Aitken Alexander to Andrew Kidd and Matthew Hamilton, both of whom helped the book to get made; at Casarotto Ramsay to Christine Glover; and to my darling wife Rachel, with love and gratitude as always.

Richard T. Kelly

March 2016

Also by Richard T. Kelly

ff

Crusaders

In 1996, just before the rise of New Labour, Reverand Gore returns to his native Newcastle charged with planting a new church in one of the city's rougher estates. As he settles into the local community, he becomes involved with Stevie, a local 'security consultant', Lindy, a streetwise single mother, and Martin, an ambitious local Labour MP. But when these relationships unravel, Gore finds himself drawn into a moral crisis. This extraordinary debut novel is driven by sharp social observation, dark humour and an undercurrent of impending violence.

'Terrific . . . An intelligent state-of-the-nation epic.' *Mail on Sunday*

'I can't remember a modern British debut that offers a more convincing portrait of so many different walks of life, or that paints its portrait of an era and a region with greater credibility.' *Sunday Times*

'Kelly's seriousness of intent and direct moral interrogation call to mind contemporary American giants Roth and Mailer.' *Independent on Sunday*

ff

The Possessions of Doctor Forrest

Three respected Scottish doctors – psychiatrist Steve Hartford, paediatric surgeon Grey Lochran and cosmetic surgeon Robert Forrest – have been friends since their Edinburgh boyhoods, and now live comfortably in suburban London. When Doctor Forrest goes missing one summer evening, Lochran and Hartford are alarmed by the thought of what might have befallen their friend. The police can find no evidence of foul play, but the two doctors resolve to conduct their own investigation. Soon they come to realise that Robert Forrest was not the friend they thought, and, though nowhere to be seen, he has remained closer than they could have dared imagine . . .

'A horror novel of the most enjoyably reckless stripe . . . Satisfyingly lurid.' TLS

'Will make a pleasing addition to any bookshelf already darkened by Audrey Niffenegger's *Her Fearful Symmetry* or Glen Duncan's *The Last Werewolf*.' *Scotland on Sunday*

'Richard T. Kelly has put his own stamp on the genre.' *Financial Times*